EXCEPTIONAL POINT

by

GILLIAN ANDREWS

Interstellar Enforcement Agency

(Book Three)

ISBN: 978-84-09-17851-3
DEPÓSITO LEGAL: DL PM 46-2020
COPYRIGHT AUTOR Y EDITOR @ GILLIAN ANDREWS 2020
PRIMERA IMPRESION 2020
1.0

1

I grabbed Zenzie's crest and twisted my wrist, throwing her to the floor.

The air was punched out of her lungs. "Ouch!" she grumbled.

I watched as the heavy block and tackle swept past the spot where her head had been a moment earlier. "It's all right, you can thank me later."

She rubbed at her head, glaring at me. "I am the one who does the saving around here."

Bizarrely, she said this because I had also saved her life a year ago. Unfortunately, in her culture, there is something called the Savior Protocol, which means that she now lives like my shadow in the hope that she can return the favor. I clearly hadn't been thinking that day.

I picked her up and dusted her down. "De nada."

That provoked an even crosser stare. "I would have ducked."

"Sure. You have eyes in the back of your head."

In fact, since she was the Chyzar this was almost possible. She had a Nexus inside her head that contained the link to the Chakrans, a nonlocal species whose cells could be spread apart by thousands of galaxies. Long story.

She was more shaken than she let on. Her short claws had protruded automatically, and her crest was rigid.

I finished setting her back on her feet. "There!"

She stared above us. "Who wants to kill me?" she shouted upwards, into the dark recesses of the *Aenysia*.

There was a pause and then Danaa's worried voice wafted down to us from far above. "What? Did I do something?"

"You nearly scalped me."

There was a clattering up in the roof and a large figure dropped down several stages until we could see her. "I did what?"

"You dropped that ..." Zenzie pointed, "... on my head."

Danaa's long and greenish face became longer and even greener. "Oh, Chy Zenzara, I am so sorry." The thought that she might single-handedly have finished the Chyzar off was too much for her. She sank onto the suspended platform, which swayed from side to side. "I ... I don't know what to say."

"Captain Mallivan saved me."

"Then I am indebted to him."

I didn't want another one. I held up my hands. "Quite all right. Just a little push. No need to be indebted."

Zenzie giggled.

We were still tied up to the Nepheal Gyre, while ships and crew underwent repairs after some damage during our last mission. Danaa took her new responsibilities very seriously. She had been inspecting work just done on the upper inner skin of *Aenysia's* main shuttle bay.

I stared up at the imposing height of a Nepheal cruiser. "How is it going?"

She grinned. "Very well. I have taken advantage of the repairs to ask for a few new updates. She will be faster and more reactive after this."

Zenzie stared up at the hanging platforms, which made a sort of impromptu staircase all the way up the side of the hangar. Only you had to leap from one to the other. "Can I go up there?"

"Sure!"

"No!"

We both spoke at once. I frowned at Danaa, but knew that it was too late. Zenzie rolled her eyes. "I am not a baby, Mallivan. You have to let me try things out on my own."

"You are not a Nepheal. You are less than half Danaa's height."

"So?"

"I bet you can't even do the leap up between the platforms."

She bounced on her heels. "Then you would lose, because I can. However, I do not believe that you, Captain, would be capable of it. Not at your age." She looked down demurely at the decking, knowing that she had scored a hit.

I fought back the urge to strangle her. "Of course I could."

"Really?" Her expression said she didn't think so.

I rolled my eyes. "For the Shells' sake! Oh, all right, I suppose we could both go up and take a look at the repair work."

She ran around me in a tight circle. "I will beat you to the top!"

Dream on, I thought to myself. But I refrained from saying it. I hadn't been training as hard as I usually did, having only recently recovered from being shot in the chest. I didn't feel as confident as perhaps I should. Mental note: spend more time in the gym.

"Ready?" She tensed, going onto her toes. I nodded. "Three, two, one ... go!" She leapt, like a gazelle, straight from the floor to the first platform.

I stared. Who would have thought a little thing like her could jump so high, so fast?

I jumped as high as I could, grabbing hold of the edge of the platform and trying to haul myself up. I was already regretting this.

Zenzara was waiting for me on top as I scrabbled for a hold and attempted not to show it. Her face was alive with mischief. "Well done, Mallivan. Keep it up!"

Then she vaulted onto the next platform, causing the one I was just pulling myself onto to swing from side to side. I nearly fell off.

"Oops!" She landed like a cat and put one hand to her mouth, probably to stop herself laughing too much. "Sorry!"

My hands had gone white, but I managed to drag myself up onto the careering plinth. It was supported by four cables, one at each corner. I got unsteadily to my feet and anchored myself by clutching at one of the cables with both hands. "You know what, Zenzie? I have things to see to. This is going to take too long. I capitulate. You win."

A rude sound followed me as I jumped back off the platform as lightly as I could and began to stride away in what I hoped was a purposeful fashion.

The sound turned into chicken noises. We no longer had the birds that had been famous at one time, but their sounds had outlasted their species.

I waved a hand, being above such things. Let her win this one. She needed some fun in her life.

I was surprised though. The Tyzarans frequently surprised me. They looked unassuming, but were actually much stronger than Spacelanders and other humans. Only a little taller than we were, when they were fully grown they were more muscular despite their leanness. They had bigger brains, too.

Danaa gave me an enigmatic look before scampering up three of the suspended platforms in as many bounds. Zenzie made her way onto the third platform and they tittered together. At my expense, no doubt. Not that I minded. Anything to snap Zenzie back to her old, confident self.

I left the girls behind and made my way to the bridge of the *Aenysia*. It was almost time to begin the long trek to the Vaer system, where we hoped to pick up traces of Bull Cunningham and Ramesh Chandrayanan, the Terrans responsible for the recent attempt to annihilate the Chakrans. We had to bring both of them to justice. They were simply too dangerous to be left floating around the Major Shells. Unfortunately we had no idea as to their current whereabouts.

Anzany smiled at me as I entered the large open space. She slid out of the oversized Nepheal chair and gestured for me to take her place.

I shook my head. "No time. I have a meeting with the Elder General and the rest of the Board of Elders. Not that I think they are the ones actually running the planet."

She gave a nod. It had become more and more obvious over the last few months that it was, in fact, the women who were in charge of the planet and its people. The Nepheals didn't publicize the fact; it was simply something that gradually became clear to frequent visitors. This far out into the Atlas Shell, there weren't too many of those.

Still, the façade of male dominance had to continue. I was there to thank the planet for its sacrifice during the recent troubles and unveil a plaque to commemorate the sacrifice of Agraala, one of their more senior females. Today's event had been put on the same footing as their coming of age ceremony, the *Phaala*, which meant that it was a public holiday. The ceremony would be attended by as many Nepheals who could manage to cram themselves into the Hall of Ages. I was not looking forward to it, and hoped to fit in a long walk before having to spend the rest of the day amongst the crush of attendees. I still got a little claustrophobic at events such as the one that afternoon. However, I was there as the official representative of the newly formed Interstellar Alliance. I would be expected to act with due dignity. I hoped I would be up to it.

I changed into the new and starchy formal dress attire of a captain and took the space ferry down to Retaara Park. Retaara hospital was the best on the planet, and I wanted to check in on Sammy before the meeting. He was still recuperating from his injuries.

It was a lovely day in Nepheal City. The sun was blazing. Even so, it was unable to completely heat the air that had been chilled by the snow in the nearby mountains. It had a wonderfully energizing bite to it. I felt better almost as soon as I began to walk.

I soon heard footsteps coming up behind me. I turned. It was Jaaven, the Nepheal boy who had recently celebrated his *Phaala*. I nodded to him. "How are you, Jaaven? And your father?"

"Is it true you gave Scout to the Retreat at Ayaala? To Ouraali?"

He was talking about the pet Geiga I had ceded to the Ayaala ladies. "I did. I decided to leave him here, though I don't expect it will have caused him much suffering. Ayaala, with its phyonwe trees, is the closest a Geiga can get to heaven, I guess."

The boy fell into step with me. "I wish I had been able to stay with him," he said in a wistful voice.

There was a lot I still didn't know about Nepheals. "Once you have your *Phaala*, you can't go back to the retreat?"

He shook his head – an action which is more solemn on a Nepheal due to the size and length of their skulls. "No. All males must stay on the plains after their *Phaala*. It is the time to administrate the City."

"That is only done by the males of the species, I understand?"

"Of course."

It was only in the last week or so that I had realized that government on Nephealis was considered a lowly job. It was quite unlike other worlds, where power was considered something to be sought. Here, government was merely a tedious chore. The fact that the men undertook all such tasks freed up the women of the species to dedicate much of their lives to the higher pastimes of scientific thought and research. However, there was immense respect between both of the sexes and males were also able to contribute to advances in science and technology. It was a far more complex society than I had expected.

"So you won't be able to see Scout again?"

"Rarely. When he is brought down off the mountain. Today is one such day."

"Really? I shall be happy to see him again, though I don't expect he will deign to recognize his former owner. I am sure he will have become insufferably puffed up."

Jaaven eyes twinkled. "Puffed out, I should think. He gets fed as much as he wants."

"Big mistake. The Geiga stomach expands to meet supply. He will hardly be able to walk."

"He has become rather a celebrity on the planet. Many Nepheals like to give him tidbits."

"Then they should put him on a diet. Fat Geigas only last a couple of years."

"You should tell Ouraali that." Jaaven took a small step back, as if to distance himself from the idea of telling Ouraali anything. I couldn't blame him. She was a strong-minded female. I wasn't keen to criticize her myself.

He saw the indecision in my face. "You must! Today is a good day to tell her! She will be diverted by all the celebrations around her. Promise me you will tell her today!" He stamped one foot. "Otherwise they will kill Scout with kindness. You must!"

How had I got myself into this? I blew out air. "All right."

He skipped off, immensely pleased with himself. "Thank you, Captain Mallivan."

I was beginning to regret my decision to visit the hospital. The only way was through the park, which left me vulnerable to approach. I scanned my surroundings in case somebody else was lurking ready to involve me in matters that were really none of my business. Maybe I should have stayed up on the Gyre. It was harder to get at me there. Still, I certainly didn't want poor old Scout to end up unable to even waddle from tree to tree. Even if he did seem to have forgotten the special relationship I had thought we had.

Although the bracing walk was dispelling the dull mood that had been hanging over me like an annoying cloud, I was still taut with anger at myself for not having spotted Bull Cunningham for what he was: a Terran fanatic. It stung that I had drunk with him, chatted with him, sung with him and never suspected that his ideals were so far from my own. I felt defrauded. Worse, I felt stupid. Looking back, there had been tiny signs that he might not be quite so accepting of other races. There had been a couple of snide remarks about crests when touching on the Tyzarans and a snort or two when speaking of the Nepheals. Plus, he had always waxed lyrical about the Sol system.

I had thought nothing of it. I hadn't met that many Flatlanders and I guess I was flattered that he had singled me out for such attention.

I blew out air. Now it was my job to hunt him down and arrest him. Now there were too many deaths between us.

One of my teeth hurt suddenly. I came to my senses, realizing that I had been grinding my upper and lower jaws together.

I shook my head in an attempt to dispel the darkness.

Suddenly a knee-high package rolled across the grass towards me and nearly bowled me over. It resolved into an excitedly snuffling nose and a substantially inflated body. Both tried to rub themselves against my legs. My black humor evaporated immediately. I bent down to caress the Geiga skin.

"Good morning, Mallivan Bell."

I looked around, to find Ouraali standing upright behind me. She was smiling.

I finished petting Scout. "Good boy!" Then I stood up. "Ouraali, How are you?"

"Well, thank you, Captain. I hear you are about to leave us again."

"We are." I indicated Scout, still nuzzling at my calves, "How are you getting on with him?"

"He is extremely useful as a guard dog. He can tell whenever anyone is within two miles of the Retreat."

I nodded. "Geigas are a great early-warning system."

Even I could hear the wistfulness in my tone. So, apparently, could she. She twisted her head to one side. "You miss your Geiga?"

I did. "No, of course not."

Her smile was full of understanding. "Are you sure?"

Nivala was no place for a Geiga. Not under the circumstances. His life expectancy would drop substantially. I couldn't do that to him. "I'm sure. But you must stop overfeeding him."

Her eyes shuttered and narrowed. She had not been expecting criticism. "Ah. I didn't know that he could be overfed." She made it into a question.

"I'm afraid so. They will gorge themselves until they explode, if left to their own devices. They have no internal gauge that tells them when they are full."

She seemed to make an effort to relax. "I see. I was not aware of that."

"I will send you an info vid about them. I have several."

She gave a slight inclination of her long neck. "That would be greatly appreciated, Mallivan Bell. I thank you."

I pushed Scout aside with one foot. "Enough, Scout! I am glad to see you as well, but you need to dial it back a bit."

"He remembers you with kindness, it seems."

"Yes. We have had some good adventures together."

"You could still take him with you."

I couldn't. Not when I knew how close to Geiga Nirvana this place was. I had thought him to be contented with me, but now that I had seen the way he was on Nephealis, I thought he had merely been marking time.

I looked down at him. He was giving little grumps of pleasure and his tiny tail was swirling around and around in ecstasy. I couldn't possibly remove him from this ecosystem. He was where he was meant to be.

I ducked down to tease at his ears. "Take care, old boy. I shall miss you."

He nudged at me again, head-butting me.

"I know, Hardhead, I like you too." I gave his spiky hair a stroke. "But I don't mind you staying here. I can't give you what you need on board a ship. I don't know why I ever thought I could. I guess I never really thought about it at all. Have a good life, Scout." I got to my feet again. "And don't eat too many phyonwe fruits!"

"I will limit his intake," promised Ouraali. She spotted Jaaven, who was still close to us. I realized that he had probably seen her coming. His extra height would have given him advanced warning. Hmm. Sometimes these Nepheals could be tricky. I glared in his direction. He raised one hand and beat a hasty retreat.

Ouraali, too, raised one hand to indicate I should leave. Some of the city's residents were bearing down on her, having spotted Scout. She gave me a small shrug of resignation before turning to greet them.

I glanced at my watch. I really needed an update on Sammy's progress, but I certainly didn't want to insult the Board of Elders by arriving late. I broke into a jog.

Sammy was still in a Zeroth chamber. His small face lit up when I walked in.

"Rye! Thanks for coming."

I stared at the face I knew so well. Despite everything, it was full of pleasure. When I say despite everything, I mean it. The face that used to be smooth and almost boy-like was now criss-crossed with scars. Not thin, romantic scars. Huge red and white rifts ploughed through the skin on his face.

I sat on the edge of the tank. "How's it going?"

He pulled one arm out of the gel to bump my knuckles, making a slurpy sound as it pushed through the surface. "Great! You know, they think I will be able to walk without a limp when I get out! They were able to clear up that old problem."

"Terrific. What about the more recent injuries, though?" I had not thought he would survive, but Nepheal medical facilities were the best in the Shells. They had salvaged his ravaged body with incredible speed and proficiency.

He shrugged. "Don't much care about my face in any case. They reckon the rest will be all right. Just scarring and some of the skin will always pull. The bones should be OK. Bit of stiffness, nothing more."

"What did Mel say?"

"You know women. She cares more than me about my face. Men don't worry about stuff like that, right?"

I examined the now devastated face. It was a terrible sight. "You were no work of art to start with."

"Thanks, Rye! Great to have friends."

It was my turn to shrug. "How do I know, Sammy? I'm not a girl, am I? You look the same to me, just a bit more … crumpled."

"Do you think women like crumpled?"

"You're asking me? How should I know?"

"Mel avoids looking at me so much."

Something else I didn't feel qualified to discuss with him. Whatever I said was bound to be wrong. "Don't care, Agazed. Need you back on board *Nivala*, though. We ought to be leaving soon."

He nodded, slipping easily back into work mode. "Sure, Rye. They reckon they can let me out of this boring Zeroth tank in a couple of days. How is everybody else?"

"They were able to bring in an Enif doctor to treat Didjal, while we came after you. He came back on board *Nivala* yesterday. He will be on light duties for the next week, but Eshan seems pleased with his progress."

"Stopping enlightenment hasn't changed them?"

I pulled a face. "They have spoken to a *Belofiin* about it. He was able to reverse part of the damage to their cordotonal organs. Not all of it, but he tells me that they will be able to continue with us."

"And Seyal?"

"Seyal surprised us all. She only needed two days of Zeroth regeneration. Like Anzany, who was only shot once in the fleshy part of her thigh."

"You, yourself?"

I began to laugh. "Sammy, the only thing that happened to me is that I got shot in the chest and broke a finger! My *little* finger!"

"That's a Mallivan for you," he said with a gloomy face. "Always keeping the best injuries for themselves."

I stared at his ruined face. Then we both collapsed. Tears streamed down my face. He was right, damn him. How had I got through all that with just a clean fracture in a little-used digit? Oh, I forgot, I had been shot in the chest too, but the Zeroth tank soon sorted that out. I had thick ribs, it seemed.

He was choking. "You can have some of mine, if you want!"

I knew, from his debriefing, that Bull Cunningham had personally been responsible for Sammy's torture. The thought of all he must have suffered at the hands of the Terran made me sick. I admired my lifelong friend so much at that moment. To still be able to joke about it! I realized just how much Sammy had grown up. Maybe we all had.

He gave me a deprecating grin. "Even your Geiga is better looking than me now!"

"He smells better too!"

I received a weakened punch in my arm for that. "Just you wait, Mallivan! Wait until I am out of this fitzing jelly-bath. We'll see who smells and who doesn't."

"Don't dawdle in here too long, enjoying yourself. We need you back."

"You're just jealous I got time off. Don't worry. I will be back on board by the end of the week."

"Great. I wouldn't like to leave you here."

"No. I'm not about to miss the next mission." He suddenly dropped the façade and became deadly serious. "I have a bone to pick with Bull Cunningham."

And I wouldn't be the one to stop him.

2

We slid out of the Nephealis Gyre a few days later. *Nivala* was followed out by Danaa's ship, which would complete the repairs while in transit. That meant more mouths to feed on the journey, but would save us two weeks. We simply couldn't afford to hang around. We couldn't let the trail get cold. We had to find Chandrayanan and Cunningham before they created any further chaos in the Shells.

The Vaer system is some 300 light years from Nephealis. It used to take two months to do the trip. Now, since we were equipped with ZEPH drive, we could do it in three days. However, this time we needed to take a slight detour. We would stop off at the Waypoint space station where we were to be given new ansible technology for the ship and let off the extra crew. The Macers had rushed the first of these devices through so that we could pick one up before our next mission.

Up until a couple of weeks ago, ansible devices had been in the form of intracranial implants. I had once had one myself, except that the feedback from it almost drove me crazy. So I was delighted when the Macers told us that there was no further need for secrecy. The new devices were in the shape of small metal boxes which could be set into a ship's console. They were much more robust than the secretive Tyzaran implants, and easy to fit. About a million times better, in my opinion. I could still remember clawing at my own scalp to try to tear the thing out.

Waypoint also gave me a chance to try to catch up again with Sibby, my sister. I had already sent her a tight-beam asking if she could make it over to the station, hoping that this time we would have more than a few hours to see each other.

I had chosen to travel on the *Aenysia*, which gave me a chance to get to know Danaa a little better. As she was going to be a permanent part of the Interstellar Enforcement Agency, this had seemed like a good idea at the time. Now I was not so sure. She looked set to spend the whole journey on the hanging platforms, and I had already learnt that they were not my best environment. Still, I could make myself useful piloting.

Since I had stayed, so had Zenzie. Since Zenzie had stayed, so had Denaraz. That is the way things go under my command. I suggest, but unbreakable pacts really dictate how some of us will act. I am more like an usher than a captain. There is little chance that power will go to my head.

Over the vid-screen, I congratulated Mel on her helmsmanship. Under Sammy's keen eye, she had become quite proficient at *Nivala's* pilot station. It had been one of the benefits of their close relationship. There were drawbacks, too, but so far it had been generally positive. His presence had calmed her. I had noticed that her claustronetia had been improving too. As she gained new skills, she seemed more decided, more assertive. I hoped Sammy's injuries wouldn't damage their relationship. So far, they didn't seem to be talking much. He was standing right behind her, even though he was not strictly fit for service yet.

She took *Nivala* out first, and I followed in *Aenysia*. Then we brought the ships side by side and powered out of the Nephealis gravity well.

"Can I drive?"

I looked down from my uncomfortably high perch. Zenzie seemed diminutive from this position. "No, you can't."

"Why not?"

"You are eight."

"Nine."

"Whatever. You are still too young."

"Not!"

I sighed. It was easy to see where this conversation was leading. "All right then. Just for a few minutes."

She leapt onto the seat I had vacated, a big smile cutting across the wrinkles in her face. "Thanks!" She gazed at the screen in front of her. "What do I do?"

"You touch nothing!" I had to stand on tiptoe to try to see the screen. Even so, I had a restricted view. Denaraz, who was standing behind both of us had a look of panic on his face. What? Did he think she was about to crash us?

There was a deep-throated hum of power and we suddenly shot forward. I grabbed Zenzie's leg so as not to fall. "I said, don't touch anything!"

She gave me a hurt look. "I didn't!"

"You must have! Pull that big lever back. That's the throttle."

"This one?"

"Yes! Quick! Pull it back towards you!"

She put both of her small hands on it and tugged. Nothing happened.

I swept her out of the chair and leapt onto it myself. Zenzie was thrown to the floor, landing awkwardly. Denaraz shot forward to break the fall, but was a little late.

She gave a disbelieving cry. "You hurt me!"

The ship had begun to spin. I was doing my best to keep her straight. "Sorry!"

"I could have broken a bone!"

"Yes. I know. I said, I am sorry." What had happened? *Aenysia* wasn't responding at all.

I heard clattering from behind me. Danaa ran onto the bridge. "What have you done?"

"I don't know. Zenzie might have touched something ..."

"... I already told you; I didn't!"

Danaa shoved me out of the way. It was my turn to slide to the floor, though I managed to keep to my feet.

Zenzie's crest was up and her short claws were out. "I didn't do anything!" she repeated, clearly upset.

"All right. I believe you!" I did. She wouldn't lie. Zenzara was many irritating things, but she had always been straight with me. She hadn't caused this. So what had?

Sammy must have grabbed the helm of *Nivala*, because the other ship skewed rapidly away from us, spiraling over and over in an emergency anti-collision maneuver I was pretty sure Mel couldn't have learnt yet.

Danaa was not having any better luck than I was. She pulled and pushed buttons on the console in front of her with exasperation. "Nothing seems to be working."

"Maybe it is the ongoing repair work? Maybe one of the workers cut something?"

She shook her long neck. "Impossible. We are only reinforcing the skin of the shuttle bay. There is nothing up there that could affect the performance of the ship."

Aenysia was now spinning irregularly around her long axis. It was not a smooth feeling, more like a whip that accelerated in one place and juddered to a lurching halt in others. I had absolutely no idea what could be causing it.

Then a faint hololink appeared on the bridge. It was Anzany, but her image was flickering in and out of view.

"There is some interference coming in from the direction of the Pallis Ring," she said. "A stream of data is being directed at *Aenysia*. We are ...," her image broke up altogether, then re-established, "...ing ... stop it."

Denaraz ran towards the communications station. "On it."

It took him bare seconds to find the cause of the problem. "we are being subjected to a stream of data commands that are taking over the central processor."

Ok. Now I knew what was happening. "It's Ellison."

Denaraz turned to stare at me.

"It can't be anybody else," I said. "Remember? This is almost exactly what we did to the Terran fleet. You infiltrated their central computer system and shut them out. This is Admiral Ellison's work. She's getting her revenge. Though I heard she was stripped of her admiralship by Ethnarch Locke."

Realization flooded Izan's face. "You are right. It should be similar to our hack. We need to counteract the intrusion. Zenzie?" They both moved to the nearest computer terminal.

Danaa stopped trying to get the inert panel to respond and stared at the three of us. I gave her a reassuring grin. What I hoped was a reassuring grin. From her reaction, it wasn't and didn't.

The ship was now reaching ZEPH speeds and our heading was directly into the nearest star, which happened to be the red dwarf on the edge of the Pallis Ring. For a small second I felt relieved because red dwarfs are the coolest stars. Then I remembered that they still reached 3500 degrees. That would fry us pretty thoroughly too. It just meant that we would be able to get closer before sublimating. It would prolong the wait. That thought was not as reassuring as you might think.

I hate making enemies. This is just what happens. They await their chance and then inflict revenge when you least expect it.

I pressed a button. "Ellison? Are you hiding out there? Is this your work?"

It took a few tries on different channels, but then her voice crackled back at us. "You put two and two together! How clever of you!"

"Are you going to take this all the way, or are you planning on letting us go?"

She activated the hololink, so that we could see her better. I felt, rather than heard, Denaraz's gasp of surprise and pleasure. The link was a way in, I realized. Then I would just have to keep it open. That red dwarf was getting seriously close, and the temperature on the bridge was going up.

"You look well, Admiral."

"I am no longer an admiral."

"That is short-sighted of Ethnarch Locke. He will need people of your expertise."

"I have you to thank for that. However, revenge is not the motive for this ... situation." She looked up at the ceiling for a moment, as if her conscience were demanding clarification. I would be surprised to find she had one. "Well, not only. The real reason for this ... demonstration ... is to present my ... our ... new business venture."

My heart missed a beat. Something told me that I wasn't going to like the next sentence.

I looked at her more closely. She seemed rejuvenated. The last time I had seen her, in the aftermath of the Battle of Zuben, as it was becoming known, she had been a beaten, diminished woman. Now she was well presented and confident. Her hair had been cut short and she dominated the room, even though she was only present by hololink.

I knew what she was going to say before she said it. There were only a couple of people in the universe who would orchestrate this sort of revenge on me and she hadn't done this on her own. She wasn't influential enough. This had all the hallmarks of a really influential family. Now, which one of my acquaintances had been elevated recently to Omnial status?

Her lips curved. She was really enjoying herself. I tried to remember that my primary aim was to keep her talking. I was vaguely aware of Denaraz and Zenzara working frantically in the background. I had to keep a grip.

As she opened her mouth I held up a hand. "I hope you haven't gone into business with Bull Cunningham," I told her. I made my voice as severe as I could. "We are going to arrest him."

She began to laugh. "You are going straight into Pallis Epsilon," she told me. "And I am relaying this to … all interested parties."

Again, I felt rather than heard Denaraz's interest sharpen. "Are there many? Interested parties?"

"You might be surprised."

"I am unsurprised that Cunningham wants me dead. He is looking to save his own skin."

She tssked. "We are simply demonstrating a new Terran product."

"To possible purchasers? And who might they be?"

She smiled at me. "Do you really think I am stupid enough to tell you that? Even if you *are* about to be incinerated?"

"I have never thought you were stupid. In fact, I think you were very clever during the Battle of Zuben. You managed to regain full control of your ship."

She put her head up. She looked almost regal. "I did. That must have disappointed you."

Zenzie suddenly gave a small skip. I knew that we were close.

"It did. At that point we did not know that the Chakrans could or would intervene."

"If they hadn't, we would have won."

"Yes. If you can call destroying the whole universe winning."

Her chin came up. "A win is when you do not lose. We should not have lost. We will not lose in the future. The Chyzar is with you now. And the Chakrans might be able to expand molecules, but I doubt they can move a whole ship bodily from one point to another."

"They certainly haven't. So perhaps they can't." In fact they had, and they could, but all that was in the past. Such things threatened their very existence. They had already told us that they would not allow wormholes through their quantum structure again.

"Bull Cunningham is a loser." I stared straight at her and hoped the transmission was reaching him too. "And a liar."

She reddened. "Those of Omnial status may not be insulted!"

"Really?" I noticed the vibration of the ship slow significantly and just caught the quick fist bump that Denaraz and Zenzie exchanged. "Tell him to watch his back, will you? Because we *will* find him. And Chandrayanan."

Aenysia was responding to Danaa's hands on the controls. I saw the ex-admiral's eyes turn towards the console. They narrowed. She swung quickly back to demand an explanation from the person behind her. "What is happening? They have got control back!"

I tried to see past her, but the hololink was already fading. Danaa fought to tear the ship out of its dive into oblivion. *Aenysia's* plating screeched with indignation. Every part of the ship seemed to rattle as she slowly began to follow the commands.

I turned to Denaraz. He put both thumbs up. "That was close. Having her on hololink was great. I could patch into their network. Once I did that it was much easier to pinpoint their entry point."

"Well done!"

He nodded. "We are going to have to shore up our systems. I have sent this patch over to *Nivala*, in case they try the same thing with them, but they will iterate with tiny changes and eventually find a way past. We are going to have to invest in software protection."

"At least we survived!"

"This attack. We may not survive the next."

His face was very long. I saw that the effort had exhausted him. Zenzie, too, was looking limp with fatigue. He bit his lip. "It seems that Cunningham is not simply going to sit and wait for us to find him."

"No. He is going to attack us first. He is very clever. With Vaer backing and Omnial status he has the funds to do just what he wants. Unfortunate."

"Lucky I know where he is then, isn't it?"

My eyes shone. "You do?"

He grinned. "He was one of the onlookers. I know where he is, and I know where the others are. The only onlooker not inside Sol's

Termination Shock was in the Vaer system, as we suspected. Though I can't give you a definite geolocation for him until we are much closer to the system ourselves. Then I should be able to pinpoint exactly where that link was going. That will give us an edge."

"More than that. It gives us a chance!"

3

We came into the Waypoint space station some twenty hours later. I found myself peering out of the viewport to try to catch a glimpse of those waiting for our docking. I really wanted to see Sibby. Our last face-to-face meeting here had been cut shorter than I would have liked, on Supreme Oznard's instructions. And I loved my sister. She was the one encouraging constant in my life. She had adored her elder brother (by two months) when she was little. She had always been there for me. She had always seen the world from my point of view. I suppose that makes her a bit too unconditional, when you think about it from an adult perspective, but I never had.

Both ships edged into neighboring docks and shut down their engines. I was first at the disembarkation hatch, ducking through it before it was completely open.

A long pair of slender arms wrapped themselves around my neck. I hugged my sister's wiry body. "I missed you, Sibby!"

"It hasn't been long, but it feels like an age." She pushed away from me and examined my face. "You look a lot older."

"Do I?" I suppose I was bound to. A lot had been happening. I wondered where to start. "Do you want some coffee?"

"Does a cat lick its paws?"

Some things never change. My sister's addiction to caffeine is one of the great constants of life, up there beside Compton, Planck and Boltzmann.

We made our way to the nearest automatic vendor. They are about ten a penny on every deck of space stations. Machines dispensing desserts and beverages. Astronauts seem to want sweet things when they come into port. Cakes and biscuits, that sort of thing. I guess that is because sugary foods are usually not served on board any ship. Initially, the Space Trust found a high correlation between shipboard obesity and sugar intake, so it became frowned on to include anything sugary in the usual diet on board their ships. The lack of exercise that Spacelanders were forced into by close confinement makes them more propense to converting sugars to fat. So sugar was virtually outlawed and exercise encouraged. There are very few ships nowadays that do not have a gym of some type incorporated. And you won't find vending machines like the ones on the Waypoint station anywhere on spacefaring vessels.

Sibby slipped her personal counter in and out of the slot. The machine verified her iris and then offered up its contents. She looked at me and grinned. She didn't have to ask. She knew. "Two Tessara cakes and two Landau coffees, please."

The machine hummed as it began the manufacturing process for the coffees. The Tessara cakes were one of the staples in these things. Those were dispersed immediately. I tore the wrapping off mine and sank my teeth into it. It was so good I didn't talk until I had swallowed it. All of my taste buds stood on end and clamored for more. These things are not called the Astronaut's Drug for nothing.

"Now I understand Scout's obsession with phyonwe fruit."

Sibby looked behind me. "Where is he?"

Oh. I forgot. She didn't know. I looked down at the planking. Perhaps I should have consulted her. She was very fond of Scout herself. I explained about his reluctance to abandon Nephealis.

She laughed. "So Scout is now a well-loved Nepheal mascot? Good for him! Phyonwe fruit all day long? I imagine he is in seventh heaven!"

We waited until the coffees arrived in their soft packs and then began to stroll around the outer ring of the space station. "I will miss him. I ... maybe I should have asked you about it."

My lovely sister shook her long hair. "No. Why should you? He is yours, not mine."

"I know. But you have looked after him for so long, Sibby. I'm sorry. I should have consulted you."

She held up one hand to stop me from talking any more. "No problem. I would have told you to leave him where he was most happy. And that certainly wasn't with Mother."

"How is she?"

Sibby rolled her eyes. "She called Uncle Gunnar in. To pilot the new ship."

"Yes. I saw the ship. Leaking radiation."

Sibby nodded. "It was all that could be afforded. Still, Uncle Gunnar has managed to get her going. He has taken over the children's navigational tuition, too."

"How are they?"

"Good. Yours are all hoping to go for navigation. Two of mine want engineering."

"Really? Congratulations! Which two?" Engineering is the most highly paid profession in space. Piloting a spaceship, for some reason, is generally more attractive to young generations than caring for engines. More pilots means fewer engineers which means higher pay for engine jobs. That is why so many Enif are contracted on Spacelander vessels. They make excellent engineers, though their services do not come cheaply.

"Alisevola and Orin."

"Prime must be pleased with that." My mother was also the matriarch of our space family. I addressed her therefore as 'Mother' when referring to her role as my parent, and 'Prime' when referring to her in her role as matriarch of the family. Whereas Mother probably couldn't care less what my progeny did, Prime would very much appreciate the cheaper cost of fueling the engineering department with home-grown spacers. I had had my problems with both of her personas.

"She is." Sibby's mouth turned down. "Err ... Mall?"

That was her you-might-not-like-what-I-going-to-say tone.

"What?"

"I was ... wondering ... if ..." She went a little pink.

"Come on, Sibby. Spit it out."

"Would you take me with you?"

My jaw dropped. Sibby was going to be the next Mallivan Prime. That had been set in stone for as long as I could remember. If she signed onto *Nivala*, the current Prime would have a fit. It was very tempting, I had to admit.

"Have you thought about this?"

She gave a definitive nod of her head. "I have. I need some space. Some time on my own." She clocked the lift of my eyebrow. "Well, obviously not completely on my own, since you would be there, but some time away from *Bellaris*."

Bellaris is the family shipstation. Mother's domain. She rules over it with an iron fist and a very sharp tongue.

"OK."

"Just like that? You don't have to think about it?"

"No. Why should I? I always said I would love to have you aboard."

"Prime won't like it."

"I know. But I tried not to be swayed by that."

Sibby hugged me. "You are the *best* brother!"

"You will have to behave yourself, mind!"

"I will do whatever you say. I hope you need a nanotech engineer?"

"I do have something in mind. We picked up an artifact on our last mission and I was hoping to develop it further. We call it the carbon cloud." I realized something. "Damn!"

"What?"

"You would have to work on board *Aenysia*, not *Nivala*. There is far more space for trials over on the Nepheal ship."

Her eyes shone. "You are kidding, right? I get to work on a Nepheal ship? They are said to be fifty years in advance of our own."

"Want the job, then?"

"I do. Please!"

"I'm not going to be the one to tell Prime."

"Oh." Her face fell. "Please, Mall?" She dropped her head onto my shoulder.

I shook her away. "Not a chance, Sib. If you want to get away from her, you can tell her yourself. I am not currently in contact with her."

"I bet she would love to hear from you."

"I bet she wouldn't."

"Spoilsport!" She pulled the old face that used to work on me. Unfortunately Zenzie had already found and exhausted that way to extract sympathy. "Yes. Sorry."

She gave me a punch on the forearm. "Oh, all right. I will talk to her."

"Is the shipstation back in profit again?" It was the only thing that had kept me from sleeping. The fear that the loss of *Faraday*, my ship, would lead the whole family into ruin.

"It has been tough, Mall, I won't lie to you. But we are beginning to come about. I think the shipstation will be back in profit within a year. Maybe less with your help. That money you send every month is very useful." She squeezed my elbow. "It wasn't your fault. I know you had no other choice."

"They would have killed the others if I hadn't agreed."

"I know. You couldn't have allowed that."

I wondered if Prime felt the same. Something told me that she would have willingly tossed ten of our crew members into a black hole if it would have benefited the family business.

"Do you think you will ever go back?"

She hesitated. "Yes. I think so. But I want to be a different person to

Prime. A different type of leader. I want to see more of the universe first."

"She won't understand."

"No. She thinks she is the best example for a future matriarch." Sibby shrugged. "And maybe she is. Maybe I will have to make horrible decisions, too. But I want to base them on other criteria. I want to see other species, live a different type of life first. I think the Spacelanders ... the shipstation ones, anyway ... have become too inward looking. Don't you?"

I had certainly changed over the last few months. The feeling of lack of control had disappeared altogether. And I used to be more of an angry person. "Yes. I do."

"We haven't traveled together since ... what? That first training course on Rasseny?"

"Ten or eleven years ago, right? That seems a long time ago, doesn't it?"

"You know something, Mall? You look ... more settled than I have seen you for a long time. A very long time."

"Yes. I guess I needed to get away from the family, too. I needed to breathe. But I still feel terrible about *Faraday*."

"Don't. You already signed over the first three years of your new salary to the shipstation. All that will pay off any hypothetical debt you may feel you owe. You can forget all about it. Really."

I drained the dregs of the coffee. "Let's get you on board *Aenysia*. I'll introduce you to Danaa. You will like her."

We stopped by *Nivala* first so that Sibby could say hello to Sammy and Mel. There were several minutes of mutual shrieks and hugs and jumping up and down.

Zenzie looked on in some confusion. "You aren't very much alike."

"Of course we are."

"*You* don't act like that."

"Like what?"

"Happy."

"Sure I do! I'm a happy sort of guy."

Her forehead crinkled even more than usual. "If you say so, Mallivan."

"I do."

She gave me a look and rolled her eyes.

She was nine. What did she know? "What do you expect? People have been injured around here. What am I supposed to do? Dance?"

She raised an eyebrow. "I just said you weren't very like your sister."

"Well, we are. Always have been."

"Ohhh-kaaaay."

"Haven't you got anything better to do?"

She shook her head. "Nope."

"Then go and help Seyal with Segaton."

She gave me a pitying smile. "You can't help being grouchy, you know." She skipped out.

I stared after her, shocked. "Grouchy? Me? GROUCHY?"

She had already gone. Giggles echoed back along the corridor to me. I shook my head in disbelief and turned back to the conversation in front of me.

I wondered if Sibby would pick up on any problems between Sammy and Mel. She didn't. That made me discount Sammy's comment back on Nephealis. I thought that Sibby, who was very intuitive, would have picked up on any undercurrents. It looked as if he had just been oversensitive about his injuries, something I could well understand. I was glad. I hadn't thought Mel the sort of girl to concentrate only on the physical.

I let them catch up and then led Sibby out of the bridge and down one floor to the weapons bridge. I wanted to introduce her to Anzany and Denaraz, who I knew would be overseeing the new munitions we were taking on.

Denaraz didn't see us coming, so he jumped slightly as I touched him on the arm. I grinned and then turned back to my sister. "Izan, this is my sister, Sibby. Sibby, Izan Denaraz, Adjunct to the Chyzar."

She was staring over my shoulder at the tall Tyzaran. I waited a moment for them to break eye contact, but that didn't happen. I turned around.

Denaraz was standing like a stone, both crests absolutely perpendicular from his scalp. His eyes were linked to Sibby's and his breathing was almost imperceptible. His skin had taken on a purple tinge.

I nudged him. "Denaraz. Denaraz! DENARAZ!"

It took a harsher nudge to snap him out of his reverie. "What? Oh! Oh, sorry, Mallivan. Your … your sister, did you say?" He bowed to her. "Hello!"

Sibby had gone pink around the edges. I was quite amazed. She was so level-headed.

They were still staring at each other.

I took a step back and looked around. Anzany was watching them, a wry smile on her face. She met my gaze and jerked her head backwards. We were quite definitely not wanted here. I guess the munitions would just have to wait. We stepped quietly backwards out of the weapons bridge and into the corridor.

Anzany began to giggle. "I think Denaraz just met his destiny."

I wasn't at all sure I approved of what we had just witnessed. "Does that happen to Tyzarans? What do you call it? Instant love?"

"We call it," she thought for a moment to get the right words in Universal, "'soul mixing'. It is very unusual. To have that physical reaction of the crests just to the presence of the other person hardly ever happens. It is a sign of great compatibility. Usually those who experience it are together for the rest of their lives."

I wasn't sure I approved of that. But something had clearly taken place between them, and I also had the feeling that it was one of those things that could never be undone. It looked like Sibby had found her

future. I knew only one thing for sure: both my mother and her alter
ego the Prime were going to hate it.

I could only leave them together for a couple of hours. Sibby, when I
went to collect her, was looking shell-shocked. She could hardly get a
sensible word out of her mouth.

In the end I gave her a hug and told her not to bother. "I think you
just found your kindred spirit. Good for you! I thoroughly approve,
and I like Denaraz, so don't worry about a thing." I gave her another
squeeze. "Well done!"

She shook her head. "He is Tyzaran!"

"Yes. I noticed." I pointed to my head. "You know, those cresty things
rather give him away ..."

She pushed at me. "Ryler Mallivan! Stop it!"

"You are sunk, Sibby. I don't know what the future holds for you, but
I am reasonably sure a long and lanky Tyzaran male is going to figure
prominently in it."

She pushed at me again. "You are getting ahead of yourself."

I gave her another quick hug. "Apparently they call it soul mixing.
You just had your soul mixed with another person's."

She gave a ragged sigh. "It does feel as if I just went through a fusion
tumbler."

"Never mind. I like him. He has saved my life several times. Thing is,
Sibby, he has to go where the Chyzar goes. That is going to be a big ...
BIG ... problem for the family shipstation."

She went quite white. "I hadn't even considered Prime," she
whispered. Her hands went to her head. "Shells! She will go off like a
nova!"

"Supernova. Hypernova." I knew my mother. Nova came nowhere
near the reaction she was going to have. "But you don't have to tell her

yet."

"No." She bit her lip. "It is far too early." She looked suddenly more chirpy. "Maybe it will all fizzle out in a week. Then there would be no need to tell her anything."

"Well, you will have time to think about it. Izan will be on *Aenysia* for this next trip. You can get to know him better. I'll schedule you to work with him."

She went a brighter red. "You don't have to."

"I was going to, anyway. You will need him to organize the project you are going to work on. You are the best nanotech engineer I know; he is the expert in software. He can hack just about anything." I realized I was forgetting somebody. "Well, he and Zenzie together."

She looked at me.

I spread my hands. "They come as a package. What can I say? You will see what I mean. Now, I suppose you want me to stand beside you while you set up the hololink with *Bellaris*?"

Sibby threaded her slim arm around mine. "Please!"

My mother's face started stiff and then gradually hardened until it could have been mistaken for concrete. "What do you mean 'a couple of weeks'?" she demanded.

"Well, there is a job I can do for them, and I thought it would be nice to help out for a bit, that is all." Sibby's excuses sounded lame, even to me.

"I fail to see why they should need your help. Surely this new Interstellar Alliance has people of their own?"

Most people assumed that. It wasn't true. Yet.

My sister spread her hands. "Mother, you know that I have had no breaks for the last couple of years. I am merely taking one now."

"It is extremely inconvenient. Work has to go on, here, you know.

Especially ..." her eyes tracked accusingly over to me, "... after what your brother did."

"We are coming out of that now. And you know that he is contributing his wages to the family. That will make a difference."

"It won't bring *Faraday* back."

My sister straightened her shoulders. "No, it won't. But that doesn't mean I have to be anchored to *Bellaris*."

My mother sniffed. "Personally I would have thought you wouldn't *want* to be away just now."

"I think it is a very good time. Uncle Gunnar seems to have it all under control."

"The family is dependent on a rust bucket that should no longer be flying. I fail to see how you can qualify that as 'under control'."

"I am not coming back yet, Prime," Sibby told her, assuming a more formal tone. You could never get anywhere with my mother. She won every argument, at least in her own mind.

That was met with another sniff. "I suppose that brother of yours has been corrupting you. I might have known."

I opened my mouth, but Sibby stood on my foot, leaving me gasping like a landed fish. "It wasn't his idea. It was mine. I will be in touch in a couple of weeks. Cutting the connexion."

She put action to words. Then she turned to me. "You always did challenge her, Mall. You shouldn't bother. Nothing changes her opinions. You ought to know that by now."

I sighed. "When did that happen? I vaguely remember a person who laughed and played with us. But those memories are so far away that I am not even sure they happened."

"When Grandmother died she changed. It was as if she became a different person overnight, one weighed down with responsibilities and burdens. She has never been the same since." There was a short silence, before she went on, "I don't want that to happen to me."

"No."

"Sometimes," she said in a small voice, "it terrifies me."

"Denaraz will stop that. He will want you to be happy. The Tyzarans enjoy life. Generally."

"Yes. But it will make Prime even more bitter. I never would have wanted that, either." Tears came to her eyes. "It is as if I am making everything worse for her."

"Everybody should have the right to choose their own path. Seems to me, at least."

She pulled a face. "Things haven't been like that for centuries. If I don't take over *Bellaris*, the shipstation might fail. The Mallivan legacy could be lost. That is why everything is so regimented."

And that in itself was ironic. The first Spacelanders originally took to space to get away from the regimented life imposed on them by the Omnistate. "Sibby, nobody should have to sacrifice themselves, even for their family. I won't let you do it."

She smiled, at last. "There is still time, Mall. Maybe it will all work out."

"It did for me."

"Yes. In a strange way, I think it did." She kissed me on my cheek. "Now, are you going to show me this strange artifact you want me to work on?"

Sibby settled into the crew of *Aenysia* as if she had always been there. She and Denaraz pursued some sort of a relationship. I didn't inquire how far it had gone. It was none of my business. I just know that every time she walked into a room, Izan's crests came up.

He hated it and loved it at the same time. It was a source of infinite embarrassment to him, but the depth of his feeling for her was so blazingly obvious and so strong that it formed something of a shield around them both.

The rest of us refrained from comment. I, at least, found that quite difficult. But there was a sense of fragility about Denaraz that prevented us from inflicting any jokes on him. I had not thought of him as vulnerable. Now he was.

Even Zenzara treated him circumspectly. I noticed that she gave him as much space as she could. I asked her about it on one occasion.

"Not many Tyzarans experience soul mixing," she told me, her eyes wide. "Those who do are changed by the experience. They are known as the multi-layered, because they are thought to be imprinted by the soul of the other person, as well as their own."

I thought this was going a bit far, and told her so. She bristled. "And just what would Spacelanders know of such matters?" she demanded, her crest rising indignantly. "You don't even form couples anymore. You procreate in test tubes!"

She had a point. "You're right. I apologize."

A doubting huff of air answered that.

I ignored it. "How is the research going? Have they managed to get the carbon bubble to work?"

She nodded. "Yes. They can make it deploy, but Sibby says they need to find something suitable to line it with. I explained about the atmosphere around the third planet in the Ebyssia system, but she thinks she can come up with something new. Something about non-hermitian waves."

Danaa, who had been nearby, chipped in. "Exceptional points," she told me helpfully.

I frowned. "I thought that was something the ZEPH drives utilized?"

"It is. In a way. Exceptional points have many uses. In this case, Sibby is talking about using macro exceptional points contained within wave guides."

"Which will ...?"

"Which will cause all electromagnetic waves to slip past the cloud." She took in my expression of incomprehension and decided to elaborate. "It would act as an unbreakable shield and would have the advantage of keeping us almost invisible from onlookers."

"Better than the original carbon cloud, then?"

"Definitely. Because it would actually shield whatever was inside. But Sibby is having quite a problem trying to adapt current technology. She isn't sure it can be done."

"I will ask Didjal to join them. It sounds like the sort of thing it would be good at."

The two girls exchanged a glance. Zenzie nodded. "Maybe. It does have quite an extensive knowledge of that sort of thing. And it has studied the ZEPH drive in the last weeks. I will go to tell it." She skipped away. I had only recently allowed her to take the shuttle between ships on her own, and she was still at the stage where she loved the freedom. I could have had her relaying food backwards and forwards all day if I had wanted.

Danaa watched her go before she turned back to me, her face thoughtful. "Captain?"

"Hmm?"

"I have something I wanted to run by you."

"Go ahead."

"Well, it occurred to me that we are limited by *Nivala's* speed. *Aenysia* can go quite a lot faster, with these newly upgraded engines, but of course she has to fall into convoy with *Nivala*."

I felt obliged to defend my ship. "*Nivala* isn't that much slower."

"No. She isn't. However, a journey of 500 light years still takes us around six days, allowing for acceleration and deceleration. *Aenysia* could cut that in half."

"Three days? That *is* fast. So what are you suggesting? That *Aenysia* scouts ahead?" My mind was already racing. The idea was not outrageous, but would be dangerous for the Nepheal ship.

But Danaa was already shaking her head. "No. I am suggesting that we take *Nivala* on board *Aenysia*."

I blinked. "Excuse me?"

"I have been looking at the dimensions of the main shuttle hold. The one we have been working on. In fact, it was that work that got me thinking about size." She dropped to all fours to be closer to my level. "I checked. In theory, *Nivala* could fit inside that hold."

I blinked again. "Surely not?"

She grinned. "We might need Sammy at the helm for the maneuver, because it would be a tight squeeze, but … in theory … yes."

"But … but …" It was outlandish. Surely the holds on *Aenysia* couldn't be that big? I realized that my mouth was gaping open and shut it with a click. "Take me there. Show me."

We made our way down to the main shuttle bay. Danaa led me right into the middle of the space. "It is twenty of your stories high," she pointed out. "*Nivala* is fifteen. And there would be around six feet to spare on each side of her too."

I whistled. She was right. On paper the Tyzaran ship would fit inside the Nepheal one. But it would be tight. Very tight indeed. I didn't think I would be able to pilot her to such exact precision. Sammy, now … Sammy just might. I pressed a button on the wall. "Tell Zenzara to wait for me. She can take me over to *Nivala* with her."

Anzany's voice floated out of the comlink. "Yes, Rye." There was a brief pause, until she came back to me. "She says she will wait, but she wasn't best pleased."

"Tell her I will let her attempt a barrel roll pass with me as a passenger." Since this involves turning the shuttle upside down and skimming the length of a larger ship I suspected it would more than compensate for the wait.

There was another pause. "She says she will do her best to make you sick!"

Anything for a happy crew.

She didn't manage to make me physically sick, but I was as close to screaming as I had been in quite a while. Tyzarans have a great spatial sense, which Zenzara might not have inherited. She scraped our shuttle against the outer hull of *Aenysia* twice. I found myself preparing for imminent death.

As we exited the shuttle, once safely docked inside *Nivala*, she managed a couple of skips. "That was fun!"

I growled.

"What? Oh, you mean because I clipped the hull? I was just getting a sense of the distance."

"Do that again and you won't be flying another shuttle until you are twenty."

She looked hurt. "I wasn't *that* bad!"

I prudently refrained from a reply.

"Was I? Come on, Mallivan! I did well!"

More silence.

She got annoyed. "Well, I don't see how you are supposed to learn if you aren't allowed to clip a few ships from time to time."

I looked away.

"Oh, all right. I won't do it again. I just wanted to scare you a bit."

It worked. "It takes more than that to scare me."

"Well, it shouldn't." She sounded cross. "I even scared myself, a bit. These things are hard to stabilize once they hit something."

My own heart rate was only just beginning to normalize. "Yes. You need a few more courses on the simulator."

Her face was all wrinkles. "No! Oh, please, no! They are so ... so ... *boring!*"

"Fifty hours before your next flight."

She hopped from one foot to the other, scandalized. "Please, Mallivan, don't make me use the simulator. I promise not to scratch any more hulls. Honestly!"

I remained immovable. She made various attempts to win me over before stomping off to see Didjal.

I waited until she had left before leaving. I wasn't sure my legs would respond. Her near misses in the shuttle had turned them into spaghetti. I was getting too old for this kind of thing. Dealing with a nine-year-old Tyzaran was enough to make *anyone* grouchy.

Getting the *Nivala* inside the *Aenysia* was a bit like a reverse Matryoshka doll. First, we had to take *Nivala's* main shuttle and put it inside *Aenysia's* shuttle. Then we had to take *Aenysia's* main shuttle and put it inside *Nivala*. That left *Aenysia's* main hold almost empty, so we were able to concentrate on edging *Nivala* herself inside *Aenysia*.

Sammy was so concentrated that he bit his lower lip. He seemed quite unaware of the occasional drop of blood running down his chin and dripping onto the console. Luckily they were falling onto the outside casing, where they could do no harm.

I must say, it was a tight squeeze. He was sweating as we slipped past the shuttle bay doors and began to ease our way past the bulkheads. We could have reached out to touch them. In fact, I think I saw Seyal duck on one occasion, when we seemed certain to scrape one of the thick girders that bordered the hold.

Aenysia was stationary in open space. I had decided that this operation was one that we would keep very much to ourselves. It could be to our advantage to be thought slower than we really were, and I was still unconvinced of the innocence of the Tyzaran Supreme Council. They had, at one stage, sponsored Bull Cunningham's work. They claimed now that they had had no idea what his intentions had been, but I remained skeptical. I thought that it would be worth watching some of their members. I definitely wasn't going to confide our plans to *them*.

We slipped inside the Nepheal hold with a couple of feet to spare on either side. Finally, Sammy lowered the ship onto the deck plating. There was a collective sigh of relief as the tension drained out of us. We made our way down to *Nivala's* shuttle bay and walked out into the enormous hold on the Nepheal ship.

I looked back at *Nivala*. Sure enough, there was space to spare above her. Even the two characteristic EP prongs that protruded from the bows fit comfortably inside the huge hold.

As I looked on, the enormous shuttle bay doors slowly clamped into place, closing out the view of empty space. The lower door formed a ramp when open. The top door came down from above, forming a horizontal seal where both doors met in the center. The shuttle bay was of the same FLOW (Fly Load One Way) stacking system as *Nivala*, where shuttles enter via the stern doors and exit via the bow doors. A sort of space 'roll-on, roll-off' system. It generally works very well, since the ships do not have to be turned around. Most space shuttles have a cumbersome and inefficient reverse thrust mechanism. Without the FLOW stacking system, we could never have put *Nivala* on board *Aenysia*. We might have got her on, but we would never have got her off again.

We dropped into orbit around a small moon of one of the outer gas giants in the Vaer system three days later. I had decided to take it easy for this first transition using ship embedment. In actual fact, it had gone remarkably well. The two cojoined ships traveled perfectly and there were apparently no ill effects on either of them. It had also given both crews the chance to spend time together, which was a bonus.

As we stabilized *Aenysia*, I turned to Denaraz. "Have you been able to trace that link yet, Izan?"

He finished a tense examination of the console in front of him. "I have."

"So, what is our heading?"

He held up a warning hand. "I only know where Cunningham was a week ago, remember? He may have moved since then."

"I realize that. But we will be a week closer to him. It is, at the very least, a good starting point. Whereabouts on Vaer Nova was he?"

"He wasn't on Vaer Nova."

I stared. "Then where was he?"

"He was on Vaer Prime. In the Northern Hemisphere."

That did bring my eyebrows together. I had expected him to be in the Vaer system somewhere, but never on Vaer Prime itself. That made things very much more complicated.

Vaer Prime was once the only inhabited planet around the Vaeris star. Its inhabitants were reclusive and xenophobic. They discouraged any contact with other species in the Major Shells, dismissing such species as inferior.

Over time, Vaer Nova, the third planet out from Vaeris, became home to a fairly prosperous and extremely ruthless group of misfits and deported criminals who saw a better future dealing with the alien races of the Shells rather than with their fellow Vaers. Some of these traders became extremely rich and formed the Propter Faction. Others lost all their money. The rich traders 'encouraged' such unsuccessful traders to move to the Southern Continent, where life was extremely hard but where their envy would not be a threat. It was generally considered a bonus that such individuals tended to succumb quickly to the dangers of the south. Those few who did manage to survive founded the Sellica faction.

From these innocent beginnings, Vaer Nova has developed into a very dangerous place to live. Vaers finding Prime too rule-bound and restrictive move to the new colony. Such individuals tend to have fewer principals and are motivated by money more than anything else. Many of them consider killing to get what they want an acceptable option. Life on Vaer Nova only cements such tendencies. Those who murder their competition survive.

This was especially true in the Southern Hemisphere, where the Sellicas began to eke out a resentful existence. Since Nova's bad beginnings, things have only worsened. The Propters, as the Northern faction is known, have been at war with the Sellicas in the South for over five hundred years. Hatred became endemic between the two factions, fuelled by poverty and the desire for revenge in those forcibly sent South and a strong desire to maintain the status quo by those privileged to enjoy the meager comforts of the North.

More and more of Nova's inhabitants situated themselves outside Major Shell law. Conditions in the South were so inhospitable that stories of cannibalism began to abound. Certainly the conditions there forced the Sellica Vaers to discard any traces of integrity they may have retained. Nowadays, the Southern Continent of Vaer Nova is a no-go zone for anyone not part of the Sellica faction. I have heard that the price of a life there can be as little as a hot meal.

However, it is certainly the place to go to buy arms and weaponry in general. Many of the Nova Vaers, especially the Sellicas, became rich by trafficking in stolen goods, and, if the stories are to be believed, people – including their own species. This encouraged daring pirates of any origin to gravitate to that area, where they lost little time in building heavy bunkers which they could easily defend. Unscrupulous individuals still gravitate to Vaer Nova. Naturally it was where I had expected to find Bull Cunningham.

There is another consideration when thinking of Vaer Nova. Until recently we had no idea what Vaers did with the money they made. However, after finding the Ebyssia moon, we had our suspicions. Vaer Nova is not a secure place to live. We now knew that at least some of them had branched out into other parts of the Major Shells, seeking uncontested moons and forming tribal colonies. It made sense. Families clearly didn't survive long on Vaer Nova. If I lived there, I would be pretty keen to get off it too. I thought the chances were high that each family was seeking some sort of refuge off-planet. If the Ebyssia moon was anything to go by, they were choosing locations where they would not be discovered, where there was a side business that could cover running costs, and where they stood a very good chance of not being found. The whole of space could be peppered with

Novans. Who knew?

I stared at Denaraz. "I thought the Terrans were under the protection of the Sellica faction? Surely they would go to the Southern part of Vaer Nova?"

He shrugged. "According to my readings, they were on Vaer Prime."

That was not good news. Vaer Prime was inaccessible to anyone not a Vaer Prime. The Novan Vaers were not allowed to set foot on the planet either. Primes detested the Novans. I didn't understand how Cunningham could be there. We would certainly stand no chance of getting on the planet unnoticed. None of us looked remotely like a Vaer. I bit my lip.

Sibby grinned around at us, still eager to see some action. "So," she said expectantly. "What's the plan?"

Good question.

Seyal had the answer. "We need a Vaer or two," she said immediately. "Ones that will be loyal to us."

"Is that even possible?" Sammy's tone was skeptical.

Seyal treated us all to a severe look. "We only have to find one who is being mistreated," she pointed out. "From what you have said, that will be quite a large pool to dip into."

"On Vaer Nova, yes. I have no idea about Vaer Prime."

She spread her hands. I got the message. So did the others.

Denaraz stepped back. "Oh, no! We are not ... NOT ... going to crash some slave pen on Vaer Nova and rescue all the slaves! Tell me we are not!"

Sibby's face was alight. "Yes!"

Danaa and Zenzie both danced on the spot.

The rest of us stared at each other. I couldn't see any other way to get the intel we needed from Vaer Prime. I sighed. "If anyone can see a better way ...?"

There was silence.

I sighed again. "Very well. Sibby, you and Zenzie will stay here with Denaraz."

The outcry was so loud that I found myself ducking backwards.

"I am going!"

"I haven't come this far to stay on the ship!"

"We should all go!"

It was Sibby's voice that sounded above the rest. "This is my time, Mall. Don't take that away from me."

She reached up and gave me a hug. "In any case," she whispered in my ear, "there is no way Sammy can go. He is still in recuperation. We have to leave him on board."

I knew all that. She was right. But she was my sister, and I had no wish to send her into such danger. What can I say?

They were all looking to me to make a decision. My eyes tracked to Sammy, whose eyes were hopeful but resigned in his scar-crossed face. I looked at his hands. They were trembling.

He saw where I was looking. His face fell as he covered one hand with the other and leaned them both on a console. He knew I had seen. He knew I knew he wasn't ready. His whole bearing slumped.

I felt so sorry for him. The last time he had been left to look after a ship while the rest of us carried out a mission he had been tortured by Bull Cunningham. It couldn't be easy for him. "Seyal will stay with you," I decided.

His eyebrows went up. Mel seemed relieved. Seyal opened her mouth but closed it again when I motioned her to stop. I couldn't ask Sammy to look after Segaton again. It simply wouldn't be fair. And Seyal herself was also still in recuperation. Sitting this one out would do her no harm.

I caught Danaa's eye. "Are you up to this?" The Nepheals hated the Vaers, who had been their natural predators for many millennia.

Danaa stiffened, offended. "I already proved I can act against the Vaers."

"Very well then. The rest of us need to get in and out as silently as we can."

Zenzie was smiling.

So was Sibby. So was Denaraz.

"What? Am I missing something?"

Zenzie began to bounce on the spot. She was bursting with news.

Sibby laughed out loud. "Go on, Zenzie. Tell him."

It came out in a rush of words. "We can use the carbon cloud."

"You got it to work?"

Sibby and Denaraz both grinned. "We perfected the design. Using the artifact that was procured from the Vaers, we can deploy a sphere around any ship. Now, the Vaers were using the carbon atmosphere of that Ebyssia planet as a filler or liner. That worked very well, but Sibby here has been able to come up with a much stronger barrier. She has been able to make a sphere of exceptional points. This uses parity-time symmetry, among other things, and acts as a protection for whatever is inside. It has the added bonus of using waveguides, which means that anything hidden remains truly invisible."

I slapped him on the back. "Well done!" Then I hugged Sibby. "I knew you would be able to come up with something!"

Zenzie was waiting for her accolade. I rolled my eyes. "Well done, kid."

She looked delighted. It had been a long time since I had called her kid.

I narrowed my eyes. "How close can that get us?"

Denaraz considered. "It will be more difficult to maintain the sphere intact in a gravity well, but it has a fairly robust design. I doubt they will detect us, even on the ground."

Sibby looked pleased with herself. "I thought we could call it the Exceptional Point Spherical Buffer?"

I shook my head. "Carbon cloud."

"But it doesn't even use carbon now!"

"Good name, though. It would confuse everyone if we changed it now. Yours is too long. I have already forgotten it."

She gave a long shake of her head. We had had this sort of argument before. I love my sister, but sometimes she isn't practical. I can remember when she wanted to call Scout "Emperor of the Upper Landau Stretches". I soon put a stop to that one, too.

I was feeling much better. "Separate the shuttles and then fit the carbon cloud to *Aenysia's* shuttle," I told Didjal. It nodded.

4

The carbon cloud seemed to be working just fine. Anzany and Neema brought the shuttle down onto the cold steppes in the Southern Hemisphere of Vaer Nova without any signs that we had been spotted. There was a little difficulty with the new shield when we hit atmosphere, but we had timed our approach so that the most noticeable trails would be well-hidden by the prevailing bad weather. We hoped.

Once down, the carbon cloud settled easily into place, spreading out slightly where the ship touched the surface of the planet. It made us invisible. We would only have been discovered if somebody had tried to drive straight through us. That was unlikely. Not only had we put down amongst some quite large boulders, but we had made sure that there were currently no Vaers within a hundred kilometers on any side. The shuttle should be quite safe.

Just in case, we decided to leave Didjal to babysit it. The Enif was another who was still in recuperation. It would be better for it not to have to traverse hundreds of miles of rough terrain. Its thin body seemed almost forlorn as it waved us off and then ducked back inside.

That left Eshaan, Danaa, Anzany, Neema, Mel, Denaraz, Sibby, Zenzara and myself. Nine of us. Thousands of them.

Not the best odds.

However, we were not planning on announcing our arrival. The idea was clear: Find a Vaer camp where resentful slaves were being held, liberate them, persuade them to work for us. What could possibly go wrong?

We piled onto four mag sleds. We had no idea how many Vaers we would be coming back with, and Vaers were big. We would only be able to bring a few back. Though even just one would do, if it had solid connections with Vaer Prime.

Denaraz had pinpointed a small settlement some 120 miles to the north of our current position. We spread out across the terrain and set off after agreeing a rendezvous point.

I was with Zenzie, who had of course refused to leave my side. Next to us, Denaraz and Danaa were staying just within sight. Sibby was with them. Beyond their mag frame were Eshaan and Mel, and the outriders were Neema and Anzany.

I looked across the planet with interest. It was utterly barren. We had landed near what looked like a dried-up river bed, one that had not seen water for hundreds of thousands of years, I thought.

There were no trees or houses. Nothing moved in a monotonous and freezing landscape. No animals. No plants. No water. Wherever the weather we had come through was discharging its rain, it was not here. The mountains were of an endless dark grey, only broken up here and there with a lighter grey stone which ran in seams through the stronger color.

I shivered. It was a desertic and frozen wasteland. Nothing was alive. The mountains seemed like doomed sentinels defending only age-old rock. It was silent, morose and very, very inhospitable. I would not like to be trapped out here in these expanses. I suspected that the survival rate would be pretty low.

Zenzara shivered, despite the heavy protective clothing I had insisted on. She pulled the collar around her thin neck. The folds of skin on her face were turning blue. Her eyes were barely open as she peered through the icy winds.

I pointed to the goggles that were dangling around her neck. "I told you to put them on!"

She glanced down and found them, gratefully slipping them in front of her eyes. "That's better!"

"You should listen harder at briefings."

"I did listen!"

"Sure you did."

She didn't reply. Talking was not easy in that temperature. My lips went icy dry every time I uncovered them. It simply wasn't worth it. I had thought of wearing IEVA suits under the outer layers, so at least our bodies were well insulated, but they would have been far too cumbersome for fighting in this gravity, which we could well end up doing. They had been designed for space travel only. The clothes we were wearing were the heaviest we could find, but, as the temperatures dropped with the approaching night, it was getting more and more gelid.

The mag sleds sped on through a light that seemed perpetually dulled. We kept to the floor of the valley, pressing close to the ground. It seemed unlikely that we could be tracked in such rugged country, but we would draw as little attention to ourselves as possible.

Mag sleds travel pretty fast. It was perhaps an hour later that we began to decelerate. We were approaching the rendezvous coordinates.

My own face felt as though it were cracking. Zenzie's was the opposite: her wrinkles had become stiff and unresponsive. One of them had curled over the rim of her goggles and seemed to be clamping them on her face. I felt bad for her. Maybe we *should* have used the IEVA suits and helmets.

The other mag sleds slid into place. We left them parked under an outcrop of rock where they would not be obvious to any overhead surveillance and then inched our way to the crest of the nearest ridge.

Sitting right in the middle of the next valley was a large compound. I pointed a zoom lens at it. After a few seconds it tuned correctly to the distance and displayed the compound on the accompanying screen.

The buildings were all old-school. Concrete walls and floors, with flat concrete roofs. Roofs like that confirmed that snow was unheard of around here. I guess rain was too. The total lack of any vegetation was a bit of a giveaway there.

The compound was set out in regimented squares. At the back were ten large huts that looked residential. In front of those were two halls that seemed more social. Closest to us were around twenty much smaller facilities. These were each individually enclosed with barbed wire that reached around three meters high. The whole compound was enclosed by an even higher barbed wire fence, one that looked to be around four meters high. Then there were two further barriers, both of these of endless loops of concertina razor barbed wire that was free to move between the concrete posts which were set every ten meters.

To our left, just outside the exterior barrier, was a small spaceport. It was very basic, almost jury-rigged to my eyes, but it was certainly enough to provide a landing pad and fuel to a couple of shuttles. There were no ships currently on the pad, though I could see a few hover sledges parked around the periphery.

I signaled to Denaraz. He pulled his way over to me on his elbows.

"Can you see any vigilance?"

"No, but it has to be there. These Southern Vaers are known for short and sharp incursions. Nobody would leave a compound like this unguarded. We just can't see it."

"So how do we get in?"

He shrugged. "Knock at the front door?"

"Very funny." I tried to think. My brain felt as though it had turned into a block of ice, so that wasn't exactly easy.

I felt Sibby's presence nearby and turned. She was looking pleased with herself.

"You got something Sibby?"

"I think so." She put her tablet screen on the ground and crouched down, pointing to a dark metal box that stood out against one of the roofs. "See that?"

I squinted. "Maybe."

"That is a DEX repeater point. It means they are utilizing quantum radar to detect any anomalies in their surroundings."

"And …?"

She pulled out a tiny drone and a much larger tool kit.

"Shells, Sibby, do you always travel around with one of those?"

She grinned. "I am a nanotech engineer, remember. I never go anywhere without one."

I began to feel better. "Does this mean you can do something to block their network?"

"I can do better than that. I can collapse it completely. It will take them at least an hour to get it back up again."

"Only an hour?" That might not be long enough.

She looked up at the heavens. "Honestly, Mall! You should be grateful, not complaining about it!"

"Sorry. I am. It is going to be tight though."

Denaraz shook his head. "We only have to get back to the mag sleds. There are no shuttles currently at the spaceport. I think the top Vaers must be away. I doubt they have anything that can catch our sleds."

Zenzie was peering down at the huts. "We have to let all of them out. That will keep them busy rounding up the escapees. They may not even realize there has been an outside influence at work."

I nodded. "Good enough. As many as we can, at least. Zenzie and Denaraz, you are with me."

Sibby stopped work on the drone. "I will have to come too."

I sighed. "Sibby …"

"I have to, Mall. The drone itself will fall into the compound. I cannot risk my tech being picked up by the Vaers. I will put a trace on it. My job will be to recover it."

I hesitated.

"You won't be able to go at all if I don't put these things together and find a way to make their system decohere."

She wasn't wrong. That didn't make my decision any easier.

"This won't work at a distance. And I have no intention of letting the Vaer know how I can crack their quantum radar."

I wondered when my sister had become so decided.

"All right. But I want Eshaan beside you."

The Enif looked gratified. "Of course."

I considered those left. Danaa was too large but could run faster than any of us. She was in. I waved her to the front.

I looked around at the others. "Any of you speak any Vaer?"

To my amazement, it was Mel who answered. "I do. I studied it for four years on the shipstation."

She must have seen my slack jaw. "My father made me choose a language. He wanted me to learn Nepheal or Tyzar, but I chose Vaer to spite him. I knew he couldn't speak it himself so he would never be able to test me on it. It set me free; the others had to speak Nepheal or Tyzar at the table."

I couldn't help laughing. The thought of meek Mel choosing to study such an aggressive language just to avoid her father's annoyance with her made me chuckle.

I was one of the few people who knew just how much she had suffered at his hands. He had never accepted her claustronetia. His view had been one of irritation at such nonsense. He was of the opinion that total immersion would cure any silly phobias. He had been merciless in his continual denigration of his small daughter's weaknesses. Mel's life had been one of pure misery. No wonder she had become such an unassuming adult.

However, here she was now, standing tall in front of me, willing to risk her life for the Alliance. I was so proud of her.

"Good for you, Melly."

She flushed. "Never thought it would come in useful for anything."

"We certainly need it now. I doubt any of the detainees being held inside that compound will know much Universal. We will have very little time to decide who to take with us and who to leave to escape on their own. In this isolated spot, that might be equivalent to leaving them to die."

She gave a philosophical shrug. "Some of them would probably prefer that. I know I would."

Neema moved and gave her a quick slap on the back. "We can save some. That is something, at least."

"If they want to be saved."

True. That comment hung over us, bringing uncertainty.

I asked Neema and Anzany to stay with the mag sleds until the seven of us got back. They nodded, though neither of them seemed thrilled to be excluded from the main action.

We waited for Sibby as she tinkered with the internals of her drone. It was small enough to sit on her hand. We turned the sleds around and made sure there was plenty to hang onto, rearranging the backs a little to protect whoever was riding them. It was the best we could do.

Sibby worked away on the tiny drone. She seemed worried about the cold temperature. She had taken her gloves off to effect the minute changes in the circuitry. Her hands had gone blue. She blew on them from time to time, until Denaraz squatted next to her and quietly took one of her hands between his.

There was a small pause, then Sibby looked surprised. "You are making my fingers warm! How can you do that?"

He smiled. "I can change my body temperature at will. I simply think that I want my hands to warm and they will. Around ten degrees, anyway." He dropped the first hand and picked up the second. "Better?"

She stared at him. "Much!"

Zenzie kicked at the ground. "Bet *you* can't do that, Ryler Mallivan!"

"Nope."

She gave me a so-why-are-you-the-captain look. I bristled. "I can do other things!"

"You can?"

I began to laugh. "Yes, I can, you abominable young thing. Now stop trying to get a rise out of me."

This mission-critical conversation stopped there. Most of us went back to the sleds, where we huddled under what little protection there was as we waited.

Half an hour later, Sibby stood up. "Done!"

"How close do we need to be?"

"Within a hundred feet of the fence."

I signaled to the others. "Let's go, then."

We decided to aim for the second hut on the right. It was one of the furthest away from the small spaceport, but more in the shadows than the far corner hut. Denaraz armed himself with a large pair of wire cutters and tough gloves. I did the same. Then we said our goodbyes to the two we were leaving behind. They promised to have the mag sleds ticking over and ready to depart.

We crept down the mountain trying not to make a sound. Sibby thought that the quantum radar would extend for a quarter of a mile in all directions, but that was from the source, which would be in the centre of the complex. We hoped that we could get to within a hundred feet of the fence without triggering an alarm, but it was a chance we had to take. Sibby was reasonably confident. She reckoned that the range of the DEX network would be closer to the fence than that. Even so, it was a tense approach.

Finally Sibby signaled a stop. She was where she needed to be. I could see her consulting a hand-held receptor of some sort. She nodded to herself and slowly began to make the drone ready.

The small craft hovered for a moment above the ground, and then rose very swiftly in the air. Sibby let it go straight up until we could no longer see it.

"I want to invade the barrier directly over the main DEX hub," she explained. "As close as I can get, anyhow. I don't want them to be able to deduce a vector for us."

That made good sense.

We hunkered down and tried not to move. They were using quantum radar, but that didn't mean that they didn't have eyes.

Sibby was carefully monitoring the drone's progress. At last I saw her shoulders relaxing. She shot a sideways glance at me and her fingers danced over the controls. "Any ... minute ... now," she murmured, more to herself than to anybody else.

"Will we see anything?"

"You should be able to pick out ...." She paused. "—There! See?"

Not really. I might have picked up a tiny flash of luminescence, but it was barely noticeable, even in the dark night that had settled over the land.

She turned to the rest of us. "We can go in now."

Denaraz was the first to move. Pulling out the large wire cutters, he ran across the open terrain to the first fence. Danaa overtook him before he reached it and Zenzara was not far behind. We followed as fast as we could.

We reached the first barrier to find it cut. They had been quick. The edges had been pulled back to allow us passage through. So far it seemed that we had not been spotted. That was sheer luck. The Vaers were known for their excellent sight. They were, however, historically day fliers, so their night sight might not match up to the excellence with which they had evolved to pick out victims at a large distance. We could hope.

Denaraz already had the second razor concertina rolled back for us when we reached his position, and had moved to tackle the first of the upright fences.

The light was better here, but there was nobody in sight and I could see no cameras on the corner positions.

We were soon through that, and the final fence. We split up. Zenzara and Denaraz peeled off. Their function was to facilitate the escape of the other huts but not to actually come into contact with the residents. After some discussion, we had decided to place small charges against the locks. These would eventually be traced to outside influence, but we were hoping it might take some time in the confusion and chaos of a break-out.

Sibby and Eshaan continued straight on, right into the center of the compound. My heart dropped a little when I saw my sister walk, head tall, straight into danger. I had to look away. This was not a good time to lose my own concentration.

The rest of us headed straight for the second hut, the one we had earmarked as the most shadowed.

Mel ducked and pressed some Lastek explosive around the lock. Then Danaa and I stepped back as she detonated it. There was a dim thud, followed by squawks of surprise from inside the hut.

We stormed in, guns at the ready.

The squawks doubled in volume.

I tried to get my bearings as quickly as I could.

There must have been thirty Vaers inside that hut. They were shriveled and shrunken in comparison to the individuals I had come across before. Captain Frynee being the one who came unbidden to my mind. I wished he hadn't.

These Vaers were in a sorry state. They had obviously been made to work in extreme conditions and I didn't think they could have been fed for days. Their bellies were concave, their feathers bedraggled. They huddled together in shock, their eyes wide and staring.

I looked for Mel. She came up beside me.

"Tell them we are looking for four volunteers."

She began to speak in Vaer. Their eyes immediately switched to her.

"Tell them they can make their own way to freedom, risking the terrain. Or they can come with us."

She did so. All of them took a step back, distancing themselves from us.

Mel stopped waiting for me and spoke out on her own. I had no idea what she was telling them, but I could see it was not working well. The expressions of utter distrust were not changing.

Just when I thought none of the prisoners would come, two of the smallest shuffled forwards. Mel walked quickly over to them. There was a quick interchange, and then Mel beckoned to Danaa. The Nepheal girl gestured for the two Vaers to follow her.

But there had been a cry of outrage and a surge forwards of the remaining Vaers. We were forced to fire warning shots. Danaa, who was the recipient of most of the acrimony, looked alarmed and moved even more quickly. The two volunteers, who looked like children and had clearly been mistreated, scuttled after her.

The warning pulser beams stopped the massed Vaers.

There was a moment ... just a moment ... when everything was completely quiet.

Then all hell broke loose.

The Vaers in front of me erupted in a sea of panic.

The two small prisoners slipped out with Danaa and disappeared.

I signaled immediate retreat.

The dull thumps of more Lastek explosive indicated that Zenzara and Denaraz had completed their tasks and would already be retreating back up the hill.

We were done. Our position was as exposed as we could afford to be without getting ourselves killed. We needed to get out of there.

We tumbled out of the hut as fast as we could go, the horde of Vaer prisoners streaming out behind us.

Luckily, we knew where the cuts in the fences were. That gave us the small edge that we needed.

Up ahead, I could see Danaa racing up the hill. The two Vaer children must be very weak, because she had dropped to all fours and placed them on her back. I could only imagine how difficult that must have been for her, knowing that the Nepheal were the natural victims of the Vaers. However, she was making good time up the slope, the Vaer children clinging on for dear life and bouncing all over the place.

I stared back into the compound. There was no sign of Sibby and Eshaan. Where were they? Had they managed to recover the drone? How could I leave without them? I told Mel to go on alone, but she shook her head and slowed her pace to match mine.

Just when we were about to stop altogether I caught sight of one of the strangest sights I had ever seen. Eshaan was running towards us, its long body bounding across the compound in huge strides. It was under fire; I could see the flashes as ABlasers rebounded off its hard carapace. Like a limpet, my sister was clinging on to its chest for dear life. She was pressed to its frontal carapace, her legs supported by its two lower forearms, her face ducked under its chin. Eshaan had found a way to protect her from the fire. I couldn't see well enough to register if they had picked up the drone or not.

Mel and I picked up speed again, turning all our attention to escaping up the hill. We exchanged quick smiles of relief. I felt a surge of something like euphoria to see Sibby coming out of that alive.

Enif can run very fast. It didn't take this one long to overtake us. Eshaan nodded to me as it thundered past. I spotted the drone clutched in one of Sibby's hands. That was great news. The tech would live to fight another day. I would have to ask Sibby to train us in its use before she left. If she ever left.

Mel stumbled, but I managed to slip my hand under her elbow, just stopping a fall. At that moment, lights came on in the compound. We reached the holes in the fences, and flung ourselves through.

As we tore up the hill, the escapees flooded in our wake, realizing that there was, after all, a way through all that barbed wire. Shots rang out as guards arrived on the scene.

We scrambled up the slope, just glad that the floodlit areas did not quite reach out to us. The lights had found scores of the Vaers we had left behind. At the moment, they were the ones who were attracting fire. But they were responding, some of them lying in wait for the guards and then attacking themselves.

Of those who had made it as far as the gaps in the fencing, most scattered when they ducked through the last barrier. Only one or two decided to follow us directly. I didn't think they were planning to join us. We had been looked down on by the Nova Vaer for too many generations for any of their number to accept us as friends. They were following because they knew that we must have some kind of transport out of here. They were following to wrest that away from us.

I shifted my rifle to my shoulder and turned back for a few seconds. I didn't aim at any of the following Vaers. I simply loosed off a volley of fire in their direction, just to hold them up.

It worked, but we still might not get away in time. Hopefully Danaa would have settled our two volunteers safely onto the mag sleds, because we were coming in hot. I could now see armed and extremely large and well-trained guards pounding up the hill in our wake.

They, too, were now firing on the escapees behind us. The only difference was that their shots were hitting their mark. And they were aiming to kill.

Just when I was almost sighing with relief, sure that we would make it, two air bikes shot over the fence and sped in our direction. Now that, *that* was going to be a problem.

I was still holding Mel's elbow. I gave it a shake. "Get back to the others. Tell them to get away. Now!"

Mel started to open her mouth to protest. I shook her again. "Do as I say Mel! I will hide out in the third valley from here to the shuttle. Ask Sammy to come pick me up in the night. Sibby will have some sort of gadget that will find out where I am."

She had gone white. I contemplated holding my gun in her face, but I wasn't sure that trick would work a second time. I stared right into her eyes. "Please, Mel!"

She gave a small moan, but turned and began to run further up the hill.

I ducked quickly to one side, where there was a small rocky outcrop. It only took a moment to slip behind the largest rock. I took careful aim with the M596.

The first shot missed, but I did manage to clip the lead air bike with the second. The bike skewed to the right, almost unseating the rider.

I tracked the second air bike. This time I had more success. The first shot powered right through the front casing.It must have hit something important, because the bike veered off line and dropped like a stone onto the ground. Its rider was thrown clear, but must have been stunned since he didn't get back up.

The other air bike had straightened up again and was now firing on my position. I ducked down, but aimed the rifle up in its general direction and fired. I didn't want to let it beyond my position, where it could attack the mag sleds from a distance. The air bikes would be armed with small air to ground missiles; our mag sleds were not. Rifle fire from the rest of my group would be useless. The rider of the air bike would never let himself get that close.

But he would have to get close to me in order to go over my position. That is what I was counting on. That is why I had stayed.

The rock next to mine exploded. My gun flew out of my hand and landed about ten feet away. I cursed to myself. I would have to risk exposure to get it back.

At that moment I heard firing from behind me and flung myself flat to the ground. ABlasers illuminated the air. Most of them impacted on the remaining air bike.

My mind, still in whiteout from the rock explosion, trailed behind. Understanding only clicked into place when two shapes dove behind my rock. Denaraz and Zenzara.

I was enraged. "Get the fitz out of here!" I waved at them.

Denaraz grinned back. "I only came because she threw herself down the mountain," he told me.

Zenzara was huffy. "I didn't ask you to come!"

"Well. We're here now. Do you think you can walk, Rye?"

I brushed myself down. "Of course I can walk! Why wouldn't I be able to walk?"

"Then we should get going. Those bikes are down for good now, but the infantry is almost on us."

"I thought I told Mel to clear out!"

"Mel and Danaa *have* cleared out! They took the volunteers and two of the mag sleds. Eshaan and Sibby went with them, though Eshaan had to restrain Sibby to stop her from coming to look for you. I don't think Sibby was best pleased. Neema and Anzany have the remaining two sleds prepped. Come on!"

Zenzara dragged at one of my arms, Izan at the other. Between them, they pulled me off the stony ground. Both of them were firing down the hill as they did so.

Luckily for us, some of the guards had caught up with the escaped Vaers that were following us. They tried to slip past, but the prisoners were having none of that. They threw themselves onto the guards with gusto, determined to get control of one of the weapons. There was a hiatus in the chase.

That left only the two air bike riders. Although they were now bikeless, they were both up and running, though one of them had lost his helmet. They were firing on us, and the ABlasers were bouncing off the rocks that we passed. We tried to put their aim off by zigzagging, but it quickly became evident that we would have to stop and deal with the threat. They were too close, and their weapons were too good.

Izan indicated a row of large boulders up ahead and I nodded. We threw ourselves behind the cover.

The two Vaer guards saw what we were doing and themselves ducked for cover.

"Keep shooting," muttered Zenzie, from behind us.

"If I had something to shoot at, I would," I replied grimly. "Zenzie, make sure you ... *Come back!*" The last was issued in a fierce whisper, but it was far too late. Zenzara had crept sideways and was making her way stealthily towards the Vaers.

"Keep firing!" I snarled at Denaraz. There was nothing else we could do. We would have to trust that the Tyzaran girl knew what she was doing.

Denaraz had gone white, too. He very nearly got his head shot off his shoulders by returning fire when he shouldn't have.

"She was right behind me!" he hissed.

"Yeah, I know. We should have tied her to one of us."

Now she had taken that route, our only positive action was to support her. We separated slightly, to increase our angle of fire, and followed her progress towards the low rocks that sheltered the Vaers.

Zenzie moved across the terrain with great ease. Her movements were quick and measured. She was so small that she was able to move stealthily. I had to admire her grit and determination. She looked as if she had been doing this all her life.

Denaraz was admiring, despite his worry for her. "We train to attack Vaers," he told me. "Avaraks are considered the main threat, but she will have had lessons on how to eliminate a Vaer as well."

And she did. One moment she was ten feet away, hidden from the Vaers by a large rock. The next we opened serious fire on them, careful to avoid going near Zenzie's position.

Then she was up and over the rock, nivala in one hand and thoria in the other. There was silence for about thirty seconds, then she reappeared, running lightly towards us.

She bounced over our cover and continued running.

"You two coming?" she demanded, over her shoulder. "We haven't got all day, you know."

Denaraz and I eyed the remaining guards, who had just about eliminated the prisoners between them and us. It was quite definitely the right time to leave.

We sprinted up the rest of the hill, leapt onto the waiting mag sleds and collapsed as Neema and Anzany forced the throttles down as hard as they could. Denaraz glared at Zenzara from the back of Neema's sled. I glared at her from closer, since she had pulled herself onto Anzany's sled with me.

She shook her crest at me. Bits of sharp flint from the rocks flew off it. "What? We made it, didn't we? You can thank me later."

I had to laugh. I knew she had been waiting to throw that one back at me.

5

We found the concealed shuttle waiting for us, engines on and ready to go. As soon as our two mag sleds were aboard, the engines began to whine.

Anzany's voice came over the com-link. "Strap in, please."

That didn't give us much time. We all leapt for the straps set in the walls of the shuttle bay. Anzany wasn't hanging around.

I finished adjusting the straps. Zenzie, beside me, had done the same. Denaraz already had his in place.

Then we were thrown out from the walls and backwards as the g-forces began to pile on. I looked at Zenzie and burst out laughing. Her wrinkles had been dragged down so far that her face looked just like a melting clock.

She let me know what she thought with her eyes. None of us could have spoken.

The shuttle began to creak and shake as it hauled itself away up the gravity well. Even though it was designed for planetary landings and takeoffs, it didn't seem to like the higher forces it was being submitted to.

I realized that we were being chased when the shuttle began to buck even more than usual, around the middle of its takeoff. My teeth shook as a huge shudder ran through the fuselage.

Anzany's voice clicked through on the com-link. "Don't worry. They can only trace us because of the heat and air friction trails we are leaving through the atmosphere. Once we reach the ionosphere I will be able to shake them off easily. With the carbon cloud they will not be able to follow us."

There was a crump and a shudder as something else it hit. They were using rail guns.

"—Though you may experience some turbulence in the meantime," Anzany's voice added, sounding for all the world like a stewardess on an interstellar liner.

A few subdued catcalls greeted her words.

But she was right. She managed to get us safely back to the waiting ships up in orbit, and we took some time to re-embed the shuttles. First the larger shuttle was squeezed back inside the hold of *Nivala*. Then all that remained was to slide *Nivala's* shuttle inside the larger shuttle, and we were good to go. Sammy took his place in the pilot's seat of the Nepheal ship and edged his way cautiously out from behind the moon with no further ill effects.

Once we were set on a course for Vaer Prime, I went in search of our new volunteers. Neema had taken them to the sick bay, where she had slapped portable triage units on both of them.

Our two Vaers were certainly children. Or young adults, perhaps. Although they towered over me, they had none of the solidity of a fully-formed adult Vaer. Apart from this, they had been mistreated.

Neema's face was grim. She had one of the female child's wings extended, and now that she had, it was easy to see the missing feathers. At least half of the primary and secondary feathers had been pulled out. Only the smaller coverts were left, those that lay close to the radius and ulna at the front of the wing.

"Who did that to you?" I disliked the Vaer species in general and some members of it in particular, but found it horrific to see deliberate mutilation in such a young creature.

I had to wait for an answer. Both of the Vaers stared at me in incomprehension. It wasn't until Mel slipped through the door and began to translate that we heard their story.

They had been traveling from one part of Vaer Prime to another. Their family owned a holiday property in the Southern Hemisphere of the main planet. Their plane had been ambushed by the Sellica faction of Vaer Nova, and they had been abducted.

The female began to cry. "The factions hate us. They blame us for forcing their ancestors to leave Vaer Prime. The pirates laughed at me and my brother. They made us clean up after them. Made us do tasks for them. Every time we were too slow they pulled out another wing feather."

I frowned. "Why did they abduct you? Did they want your family to pay to get you back?"

More tears. "No," she wailed. "My family would never take us back now. We have been defaced. Vaer feathers don't grow back. We can never go back to Vaer Prime."

"Then why did they take you?"

She gave a huge sniff. "Because the Sellicas trade anything. Anything. Anybody." She looked at her brother. "They traded our plane. They traded our pilot. Our nurse. Our cook. Only, when it came to trade us, the pirates had pulled too many of our feathers out. The lead Vaer in the compound was cross with them when he saw us. It made us difficult to sell. Nobody wants a bald-winged Vaer. He told them to throw us into the huts." Now she really began to sob in earnest. "Nobody ever comes out of those huts alive. They only throw in enough food for half the numbers. We haven't eaten in five days, since they threw us in. And it was so cold. Without all our feathers it just gets so cold."

Her brother had the fixed stare of somebody in shock. He couldn't even speak.

"How old are you?" I asked.

"Thirteen. My brother is fourteen."

"All right. We will get you some medicine for your injuries and some food and water. Then we can talk."

"Are ... Are you going to torture us?" Mel's voice broke as she translated. I looked at her.

"No. Of course not. All we want you to do is to help us find out where somebody is on Vaer Prime. Then we will drop you off wherever you want to go."

The female said something to her brother, but he shook his head.

"We cannot go back. We have nowhere to go."

I didn't even think about keeping them on board. These two souls needed to get back to their family. They weren't like Zenzara.

"Well, you can think about that later. Rest first."

I was glad we had managed to save these two youngsters. From the girl's account, they wouldn't have lasted for much longer in that hut. In fact, I was surprised that they hadn't suffered even more aggression inside. Perhaps their youth had saved them from being challenged.

The problem was, if they wouldn't be accepted on Vaer Prime, they were limited in their usefulness to us. I had hoped to get a spy out of our dangerous incursion on Vaer Nova. What we had actually obtained were closer to two liabilities.

I sighed.

The boy seemed to sense my disappointment. He leapt up, breaking the sensors that crossed to him from the triage PTU. He thrust his small beak right in my face and words poured out of him. I couldn't understand any of them.

Mel began to have trouble translating, but got the gist. "He is basically saying that they will be useful to you. That you will see. That you won't regret rescuing them."

I knew how to answer that. "Tell him that I will not harm them. That they will be safe now. Tell him he can relax. Nobody will hurt his sister. Or him."

The Vaer boy stopped, mid sentence, as her words percolated.

Then he subsided again and allowed Neema to reattach the sensors. I thought I saw tears in his eyes, as well.

I took Neema aside. "Can you check with the other Shell species? See if any of them know how to regenerate feathers?"

She nodded. "The Nepheals might. Or the Tyzarans."

"Yes. At least we will know where we stand then."

She checked the PTUs. Then she turned to the two Vaers. "You are both dehydrated and undernourished. There is severe scarring along the wings, and you have heavy bruising all across your bodies. Apart from that, both of you have fractured phalanges in the wing tips. I am going to ask you to submerge what you can of your wing injuries in Zeroth chambers for the next couple of days. That should be sufficient, although unfortunately you won't fit in completely."

Mel translated. The boy nodded solemnly. The girl's eyes opened wide at the idea of going near a Zeroth chamber, but her brother spoke sharply to her and she acquiesced.

Neema smiled. "You will both be in the same room. You will be able to talk."

That quieted the girl down.

I left them to it.

Zenzara caught up with me in the corridor. "You look tired, Mallivan Bell."

"I am. It takes longer than you think to get back to normal after injuries."

"Yes. What are you going to do with the Vaers?"

"I don't know. They say they can't go back to Vaer Prime." I explained about the missing feathers.

"But the Vaers don't even use their feathers! They lost the ability to fly centuries ago. Didn't they?"

I shrugged. "So the rumors say. Search me."

She became thoughtful. "Hmm. It must be a bit like walking nude along a Tyzar street. Not socially acceptable."

"Maybe. We will have to wait and see what we can do for them. It isn't their fault."

"Nobody is blameless."

I flared up at that. "This is not their fault! They are victims!"

"Yes. But they are Vaer victims. Vaers promote aggression. You see?"

"No. I don't see. These are innocents."

"We don't know that."

"They are young!"

"So am I, yet I am already the Chyzar. A lot of people would like to kill *me*. Age doesn't always matter. We should withhold judgement. We don't know."

She had a point. I hate it when Zenzara has a point. I gave a grunt. She took that as agreement and looked smug.

I told Danaa to take it easy as we flipped across the system towards Vaer Prime. If the two Vaers needed a couple of days in a Zeroth tank there was little point hurrying.

I decided to get Sibby to use that time to make up a few high-tech gadgets that might come in useful. Mainly small adornments that would record conversations. I did try to get her to make individual carbon clouds in the hope that they could act like personal invisibility cloaks.

She stared at me. "I already told you that was impossible. Sometimes, Mall, I think you don't even listen."

"I do. I just wondered if you might have come up with something. Since then, I mean."

"Well, I haven't. The technology needs a huge amount of energy. Unless you can wander around with a 200 pound set of batteries on your back, it won't work."

"Pity." It would have made life so much easier.

"Yes, but you knew that."

"Hmm. Beggars can dream."

She was taken aback. "Are things that bad?"

"No. Bad? Of course they aren't. I was merely exploring all possibilities."

Denaraz walked in and my wonderful sister blushed right to the roots of her hair. "Hello," she said.

Izan bent to plant a small kiss on one of her rosy cheeks. "Hello."

It felt as though that had been a whole conversation. I rolled my eyes. I couldn't help it. I may have muttered something under my breath.

"Don't be jealous, Mall. It may happen to you one day."

Not a chance! I like to go out as much as the next man, but there was no way in the Shells that I was about to align my path with somebody else's. Mine is single track.

I left them to it.

A day later we were hanging tucked in behind the smallest moon of Vaer Prime. I was back in the med bay, checking out our visitors.

They already looked better. Their skin was taut and their flesh seemed to have filled out. Mel translated my question as to whether they were feeling better.

"Thank you. We are stronger. Neema has indicated that we can take our wings out of the Zeroth chambers this afternoon." They looked relieved. Our Zeroth chambers were far too small for Vaers, and it must have been tedious to have to squeeze parts of their bodies in. They would have to remain doubled over for hours at a time.

I nodded. "Then I can talk to you about the task at hand?"

The girl didn't answer. She looked towards her brother. He peered over at me, twisting his head from side to side to examine me with both eyes. "You can."

"We believe that two Terrans have taken refuge on Vaer Prime."

His dark eyes flashed, making him look more like the predator his species had always been. "Impossible!"

"How so?"

"No foreigners are allowed on Prime soil. It is forbidden."

"Then how is his signal coming from there?"

The boy shot a question at his sister in Vaer. She frowned and considered, replying at length. I raised my eyebrows at Mel. She shook her head. "That is some sort of dialect. I don't understand it."

I saw the flash of amusement that passed between them. They were happy that we couldn't understand everything they said. Zenzara's warning popped back up in my head. I couldn't afford to trust these two, however young and apparently innocent they were.

The boy turned back to me. "There is only one logical answer."

"And that is ...?"

"They are on the Atmospheric Research Facility."

"What is that?"

The girl tucked her beak into her neck. "It is the only place any Terrans ... any foreigners ... would ever be allowed. Even then, I have never heard of such a thing happening. The Atmospheric Research Facility is on a geocentric stable platform in the stratosphere of our planet, above the equator. There is a ... a ... rising platform to take visitors up from the planet, and a small space port for shuttles to land."

"A lift? A space elevator?" I was impressed. "Nifty!"

They seemed confused. Mel glared at me. "Don't use words I can't translate!"

"Sorry. So, how can we get you on this facility?"

They both shook their heads. They seemed pretty definite. It wasn't possible.

The boy finally deigned to explain. "We are young. We are now without feathers. There could be no possible reason for our presence. It is quite out of the question."

I sighed. But it was what I had been expecting. However, I wasn't going to give up. Not that easily.

"What about your parents?"

"What about our parents?"

"Would they help us if we could get those feathers to grow back?"

His eyes hooded over and then cleared. "They might. We are their only offspring. Can we be cured?"

"The Tyzarans say they can regenerate the feathers you have lost. It will mean four months sleeping in modified Zeroth chambers, but you could spend the days as you liked. It would have to be on Tyzar, however. That's the only place they have Zeroths big enough for you. You would have to go into their main treatment facility. They are willing to allow you safe passage and a secure stay in their capital."

He was suspicious. "How much would it cost?"

"It would be free. The Alliance would pay for it. I have consulted the Macers."

"My father would not betray his people. Even for us." The boy's voice was choked. It was a reality he would rather not have faced.

"I don't think we are asking him to do anything treasonous. These are not Vaers. And you can explain to him that the two Terrans are in possession of the most dangerous technology that exists. They cannot be trusted not to use it. All I am trying to do is flush them out of the sanctuary of Vaer Prime. I wish no ill to the inhabitants. And, he should know that they are in league with the Sellica faction of Novan Vaers."

"I find that hard to believe. Our government would never enter into an agreement with the Sellica faction."

"I have proof."

His gaze stilled. His eyes hooded and he examined my expression. Then he scraped his beak lightly on the side of the Zeroth chamber. I think he did it to gain time.

"Do you have proof that the Tyzarans can heal us?"

I nodded. "I will bring you the confirmation, together with evidence of the Sellica faction's involvement."

"Then I will talk to my father."

"Good. Tell him we would need him to facilitate access for us to the research facility."

"The ARF, yes. My father would find it difficult to access, but perhaps not impossible. He would no doubt want reassurances that his action could not be traced back to our family. Some Prime Vaers would not understand it."

"If he does not betray us, I think we can successfully cover his tracks."

"Then, as soon as we are free of these regeneration tanks, I will attempt to persuade him."

"Thank you. If he refuses, we will take you to wherever you want." I didn't tell him that we would arrange for the treatment in any case. He didn't need to know that.

"You will not punish us?"

"We will not. Although we would of course be disappointed if you did not fulfil your promise to us."

He dipped his beak. "I see."

That evening, we were all on the bridge to witness the conversation between the two Vaer children and their parents.

At first, there was great happiness on the faces of the parents. Then the reality of the mutilations set in. Their father's face turned to stone.

"What have the barbarians done to you?"

His son correctly identified the barbarians as us. He hastened to correct this mistake. "No, Father. This was the Sellicas. We were captured by Novans."

"Then why are you with foreigners now? Have you been traded? I will punish them for daring to trade Vaer children!" His expression as he said this was dire, and since he was looking directly at me I took a step back.

Mel, who was translating, told us that the boy was now explaining exactly the agreement he and his sister had undertaken. The father did not look much happier.

"The agreement is null and void," he said sharply. "Neither of you may come back to Prime. Not like that."

"We know, Father. However ..." He went on to explain about the

Tyzarans and our proposition to cure them both, finally holding up the written guarantee he had himself sought. "It is true. It can be done."

"And what do the foreigners want in return? What will it cost me?"

I stepped forwards at that. I thought that these Vaers would speak some Universal. They were fairly important people on Vaer Prime.

"Let me explain." I started to tell him who Bull Cunningham was, and what he had done in conjunction with the Sellica Vaers. I ended up telling him where the signal was coming from, and that we now believed that they were on the ARF.

"You wish me to betray my people?" His chest puffed out with outrage.

I held up my hands. "Not at all. Your people have already been betrayed. Why should the Sellica faction have any influence here on Prime? Has your government somehow been infiltrated? I believe that we have uncovered a plot of some sort and this will allow you to avoid catastrophe."

He fell silent, mulling my words over. "I will need proof," he said eventually.

"Naturally."

"It would be hard to intervene successfully."

"We have looked you up. I believe you are a member of the Vaer Prime Sub-delegation?"

"I am."

"Then you are in a good position to investigate. I would, however, urge you to take care. The stakes in this are very high. Those involved will be on their guard. Bull Cunningham knows that we will attempt to find him. He will be expecting trouble."

"The Terrans do not interest me. If what you say is true, we must root out the Prime citizens who have committed treason. It is an offence to trade in any shape or form with any Novan Vaer. It is one of the worst offences in Prime legislation."

"Yes. I know. Which is why I believe you will help us. All we request is permission to land on the ARF when the time is right and permission to extract Bull Cunningham and Ramesh Chandrayanan. We have no further interest in the matter. However, the Interstellar Enforcement Agency is required to escort those two Terrans back for trial."

The small protrusions on his beak twitched a little. I saw his children look at each other with something like panic. Finally he gave a slow nod and they relaxed. "Send me the proof. I will examine it and let you know."

I let out a long breath. "Certainly."

We cut the hololink. Everybody smiled. Even the Vaer children looked happy for the first time.

I went up to them. "What are your names?"

The boy understood without translation. He pointed to himself. "Emereen." Then he pointed to his sister. "Marivee."

"We will get you back to your family yet, Emereen."

He looked over to Mel inquiringly. She translated. He made a strange chattering sound with his beak.

"I think he is saying that he hopes so too," said Mel with a smile.

It didn't take long for Sub-delegate Belzeer to get back to us. He was short and to the point.

"I will require a written agreement, which is to remain private between the two signatories, but binding on the Interstellar Alliance."

"Very well."

"And if the treatment is not successful in either case, the child in question will be cared for on Tyzar until puberty and then allowed to choose a career within the Interstellar Alliance."

I had to be careful there. "*Within* the Alliance, yes. *For* the Alliance will not be possible, unless the Vaers are full members."

The tips of his beak crunched together. "Acceptable."

I felt huge relief. "How will you get on board the Atmospheric

Research Facility? Will that be difficult?"

He shook his head. "I have already initiated preparations for a visit. Ostensibly it will be to honor one of the long-time scientists who works there. He is being awarded what we refer to as the black cross, which is within my purview. It is one of the most prestigious awards that a scientist can get."

I was impressed. Belzeer didn't hang around once he made up his mind.

"How many will there be in your party, Sub-delegate?"

"I am taking twenty of my closest collaborators. Those include three who work for state security. They are trained to evaluate things that pose a threat to any Prime citizens."

"Have you informed them of the real reason for the visit?"

"I have. I would never ask them to walk blindly into a dangerous situation. I have not, however, told them of the situation of my children. That will remain strictly between us."

"Of course. We have already agreed that point. How can we get onto the station?"

"You can't. Your presence there is not acceptable. However, what happens out of our Prime orbit is outside our control. If any Alliance citizens were to be found outside our boundaries, it would be none of our business what happened to them. Our focus is always on our own citizens."

"You would let them escape?"

He spread the tips of his wings. "How could we stop them if they decided to take a waiting ship? Such things can happen, you know."

"I see. Would ships such as the one you are discussing have trackers implanted in them?"

"That cannot be arranged, I'm afraid."

"Then perhaps the waiting ship could be an old one. One with high emissions?"

"That could probably be arranged." He puffed out his chest a little. "Good. I am glad we do understand each other. As a loyal subject, I owe my allegiance to my people. I could never – under any circumstances – allow family expediency to come first."

"A true patriot." Who had one eye to the main chance, like many. I could not blame him for that. I would have done exactly the same thing. At least, I think I would.

"Perhaps you wish to speak a little more to your children?"

"If you do not require the bandwidth, I would appreciate that."

I left them talking. Mel was recording the conversation and listening intently, just in case there were indications of any sort of subterfuge on their part.

I beckoned to Denaraz and Didjal. We walked a little way apart.

"Didj, we are going to need full power. Can you make sure that the engines on both ships are running optimally?"

It nodded. "Sure. Are we going to disembed them?"

"No. Not at first, in any case. But we will move all unessential personnel onto *Nivala*. They will be safer within two layers of hull."

Didjal walked away to get a start on that, and I turned to Denaraz. "Izan, can you and Sibby make sure we have carbon clouds ready for both ships?"

"That might be difficult. We would have to readapt the one we used in the shuttle on Vaer Nova. We have only been able to reverse engineer one copy so far, because we don't have enough prime materials on board either ship."

"But we can disguise both *Nivala* and *Aenysia* at the same time?"

"In theory. Sibby and I will need a day or two to set it up correctly."

That was a relief.

He gave me a strange look. "What is on your mind? You seem worried."

"I just can't see why Cunningham would come here. There had to be some very good reason. He was protected by the Sellicas, or part of the Sellicas. They don't get on well with the Vaer Primes. We know that. It simply doesn't make any sense."

Denaraz huffed. "Perhaps they just needed something they couldn't get on Vaer Nova."

"Exactly. That is what is bothering me. What was it they needed, and why did they have to come here to get it?"

Izan grinned. "Research. You need Seyal for that."

He was right. I had forgotten how good she was at it. I would put her with Mel to sift through the unique things that could be found on Vaer Prime. They would soon figure it all out. Because I had a really, really bad feeling about it.

Then I realized that I could get information more quickly. It made me interrupt the conversation Marivee and Emereen were still having with their parents. They all looked up at me, expectant.

"Sub-delegate, can you tell me what reason the Terrans might have to wish to use the ARF?"

The Vaer's nostrils flared. "The only thing on that station, apart from the research team, is the link to Vaer Prime's only supercomputer."

I felt the bottom drop out of my stomach, and exchanged a look of concern with the others on the bridge. We all knew what that meant. Chandrayanan was not done. Cunningham must still have the capability to open that traversable wormhole they had been planning for so long. We had damaged the supercomputer on Ebyssia that they had been using. There was no such thing anywhere on Vaer Nova. And we would have caught up with them long before they could reach the Sol system. It was all beginning to make horrible sense.

I tried to smile although my lips felt like rubber. "Could you hook us in via hololink when you go into the ARF? In a private way, so that we could talk to you via tight-beam and you could consult us if you thought it were necessary?"

He huffed a little, uncertain.

I hurried to give him a reason to comply with my request. "I believe we might be able to help identify any devices that could compromise the safety of your planet."

He took that on board. Then nodded, albeit rather reluctantly. "I will arrange for that. I can hook up hololinks to myself and to my two most trusted advisors. However, you will only be able to speak to me. I will tell the others that I wish for a multi-angle recording of the investiture."

"Thank you. When is the visit programmed for?"

"Two days from now, in the middle of the day. Refreshments are to be provided up on the facility after the ceremony."

"You need to organize a visit to all of the areas of the facility."

"Obviously." He glared. Now he had undertaken to carry out this plan, he needed to feel very much in charge.

"Thank you Sub-delegate. I believe you will find ample justification once on the ARF."

"If that is true, then our agreement will have been sweeter than I currently find it."

I smiled and allowed them to say their goodbyes before cutting the connexion.

Two days later we were all clustered around the hololink, except Seyal and Eshaan, who were embedded in *Nivala*, inside *Aenysia*'s huge shuttle bay. They were accompanied by the two Vaer children and Segaton. Eshaan was beginning a huge painting which would depict the fight for the Chakrans at Ebyssia. The Enif artist had been getting more and more fidgety since then. Didjal had explained that this was always the case.

"My *faliif* needs to get a painting done. Until then it will feel restless and unhappy. This is going to be an important painting. It is the place we were meant to die, the place we were meant to undergo our state of enlightenment. Eshaan is eager but apprehensive at the same time."

"How are you feeling about not completing your state of enlightenment, Didjal?" I still felt a little guilty about bringing them back. I knew how important it was to the Enif.

"Now that a real *Belofiin* has authorized it, we have come to terms with it. But this painting is crucial. Nothing like it has ever been attempted before. We are hoping that it will give reason to the delay in our enlightenment, that all will become clear when we see it."

"That is a lot to ask of a painting."

"Paintings can sometimes give a lot."

That was true. And Eshaan's had been so striking recently that they certainly left a lasting impression.

"Do you know what it will be of?"

It nodded. "When the hypersphere turned inside out … when it everted and there was that fierce flash of light. And you, unlocking the casket. At that moment, you were surrounded by pure energy. I think it will be a very great painting."

"I hope so."

"I know it will."

There was a crackle and then the hololink appeared. Sub-delegate Belzeer was wearing the camera somewhere on his ample chest. We could see the forward view. Quality was very good, and we could hear the conversations, although Mel was straining to understand what was being said.

"Those six Vaer in the front are the station heads," she told us. "They are giving a welcome speech. The one to the right, the taller, thinner one, is the scientist who is to receive the award."

During the ceremony there was nothing of interest to us. The visiting group stayed in the reception areas of the facility and there was little to see on any of their three holo recorders. I hadn't expected there to be.

However, once the investiture was over, it was another matter. Our group of infiltrates was escorted towards the laboratories.

On *Aenysia,* thousands of miles away behind the small moon, we all sat up and began to pay more attention. I scrunched up my eyes, determined to spot as much as possible in the background.

The first three labs gave us nothing. It was the fourth where we spotted something of interest.

Sammy nudged me. "Look through that hatch," he hissed. "Can you all see it?"

Sure enough, tucked just in view behind the hatch was a small IEVA helmet, hardly noticeable amongst the background mess. It was much too small for any Vaer.

I immediately instructed Belzeer to make his way through that particular hatch. He took his time to understand which hatch I was referring to. He dropped a couple of paces behind the others, seemingly straightening the lie of his main feathers with his beak, then darted towards the hatch in question and was through it in seconds. He did a full 360° turn slowly, to enable us to see everything there was.

I could hear the rest of the party crowding in behind him. There was confusion as to why he had entered that particular laboratory. As we listened to him explaining that he thought he had seen someone wave to him, we rescanned the images he had sent.

"There! Stop!" It was Zenzara who had the sharpest eyes. "There is somebody behind that door ... the one which has all those yellow stickers on it."

She was right.

I asked Belzeer to push that particular door open.

He edged over and leant against it, pretending to be startled when it began to open. There was an alarmed shout from the others in the group. One or two of them wailed. He half fell inside, grabbing the door frame to steady himself.

As he straightened up again, his camera caught Bull Cunningham full face on to us. Bull's face showed surprise, followed by wariness. He took a step back.

Belzeer's whole body language changed. "What is a Terran doing on Vaer Prime?" he demanded, his voice crackling with outrage.

"No. Err ... Sub-delegate Belzeer ... err ..."

"Are you trying to tell me I am not seeing a Terran in front of me?" Belzeer shoved his beak into the other Vaer's face. I could tell that he was extremely relieved. The discovery of the Terran had given him the power of righteousness. He had shed his air of doubt and now was standing solidly with an accusing air and the aura of somebody who had just seen a promotion in his near future. The man who had spoken shrank back. "No, Sir."

"Then explain yourself!"

I pointed out to Belzeer that while he was busy being horrified, Cunningham was retreating slowly towards a small exit door. Belzeer waved his wingtip at a couple of guards, who stepped smartly forwards and retained Cunningham. Bull's face was one of confusion. He had not expected to be discovered. His glittering eyes were searching those crowding into the laboratory, as if he expected to see me.

I was aware of a sudden surge of triumph. It was a great feeling. I had to stop myself. There was still a lot to do.

"Tell them to search for more Terrans!"

Belzeer obeyed me, then turned his attention to the head of the facility again. This worthy had hung his beak and his head. Belzeer repeated his previous words. "Explain yourself!"

Mel struggled to understand the reply, muffled as it was by feathers. "He is saying something about a family difficulty, illness, lack of funding, opportunity, not intending any harm."

Belzeer seemed unimpressed by the explanation. With another flick of his wingtip the facility leader was escorted out of the laboratory by a guard of six stern Vaers. We could hear his protests as he disappeared down the corridor.

Belzeer regarded the rest of those present. Finally, his gaze fell on the scientist recently decorated, who was covering the new insignia on his breast with one wing.

"I ... I ... know nothing about it, Sub-delegate!"

"Nothing at all?"

"NO! I never saw this Terran. I swear to it!"

"What is the purpose of this laboratory?"

"I don't know. I have never set foot in it before!"

"Then find out! You have ten minutes!"

The utter relief on the Vaer scientist's face was almost comical. He signaled to three other men who had formed in a phalanx behind him. Actually I think they had been hiding behind him. All four scurried to some consoles in the room and began to investigate.

All the time Belzeer stood. The only sound he made was of one claw slowly tapping on the steel decking. It made a hollow, scratchy sound. I found it very irritating. I think the scientists did too, for they kept glancing towards his feet.

After a few minutes, the head scientist reported back. His eyes were wide with news that frightened him. "They have been running a computationally intensive quantum simulation, Honorable Sir!"

He frowned. "A simulation? What sort of a simulation?"

"We do not know more, sir. I regret that a high level of encryption has been used. We know that the results are being off-loaded and then erased. We are unable to recover any of it." He stared miserably at the floor. "I regret this, Honorable Sir."

"Who knew about him?"

There was a pause.

"Come on! Somebody had to give him access to our only Supercomputer! Anyone who saw a Terran wandering around a secure Vaer facility without reporting it is guilty. Tell me!"

"We work in three shifts here on the facility. For my shift, this door has always been locked. The laboratory is marked as reserved for the third shift. They told us they were running a highly sensitive no-atmosphere experiment and that this section was open to the vacuum. Nobody has opened this door for a long time."

Belzeer snarled to himself. "Arrest all the third shift workers. Every single one of them. Including all supervisors."

"Yes sir." Rapid orders were snapped out. A few seconds later, an alarm began to sound.

The original guards came back, dragging a scared Ramesh Chandrayanan between them. His legs hardly scraped the floor. They dropped him in front of Belzeer. "We found this one, Sir."

Belzeer switched to Universal. "Good morning. What are you doing here?"

"None of your business!" But I could see the whites of the scientist's eyes.

"Why did you need access to our supercomputer? What have you been running? Have you infected it with some virus? Speak!"

"I have done it no harm!" Chandrayanan muttered, shifting uncomfortably.

"Then, what were you doing? And who gave you access? I want names! I presume you were infiltrated on this platform by Novans?"

"It has nothing to do with you!"

"I'm afraid it has everything to do with me." I noticed at this point that the television cameras were still running. No doubt some of this footage would later make it into the public domain on Vaer Prime. I had the strangest of feelings that Sub-delegate Belzeer would shortly be a much more important person that he was now. Well, I certainly didn't begrudge him that. I would prefer to have a Vaer I knew amongst the ruling delegates. For sure. Especially one who had already shown himself to be slightly flexible with the rules, if only for the sake of his children.

I grinned. I was pleased with myself. Now all we needed was to pick up the two Terrans once they were away from Vaer Prime and escort them to Ulon Prime. They would be tried there. I was pretty sure that neither of them would get to see a starship ever again.

If I hadn't been sure the Sellica faction would spring them, I would have been tempted to leave them to their fate here on Vaer Prime. But the very presence of the Terrans on this Atmospheric Research Facility was a sign of just how far the Sellicas had managed to infiltrate Vaer Prime.

Now Belzeer's men were pushing Chandrayanan along in front of them. They were walking out of the laboratory and towards the entry point.

I coughed. This was where Belzeer was supposed to facilitate an escape. So far we had fulfilled our word to him. We had given him an infiltrated research station. Now he had to give us what we wanted.

The Vaer stopped. He knew what I expected from him. He was just finding it slightly more difficult than he had anticipated. I suppose he thought he was committing treason against his people.

"No-one need ever know," I whispered. "You will be doing the right thing. These two individuals are extremely dangerous. They could blow up the entire planet with their experiments."

His shoulders relaxed and I breathed again. For a moment there I had thought he was going to insist on taking them into Vaer custody on the planet.

He gave the smallest of nods, which we could see from one of the other cameras in the facility.

"Take them to the elevator!" he ordered. "They are to be escorted planetside and delivered to the Delegation Police."

The guards inclined their heads and ushered the last prisoner out.

We had discussed this. Belzeer did not want to be anywhere near when the two prisoners escaped. That meant presenting the possibility of breaking free and assuming that Cunningham would take advantage of any way out of his current situation. It had to be subtle, yet obvious.

In the end Belzeer had decided to pre-arrange a small accident as his men passed. He had been more than cagey about who he had sent up to the research facility, something that had made me think he might know more than he had revealed about the Vaer Secret Service. It seemed that a cryogenic ball valve would spring a leak in one of the refrigeration systems as the group passed. This would result in a fine spray of potentially dangerous cryogenic liquid. Not only would it burn anybody dumb enough to stay in its path, but it would condense any water vapor in the air, creating a dense fog.

I rather thought that would be enough for Cunningham.

However, we had made sure that there were two vessels tied up to the space platform. He had his choice of an interplanetary shuttle or a Vaer cruiser. It didn't matter which he took. They would take him so far, but not far enough, and we would be able to trace either of them.

I saw Belzeer turn to the television cameras. His very best alibi would be to be seen standing in a public place as the escape was effected. Neither of us had wanted him to become implicated.

I didn't think Cunningham would lose their research. We already knew they had been uploading the results somewhere. He wouldn't want to hang around the facility. I was pretty sure he liked his newly-found Omnial status too much to risk his own hide too much.

In the end he took the cruiser. He must have been planning a longer voyage, and he liked his creature comforts. He left the escorting Vaer guards doubled over and coughing up their lungs and was gone within seconds of the cryogenic fog settling over them all. You had to admire his quick thinking.

Five minutes later, the cruiser lifted gently away from the station, turned and went into hyperdrive far too close for safety. The whole platform shook with the shockwave. We stared as all our live feeds stuttered and jumped, the cameras tumbling to the floor with their owners.

There was screaming and real panic now on the Vaer faces as the cameras refocused.

I just hoped that the space elevator had not been compromised by that shock wave. Thankfully it was not my problem.

I muttered a goodbye to Belzeer, with no idea whether or not he was able to hear me. Then I nodded to Sammy. We slid out from behind our moon and began to track the Vaer cruiser. We were close.

I couldn't wait to be closer.

6

Apart from the radian emissions, the hypertrail it left would have given the Vaer cruiser away. Bull was putting every smidgeon of power the engines had into moving as far as he could as fast as he could across space. The ship he had stolen wasn't equipped with any kind of carbon cloud, and I doubt it could have completely shrouded them even if it had been. Not at those speeds. Even *Aenysia* was hard put not to lose ground. With *Nivala* embedded in her hold our acceleration was affected. We were not going to be able to overtake. Not unless Cunningham throttled back.

There was little chance of that. He tore out of the Vaer system and made a direct dive towards Yamis: a large system about half way towards Heisenberg's Halo. It looked to me as though he would keep going through the Halo and try to reach somewhere in the Landau Rift, my home territory. Beznik would be the easiest to reach from his specific vector.

That made me wonder. Beznik was famous for its inhospitably hot weather. Conjunctions of its three suns were so dangerous that in ancient times they had been known to wipe out two thirds of the planet's inhabitants in one pass. It had kept their development back to the point that they were still considered an indigenous tribe and not one of the major races. The Bezniks were left alone for the main part, although a small part of the planet's northern hemisphere had been developed as a holiday resort for tired Spacelanders. Sorrengaria was ideal for those hardy souls who needed to bake in sunlight for a couple of weeks to boost their vitamin D levels. Even with modern additions, however, Beznik still remained one of the most dangerous planets in the Landau Rift. I could think of nothing there that would be of help to the Terrans.

Which reminded me. I hadn't seen much of Seyal recently. I went in search of her.

She was sitting in the mess hall in *Nivala*, devices spread all around her. She made a small figure, hunched over against the backdrop of Eshaan's wonderful painting of the Avaraks saving *Nivala* from the Terran attack, back in the Adhara Corridor.

I took a moment to remember back to that moment. So many had died.

Seyal looked up. "Captain?"

"Have you got anything on Beznik?"

"I have already started looking." She put her finger on the page to keep her place. "The thing they are most famous for is a substance called alkel, made from the sand there. It is a special sort of glass, very much stronger than that produced elsewhere. However, it is reserved only for the Bezniks. They refuse to trade it with any of the Shell races. They do not consider us worthy of their produce."

"Why is that?"

"They say our standards are inferior."

"Really? Wise people, then."

She stared at me in a bovine sort of way and I raised my hands. "Just a joke. Take no notice of me. What else have you found?"

"Not much. There are believed to be extensive enzenium deposits on the planet, but that is all. They are not currently being tapped."

I gave a hollow laugh. "As far as we know. They may be trading it with the Novan Vaers. We probably would never find out and the Vaers on Vaer Prime would never sell their own enzenium to the Sellicas, or any Novan. That would mean that if they wanted it they would have to go elsewhere. Enzenium can be weaponized. The Primes don't want the Novans to develop weapons. Not nuclear weapons, and not that close by."

I shared that dismay. I wouldn't like Vaers like Frynee hovering over me with quantum bombs in his holds.

Seyal managed a small quirk of her mouth. It was almost a smile.

I pressed my own lips together. "So, perhaps Bull needed more enzenium. Or possibly alkel. Or both. That seems to be the only reason for coming right out here to the back of beyond. I wonder which of those is so important?" I nodded to Seyal to accompany me and we made our way back up to the bridge on *Aenysia* to call a meeting of the others.

Didjal pointed out that we had encountered enzenium previously.

"They were using it to act as a binding agent in the carbon clouds, back on Ebyssia, remember?"

I did. "Yes, and I guess our blockade has cut them off now from that supply. However, I can't see that the carbon clouds would be important enough to justify the risk of spending time on Vaer Prime. They could have been discovered at any moment, and Vaer Nova undercover operatives will have been burned by the operation. It has to be more than that. Anybody?"

Danaa wrinkled her nose. "Where ...," she said slowly, "... did I hear the suggestion that enzenium could be added to glass?" She frowned, then her eyes widened and she swung to look rather fearfully at me.

"What is it, Danaa?"

"— Agraala's last thesis," she whispered. "Chandrayanan must have figured it out, too. Or somebody told him what was in it."

She saw my incomprehension. "Agraala's latest, unpublished thesis, explored a possibility that was only hinted at in her previous thesis.

It was thought to be a possible danger to the Chakrans, so Ouraali destroyed it after Agraala's death. It detailed how to make a quantum resonance chamber from a compound of enzenium with strengthened glass." Danaa's long face grew even longer. "Agraala also suggested that the no-cloning theorem is wrong, that quantum waveforms can be at least partially cloned." She gave us all a long look of sadness. "You can see why it had to be destroyed."

I couldn't. But my sister had stopped moving. I knew that meant that her brain was outstripping her consciousness. I held up my hand to tell the others not to speak. We watched her for some minutes, until her eyes suddenly came into focus again. She immediately went white. "Oh no!"

"What?"

"If Chandrayanan has found a way to copy individual Chakran strands, he could build a Quantum Farm."

"You mean he could duplicate a strand? As many times as he wants?"

"Sort of. It is a bit more complicated than that, which is where the resonance chamber comes in. He would have to dismember the strand and replicate only that part that resonates as negative energy. That means destroying the strand."

A very small voice interrupted her. "—Which means that he still has some of the missing strands. We know two of them died in the wormhole he built. I thought the last two must have, too. They can't have. That means he is going to kill them anyway?" Zenzie had started to shake. Mel gave her a hug, as we went on with our discussion.

I gave a grim sigh. "Yes. He must have those missing strands. You are right, kid. Nothing else fits the facts."

"And if the Terrans are headed straight for Beznik they must need more enzenium to build this chamber." Seyal was ahead of me. "And the alkel, of course. It sounds as though it is much stronger than ordinary glass. It will work even better."

I frowned. "But they already had the canisters. Those held the Chakran strands trapped, didn't they? Why do they need something new?”

Sibby spoke hesitantly. “This isn’t just a trap, Mall. It would be a way to strip the negative energy from the strands. To clone only that.”

“And discard the rest?”

She nodded dumbly.

“Surely that would terminate the Chakran being?”

She nodded again. “Probably. If not, it would be crippled.” I saw tears in her eyes.

I blew out air. “Then they could still make a traversable wormhole.”

Seyal’s face was remarkably smooth. “Such a quantum farm would indeed constitute a threat. What are we going to do, Captain?”

Seyal’s ability to adapt was truly amazing. Only a few short months ago she had found it hard to speak Universal. Now she spoke and read it fluently, had managed to assimilate three other languages and was able to research anything we wanted. The nursing skills she had come with made her an asset, but her unexpected facility for learning had made her indispensible.

“What do *you* suggest?”

Her eyes took on a surprised look. “*Me?* You are asking me?”

“I am.”

There were a few seconds silence as she collected her thoughts. “We can’t catch up with them at the moment. Our only choice is to follow and then attack when they are on the ground. On Beznik, if that is their final destination.”

It was. Beznik hove into view some five days later.

We were close behind, carefully concealed by Sibby’s wonderful new carbon cloud.

There were fewer of us on board. We had docked with a Tyzaran cruiser briefly, just above Yamis’s gravity well. There, we extended a docking tube between the two vessels and sent Emereen and Marivee over to the Tyzarans.

The two Vaer children were almost reluctant to go, but I insisted. "Your father upheld his end of the bargain. I must uphold mine."

"We could go with you," said Emereen, a hopeful look on his face.

"No, you couldn't. We have already put you two into too much danger. You need to grow those feathers back and then you will be able to decide what your next move is. You will be free to go back to Vaer Prime."

Emereen looked down his beak at me. "And if our feathers don't take? Don't grow back? If we can't go back to Vaer Prime?"

"Then we will find somewhere else for you to live. For you to make your home. I already promised that."

We waved them off with some relief. Although we had got used to them, it would be a worry to have them aboard where we were going.

I had suggested Sibby go with them.

She just laughed at me. "You aren't going to get rid of me that easily, Mall, and neither is Izan."

"It seems serious between you?"

"It is." She must have foreseen my next question because she warded it off with her forearms. "I don't know what I am going to do. I am living in the moment, because it is a *good* moment."

"Can't say as I blame you."

She stretched up and kissed me on the cheek. "Thank you, brother."

"I didn't have much choice. Denaraz took one look at you and melted into a puddle."

"You do like him, don't you?"

"He's all right, I suppose."

She gave me a small push. "Come *on!*"

"You know I like him. I just wouldn't have chosen a Tyzaran for you, Sibby."

"No, that's true. *She* won't like it."

"No. She won't."

Truth be known, my esteemed mother was going to scream her anger to the four moons. She had steadily been working towards passing on the *Bellaris* shipstation to Sibby.

First I had lost *Faraday* to the Vaers, now Sibby might abandon *Bellaris* altogether for a Tyzar. For life on a spaceship. It wasn't going to go down well. If I were Sibby, I would tell my mother with at least one whole Shell between us.

I scratched her head. "Never mind, Sibby. You can't help who you fall in love with."

"It is why they keep us on the shipstation, you know."

I frowned. "What do you mean?"

"The fewer people we meet, the less chance there is that we might run off with somebody."

"You have left *Bellaris* before."

"I have, but not very often and not for very long. It is a sort of faux freedom. Just enough to give you the illusion of free will." She sounded bitter.

"Have you always felt trapped?"

"Maybe. I just didn't really realize what was wrong with me. I think some of the Spacelander Trust stuff needs to change. It isn't fair to have to inherit all the problems just because the Space Trust says you must."

I could feel one eyebrow going up. "What is the alternative?"

She sighed. "*Bellaris* would be forfeit on Prime's death. It would be adjudicated to another Spacelander family. One of the new ones from Tevan 321. Our family would be granted nomader status."

I winced. Nomader status was generally considered to be the dregs of Spacelander society. It encompassed all those who belonged nowhere. Drifters, seasonal workers and men who hired out their small ships for transport or odd jobs.

The Mallivan Bells had long been one of the oldest and more settled Spacelander families. That would all change. Not only for us. Our children ... at least the ones on *Bellaris* ... would be send back to

Zenubi, to the Genetic Institute. From there they would be assigned new families.

I felt I could actually see the weight on Sibby's shoulders. It was enough to bow anybody down. She gave me a bit of a shrug. "No, it definitely isn't going to be easy."

"No." Then I tried to cheer her up. "But things are changing. With the Alliance. Maybe the Space Trust will have to modernize too."

"I hope so."

We hung well back as a shuttle cleared the Vaer cruiser's hold and began to drop down onto the planet. It was not in my plan to be spotted this soon.

"First we secure their ship," I ordered. "We don't want them slipping away from us again. Then we can get down to the planet."

So Sammy and Anzany took one of *Nivala's* shuttles to rendezvous with the Vaer vessel. The rest of us stayed on board *Aenysia*, watching as the shuttle made its way out of our hold and carefully skipped across the dark sky to the now geostationary cruiser.

I wasn't expecting any resistance or I would have sent more hands over. On the ARF on Vaer Prime, both ships had been left empty deliberately. The cruiser ought now to be unmanned. I was pretty sure that Bull would never leave the physicist alone in a ship. I didn't think he trusted him that far.

And I was right. Sammy was soon on the hololink. "No problems. Nobody on board."

"OK. Get a tow cable across to *Aenysia* once we disembed *Nivala*. Then you two can stay on *Aenysia* and monitor the situation of the Vaer cruiser from there. That should keep you out of trouble. We will rendezvous with you once we manage to grab the two Terrans."

"Copy that."

"Can you search the whole ship meanwhile? Check that they haven't conveniently left any trapped Chakrans about?"

"Anzany is already on it. We will get back to you when we can."

I didn't think they would find anything. Bull had got this far by keeping everything close to him at all times. If they did still have two untouched strands, they would be on some other Vaer or Omnistate ship. They would never have risked taking them to Vaer Prime. Still, we couldn't ignore the possibility.

It didn't take them long. The hololink was back within the hour. "We checked the vid recordings," Anzany told us calmly. "Both men went down to the surface of Beznik, and they also loaded two small empty crates on board the shuttle. We have searched all the areas they visited and found nothing. It was easy to access the recording logs."

"As expected. Right, Tell *Aenysia* to slip away with her tow and hide out behind that moon. We will try to keep you updated, but that might not be possible."

"I will give you five days, then I am coming to get you!" Sammy sounded quite determined. I certainly wouldn't put it past him. I gave Mel an accusing look. She held up her hands.

"Nothing to do with me!"

"Sure, Mel." I sighed heavily. "Too many relationships on this barge, if you ask me.

Neema, Denaraz and my sister all glared.

I ignored them.

Zenzie chuckled.

We had extracted *Nivala* from *Aenysia* before the tow line was set. Otherwise Danaa would be dealing with an extremely complicated situation. In any case, whatever happened down on Beznik, the time for stealth was probably over. And we might just need *Aenysia's* top speed. I decided to keep both ships segregated for the time being.

That meant leaving more of my crew up in orbit. I had decided to ask Danaa to stay on *Aenysia* because of the heat on the planet's surface. The Nepheals are not so adaptable as other species. They find extreme heat very challenging. She took charge of the Nepheal cruiser with Sammy and Anzany to help monitor the towing of the Vaer cruiser.

And I left Seyal in charge of *Nivala*. Although she was disappointed not to be going down to the planet with us, her eyes shone as she realized that I trusted her enough to look after a whole ship. She tucked Segaton firmly on one hip and straightened up. "I will not let you down, Captain."

"I know that, Seyal. Otherwise I wouldn't leave you in charge. You can and will take any decisions necessary."

"Yes, Captain!"

She had never been allowed to take a decision in all her lifetime with her own Avarak people. She needed the experience.

That left the two Enif, Sibby and Denaraz, Zenzara, Neema, Mel and myself. Eight of us. We took two shuttles and followed the same line that the two Terrans had taken. Once close to the ground, however, we shifted our course so that we could put down behind some local hills, just about five miles to the north of the Vaer shuttle. We didn't want to let them know that we had already found them.

As the shuttle hatches went down, we all gasped. The air was so hot that it scalded your throat. Any secretions evaporated instantly, leaving you longing for a cool drink of water at any price.

I signaled to them all to put their IEVA suits on. That would keep our bodies insulated from the harsh temperatures. Sibby and Denaraz had modified the IEVA helmets with an exterior cooling tube so that we could breathe the outside air freely at a temperature that would not damage our lungs. It was still hotter than comfort decreed, but it would now not actually harm us.

I looked around the rolling dunes of this part of Beznik. There was sand everywhere. The heat rising off it created small wispy clouds which formed trails up to the sky. I wondered what phenomenon that was. I had never seen it before.

As we got a mag sled out of each shuttle, Zenzie bounced over. "Have you seen those vapor trails, Mallivan Bell? How does that work?"

I looked towards Denaraz, our resident expert on all things alien, but he shrugged. "New to me. Very odd." He stared at our surroundings. "No wonder there is no plant or animal life. I can't see anything surviving."

Neema nodded. "Most species indigenous to Beznik evolved underground."

"I hope we are not about to meet any of them?"

She giggled. "There isn't anything dangerous, I don't think. Though there haven't been many studies done on the planet. Most were done in the North, around Sorrengaria. The rest of the planet is pretty inhospitable. Apart from the Bezniks, who are highly reclusive, the biggest mammals are half the size of a Geiga."

"I hope they have smaller teeth!"

"They live off some sort of mushroom that grows in caves."

Zenzie didn't like being upstaged. "How do you know so much about it?"

"I looked up our archives on the way."

"Huh."

"You should try it sometime, Zenzara." I couldn't help myself.

"You're the captain. Aren't you the one who is supposed to know all this stuff?"

I treated her to my most pitying look. "I know all about the planet."

She bristled. "You do? What is the population?"

"Err ... around 6,000."

"Wrong. 13,500."

"So you did check. Good."

She huffed. "Of course I did."

"How are we going to find the Terrans?" asked Didjal. He and Eshaan were busy unpacking one of the sleds.

"Hopefully they will have left a trail on the sand."

Zenzie sniffed. "As long as one of the famous northerly winds doesn't spring up."

"Is it that time of year?" I asked. I couldn't resist.

"I ... I ... I don't know." The Tyzaran girl's crest twitched. So did my lips. She noticed, and reddened.

"Neema?"

The Spacelander gave an apologetic glance sideways at Zenzara before answering. "No, Captain. The winds are unlikely at this time of year."

I distinctly heard Zenzie grind her teeth. I answered before she could.

"Never mind, *Chy* Zenzara, I expect you are above such things as normal study hours."

That hit home. She actually recoiled. "I am not arrogant!"

"I didn't say you are."

"You implied it!"

"Did I? No. I don't believe so. I just said that, as Chyzar, you probably wouldn't be required to be knowledgeable about anything else."

She stamped one small foot. "You are suggesting I am opinionated! That I need to study more!"

"On the contrary, I said outright that you had reason not to bother studying any more. You are, after all, already one of the most important people from your planet. Who needs learning?"

She gave a sound like a strangled sneeze. "I never want to become self-important."

"Neither does Neema. That's why she studied the planet we were visiting."

"I hate you!"

"No you don't. I am only saying what you already know. Inside."

Her shoulders slumped. "All right. I will make sure I keep up with my lessons."

"I think you will feel better if you do."

"I don't see how anything I do is any business of yours."

"The Savior Protocols work two ways. And I *am* your captain."

She went even pinker. "I'm sorry."

I started to number us off into two groups, one for each mag sled. "Denaraz, Sibby and Zenzara with me on this one, Eshaan and Dijal, Mel and Neema on the other."

The chance to chat disappeared as we separated to our respective sleds. I wasn't sorry. Zenzara was furious and I suspected it was mainly directed at me. I couldn't blame her, but she had needed a small wake-up call. Ever since she had been kidnapped by Cunningham and the faction, she had been unable to concentrate. It was time she snapped back to her usual self. It was my job to motivate her and nicety hadn't been having much of an effect.

I could feel her eyes on me. I put my chin up and tried to appear unconcerned. I wasn't.

We came across the Vaer shuttle some six kilometers to the south. We approached with some care, but it turned out to be unnecessary. The Terrans were long gone. There was the soft trail of some hover-based vehicle leading away to the west. At least that should make it easier to follow them.

I signaled to the other sled to follow after 15 minutes. There was no point in putting both sleds within the same small area. It only increased our risk. We would be better to divide our efforts.

We kept very low to the ground to avoid being seen. In the end, it didn't matter.

The sand had been sculpted over centuries by the harsh sunlight and the winds. It was now piled in hard, tight folds. They lay glistening in the blazing light like giant loops of hair that had been plaited together. Where one dune twisted over another there were dark recesses. Some of these were mere areas of shadow, some seemed more like caves, openings in the continual dryness. It was from some of these that the puffs of water vapor were emanating.

The Vaer vehicle had been struggling to navigate such hostile terrain. There were clear indications where its intake had become clogged by loose piles of sand, where its riders had been forced to set down to clear the valves.

We had no such restrictions. The mag sleds flew over the rough ground. The only problem the folded dunes gave us was one of equilibrium. Mag sleds are designed to travel horizontally to the ground. Which means that, when you are traversing steep slopes up and down like we were at that moment, the sled bucked and reared like a living monster, tossing us against the benches and forcing us to cling on for dear life.

I bit my own tongue twice and my cheek once. So the metallic taste of blood was just another joy. I wasn't the only one. I could see small traces of blood trickling down Mel's chin and red stains on Sibby's neck. Great.

We followed the tracks for an hour and a half across the Beznik desert. If anything, the ride got worse. As we headed west, the solidified dunes became higher and higher, and even though we throttled right back, progress was limited.

I thought back to Vaer Nova longingly. It now seemed quite a benign sort of planet.

Then Denaraz, who was driving, slammed on the brakes. The whole sled shuddered, and I only just managed to grab Zenzie as she shot towards the front and was nearly thrown out altogether.

Denaraz whipped us around and held up one hand to silence any comments. He settled the mag sled as evenly as he could on the first shallow depression he could find.

"Their hover sledge set down by that cave opening," he whispered. "It has been moved now, but they disembarked here."

I nodded my understanding. We asked Sibby and Zenzara to wait by the sled to intercept the others and stop them, then we staggered up the slopes until we reached the summit of the highest one. Stagger was the right word. Although the dunes were hard on the surface, they didn't hold our weight. Each step broke through the crust and then buried our feet up to our thighs. Reaching the crest of the ridge took a long time and left us both utterly exhausted.

I peered over with caution, attempting to keep my ragged breathing to a low sound level.

There was a dark opening to what looked like a cave. Small wisps were rising out of it and trailing up into the sky where they gradually became thinner and thinner puffs of white and then evaporated altogether.

"So. Now we know why they came here."

Denaraz nodded, but pointed to one side of the cave. There were many footprints around the entrance. Many and various. This cave, or whatever it was, had been in use before Cunningham and Chandrayanan had arrived.

I sighed. This was not going to go well. I could feel it in my bones.

I swiveled around as something touched my boot. It was Eshaan. The second sled had arrived. The Enif had made irritatingly good time over the sandy surface.

I glowered. "How did you get up so quickly?"

It hummed. "I swam."

Denaraz's eyebrow nearly reached his crest. "Swam?"

The Enif demonstrated. It fell onto its carapace, rather like a turtle, and used its feet to dig small steps in the sand and use those to push itself up and along.

Denaraz looked sick. "Why didn't we think of that?"

"Because you are mammals," Eshaan suggested, completely seriously. "Our brains are better at lateral thinking." It looked smug.

I thought of the way we had been buried up to the crutch with each step. Maybe Eshaan had reason to be feeling superior. Now I knew how to get up and down the slopes, our effort seemed quite ridiculous.

I turned back to the scene in front.

"We will have to go in."

"Of course, Captain. That is, after all, why we are here, is it not?"

"It is. It seems a little rash." I pointed out the many footprints. "They are not in there alone."

"Wait here!"

Eshaan flopped back onto its rear carapace and allowed itself to slide down towards the entrance to the cave. It took it about three seconds. We watched as it tracked backwards and forwards outside the opening to the cave. Then it slipped inside the dark shadows and disappeared from sight for some ten minutes.

We used the time to get the others up to our position, making swimming gestures with our arms to try to explain. None of them got it until Didjal started to make its own way up. It fell frontally onto the sand and paddled up the slope in about half a minute.

There was excitement amongst those left. Finally they all flopped onto their bellies and began to kick their toes through the crust in order to get enough traction to move up the side of the dune to our position, on the crest.

It took them five minutes, but it was infinitely easier than Denaraz and I had made it. Sibby and Mel were first, followed closely by Neema. Zenzie trailed rather at the back. She was so small that she didn't have the strength to kick through the crust.

I couldn't help laughing at her plight. Her face was going red as she gouged again and again with her small toes at the desert crust. Then she tried to pull herself up with her hands, but they slipped over the crust. She began to slide slowly down the slope again, much to her chagrin.

Finally Didj took pity on her, glided down, dragged her onto its back and was back at the crest within a minute. Zenzie was hot, thirsty and humiliated. She was not having a good day. She definitely didn't look like the Chyzar at that moment.

"If I catch anybody laughing at me ..." she threatened.

We all looked hurriedly away.

Eshaan slid back out of the dark hole in the sand at that moment. It was up beside us very quickly.

"There are no guards on or near the entrance," it told us. "Though, of course, there may be some further into the structure. We seem to have escaped notice so far. If we are going to make a move, it should be immediately."

I nodded. We all threw ourselves onto our backs to slide down the slope into the entrance gulley, the two Enif leading.

We gathered at the black mouth of the cave. It was in a triangular shape, pointed at the top. The sides had been sculpted by the weather over many, many years. It was big enough for two of us to walk in side by side.

The blackness beckoned.

We ducked into it.

7

The entrance to the cave narrowed as we walked. It only went about fifty meters into the rock before petering out. Eshaan, who was leading the way, took us behind a small outcrop of rock.

Sibby gasped. There was a hole in the ground and what seemed to be a sheer drop down. She had always hated being under rock. The light wasn't strong enough inside for me to see her face clearly, but I sensed her dismay.

I moved forwards. "How far down does it go?"

Eshaan chittered to Didjal, who answered. "At least fifteen meters."

"Sibby, go back and keep—"

My sister straightened up. "I am coming with you."

"But—"

"No buts, Mall. I have to come with you. I have no intention of leaving Denaraz, and Denaraz will follow Zenzara, who will follow you. That makes us into a group of four. I cannot stay behind."

"I know how you feel about being underground."

"So? I will just have to get over it. I am old enough to be able to cope with my fears."

Denaraz squeezed her arm. "Are you sure?"

She smiled up at him. "Totally."

He met my eyes. "We will all go."

I harrumphed. "Fine. Let's all go. But if she has a screaming fit, it will be up to you to look after her."

Sibby seemed to shrink. "That was unkind."

It was. "I'm sorry. It is just that I worry about you."

"You will need me in there. How many nanotech engineers do you have?"

She had a point there. And she was right. She was a grown woman. I would have to wipe the memories of a panic-stricken teenager in the Lycara mines. They really shouldn't be dictating my actions now.

I dropped my own head. She was my sister. I shouldn't be humiliating her in front of the others. What had I been thinking?

I shuffled forwards and grabbed the rope that Didjal had been deploying while we all talked. He had been about to go down himself and seemed surprised when I pushed in front of him.

I slid down into the darkness still angry at myself. Now I had put my own sister into even more danger. There was no right answer, which frustrated me. And I hated being petty.

I was in such a glow of disgruntlement that I never even saw the Vaer until he was on top of me.

He had been waiting in the shadows for me to touch down on the floor of the newer cave. As I let go of the rope, he lunged across from the side walls and took me down.

He trumpeted a challenge. I grunted as the wind was forced out of my lungs. He pecked at my face as he landed on top of me. I struggled, but found myself pinned to the floor. This is what happens when you stop concentrating on what you are doing, I thought. This is all Sibby's fault. Then I grinned to myself. I sounded like a six-year-old. How hard it is to break the habits of a lifetime!

The Vaer on top of me was now clucking in what sounded very much like satisfaction. He knew that I was trapped. I saw him pull his head back, readying a final attack. I realized he was about to take my right eye out with his beak. My heart froze.

Then there was a flash of metal in the blackness surrounding us. I saw the head above me shudder. A thin shower of blood and brains soaked my face and the inert body of my attacker slumped onto me, clogging my eyes, nose and mouth. I began to choke.

Voices appeared from a great distance and I felt the huge weight on my lungs gradually shift and then disappear. Somebody was wiping my face with a damp towel. I could hear Zenzara muttering to me.

"Are you all right? Speak to us!"

I spluttered and spat out some blood. It wasn't mine. I gagged.

"Th-thanks, guys. I ... I wasn't looking where I was going."

Neema's voice cut through the darkness. "He was alone. He must have been left as a rear guard."

Denaraz was helping the two Enif drag the corpse away into a corner. "We may not have much time, then. There could be more of them around."

Mel helped me to my feet. Sibby gave me a fierce hug.

I returned the favour. "Sorry, Sibs. I shouldn't have said what I did."

"S'all right, Rye. You were just looking out for me." She gave me a nip on my forearm, which I felt even through the IEVA suit. "But you have to remember I am a big girl now. I don't need my big brother to look after me. Right?"

"Right." I gave a rueful nod. "Was it you who killed the Vaer?"

She shook her head. "Zenzara. She pulled something off her jacket and threw it at him. It went straight through his forehead." She gave a shiver. "Looks can be deceptive. She seems so cute and innocent."

"Hmm. All Tyzaran children are taught stuff like that."

I put my sister down and watched as Zenzie tugged her nivala out of the Vaer's skull, cleaning it roughly on her boot before replacing it onto her jacket. "I appreciate it, *Chy* Zylarian."

"It is why I am here," she replied, in a formal tone. "You are very welcome, Mallivan Bell."

"Does that make us quits?"

She frowned, making the wrinkles of skin around her eyes fold even more. "Quits?"

"Is your debt now paid?"

"Of course not. The Savior Protocols will be in place for your entire lifespan. I would look pretty stupid if I saved your life today and then someone took it tomorrow, now wouldn't I? Every day of my life is due to your action. So every day of my life I must be ready to repay that. One, ten, a thousand times. It does not matter."

I couldn't help sighing. "Maybe I should have left you on *Commorancy*."

"You are in a bad mood today," said Mel, shaking her head. "If that is your way of saying thank you, then you need some lessons on diplomacy."

Zenzie laughed. "It is because he is so old. He gets very grumpy."

"I am not old. I am only just coming up to thirty!"

She shrugged.

"That is young!"

She shrugged again.

I gave up. In any case, I wasn't feeling very sprightly at that particular moment. I ached all over and was still wiping brains off my chin. Maybe I *was* getting old. I should have been happy they weren't my own.

Neema came back. "The next drop must be much further down. They have set up a paternoster lift. It takes one person at a time, and those of us who are bigger may have to duck as we get in. It was not running but I pushed a red button beside the two canisters and it started up."

"What is a paternoster lift?" Denaraz asked.

"It's a lift that is on a continual loop up and over. One canister goes up and the other side goes down. You have to step on and off while it is in motion."

Denaraz raised an eyebrow. "We don't have those on Tyzar."

"No. They are not used anymore."

"What happens at the top?" Of course, that would be Zenzie.

"There will be a wheel that moves the capsule across from the upstream to the downstream, or vice versa. Paternoster lifts were used in ancient times, back on Earth. They were reasonably safe."

Zenzie gave a snort. "Sounds like it."

Neema was not looking at all keen. There was something she wasn't telling us. I raised my eyebrows at her in encouragement. She gave a sigh. "These capsules seem to be made of some special kind of glass. They don't look very resistant." She glanced at Mel. "I imagine they will be shatterproof."

Sibby nodded. "That will be the alkel glass the Bezniks rely on. Apparently they use it for everything."

The thought of trusting my life to some glass coffins that transport you through solid rock wasn't particularly appealing. I glanced around at the rest of my group. Their expressions ranged from mild interest to full-blown panic.

Mel swallowed. Then her eyes slid to Sibby. "I will be all right. Don't you worry about me."

"Sure?"

"Of course."

Sibby walked up to her and put an arm across Mel's shoulders. They had known each other for years. They knew each other's fears. "Well done, Melly!"

"You too!"

"I will go first this time," offered Denaraz.

"Go ahead." I needed the few extra moments to catch my breath. "I will bring up the rear."

"Be ready for anything at the bottom. We have been lucky so far."

We all nodded.

I watched as, one by one, they each stepped warily into a moving glass canister and disappeared into the ground.

Zenzie was the last before me. She was lucky, she fit with room to spare.

Just before it was my turn to get into a canister, I realized one other thing. These things were not made for Vaers. There was no way an adult male Vaer could manage to squash himself inside one of these things. No way.

Which meant that there would be no Vaers below us. And it also explained why my attacker had been waiting at the base of the previous descent. He must have been one of Bull's collaborators from Vaer Prime, must have accompanied him here in the Cruiser.

The paternoster lift trundled on its way. Unlike a normal lift, there were no intermediate floors. All I could sense was flat black rock passing in front of my eyes. It was a horrible experience. And it went on forever. Or seemed to, at least.

I had begun to feel that there was no air left in the canister by the time I reached the bottom. And it was only by a change in the air pressure that I realized I had descended as far as the thing was going. That and the sudden appearance of lighting.

I stumbled out of the canister, almost falling out in my panic at being wedged so tightly that I wouldn't be able to get out before the lift swept me past the gap.

Then I stopped, dumbfounded.

I blinked. Everywhere, the lights reflected off black water. We were in an immense underground cavern with a lake that stretched out as far as the eye could see. The lift had deposited us on a small pathway skirting the lake.

We were all struck dumb. The last thing we had expected to see was a body of underground water of this sort of size. It seemed as big as a continent, from where we were standing. Now I knew what the wisps of smoky vapor were on the surface of the planet. Now it all made some sort of sense.

Denaraz was examining our surroundings, but so far we had not been attacked. We regrouped, the two Enif at the front and Denaraz at the back with Sibby. They didn't have to ask me what direction to take; there were marks in the ashy sand underfoot leading along the bank of water towards the north. We followed, taking care to make as little noise as possible. In a place like this, noise would carry various kilometers.

We also extinguished our torches. They were weak, but again they would be beacons for anybody checking. It meant stumbling along the side of the lake and slipping on the dark sand. We found ourselves clinging to each other. It was a most unsoldierly way to proceed. Zenzie was giggling.

"Stop that!"

"I c-can't! We must look like half-drunk crabs!" She tittered again.

"Shhhh! They might hear us!"

"Who might?"

"Cunningham and Chandrayanan. Or the Bezniks!"

"I don't suppose the Bezniks would do much to us if they did hear us. We don't exactly seem threatening. We are having trouble standing up."

"That has nothing to do with it. It is a question of protocol."

"Ohh, *protocol!*"

I was about to reply when, unfortunately, I slipped. She had to put a hand over her mouth to cover the gales of laughter.

I could see that it was useless. "Oh, never mind!" I said with as much dignity as I was able to muster.

She disappeared into the gloom, but I could still hear her hiccupy way of showing her amusement. It was extremely irritating.

Then it was brought short suddenly.

We were all brought short suddenly.

Six armed figures had appeared without warning on the path right in front of us. They were of human shape, but much smaller than we were. They were only a few inches taller than Zenzie, though they were much more heavily built than she was. They were holding weapons on us. At least, I assumed they were weapons. They were strange cylindrical objects that looked to be made from the same glass compound we had seen in use in the paternoster lift. I had never seen anything like them, but the way they were being held made me think they would be used if we caused problems.

I shouldered my way to the front. "Good morning!"

"Who are you, and what are you doing down here?"

"Err ... we are members of the Interstellar Enforcement Agency, and we are in pursuit of two escaped criminals. We have followed them down here. I am hoping that you can help us."

The glass weapons held on us didn't so much as twitch. "You are talking about the two Terrans?"

"Yes. They are wanted for crimes against the Alliance."

There was some muttering between the six men. Then the front one spoke again.

"We do not know what this 'Alliance' is. Your account does not tally with theirs. We will need some time to deliberate before we can allow you to undertake any operations on Beznik soil."

Zenzara coughed. "Actually, we are *under* Beznik soil."

They all stared at her.

She took a small step backwards. "Not important. Sorry I spoke."

She would be. I gave her one of my special stares.

"May I ask if you are the Bezniks?" I queried.

"We are."

The lifts suggested that this race was far more advanced than I had previously thought.

"You don't live above ground?" I asked.

One of the men curled his lip. His face was close enough to mine for it to be quite clear to me. "The tourists go to the place they call Sorrengaria, on the Northern peninsula. They live above ground. They stare at our three suns and oooh and aaaah over them. What do they know about our culture, our history?"

"I don't think they even know you live ... err ..." I waved my hand weakly to indicate our surroundings, "... here."

"We make sure that very few people know about our existence."

"What do you call yourselves? Your planet was named by the Space Trust, wasn't it? Beznik can't be the name you use."

He tipped his chin up, looking proud. "We call our planet Alkelala. So we are the Alkelalavazalans. However, you may call us Bezniks."

That was a relief. I wasn't at all sure I could get my tongue around 'Alkelalavazalans'. "Pleased to meet you." I proffered my hand and, after a small pause, he shook it. I then went round the other five with the same gesture. They all returned it.

"Then, you must live underground. Did you make the paternoster lift we just came down in?"

"Paternoster lift? Oh! you mean the surface pulley! Yes, we made it. There are many of them, all over the planet."

I pointed to their weapons. "You seem to use the same substance … alkel is it? … for many uses?"

"Of course. Our special sand is ubiquitous on our planet. So is heat, which occurs here at every conjunction of the suns. Heat and this special sand naturally become alkel. It is like your glass, but pliable and much stronger. Everything we use is based on alkel. Our ancestors discovered how to encourage it to form. Now we have alkel manufacturing plants in many locations."

It was logical. I had seen no trees or rocks on this planet. They would not have been able to use wood or iron for their needs.

"I see. But … if you live underground … why do you need so many of these paternoster lifts … err … surface pulleys?"

"We have to visit the surface for at least two days a month. Otherwise we can become ill from a vitamin deficiency."

"Vitamin D?"

"We call it the sun vitamin. I do not know what you would call it."

"Why have you not claimed your own planet?"

He frowned. "Why should we claim what is already ours? We do not care about the few thousand interlopers who live in Sorrengaria. They do not affect us." He smiled. "In fact, we have learned from them. They have brought us new ideas, new technology."

And, thankfully, the Universal language. I would have had trouble communicating if they hadn't. "All the same, you need to know about our new Alliance. You are part of it ... at least, I think you could be."

"They will leave us alone?"

"Of course. If that is your wish."

"We do not like to mix with other races. It is not our way."

I understood. Living underground as they did was bound to make them leery of strangers. I couldn't blame them. But I would have to do something about this. They were certainly far more advanced than they had led the Space Trust to believe. Their sophistication meant that the Shells contained nine advanced sentient races, instead of eight. That was a massive discovery!

"I can put your case before the Macers, if you wish. But first, can you help us find the two Terrans?"

"We cannot. They have paid us for safe transit through the caves. We keep our word. You must go back." He made a hand signal to the rest of his men, and these sat down in a line across the path, blocking our way. Although they were no longer pointing their weapons directly at us, they still held their fingers on the triggers. We could not pass by them without attacking.

I laid down my own pistol. It was time to practice some of those diplomacy skills I was so lacking.

"I understand. They have paid you for safe conduct. You have guaranteed it. But does that safe conduct extend to the surface of the planet?"

"It extends to the first entry level. Where they left the Vaer."

That was a relief. I hadn't been looking forward to telling the Bezniks that we had already eliminated one of the Terrans' party.

"Then we will go back to that point. We will capture them there."

There was a quick discussion on the part of the Bezniks. At length, the leading man shook his head. "They are not going to exit the lake through the same surface pulley. They will exit from one about fifty miles further north, when they have what they are looking for."

Then why did they leave the Vaer in the first cave? I almost asked the Bezniks that question. But the answer was blindingly obvious. Bull had no further use for him. And Bull was not one to take deadwood with him. The Vaer had been abandoned. There had been no rope hanging through the 15 meter drop to the first level. And I didn't think a Vaer of his weight could possibly have climbed the shaft without one. He had been left to die there. That is why he attacked!

I wished I had known. In retrospect, his life could have been saved. He must have thought we were there to kill him. He must have been quite desperate to save his own life.

I stared at the floor. We were going to have to remove that body. We couldn't leave it there for the Bezniks to find.

"Then we will retrace our footsteps and exit from the same paternoster lift ... err ... surface pulley ... that we used to come inside here. Would your guarantee to the Terrans allow you to tell us where they will exit?"

"No. However, it would allow me to tell you where we were asked to take the vehicle they were using. One of my men has driven it to the Okakuara entrance."

"That is most kind. Would the Okakuara entrance be easy to find?"

"It would be easy if you had a map of Beznik. A true map."

"And how much would a true map cost?"

He held up a rolled parchment. It looked to me as if it were drawn on what looked like transparent paper. Perhaps it was some refined form of their alkel glass. But then, how would the Bezniks make paper?

"What can you offer?"

I held out my pistol. "A Tyzaran ZR pistol?"

He turned it over and over in his hand. "Hmm. Very nice, but perhaps not quite enough."

Sibby slipped forwards. She pushed something into my palm. I trust my sister. I held it out to him.

"What is this?"

She ducked her head as a sign of respect. "It is a perpetual light," she said in her usual quiet voice. "It will never run out of battery. You can switch it on and off at will, but it will last forever."

The man pushed at a small button on the top of the gadget. A coherent beam of light shone out, illuminating at least fifty meters of the path.

The Bezniks muttered to each other. I could hear admiration in their comments.

"We want more of these," said their leader. "Five, for the map. Plus the pistol."

I shook my head. "I am sorry." I began to stand. "We only have the one. If you give us the map, we will give you the pistol and the light. I have nothing else I can barter. Though I promise I will bring your case to the attention of the Alliance."

There was a short pause, then he passed over the map. I unrolled it. Sure enough, there were many places marked on the parchment. Since one was marked Okakuara, I assumed that the dots were actually entrances to the underground systems.

There was another dot almost due south of Okakuara. It was marked Rooshaka. I poked at the map. "Is this where we came in?"

He peered over. "Yes."

"Thank you. Can you ... can you tell me what the Terrans were looking for?"

There was a quick discussion. "They were here to purchase enzenium ore. It lies abundantly just to the south of Okakuara. We do not use it ourselves, so we were able to come to an agreement with them. They also required alkel granules. We agreed to trade them a very limited amount."

"Thank you for your help. Is there any place where the Alliance could contact your representatives?"

More discussion. Then he bent down and put a grubby finger nail on a spot some way to the west of our current position. "Here. Ababuka. It is our ... our main place. Tell them to go there. But when they use the surface pulley they must remain close to it. We will find them. It is forbidden to wander around the great underground lake. It is an offence."

"We will tell them. Thank you." I gave him a vague attempt at a bow. He did the same to me. There was a moment of bobbing and nodding between all of us and all of them. Then we turned and began to make our way back to the paternoster lift.

It was easier going than coming. The Beznik walked ahead, allowing his new torch to light up the way in front. We made good time.

"When did you pull that together?" I whispered to my sister.

She shrugged. "I just thought it might come in useful. You know, when we saw the shaft down."

"You are amazing. Only you could invent a permanent light in ten minutes."

She smiled. "It really wasn't difficult. It is just something nobody has needed until now. Any decent nanotech engineer could have cobbled one together. It is a simple quantum device."

"Thanks. Look how useful it will be to them."

"They see in the dark. It is like a toy for them. Not something they really need."

"How do you know? That they see in the dark, I mean."

"They have to. Stands to reason. They came up on us with no lights whatsoever. Their eyes have evolved to see in really low light."

We were soon back at the paternoster lift. It had switched itself off, so our escort pushed a large red button near the base of the structure.

"It is programmed to turn off after two turns with no weight."

That gave me a funny feeling of being stuck inside half way up and being found decades later as a mummified clump of flesh. I shivered.

Both Mel and Sibby were staring aghast at the man. It wasn't hard to see that their thoughts had gone in that direction, too.

He picked up on their doubt. "I will stay here until all the cylinders come around again," he reassured us. "You have nothing to worry about."

Neither of the girls seemed very convinced, but there wasn't really very much that they could do about it. They didn't want to stay down here, either.

I grabbed Sibby and thrust her into the first of the canisters. She made a small squeak and then closed her eyes and her mouth.

"See you at the top, Sibby!" She disappeared slowly.

I grabbed at Mel and shoved her into the next cylinder. She was completely mute, though her mouth moved. She might have been praying. She slumped against the back of the glass container and disappeared upwards.

I stepped back and let Denaraz load up the others.

Then I shook the hand of the Beznik leader. "I appreciate your help."

He grinned. "You have made it worth our while."

"Do you really spend all your lives down here?"

"You get used to it."

"And you never felt like contacting the visitors at Sorrengaria?"

"We sent a few of our people out when they first arrived. They didn't pass our tests. We were not ready."

"Are you ready now?"

He hesitated. "I ... am not sure. You have passed our test. We must discuss our position."

"I will inform the Macers. Perhaps a small group of your people ... a delegation ... would consent to being transported to Ulon Prime? You could give the Macers your tests and decide after that?"

"I will put forward your suggestion. But please come back yourself to find out. If you approach us through the Ababuka surface pulley, you will find it manned at all times. Give my name – Obari – to the guard."

I thanked him and gave him my own name. "Perhaps we will see each other again, then?"

"I hope so."

I stepped into the next canister and pulled my body in as it began to rise. He watched with amusement. I suppose they were so used to the paternoster lifts that they found our reserve amusing.

By the time I reached the next level I felt unable to breathe. The air circulated well along the underground lake, but it certainly didn't feel as though enough of it had made its way into my cylinder.

Sweat was pouring off my face and I was panting when, at last, the glass casket edged out of the rock face and I felt fresher air on my face. I staggered out of the thing with huge relief, vowing never to take another one of the things in my life.

Zenzie was waiting for me. She handed me a pack of water. Her own face was shiny.

I used my top to wipe off some of my own sweat.

She nodded. "It *was* unpleasant, wasn't it? For some reason the amount of air in the canisters has thinned. Sibby says it must be due to outside temperatures. She thinks we may be in a conjunction of the suns. That puts the outside temperature up by 35 degrees. She says that could cause pockets of thicker and thinner air."

I took in a deep breath.

Zenzara rolled her eyes. "We are in a pocket of thick air here. You can't store oxygen up in any case, you know."

"Of course I know that. I was … yawning."

"Really? Are you tired?"

The thought of not having enough air triggered an involuntary response in my brain and I really did begin to yawn. It brought tears to my eyes.

Zenzie opened her mouth, but since I knew the gist of what was about to come out, I pushed past her and made my way to the others.

They were clustered around the body of the Vaer. Denaraz had already slung a rope around the body and the girls had collected most of the shattered head fragments into a cloth which they had found in the first aid kit.

Izan gave me a brief nod of acknowledgement. "I will go up first, then Eshan and Didjal. The three of us will haul up this body and then the box of head parts. Then the rest of you can make your way up in your own time.”

He glanced to me for the go ahead. I nodded.

As the three leaders began to climb up the fifteen meter rope length, I sat down next to Sibby and Mel. Neema was moving from one to the other behind them, giving neck massages in an attempt to make them relax.

I took Sibby’s hand. “All right?”

She was grey. “Sure, Mall. Just don’t ask me to do that ever … EVER … again, right?”

“I won’t. Neither of you will have to.”

Mel was still gasping for air. “I would ap-ap-preciate that Cap-captain!”

“Will you be able to get yourselves up that rope?”

Sibby pointed to the rock above us. “I certainly have no intention of staying here! I will find a way to get myself up.”

“Me too.” Mel made as if to get up already, but Neema pushed her back down. “Rest a little longer.”

Zenzie had walked over. “She nearly went round again,” she told me conversationally.

“Who did?”

“Mel. She lost consciousness on the way up. If Neema hadn’t been watchful, she would have gone around the whole loop again.”

Mel shivered at the thought.

So did I. I wasn’t sure she would have made it out. “Well spotted Neems!”

“We nearly didn’t get her out. Luckily Eshaan was close enough to sprint over and give me a hand. We only just dragged her off the platform before her capsule disappeared again into the rock.”

I swallowed. Just the thought of it made the roof of my mouth dry. I needed to look after my crew better.

“Thank you.”

Neema concentrated on Mel’s neck, although she had gone pink. “Just doing my job, Captain.”

I examined Mel more closely. She was a pasty shade of green. I really shouldn't have put her through that.

"You go up next," I told her. "They can pull you up first. Tell them to send me the rope down after."

She tried to stand up obediently. Her legs were rubbery and she almost fell. I walked her over to the rope and tied it around her like a harness. She clutched in a floppy sort of way at the rope.

I gave it two quick pulls. Effortlessly, Mel began to rise, swaying to and fro as she did.

"Mel, keep yourself clear of the sides with your feet."

She met my gaze and nodded.

In a few seconds all we could see of her was her shoes moving away from us as she was winched to safety.

I turned my attention to Sibby, but she held up a hand. "I will be all right. Get the Vaer ready. I can make it up on my own."

"Sure?"

She nodded. "Positive."

I gave her a hug. "Well done!"

She groaned. "I might not have been so keen to come at all if I had known what it was going to entail."

"Come off it, Sibby. You would never have met Izan if you hadn't!"

Two spots of red appeared on her cheeks and blossomed outwards. "I guess that is true."

I dropped a kiss on top of her head. "Proud of you, kid."

She glared. "Don't 'kid' me!"

I held my hands up. "OK. Old lady then."

She pinched me.

The Vaer's body was now inching its way upwards. I felt a real regret as I watched it go. A real case of the wrong place at the wrong time. I just wished he had thought to ask us for help instead of attacking me. Too many people died in Bull Cunningham's wake. He was toxic in the true meaning of the word. I couldn't wait to lock him up somewhere very, very safe.

The box of head parts went up next. I moved over to check the area we were leaving. There was still blood on the floor, but we couldn't do anything about that. I kicked what loose sand I could find over it and spread it around with my shoe. Eventually it looked pretty much like the rest of the ledge.

Sibby went up the rope without help, though I could see the strain around her neck and shoulders.

Neema has always been very athletic. She swarmed up the rope with no difficulty whatsoever. Then Zenzara made short work of it too, making it look easy.

I took one last look around the penumbra on the large shelf, before reaching for the rope myself.

It took me a little longer. My build is more for stamina than speed, I like to think, though I am pretty sure Zenzara would put it another way. In any case, I made it out in the end, emerging from the shaft to a ring of anxious faces.

"What? Did you think I couldn't make it?"

Denaraz and Eshaan pulled me out and then pulled the rest of the rope up.

Didjal had been scouting outside the entrance of the cavern. "It is really hot out there. I think you will all need to helmet up again."

We had left the helmets at the top of the shaft. We bustled over to separate them all out and position them safely again.

"What is the temperature out there, Didj?" I asked.

"Between 75 and 80 in pure sunlight."

I stared. "Celsius?"

"Celsius."

"Can we survive that without the full EVA helmets?" We had brought them on the sleds, just in case, but they were cumbersome and would mean putting on full EVA. Full EVA of course can withstand intense cold and intense heat, but is much, much more comfortable in intense cold. It really can become extremely humid inside in full EVA at high temperatures. If possible, we needed to stay in IEVA. Even that was severely limiting.

Sibby was still securing her helmet. She stopped to answer me. "It is right at the top of the range. We should be fine for an hour or so. The cooling tubes will bring that down to around 50 by the time it reaches the lungs, and of course the air will be heavily hydrated. That will help. We should be all right, though the main danger is that the heat could trigger an asthma-type response. We will have to monitor ourselves closely."

I turned to the Enif. "You, Didjal? Can you and Eshaan manage at temperatures like that?"

It nodded. "Certainly for an hour or two. We would be uncomfortable for much longer than that."

"Then we go forwards. Let's get ourselves to the sleds and set a course for Okakuara. This is going to be unpleasant."

8

That journey across the Beznik desert was one of the closest things to hell I had ever experienced. The sleds hammered over the dunes, unable to cope well with such broken terrain. We reared upwards, only to slam down towards the next trough. The only ones of us not to vomit were the two Enif. Even Denaraz found his stomach unable to cope.

You should try vomiting when you are wearing a helmet designed to save your face and lungs from being burnt away. First you pull your helmet away from your face, whilst leaning out from one side of the sled. Then you are violently sick while trying not to breathe in superheated air that sears your throat even more. Then you slap the helmet back over your burning face and blow out in order to clear the coolant tubing. By that time you don't know if you are going to be sick again or asphyxiate. The sight of your companions doing exactly the same thing only serves to prompt your stomach to go through the whole thing all over again.

We were lucky that the two Enif were unaffected, relatively. Eshaan took the controls of one of the mag sleds and Didjal the other. I don't think we could ever have made it to Okakuara if they hadn't.

The temperature was so unpleasant that those moments of nausea were enough to leave us all with red facial burns. Taking that helmet off was like putting your face in a sand blaster. Instant facial peel, and then some. Mine felt as though it was down to the muscles. Maybe even the bone.

Not only that, but the helmets didn't really protect our eyes adequately from the three suns. The light pouring down on the sand was so bright that, even with the helmets on, our eyes refused to open. My own eyelids had sealed tight as we came out of the cave. I was reminded of a childhood experiment where we had focused the rays of the sun with a magnifying glass on paper. Within seconds it had begun to burn. That was exactly the sensation on my retinas. That was with the helmets on. Without them, it was necessary to ball up your hands to cover your eye sockets. All done whilst leaning over the side of a plunging platform that reared and plunged, slamming through crusted peaks and troughs.

I was only just in time to stop Zenzie from falling off the sled altogether. She had been jolted loose while leaning out. Luckily I was able to grab the collar of her IEVA suit and haul her back on board. She was having the worst time of all of us. All those loose wrinkles exposed a larger surface area of her face to the elements. Her eyes were dark sparks of agony in a red sea of pain.

I tucked her under my arm, trying to offer comfort. She thanked me with a squeeze of my arm, then pulled away to vomit again. I kept a hold on her sleeve as long as I could, just in case.

We pulled up in front of a new cave entrance what felt like some days later. Actually it was under an hour, but I would never have guessed that less than sixty minutes had passed.

If Cunningham had been waiting for us, he could have wiped us out easily. For my part, I simply tumbled off the mag sled and lay panting, face up, on the sand. Even the two Enif had their shoulders hunched.

Didjal waved to me to get out of the elements. He and Eshaan quickly disappeared from my sight as they began to reconnoiter the surrounding areas. I felt relief. I couldn't have done it myself.

We left the sleds and staggered quickly out of the sunlight. The entrance to the Okakuara shaft was almost identical to the one we already knew at Rooshaka.

We scuttled down the dark tunnel as fast as we could. Even fifty metres of shade were insufficient. It wasn't until we had let ourselves down to the first level that we were able to remove our helmets.

I passed water around. We all made an effort to clean up our faces. It hurt just to pat my skin with cool water. I had no idea what I looked like, but if it was anything like the others, I felt sorry for myself.

Zenzie's wrinkles were quite spectacular. The crests of the wrinkles had been shaved by the superheated sand blast, leaving bleeding skin in shreds. Blood had trickled into the troughs where it had become trapped and dried. I stared and then shuddered.

"Here, let me do your face." I dabbed ineffectually at it, cringing inside as I saw the discomfort I was causing. Then I threw up.

Zenzie gave a shout and jumped to one side. "You might have told me you were going to do that!"

"Sorry. It just happened."

"And stop scraping at my face like you are peeling a carrot! You are hurting me!"

"Yes. I know."

She caught something my tone. "Is it that bad?"

"No-o-o."

Her eyes widened. "Is it worse than yours?"

I shrugged. "How should I know? I can't see my own face."

She pushed my hand away. "Give me the water. I will do it myself."

Didjal and Eshaan let themselves down the rope. They were

accompanied by a sturdy Beznik, who regarded us all with some caution, but did not seem afraid.

The two Enif were the first to recover. I knew that their race preferred cold vacuum to hot air, but they still seemed relatively unaffected by the ordeal. They quickly checked our surroundings, leaving the Beznik man next to me. There was nobody else in the wide cavern.

Didjal came back to me. "There is a similar paternoster lift."

"Good."

"It is currently switched off. It looks to me as if it has not been used in some time."

"Then we wait. The Bezniks have guaranteed them safe passage to this point. We can't go any further down."

They nodded. "We haven't missed them. This man is the driver of their hover sledge. He brought it over from the Rooshaka shaft. He was told to wait for them here."

"He was outside?" I couldn't help but admire his fortitude. As far as I could see he was wearing nothing but a thin tunic, though it did have a hood.

The Beznik inclined from the waist. "It was my time."

I remembered what the leader of the men at Rooshaka had told me.

"You needed to spend two days outside?"

He nodded again. "It is why I volunteered."

"But there is a conjunction of the suns. "You can survive that?"

He showed me his tunic. Although it seemed to move like a material, it was in fact far more resilient. "This is interwoven with alkel. It offers protection."

"But you still must breathe in the air at a very high temperature."

"Ah, yes, but we are accustomed. Our bodies do not feel the heat like yours. We can survive outside on the planet. We do not normally choose to go out during a conjunction, except for the alkel workers, of course, but we suffer no damage if we do. It is uncomfortable if we do not take protective clothing, but it does not harm us."

They were a tough people, then. I looked around at my own sorry group.

"All right. We wait here for Cunningham, then." I explained the situation to the Beznik, who had introduced himself as Etios.

"Obari was correct. My instructions are to return home once the interlopers arrive at this level. I am to tell them where to find their sled and leave." He spread his hands in a universal gesture. "What happens then is outside my ... my ..."

"Purview?" I suggested.

"Yes. It is no longer my concern." He frowned. "However, I would ask that you wait until I have left the level. I would wish to be able to report an incident-free delivery."

"Of course. We will wait over there ..." I pointed to a dark corner of the cavern, "... until we see you descend into the surface pulley."

"That would be acceptable. I thank you for your understanding."

We moved to the darkest point of the cavern, beside a couple of large rocks that jutted out of the floor of the cave and pointed up to the ceiling. We all sank to the ground. There was no point hiding yet. We would have plenty of notice of Cunningham's arrival. The paternoster lift had yet to be activated.

Sibby and Mel were trying to clean up Zenzie's face. Sibby had pulled out a tube of some sort of cream from one of her pockets, and was applying it liberally, much to the Tyzaran girl's disgust.

"That smells terrible!" She pushed Sibby's hand away.

"Maybe. But you need it." Sibby tutted and rubbed in a little more.

Zenzie cringed away from her, but Sibby simply shuffled closer again. In the end there appeared to be a sort of undeclared truce, where Sibby continued her ministrations and Zenzara accepted them with ill grace.

I pulled myself over to the Enif, who were crouched next to Denaraz. "I think they will be alone," I said, "but we can't be sure. And we cannot act until the lift containing Etios descends below this level. He should not witness anything out of the ordinary."

Izan grinned. "They have a strange sense of what is right."

"They do, but they appear to have strong integrity."

"It will be interesting to see what happens when the rest of the Shells discover there are nine sentient races instead of eight."

"It certainly will. I guess Beznik will stop being a tourist attraction."

He pursed his lips. "Maybe not. I got the impression that the Bezniks like having that tourist trade. They are an interesting race."

"Yes. I think they will get on well with the Macers."

"And the Nepheals. They will not have met either species before."

"So. We have our next mission. To welcome a newcomer to the Alliance. If they want to join, of course."

"That is a big if. From what we have seen so far, they appear to want to maintain their distance."

"They do. However, they will have to adapt once their existence becomes known. There will be a constant flood of ships here to sell them things. And that extra-strength glass they make would be very popular."

"Especially those weapons. I wouldn't mind getting my hands on one myself."

I shushed him, but it was too late. Etios had overheard. The Beznik walked up to him, holding out his weapon. Denaraz checked with me and then took it eagerly when I gave him a nod. They walked towards the lifts, chattering. Denaraz was turning the thing over and over in his hands. He looked pleased.

He asked Etios something and then peered through the sights, lining the thing up on a small outcrop of rock at the side of the cave.

He would probably have pulled the trigger, but at that moment the red light to the right of the lifts flashed, and the paternoster lift began to move. The glass cylinder to the right went up, that to the left began to go down.

We all hurried to hide ourselves, until only Etios was left. Izan patted the alkel weapon with some regret before handing it back and ducking back towards the rest of us.

Light flickered off the glass cylinders that served as lifts as each one slowly hove in and then out of view. The process was slow. Paternoster lifts have to be slow, so that there is time for the travelers to get themselves in and out while it is moving.

There was one capsule about every ten metres and we knew from Etios that the underground living level was a hundred feet down. That meant ten empty capsules before Cunningham could arrive.

We watched the shadows play over the scene as we waited. All of us had drawn our guns. We wanted to be ready.

Bull Cunningham was the first one to step out of the glass casket. He spotted the Beznik straight away. His lean figure hesitated only for an instant as he scanned the rest of the cave, his eyes wary. He must have decided that there was no danger, for he strode forward, a smile on his lips.

Etios looked nervous. I could hardly blame him. The two men met in the centre of the cave, and Etios passed a set of keys to Bull. He then pointed to the rope leading up to the outside and gestured with his hands, clearly telling the Terran exactly where to find the sled. Bull gave a faint nod, but his attention was more on the paternoster lift.

Etios moved quickly towards the lift. He was hoping to step onto the next down capsule. I was wondering what would come out of the next up capsule.

The Beznik ducked fluidly inside the cylinder. I caught his head descending into the darkness out of the corner of my eye as I focussed on the arriving capsule. It contained two large heavy sacks and one small light one. So did the next and the one after that.

Ramesh Chandrayanan didn't arrive until the following lozenge slid into view. He tumbled clumsily out, shouting something to Cunningham as he did.

Cunningham had exhausted himself dragging the sacks out of the lifts before they moved on. He didn't bother to reply to the Indian's obvious discomfort. In fact, I thought I saw a smile on his face.

We waited until they were both beneath the lift shaft before we surrounded them. I ran out of the penumbra and put my pistol against Bull's forehead.

He froze.

"Hello, Bull. How are you?"

"Ryler! I was wondering where you had got to." His handsome face actually creased into a smile. "You are looking a little peaky, if you don't mind my saying so."

My teeth ground together and I jumped as a nerve in my jaw signaled discomfort. "Damn it!"

"Have you come to take me back to face my peers, old boy? I heard they had seconded you onto the Interstellar Enforcement Agency. Well done!"

His patronizing voice irritated me beyond measure. "You won't be so pleased to see me at your trial."

"No such thing!" he seemed offended. "I was – and still am – working for the good of my people. I have merely been trying to obtain technology that should never have been withheld from us. I have done nothing wrong."

I stared. Surely he couldn't believe that? He had caused so many deaths. Did he really believe that they were justified?

"The Tyzarans have been stockpiling new discoveries for the last century," he said with a defiant toss of his head. "They have only passed on what technological advances they felt we should have. They have kept the most important discoveries very much to themselves."

"We owe the whole of our interstellar program to the Tyzarans."

"Maybe we do. But they agreed to share their technology with us. Not just some of it. The Berennis Treaty states specifically 'share technological advances'"

Denaraz was intrigued by this argument. "It does not say 'all' technological advances, I believe."

Bull turned on him. "It does not say 'some' technological advances. Your nation has been holding back all the best new technology for decades!" His voice rang with conviction.

"How can you believe that justifies kidnapped and torturing Zenzie? Exterminating the whole Chakran race? Declaring war and annexing whole star systems?"

"They brought it on themselves!"

I shook my head and passed him over to Denaraz.

The Indian was trembling. "I do not recognize the Alliance!" he kept repeating. "You have no right to do this!"

There was something about both of them that made me pause. Almost as if they were both playing a role. I narrowed my eyes and checked my surroundings yet again, but I could see nothing out of the ordinary.

I caught Denaraz's eye. He was looking watchful too.

Still, we had to get them out of the cave and secured to a sled. The conjunction would be nearly over now. Hopefully the trip back to the shuttle would be rather more bearable.

I stared at the sacks of enzenium. I was in two minds to leave them there, on the first level, except I wasn't sure how the Bezniks would take it. They seemed to be very fussy about agreements. Perhaps it would be better to take the sacks with us, at least up to the surface. Once there, I could decide what to do with them.

I asked the two Enif to organize the enzenium. The rest of us watched as they busied around, tying, hauling and transporting it up to the surface of the planet. It took them nearly an hour.

At last they were ready. Eshaan slipped down the rope again to tell us of the temperature above our heads.

"It is slowly cooling now. There is only one sun currently over the horizon, and the outside air is down to fifty-five and still falling."

I thanked him.

Denaraz and Cunningham walked up to the rope first, flanked by Eshaan and Neema. All of my crew had their guns out and trained on the Terran. None of us were prepared to give him the benefit of any doubt. We were way past that.

"Tie them up once you get to the top," I told Denaraz.

The Tyzaran nodded.

I noticed Cunningham glance at the Indian as he passed him. Chandrayanan began to moan. "I'm not staying down here with these people. They will kill me if you are not here. Let me go up first! You have to! I can't stay here! I feel sick!"

Mel gave him a small push to encourage him not to talk.

He screeched and cringed away from her. "See! They are going to torture me! I demand to go up first!"

Mel looked to me. I shrugged. "Take him up first if he wants."

I should have been more suspicious, but at the time I wasn't.

Mel, Zenzara and Sibby edged past the other four and began to make their way up the rope. Even though the Indian was escorted by the girls, he had zero chance of escape. Both Mel and Zenzara were taking their duties extremely seriously, and I had rarely seen my sister so resolute.

They managed to get him up the rope fairly quickly, though he wailed and cried all the way up.

Then it was Cunningham's turn. He had fallen silent after his attempt to justify all their actions. But his eyes moved constantly. Once or twice he seemed to be challenging me. To what, I don't know. I do know that his gaze rested on me more than once. I almost felt he was amused.

"Don't take your eyes off him," I told Denaraz, who inclined his head once. He would not allow Cunningham enough leeway to escape. I was certain. Yet something in the Terran's eyes still bothered me. I couldn't quite put my finger on it, but I was uneasy.

At last I was left alone in the dark cave. As soon as Neema cleared the rope above me, I shimmied up as fast as I could, trying to ignore the bad feeling.

I reached the surface at the same time they did and burst out into what seemed like unbearable sunshine, even though the intensity was much less now. Our stay in the darkness of the caves had allowed our eyes to rest and they resisted the sudden change to bright sunlight.

I slammed my IEVA helmet on, and after a couple of seconds, my eyes managed to adjust to the new light.

Denaraz was just pulling a pair of restraining cuffs from his belt. Mel was asking Cunningham to put his hands behind his back. The Indian was standing to one side.

Cunningham looked straight at me as I came out of the tunnel. He waited until he was sure I was looking back at him, then he smiled. It was a calculated, victorious smile.

Behind the helmet's shield, I checked and rechecked the scene in front of me, but could find nothing to worry me. There were no other people nearby. Nothing seemed to justify that cold smile of triumph.

But my heart sank.

I knew something I wasn't going to like was about to happen.

Cunningham held my gaze for some six seconds. I literally felt him gloat. Then, just as Denaraz was approaching with the restraining cuffs, he wrenched both hands in front of him. This surprised Mel and easily overpowered the loose hold she had on his arms.

He looked down at his wrists, which drew my attention to the same area.

I noticed a large metallic arm band encircling his left wrist. It was silvery, but dull, like pewter, and was embellished with studs.

I was walking towards him, my arms moving outwards in an attempt to stop whatever was clearly about to happen, but I was far too late.

He threw himself to the left, pulling Chandrayanan over with him and falling onto the sacks of enzenium. Chandrayanan put both arms out and across three of the sacks. Cunningham touched the others.

Then he turned to give me a triumphant look.

Zenzie gave a cry and raised both hands to her head. She bent over as some sort of pain dragged her down.

There was a shout of alarm and a blur of light. A dark shape hurtled past my shoulder towards the two Terrans.

Too late.

Their shapes flickered slightly around the edges and then both the Terrans and the sacks of enzenium and alkel disappeared.

We were left staring at empty air.

Didjal slammed into the ground, just where Cunningham had been. It had been a fraction of a second too late.

I proffered my hand to help it up.

It took it. It seemed unharmed.

A cold fury took me over. I began to shake. I couldn't believe that Bull had got the better of me yet again.

Both Sibby and Mel came up to me, but I shook them off. I walked away from the others. I needed a few moments to myself. If I could, I would have screamed in frustration. Why was I always a step behind? I should have seen that coming.

Denaraz was the one who broke the spell. He approached me slowly, a worried look on his face. "If they can do that ... whatever it is that they have just done ... they could come back whenever they want. They could snatch Zenzara again."

My destructive anger evaporated. What was needed now was to be constructive. And Izan was right. If we stayed where we were, they would know exactly where Zenzie was.

We had to get out of there.

The whole mission was in tatters. Over. We had failed. Not only had the Terrans escaped, but I had allowed them to escape with enough enzenium and alkel to clone however many Chakran strands they still retained. They might now be able to replicate enough to open *several* ship-sized wormholes. I had signed the death warrant on the strands they still had and possibly on those they didn't. And I had failed to consider that they might somehow have found a way to disappear at will. I was bitterly disappointed in myself.

"Zenzie, are you all right?"

She was deathly pale, but had managed to stand up again. She nodded. "I felt it when they vanished. The Nexus inside me pulsed. Everything flared up and then almost collapsed. It hurt my head. It hurt the Chakrans. They have destroyed one of the strands." She blinked in an attempt to clear her head.

I turned to the rest of the group. "Get on the sleds! Didj, can you bring the hover sledge that was left here for the Terrans? We will take it with us. They might … just might … have left something of interest on it."

We clambered onto the three sleds, dividing our forces. The journey back to the shuttle was long, arduous and filled with bitter disappointment. Although the suns were now below the horizon, the temperature was still highly uncomfortable. The best thing that could be said about it is that none of us, this time, were sick.

9

As soon as the shuttle docked with *Nivala*, I stormed to the bridge. Seyal reacted with alarm to my expression.

"Captain? What has happened?"

"They escaped. Get me *Aenysia* on the tight-beam."

Seyal shook her head. "I can't. They are behind the moon, where you sent them. They have been out of contact for the last four hours. Are they under attack?"

"I don't know. Get us over there. As fast as you can, please."

"Yes, Captain."

I plonked myself into the captain's chair and watched with finger-tapping frustration as it took us an hour to get out from our own orbit and across space to a path that would intercept with *Aenysia*. I couldn't stop thinking that if Danaa, Sammy and Anzany were dead it would be because of my lack of forethought.

Nivala raced around the edge of the moon, hoping to find two ships hidden there. There was only one. *Aenysia* hung, stationary, behind the dark curve of the moon. Her hull was pock-marked and she was venting atmosphere from two long gashes in her hull. Of the Vaer cruiser, there was no sign.

"Take us in," I snapped.

Seyal altered course. "Thirty minutes, Captain."

I glared round at the others. "Right; what happened back there? How did they just disappear like that?"

Didjal chittered, sounding unusually nervous for an Enif. "The arm band Cunningham was wearing was some sort of mechanism."

Sibby nodded. "That is some seriously advanced technology."

"Well," said Mel in a thoughtful tone, "they left the shuttle down on the planet!"

"They didn't need it," I growled. "They used that arm band thingy to transport themselves right back to their ship! Sibby, you and Didjal get started on some way to figure out what that mechanism is."

My sister pursed her lips. "That may take some time."

"We have to try. Go!"

She and the two Enif made their way off the bridge. I turned to Izan. "Can you take Zenzie to the sick bay, please, and put her through the triage unit? Make sure she is all right?"

I didn't have to tell Mel and Neema to stay on the bridge. They were both staring across at the stricken *Aenysia*, wondering how much of Sammy and Anzany would be left. Mel had been trying to establish a link with the Nepheal ship, but she now shook her head. "I can't get through to them."

Or they aren't answering.

She didn't say the words, but she didn't have to. They thundered in my head in any case.

Seyal had been examining the scanner. "I don't believe the damage is too bad, Captain," she murmured. "Those gashes in the hull are both limited to the outer hull. Nepheal ships have an outer and inner hull. They are venting water vapor from the coolant pipes, not atmosphere from the inner hull. I suspect that communications are down because they were hit by an electromagnetic detonation pulse."

I wanted to believe that. A well-aimed EM pulse could certainly have taken out all communications, along with the guidance systems of the rail guns. Another pulse to the stern of the ship would have left them dead in the water. I suppose I should be grateful that such a decrepit Vaer cruiser had been equipped with little ordinance. Cunningham would not have hesitated to eliminate the Nepheal ship if he could have.

It wasn't going to help his case.

I went to the consoles, hoping we could scan for emissions. We needed to find out exactly where they were bound. It was time to put an end to all this. Well past time.

"There is movement ahead, Captain." Seyal's voice was excited.

I leapt towards the navigating station. Sure enough, one of *Aenysia*'s shuttles had edged out of the mother ship.

"I have them on hololink!" Seyal flipped a button to allow the transmission.

Sammy appeared, a little the worse for wear around the edges, in the middle of the bridge of the shuttle.

Mel gasped. He had a bad cut along his forehead.

"It looks worse than it is," he said in a tired voice. "Sorry, Rye. The first we knew that there was anybody on board the Vaer ship was when they fried all our electronics. It has taken me a while even to get the shuttle back on line. And for that I had to get out from the main ship's shadow."

"Are the others all right?"

His holo smiled. "They are. Danaa was caught in the engine room and suffered some burns to her hands, but they are not serious. I just wish we could have done something about it. One minute there was nothing, the next they were on board the Vaer ship. We saw nothing, and believe me, we were watching very carefully. What the fitz happened?"

"They have refined their technology. They can vanish from one place and reappear in another."

Sammy whistled. "I don't like the sound of that!"

"How long will it take to repair *Aenysia*?"

"Danaa is on it, but she reckons we need at least two weeks in a full-facility repair station. She says that if we worked on it ourselves it would take months."

I checked the astrogation console. "The nearest class II full-facility is over on Javesta. What speed can she manage as is?"

Sammy's holo faded in and out as he consulted with Danaa on the main ship.

He was soon solid again. "Sorry about that. We are using handhelds since the main communications hub is down. She says it will take us a week to reach Javesta and get the necessary repairs done."

"All right, Sammy. Stick with Danaa and Anzany. Get the ship fixed. We will get word to you where to rendezvous."

Sammy hesitated. "I think they could spare me."

"No. Stay with *Aenysia*. And get yourselves fighting fit, please!"

Sammy looked disappointed. His eyes tracked to Mel. "Yes, Rye."

That was the problem about on-board relations. They got in the way. "I'm sorry, Sammy."

"I understand."

He cut the connexion and the bridge went suddenly silent. I told Seyal to stop the ship and turned my attention back to the emissions console. It was *Nivala's* turn. She would have to find them, and she was going to have to do it alone.

Neema's shadow fell over the console. "We can still track them, luckily. That Vaer ship is oozing contamination out of every pore. Their path looks like a firework on my radian toxicity screen. The Vaer ship is on a direct heading for Heisenberg's Halo."

I stared. "There is nothing up there! It is outside any Shell! It makes no sense. Why would they travel outside the Shells? Why Heisenberg's Halo? Do any of you know anything about it?"

They all shook their heads. Seyal brought up some background on the supernova. "It's the supernova remains of a blue giant which exploded around 5000 years ago. There's a ring of expanding detritus now at a distance of 10 light years. There are no planets and no other stars in the area."

I drummed my fingers on the screen, glaring at it. "This makes no sense! There is nothing there that could be of use to Cunningham! Why is he heading out into the Dust?" We were missing something, clearly. "Send a message to the *Aenysia*, will you? Tell them that our final destination is probably Heisenberg's Halo. Ask them to pass that on to the Macers. Then set a course to follow ... wait! No! Let's get one of the carbon clouds set up around us first. The last thing we want is for them to realize how close behind them we really are. Get Sibby and Denaraz to set up a carbon cloud to hide our signal. Then get us to Heisenberg's Halo. We have to get ahead of them. We have been trailing them all this time. It is time to put ourselves one step ahead."

Seyal smiled. "Yes, Captain!"

I noticed that my fingers had finally stilled. We would get there in time to put an end to all of this. We had to.

Heisenberg's Halo is outside the Major Shells, which means that it is situated in what we call 'the Dust'. The Shells are actually cavities in the interstellar medium, zones where space itself is thinner. The Dust is what surrounds the Shells, and has between five and fifteen times more material. Most of our stars are within the Shells, but that does not mean that constellations do not exist in the Dust. They are simply fewer and further between. Waypoint, for example – which is one of the largest space stations – is situated just inside the Dust. For that reason it is considered to belong to everybody. The Dust is considered neutral territory.

We trailed silently through space. Sibby, Didjal, Denaraz and Zenzara spent their time trying to come up with answers. They thought they were getting closer to putting the puzzle together, but there were too many unknowns for them to be able to foresee exactly what Cunningham was planning.

The only good news was that Heisenberg's Halo was so far off normal shipping lines that it was extremely unlikely the Terrans would be able to get reinforcements out here. The bad news was that neither would we. Unless Danaa was able to get *Aenysia* up and running much faster than she thought.

As we got closer and closer to the Halo, it resolved into a wonderful mixture of colors. I had been expecting a regular circle, expanding in space, rather like the Crab Nebula. It wasn't like that at all.

Firstly, there was a ring of material that had been ejected before the star went nova. This was its supernova wind, which in this case consisted of overlapping wisps of pure blue energy. These twisted and wrapped around each other, so that there were braids of it lying more thickly in some places than in others. As it expanded, it had clumped together so that other parts of the circle were now almost empty. The curved tendrils in places were ghost-like. In others they seemed to be formed of almost solid energy.

Inside that ring of material was a tiny pulsating quark star. In fact, the Halo had been the first quark star remnant of a supernova to be discovered. That was the reason it had been named after Heisenberg, who had first caught a glimpse of the complexities of the subatomic world in the mid twentieth century. A quark star is a variant of a neutron star, but involves exotic material. It is made of a quark-gluon soup, and is therefore very, very special. It is a brilliant white color, one that you can't bear to look at directly, even 50 centuries after it exploded.

The Vaer ship made a beeline for one of the brightest spots in the supernova wind, on the edges of the Halo. This particular spot was a deep bright electric blue.

We slid to within a thousand kilometers of the Terrans. With the carbon cloud around the ship, there was no way that they could possibly detect us.

Sibby called us all into the Weapons bridge, which is where our science laboratories had been installed.

She was not looking very happy as we filed in. She waited until we were all there except Seyal, who was still on pilot's duty.

She got straight into it. "I believe that the device used by Cunningham was a personal carbon cloud that was powered by a Chakran strand."

There was a collective gasp of concern. "How?" asked Neema.

"Chakran cells are linked by special quantum connections. Part of the reason that these connections are so special is that they utilize exotic matter. This is what keeps the links open all the time." She glanced at Zenzie. "*Chy* Zenzara has been able to document this through their use of her Chakran Nexus to force open the throat of the wormhole they managed to construct."

Zenzie shuffled her feet in an uncomfortable manner, but said nothing.

"Chandrayanan hasn't had the facilities to work on the traversable wormholes since then, but he could and probably did take the carbon cloud technology and work out what he could do with it."

Sibby stopped and swallowed. She looked sick. I wasn't sure I wanted to hear what was coming. I knew that expression well. Whatever it was, we weren't going to want to hear it.

"So, what did he come up with?" Mel was frowning.

"I told you that personal clouds were impossible because of the need for huge batteries?"

I nodded. "You did."

"He will have started there, and must have realized that he could power a personal cloud with negative energy. It would take relatively little."

Zenzie inhaled sharply. "—He used the strand they kept!"

"I think so, yes. It would have seemed the obvious solution to him. We know he does not care about dismembering the Chakrans."

"They *did* destroy it!" Zenzie had gone pale.

"I am sorry, Chyzar. I think that they did, yes." Sibby looked at her own feet. "And I am afraid that they may have gone even further than using the strand as a power source."

We were all staring at her now, afraid of what she was about to tell us.

She gave a deep sigh. "I think Chandrayanan realized that the negative energy of the Chakrans was good not only as a power source on a large scale, or to maintain a wormhole open. I think that he realized it could also be used as a transfer device on a small scale."

I scratched my head. "A transfer device?"

She shrugged. "The idea of using negative energy to propel ships is not exactly new. It goes all the way back to the ancient idea of Alcubierre drives. Even the ZEPH drive uses a positive energy variant of that concept. And we know that wormholes need negative energy if the throat is to remain open and stable."

"But those are not transfer devices!" I pointed out. "Are you talking about a propulsion device?"

"No. A propulsion device would not have allowed them to pass through the walls of the Vaer ship onto the bridge from the surface of the planet. Propulsion devices don't pass through solid barriers. What he must have developed is a small subspace link from one place to another. Since it connects places through the zero point field, it can traverse barriers. However, it is very limited on the mass it can carry and the distance it can travel. My initial calculations suggest that the link would have to be within a few hundred physical miles, and the mass would cap out at around a ton. Anything more would kill the Chakran strand used outright."

Zenzie had begun to cry. "What did they do to the strand, then? If they haven't killed it yet?"

Sibby's face fell even more. "It might be better if they had. I'm afraid it is still alive."

Zenzie stared. I put an arm over her thin shoulder, but she shrugged it off angrily. "But you said they destroyed it." she whispered in a hollow tone, her throat closing up before she could finish.

"The strand must still be alive; otherwise the device wouldn't work. They haven't had time to build the resonance chamber. That wasn't cloned negative energy. That has to be one of the strands they stole from your Nexus. I think they have found a way to circumvent the strand's free will. They have forced it into compliance. It is trapped and has already been dismembered."

"Dismembered?" Zenzie wailed.

"Yes. Chakran strands communicate via tiny links through subspace, known as EPR, or entanglement. Because of the ER = EPR conjecture and Agraala's thesis, we know that they can be used to form the traversable wormholes they want for their ships. That requires a lot of energy ... one strand is not enough. They used two for their prototype remember. To move a fleet, they would need dozens. However, one strand *is* enough to make small jumps through those subspace links. Small, discrete jumps."

"How do they know where to jump?"

"Our best guess is that they have paired it with a modified hololink. The bubble can be directed along the same path as the hololink. That is what happened with Ethnarch Locke, remember? The Chakrans were able to follow even an ansible hololink."

"I see. Thank you." I blew out air, rather shakily. "Can we rescue that strand?"

"I believe not. It has already been harnessed into the device. And it has been used. It cannot be recovered. It is alive, but agonizing."

Zenzie's claws had sprung out of her hands, which were clenched.

"How can we stop them?" I found my fingers beating a staccato rhythm against the side of the console I was standing behind. Again. I stopped and put them behind my back. "We can't destroy the device?"

Sibby shrugged. "Maybe. We have to find it first. Even then, I am not sure how to destroy it humanely. We would be killing the strand inside."

"It sounds to me like that would be the kindest thing to do."

"Yes, maybe. But will the Chakrans agree?"

"So what do you suggest?"

"I don't know." Her eyes, when they met mine, were defeated.

She was exhausted. She hadn't slept for days and it showed. I wished I could tell her to go and relax, but I couldn't.

I settled on rubbing her back lightly.

She yawned, but gave me a smile. Her skin was translucent and the smile was oddly vulnerable. She wanted to do more.

"Then work on that, Sibby. Who do you need with you?"

"At this stage, mainly Didjal." She gave a grateful look at the Enif. "It is the only one of you with a sufficiently advanced background in micro-engineering. Denaraz has been great with the theoretical research, but he is not expert in the applied stuff. Now we have to reverse-engineer their device to find any weak points, and of course without the power source they are using. We will attempt to construct something that will stop it. Even if that is possible, it will take days."

"Right. Meanwhile Chandrayanan will be working on cloning the last strand. I'm guessing he has all the research he needed. I don't think it will take him long." I looked around. "Suggestions?"

Denaraz grinned. "Sounds like it's time to go in?" He seemed quite happy about it. "We pick up the Terrans and grab the device. We rescue the strand or strands. Mission accomplished."

"We send a boarding party?"

"I can't see any other options."

"There aren't any." It was Zenzie, and her eyes were flashing. "The Chakrans want *me* to go."

"Good try, Zenzie."

She stamped her foot. "They do! I might be the only person there who can alter the outcome. I might be able to connect with the strand they have butchered. It might still be able to link with my Nexus.

Perhaps I could save it."

From Sibby's expression, that wasn't going to happen, but Zenzara clearly felt she had the right, as Chakran Chyzar, to try.

I wasn't happy about risking her again. "Who's to say the Terrans won't just kidnap you again and torture the other strands out of you? That might even be what they want, for Shell's sake! We could be playing right into their hands. I can't let you go. You know I can't."

Her crest was spiky and she looked daggers at me. "I am the Chyzar," she said in an imperious sort of way.

"You could be the Queen of Sheba for all I care. I am the one who decides what we will do."

"You think you are better than the Chyzar?"

"No. I don't think I am better than any of you. I am temporarily higher up in the chain of command."

"What do I care about that?"

I suppose, to a nine-year-old, chains of command seem pretty stupid. Not so long ago, they did to me too.

"It is decided, Zenzara. You will stay here and help Sibby and Didjal."

I thought her crest was going to fracture, it was so stiff. She stood there, breathing hard and struggling with her self-control. Then, all of a sudden, she deflated.

"Very well. You are the captain." Her crest came down. "But I do not agree with your stupid decision!"

"So noted." I couldn't help being a little sharp. It is very hard to run a ship when nine-year-olds challenge your authority. You should try it. Even Mel had her mouth half-open to argue Zenzie's side.

I stopped and looked at her, raising one eyebrow.

She subsided, closing her mouth with a snap.

Zenzie tossed her head and left the weapons bridge. "I am going to the pool," she snapped. "I need to cool down."

"Don't hurry back." All right, I know. I went too far.

"I shan't," she snapped back over her shoulder.

"Good."

The meeting broke up then. I needed time to decide who to send on the mission to the Vaer ship and how to get them on board. I headed to my cabin. I wanted to be alone to work out some of the logistics. We had the carbon clouds, but Bull would still notice if somebody opened one of the hatches from outside. We might as well walk straight up to the main visor and knock on the glass. And things were not exactly symmetrical. *We* might not be able to attack *them*, but I was pretty sure Bull would not give us the same courtesy. *Nivala* is a small ship. She is delicate. She wouldn't survive a few well-placed EM pulses, and he was bound to have saved some up for us.

I decided to go on my own. There was nobody else I felt I could take who would accentuate my chances of success. I wasn't going to allow Zenzie to put herself back in the same danger. Denaraz would stay with Zenzara. Sibby and Didjal were needed on *Nivala*. Eshaan, while very useful, was a painter and should remain that way unless there was no other option.

That left the three women. Seyal, Neema and Mel. None of them were quite right for the task. And I didn't think anybody would be coming back from this mission. It was, after all, only to gain time. Sibby would be the one who would stop the Terrans.

I walked back down to the weapons deck and drew her aside. "You are going to have to find a way to stop them," I told her.

"I know." She stared up at me, a worried expression on her face. "You will be careful, Mall?"

"I will. But you are the one who can find a technological solution. Unless we do that, I suspect they will run rings around us forever."

"I know."

She was breathing too quickly.

"What is it, Sibs? Is there more? Something you haven't told me?"

She deflated with a huge sigh. "Yes. I suppose there is. A worry more than a thought."

"Spit it out, then."

"I think Chandrayanan will succeed in cloning the strand they have left. The physics is looking solid. That will give them a new type of energy, a new form of local transport, and a new type of interstellar transport, right?"

I didn't want to say yes, but she was only stating a fact. "I suppose."

"The Terrans and the Vaers would have the monopoly on wormhole travel and such devices as Cunningham just used, plus a new energy source many times stronger than anything we currently have and—"

I was catching up with her. "—and you think they would charge through the nose for use of their technology."

"I think so. Within decades, the other races would become subservient to them. It would crown them, not just in the Shells, but in this cluster and supercluster, but that is not my main concern."

It seemed enough to be going on with to me. I waited. She looked grim. "The only thing that could prevent them from having a complete monopoly on the technology would be another source of negative energy."

The cogs in my mind clattered into overdrive. "They will have to eliminate Zenzara!"

Her face twisted. "I think they will see it that way, yes."

"—Having removed all the other strands in her Nexus first." It was obvious. "You paint a pretty grim future. I'm glad you shared that with me. My life is certainly not worth more than the survival of freedom as we know it." I gave her a hug. "Thank you, Sibby."

Tears were sliding down her cheeks. "I don't want to lose you."

"It is my job to go. It has to be me. It was always going to be me at the end. I can't let Bull go on. I just can't."

She sighed. "I know. But you could take Denaraz."

Those words cost her. I appreciated them. "Izan has a duty to Zenzara. I will not take him. Not this time."

She leant into me. "Be careful?"

I tried to smile. "I will. Now, will you do as I have asked? Promise? I think the whole future of the Major Shells may depend on you."

A shiver ran down her spine. I actually felt it. "I will."

"Thank you. You are a great sister."

I dropped a kiss onto her hair and strode away. I had a lot of things to get ready.

I was still in the arms deposit, behind the saloon on the mid deck, when Neema sent me a tight-link. "Get to the bridge!"

That meant fast, so I dropped everything and only took the time to carefully lock the arms cache behind me before I made my way up a deck at the double. There was, after all, a baby on board.

I knew we were in trouble from the look I got as I walked onto the bridge. Seyal's eyes were wide. She was expecting trouble.

I checked behind me. There was nobody.

She was expecting trouble from *me*.

"What is it? What happened?"

Neema straightened her shoulders. Her chin came up. "They have left the ship."

"Left the ship? Who has left the ship?" But in that moment I knew. Who else?

"Zenzie and Denaraz."

My heart gave a pound and almost leapt out of my ribcage. "What?"

"The first we knew of it was when the shuttle left the shuttle bay. I am sorry, Rye."

"Get them on a link. Any link."

"They are not answering."

I swore. "What other vehicles are there?"

"The smaller shuttle or the jet skis."

Damn it! She could outrun either of those. But I was pretty sure Denaraz had gone to stop her doing anything stupid. I made up my mind. We would have to get much, much closer if I was to take a jet ski over to the Vaer cruiser.

"Take us in, Neema. To within twenty kilometers."

"Yes Rye."

Nivala began to slip towards her quarry.

I was furious. I left the bridge for a moment, slipping into the gymnasium behind it. I spent five minutes hitting one of the boxing training bags, and then went back to the bridge, slightly more composed. Though Seyal still eyed me in a slightly worried way.

I grabbed a new tight-beam. I navigated the swipe menu until I found the terminal that was situated at the back of the shuttle cabin. If Zenzie was in the pilot's seat she wouldn't be able to reach it.

"Denaraz? You better answer me or I might just shoot you myself."

The new unit crackled. It had never been used before.

"Sorry, Mallivan. I only realized what she was going to do at the last moment. I was able to throw myself through the shuttle door just as it was closing, but she ..."

"She what ...?"

"... She shut me in the entry hatch." His voice was martyred.

I burst out laughing. He must have been mortified. "But you are out now?"

"I am. Unfortunately I had to swear not to make her come back in order to get out."

I rolled my eyes. Terrific. "What the fitz does she think she is doing?"

"She says that the Chakrans require her to act. They are extremely concerned. They will not allow their fellow strands to be tortured like this." He dropped his voice. "I believe her, Rye. She is not herself. I believe that the Chakrans are dictating her moves at the moment. They seem to have re-established contact through the Nexus."

I sighed. Just what we needed.

"Very well. Tell her to pull to a stop and wait where you are. I will join you with a jet ski. I will bring weapons. If she is going to do this, she has to do it with some back-up."

There was a silence on the connection and then Izan came back to me. "She agrees. Thank you, Captain."

I was mentally reminiscing about the good old days when captains could shoot people for mutiny, but I kept my feelings to myself. I didn't really know enough about the Chakrans to be able to say categorically that they couldn't and wouldn't dictate to Zenzara. After all, their very existence was in question. I certainly wouldn't blame them for getting involved. And I owed them something for the quick passage they had given us after Ebyssia. They had saved Sammy at great loss to themselves.

"I will be with you soon."

"Yes, Captain."

I put the tight-beam back into its metal support.

Determined to move quickly, I turned to leave, only to find Seyal blocking my way.

I tried to push past her.

She didn't move.

Avaraks can be ... bulky ... when they want to be. Even female ones. I realized that she wasn't going to move until she had talked to me.

"Seyal?"

"Captain. I would like to come with you."

"You have Segaton here to look after. He needs you to thrive."

"He needs the universe to continue existing to survive," she pointed out.

She must have overheard Sibby and me. My shoulders dropped. "That too, but do you think you should be risking yourself like this?"

"I do. *Avarak Karax!* After all, I am an Avarak, if only a female."

I couldn't deny that her help would be invaluable.

"All right. I'll meet you down in the shuttle bay, by the frames. Make sure you are kitted out for an EVA transfer."

She nodded. "Thank you, Captain."

I thought of something. "Mel, make sure that the other jet ski is ready and packed, will you? If and when Sibby develops some means of destroying the device and the resonance chamber, she will need a way to get onto the Vaer ship. Tell her I will attempt to disable the warning system of whichever hatch is nearest to the back tailfin. Attempt, mind you. I can't guarantee it."

Mel nodded.

"And once *Nivala* is at twenty kilometers, hold her there. You can glide in closer when Sibby is ready. Tell her to take the two Enif with her. They will be very useful."

Mel nodded again. So did Neema.

I was leaving them in charge of *Nivala*. And I had no idea what was coming. I gave them an attempt at a smile, but I suspect my face was rigid. They both drew their lips upwards and backwards in response, but it looked like a rictus. I hoped it wasn't an omen.

10

Seyal was waiting for me by the time I got down to the shuttle bay. She was wearing her full EVA suit. She was as protected as she could be.

She busied herself at the controls as I hauled all the weapons I had chosen on board.

We were just about to leave when Eshaan strode in. "I wish to accompany you," it said in a no-nonsense voice. "Didjal will bring your sister over when they have completed their research."

I gave a shrug. This was getting to be a habit with my crew. They seemed to like being independent. "Does Mel know?"

"Yes."

I stood aside and gestured the Enif onto the sled. "Be my guest." Then I asked Seyal if Segaton was comfortable.

She giggled. "He is. I am not so sure that Neema and Mel are. I left him on the bridge."

I wondered what good old Captain Tevis would have said about that. My crew would have given him plenty to huff about. I didn't think his rigid rules and regulations would have had room for a baby in them. It quite definitely didn't have room for a crew that disobeyed orders.

Eshaan was without EVA gear, since the Enif can manage perfectly well without oxygen and in a space vacuum for a few hours. Looking down at the quantity of gear I was wearing made me slightly envious. Not only that, but the Enif were virtually immune to ultrapulse fire. I wouldn't have minded having Eshaan's gleaming black carapace as well.

We slid out of the forward FLOW door of *Nivala* and headed to the shuttle's coordinates. Although we were unprotected by one of the carbon clouds, it was very unlikely that the Vaer cruiser's sensor array would pick us up. Not at this distance. The shuttle was still a long way from the cruiser. Sensor arrays are good, but not quite that good.

We skimmed the jet ski up to the rear of the shuttle and let ourselves into the hold once Zenzie had opened the back door for us. Once breathable air had been reestablished in the shuttle bay we were able to slip our helmets off and make our way into the forward section.

Zenzara gave me a bright smile. "Mallivan Bell! I am happy to see you here. It will be quite like old times, will it not?"

"You didn't exactly leave me much choice, did you?"

She seemed shocked. "That wasn't me. That was the Chakrans. I can't help what they do, now can I?"

I paused. She had this nasty habit of taking the wind right out of my sails. To be fair, I really couldn't imagine what it was like to have the Nexus of an alien species inside your brain.

Just thinking about it gave me a headache. "Well, you can tell them from me that their little ... tantrum ... is most inconvenient."

"I can't tell them that! You tell them!"

"They aren't inside *my* head."

"They might still *hear* you."

I doubted that. "In that case, Chakrans, please refrain from running off with a nine-year-old body. You are putting it at risk. Don't!"

Zenzie giggled. "They don't care about me. Why should they? I am like a speck of dust to them."

"As I understand it, you are their eyes and ears. You are the only way they have of interacting with carbon-based life. I would have thought you would be very much worth protecting. You may be only a speck of dust, but you are *their* speck of dust. Their *only* speck of dust."

She treated me to a pitying look. "Their whole existence is at risk. Of course they must act to prevent that. Anybody would."

I gave up. It wasn't going to change the current situation in any way. Now Seyal and I were here, we would be going into the Vaer cruiser. There was no time to think up another plan.

Just at that moment, there was a slight shimmer in space and ships began to appear out of hyperspace. The tight-link with *Nivala* flared, only to fall just as suddenly silent. I was glad to know that there was some quick thinking going on at Mel's navigation station.

"Get me a report!" I snapped.

Denaraz began to peruse his console. "There is a Terran battlecruiser and six smaller cruisers."

I cursed. "Now we know why Cunningham came here. He was drawing us into a confrontation, at a place of his own choice. Terrific. Ellison has seven ships against our one. How very ... fierce of her. She must be back in favour with the Ethnarch. Can they see us?"

He shook his head. "No. We are in our own carbon bubble, and moving away from their position. Unfortunately, they have come out of hyperspace very near to *Nivala's* position. Because she is behind her own carbon cloud they won't be able to detect her directly, but they may very well be close enough to detect star blocking."

I sighed. It broke my heart to have to leave the others behind. "Let's hope they can edge away, then. Zenzie, keep your course to the Vaer ship."

"Yes, Mallivan."

Denaraz muttered. I swung around. "What?"

"Several more ships have arrived." He looked up in astonishment. "They are Nepheal! *Aenysia* is leading them!"

"They must be doing those repairs on the hop." I wished we could let Danaa know our position. I wondered how she, Sammy and Anzany had managed to convince the Nepheals to send their ships. But I was very, very glad that she had.

"Wait!" Izan held up his hand. "There are even more ships emerging!" His crest twitched and then fell slightly. "They are Tyzaran. Cruisers."

"And which side are they approaching?"

His eyes didn't meet mine. "I don't know."

The Tyzarans should have been on our side. They were fully signed-up members of the Interstellar Alliance, and one of the things that meant was putting one's space navy at the disposition of the Alliance. However, the Tyzaran Supreme Council *had* recently helped Bull Cunningham and Ramesh Chandrayanan. With the stakes so high, I really wasn't sure which side of the equation they were on.

"How many ships?"

There was a pause as he counted. "Seven Terrans. Four Nepheals. Four Tyzarans."

"How are they lining up?"

More empty seconds of spacetime.

Finally, he gave a sigh of relief. "The Nepheals and the Tyzarans have swung around to form a block together. They are facing off the Terran fleet."

"Where are they in respect to *Nivala*?"

"*Nivala* is caught right between the two sides."

I sucked in air through my teeth. "Get the fitz out of there, Mel."

"I'm sorry?"

"Nothing. Just muttering under my breath."

"They will do what they have to. Don't worry about them."

"Is anybody opening fire?"

"Not right now. That doesn't mean they won't. All the ships are on alert and are standing with weapon systems live." He leaned back. "Oh!"

"What?"

"There is a Vaer Nova vessel accompanying the Terrans. It has just hopped alongside Cunningham's ship and is transferring men onto it."

"What is Cunningham's Vaer cruiser doing?"

"Opening its hatches to the Vaer Nova crew. Ignoring everybody else."

"Then we will ignore them all too. We have a job to do. This is only going to work if we assume everybody else will be able to do theirs."

Seyal glanced around at us. "The team is good," she said, a faintly proud tilt of her head making her stand out far more than she usually did. "Each component has unique input."

I wondered if that meant that she felt at home with us. It was a very long way away from her beginnings as a little more than a brood mare for Avarak children.

The tilt of her head motivated all of us. We scurried about the shuttle as it approached the Vaer ship. We needed to be ready. We might not even get a first chance at this. We certainly weren't going to get a second chance. It would have been hard enough when Cunningham and Chandrayanan were the only occupants of the cruiser. Having it full of Nova pirates wasn't exactly going to help.

The Vaer cruiser never saw us coming. In a sense, we were taking advantage of the appearance of all the other ships. Their attention must have been well and truly fixed on what was going on over there.

We left the shuttle well-disguised and half hidden inside a particularly dense clump of bright blue supernova wind. Taking care to keep both jet skis disguised by a temporary carbon bubble Sibby had managed to construct, we slid alongside the ship. Getting in was going to be a problem. We could hardly go through their main lock. We had to find something a little less obvious than that.

In the end the Vaers themselves helped us, albeit unwittingly. The cruiser that Bull had taken was an exploration ship, fitted with intake tubes to take samples of molecular clouds. It was a weak point in the ship. The tubes were around sixty centimeters in diameter, and we hoped that the hatch that opened such samples up to the ship would be unmonitored. It was a tight squeeze since we were in EVA suits, but we were just able to squash ourselves inside. Eshaan, who had none of these problems, had already fed himself easily down the starboard tube and disappeared. We followed, leaving the sleds tethered loosely to the hull, but floating some fifty feet out. We left the carbon bubble in place, so it was weird to see the tether leading away from the cruiser only to vanish into the carbon bubble. The frames were impossible to see. Sibby had set them up for us, but warned that they would drain their batteries in just an hour. After that our transports would be well and truly visible to anybody. And we might have a bit of a job switching the jet skis back on if we ran the batteries that flat. We were on the clock.

I was taking up the last spot, so all I could see in front of me as I wriggled along the tube were the soles of Denaraz's feet, which flapped in front of my eyes. I followed, concentrating on them, so as not to fixate on the feeling of claustrophobia that was threatening to take me over. Thank fitz Mel was not with us! I doubt she could have gone down the tube.

The thing was longer than I had expected. On the outside it had seemed about eight feet long, but that was deceptive. In fact it turned inside and wove its way along the space between the two hulls that Vaer ships are equipped with. Then it turned inwards towards the centre of the ship. It was formed from several sections, each around ten meters long. At the end of every section was a hydraulic hatch. One hatch could not be opened at the same time as the next, which provided the Vaers with sufficient safety to collect specimens without risking the whole ship.

At each hatch, Eshaan pressed a small electronic device that Sibby had given it against the metal plating. The device must have had some sort of code breaker, because it whirred busily for several minutes before popping the hatch open.

By the time we got to the final hatch, we must have crawled some fifty meters, perhaps more, along the ship. I had no idea where we were.

Then Eshaan was applying the device to the metal of the last barrier. I hoped that we wouldn't make too much noise as we went in. Some noise was inevitable. We just had to hope there wouldn't be anybody on the other side of the hatch.

With a hiss of hydraulics, the last access opened out into the inside of some sort of machine. Eshaan hacked its way through various filters that blocked our passage. We ignored various smaller side tubes and chose to progress directly along the shiny surface of the scientific spectrometer. Eventually we came to what looked like a maintenance hatch. Eshaan tried the device, but got nowhere. In the end it applied the bolt cutters and chopped its way through. We finally dropped ignominiously onto the floor of a scientific laboratory, falling higgledy-piggledy on top of each other.

Zenzie glared. "Did you have to put your elbow in my stomach?"

"Actually, yes."

She sniffed.

I stared around our surroundings. My first thought was to take care of any prior occupants.

There weren't any.

I hadn't really expected there to be. We knew that Cunningham and Chandrayanan had been alone on the ship. It was pretty unlikely one of them or one of the new Nova crew to board would be in that particular laboratory. Still, we needed to proceed with caution.

We were in a room about the size of a large bathroom. The only occupant was the huge mass spectrometer, which had been adapted to perform additional experiments on the molecular clouds it was examining.

I pasted myself against the door, listening intently. I could hear footsteps, but they seemed some distance away. I inched the door open and peered out.

It seemed we were in luck. I signaled to those behind me and we all ran out of the laboratory.

Eshaan and Seyal moved rapidly towards the bows of the ship. I headed for the stern, together with Denaraz and Zenzara. I needed to do something to the rear entry hatch. I needed to leave Sibby with a way in.

We ducked in and out of the doorways and bulkheads. However, we met only two Vaers on our long journey to the rear of the ship. They were heavily armed, but unsuspecting. We heard them coming long before their presence was visible, and had plenty of time to secrete ourselves in one of the cabins that led off the main corridor. The Vaer cruiser was built off a central corridor which ran from bows to stern, with all its many cabins and laboratories set off that corridor.

Once they were past we scurried to the rear of the ship. By the engine room there were several storage facilities and it was there that we tracked down an outer hatch that looked as though it hadn't been utilized for a long time.

Denaraz bent over the control panel that was set into the wall. He plugged his own small Tyzaran device and pushed a few buttons that were set into its tiny surface. Then he withdrew the cables again. "Done."

"That was quick."

"I only had to disengage the alarm system. Piece of cake."

Zenzie looked from one of us to the other. "What is cake?"

Denaraz shrugged. "No idea. It is an expression that the Terrans used. It means easy."

I couldn't help her either. "Don't ask me. It's from the old, old days. I guess it was a measure of time. You know ... only took a bit of a minute. That sort of thing."

"I see. Yes. Piece of cake. Quick. I wonder how many minutes there used to be in a cake?"

"You can ask Seyal to look it up for you when we get back."

"Yes. I shall do that."

"You should. Instead of listening to alien voices in your head that tell you to infiltrate ships without taking back-up along."

Her voice became plaintive. "It isn't my fault that the Chakrans are worried. What do you expect them to do?"

"I—" I never got the chance to finish because the deck plating underneath us trembled as a shudder passed through the ship. The plating groaned in response.

Denaraz opened his eyes wide. "Bull Cunningham has opened fire on somebody. That was an EM gun going off close to us."

I grinned. "I suspect Danaa is feeling the heat. He would hardly attack either the Vaer Novas or the Terrans."

"Sammy won't like that. But I don't think he will fire back, either. He must guess that we are on board or close to the ship."

"I'm just worried Cunningham will wing our jet frames. They are tethered close to the gun emplacements, remember?"

"Shells, yes! If he clips one of those his plan could very well backfire. He might blow all of us to smithereens."

Zenzie put her head to one side. "What are—?"

"I'll explain later," I hissed, breaking into a run. "We need to get ourselves to Seyal's position."

"Why the hurry ...?"

"Because one of the ships out there might be about to fire back!"

I grabbed one of her thin arms and propelled her along the passageway before me. I had a moment of déjà vu as I remembered the first time I ever saw her, on *Commorancy*, when I had done almost exactly the same thing.

Then she had been a lost waif. Now she was a year older, a century more experienced and the spokesperson for a quantum species that spanned thousands of galaxies. It was getting a whole lot harder to push her around. I sighed. I had the feeling things were going to be much worse when she hit her teen years.

We thundered along the main passageway. We weren't the only ones. Several huge Vaers were doing the same thing. There was a nasty moment when we crossed with three of them.

Then we were past and Zenzie was giggling like a lunatic. "They didn't even recognize us!" she panted with delight. "They thought we belonged to the ship!"

"To be fair to them, they have only just come aboard, and they do know that they are to work with two Terrans. They must have thought they were us."

"And what am I?"

"Insignificant, thankfully."

She went silent. It was an ominous silence, but even so, I was thankful for that too.

Eventually we tumbled out of the long passageway and onto the bridge. Several people turned to stare at us. They were all pointing weapons at each other in some sort of Mexican standoff. Seyal had Cunningham covered, and Eshaan had made a large Vaer stand back from the console he was manning.

Bull Cunningham moved to cover Zenzara with the ultrapulse pistol he was holding. He seemed quite relaxed. "Rye," he said in a conversational sort of way.

"Bull." I nodded. "You have been busy since I last saw you."

"You have massacred the Chakran strands," spat Zenzie.

I nodded. "You can't destroy an entire race just to give you wormholes and a convenient way to travel."

He raised his large face skeptically. "Really?"

Seyal, who still had her pistol trained on him, shifted. *I* was tempted to shoot him, too.

His eyes flickered to her, then away again, dismissing her. He seemed totally in charge of the situation. "They are the only viable source of exotic energy. I feel badly for them, but we cannot allow our enemies to get hold of all their negative energy. You are working to stop the Terran people from becoming independent."

"You can't believe that! Surely you know me better? I have no motivation to lie. I work for the Interstellar Enforcement Agency."

"That hardly makes you more credible. You are preventing the Omnistate from advancing."

I don't think he believed his own propaganda for a moment, but it saddened me to listen to him.

His pistol never wavered from Zenzara. He licked his lips. "I am glad you have brought the Chyzar with you. I was hoping you would. Her Nexus will be very useful."

"You are not getting your hands on her again."

He tutted. "No hard feelings, *Chy* Zylarian, I hope. I merely need to get control of the Chakran Nexus. It is nothing personal. If I could do it without harming you, I would."

He sounded almost believable, except that I knew better. I knew what he had done to Sammy, with no provocation. Bull Cunningham had become a sadist. His words were convincing. There was just no reality behind them.

Zenzie glared at him. I noticed that one of her hands was on her tunic, close to the largest nivala pinned there. "What gives you the right to threaten the Chakrans?"

"I never threatened anybody! But they really shouldn't go around the universe thinking that they have the right to dictate to all of the other races. Ok, they are quantum based. We know. We heard. That doesn't give them rights over us, doesn't make them more intelligent."

"Of course it does. Their brains span thousands of light years! Ours are microscopic in comparison. You have got to be joking if you think you are on a level footing with the Chakrans!"

"Can't you see that the original Terrans have been gradually pushed back, until it has reached the stage where we have to beg the Tyzarans to share their technology with us? We ... the Terrans. The *original* human species. It is abhorrent to see us becoming slaves to the other races!"

I was getting fed up. "Whatever are you talking about? You have got yourself enmeshed in your own hype, man!"

"You are a Spacelander. I do not expect you to understand."

"Just as well, because I certainly don't. All this lack of trust is completely your own Flatlander fault! You wanted to claim the whole local Shell as your own! You stole Tyzaran technology! You started a war with the Avaraks!"

"They forced us into it."

I felt like pummeling some sense into his thick head. "You can't just start a war because you have expansionist tendencies!"

"They left us no other option," he grumbled, mostly to himself, entrenched in his particular vision of the universe. Whatever I had to say wasn't going to change his opinion.

He moved slightly. I noticed his hand twitch towards his arm. I gave a warning shout. "That arm band on his wrist!"

Several things happened at once. Bull's attention left Zenzie and focussed on his own arm. She threw her nivala directly at him in one swift movement. It spun straight at his face. He twisted in mid air and fell towards her. His arm reached out to touch her. The nivala spun past him and buried itself in the bulkhead. Apart from that, another dark shape flashed past me and reached out towards Zenzara. Bull Cunningham had already encircled her with his arm and was pushing down on the buttons of his arm band. The dark shadow just managed to touch Zenzara's ankle. I realized it was Eshaan. All three of them vanished.

I gave a shout of frustration and threw myself forwards, landing too late to grasp either one of them. "No!"

I picked myself off the floor and spun around to Seyal. "Where is Chandrayanan?" I snapped, feeling sick. I told her not to risk herself!

Seyal pressed some buttons on the console in front of her. "In the Lab. We might be too late."

"Oh, I don't think so. Bull wouldn't have been up here on the bridge if they were about to test new tech. They haven't built the quantum farm yet."

I was about to ask Denaraz to and go look for the Indian when the whole ship shook again. This time we were on the receiving end of the missiles. A barrage of them exploded around the outside of the ship. Somebody was aiming at the cruiser, somebody was making a point.

They had certainly caught my attention.

The explosion hit one of the jet skis full on. It must have exploded into lethal shrapnel, which then showered down on the cruiser. Most was deflected harmlessly, but some shards punctured the outside hull. That led to a cacophony of alarms as the air pressure between the inner and outer hull plummeted.

Denaraz had pushed the Vaer to one side. He was now tying the Vaer up securely.

"The Terrans are firing on us!" Izan shouted.

"Then Bull Cunningham and Chandrayanan have somehow managed to get themselves and all their gear over to Admiral Ellison's ship. We always seem to be two steps behind!"

Another missile exploded, this time hitting the back of the Vaer cruiser. We were knocked sideways and the whole ship began to spin.

I put out a tight-beam to *Aenysia*. I knew they would be monitoring on *Nivala* too, without giving away their position.

Danaa answered in a wary voice that changed to pleasure when she realized who was calling her.

"Captain! I am very glad to hear from you!"

"Can you stop them lobbing scrap metal at us?"

"Of course, Captain. I will open fire on them immediately."

I heard Sammy's voice questioning in the background and Danaa's calm reply. *Aenysia* turned and opened fire on Admiral Ellison's ship. A couple of missiles bounced off the Terran shields.

"Like that?"

"Exactly like that. Thank you."

"Think nothing of it Captain. Err ... we are now under attack ourselves, so perhaps I should stop chatting."

I could see. Denaraz now had the situation outside up on screen. The Terran ships had closed around the Admiral's flagship, protecting it. The Vaer Novas were falling back to defend the Terran fleet, leaving the Nepheals almost on their own. True, they had the Tyzaran fleet behind them, but I could see from the marked positions that the Tyzaran ships were hanging even further back and were not firing on the Terrans. Unfortunately the same could not be said for the Vaers and the Terrans. They were collectively directing their weapons at *Aenysia.*

"They will have Zenzara on the Terran flagship! And Eshaan." I told Danaa.

"Cunningham and Chandrayanan?"

"Yes. They used a transport device they have developed. And now they have the last piece that they needed. Zenzara." I found myself ducking involuntarily as the Terrans lobbed another couple of missiles at the Vaer ship we were on. One exploded at the rear of the ship. "They mustn't get away."

"I will attempt to stop them, Captain. As will Ouraali."

"Ouraali?" I was shocked. I thought the mountain leader never left her Ayaala Retreat.

"Apparently Scout insisted. He began to detect danger from this direction. She felt she had to bring a few ships out to see what the problem was. She thought we might need reinforcements."

"Tell her I am very glad to see her."

"I will do so, Captain. Please wait as safely as possible for rescue."

The tight beam fell silent. We watched the developing scene in front of us. the Terrans and the Vaers were bombarding the Nepheals.

Luckily, the Nepheals had further range than either the Terrans or the Vaers. They were returning fire very successfully. I saw two Vaer craft hit with only five salvos. The Terrans were faced with the choice of falling back or pressing forward.

But the Tyzarans were not firing. And the Nepheals were at a distinct disadvantage as far as numbers were concerned.

Denaraz gave a cry of exasperation and leapt for the console. "Tyzaran shipping! Why are you not defending the Nepheals? Move in! Attack the Terrans!"

A hololink formed on the Vaer bridge and we all held back a groan as we recognized Spokesdesignate Xynia. "Is that you Denaraz?"

"It is," he said in a grim tone. "Why are you holding back?"

"It is a pleasure to see you too, Adjunct." Her voice was taut. "Although that title is no longer yours, of course."

His voice puffed with irritation. "Does that matter?"

"Well, it does mean that I am the apex of decision for this fleet, does it not? And I must make decisions as I see fit. We cannot fire on the Terrans. We have only recently signed a bilateral peace treaty with them." Her tones were soft and patronizing.

I knew immediately that Denaraz was not going to get anywhere with her. Denaraz was swelling up in order to respond to that provocation when I signed to Eshaan to cut the connexion. The link dissolved.

Izan's crests were rigid with indignation. "Did you hear what she said to me? I have a good mind to get straight through to the Supreme Council and complain about her attitude."

"Don't forget that some of the Supreme Council backed Cunningham and Chandrayanan not so long ago," I pointed out. "You may not find yourself very popular back on Tyzar. Plus, you just lost the Chyzar. Again."

He shoulders slumped, followed shortly afterwards by both crests. "You are right, of course."

"It is not your fault, Izan. Short of tying her up, you couldn't have stopped her. If I know Zenzara, she will be making their lives as difficult as she possibly can."

"Sure. Why change now?"

I grinned. "And she has Eshaan with her this time. Between the two of them they will figure out a way to make Bull Cunningham's life just that little bit worse."

"If he doesn't shoot one or both of them first."

My face froze. "There is that, of course."

We left the remaining Vaers on the cruiser and started our way back to the remaining jet ski. There was now no point in waiting here for Sibby to join us. Our place was close to the Terran flagship. We were going to need *Nivala*.

I opened another tight-beam to *Aenysia*. "Danaa, you and Neema are doing great work. Keep it up!"

"Understood. Thank you Captain."

Seyal looked confused. I smiled at her. "I am telling Neema and Mel to keep *Nivala* camouflaged where they are," I explained. "I can't contact them directly, and they must be wondering whether to join in the fun or not."

She nodded. "I see. Yes, of course. But will they know to stop Sibby from coming over?"

"They already knew that. They know that Cunningham and Chandrayanan are now on the Terran flagship. Do you know which ship that is, by the way?"

Seyal nodded. "The *Chibuzo*."

Denaraz exchanged a glance with me. "Well, well, well. Our old friend. They gave the Ellison her favorite ship back. I guess she made Admiral again. She regained her popularity."

"Can you get into her mainframe like last time?"

"Not from here. What do you think I am? A magician?"

"Pity."

He assumed a disgruntled expression. "Always more, more, more!"

I laughed at Seyal's face. "It is just his way of having fun; he is joking."

The Avarak sense of humor is non-existent. It was the one area that Seyal had been having difficulty with. However, she moved her lips into what she clearly thought was a semblance of amusement. Actually she looked very scary. Denaraz shook his head. "You might need some practice with that, Seyal."

Her head went up. "Avaraks do not make fun of people!"

It was the first time I had seen her confront anybody. Izan's face was a study. He stepped backwards and almost fell over.

"Right," I said, indicating the corridor behind us. "Time for a strategic withdrawal, I think. Before the Vaers on this ship decide to warp her out of here."

We hurried back along the passageway to the nearest hatch. There was no need for subterfuge now. We invalidated any Vaers by the simple expedient of stunning them before they could shoot us. Within two minutes we were outside the hatch.

I fused it shut with my ZR pistol, and then we ran clumsily across the outside hull until we were opposite the remaining jet ski. The hit on the other frame had totally vaporized both carbon bubbles, so that we could see the remaining frame in all of its glory. It was hanging on by a thread. The explosion had almost severed the thin tether that held it to the cruiser.

Denaraz didn't hesitate. He bent at the knees and propelled himself off the fuselage of the cruiser straight into space. I reached out to pull him back, but he was just out of my reach. Neither Seyal nor I touched the tether. I was pretty sure just looking at it would break the remaining bond.

The whole area was awash with shrapnel and remnants of the explosions. It was like being inside one of the rings of the broken moon, Scobis. He would be very lucky to escape with his EVA suit intact. I caught my breath as he arrowed across the gap between the cruiser and the sled.

At the last minute, the sled collided with a piece of loose piping, and Denaraz had to try to swerve to avoid being hit as the piping ricocheted off the sled at an angle.

The shed slewed slightly, too, which broke the remaining strand connecting it to the Vaer cruiser. For one terrible moment, I thought that Izan would miss the sled. If he had we would never have found him again. He would have drifted on out into space, just one more piece of flotsam amongst thousands.

My heart lurched. I put one hand over it in case it jumped out of my chest. I know. Stupid. Couldn't help myself.

But I had underestimated the Tyzaran. He gave the most peculiar twist in empty space and grabbed out with his right hand, just connecting with one of the starboard railings. His hand closed around the metal and he managed to hang on as the jerk stopped his momentum dead. After that it took him only seconds to grasp the railing with his other hand and haul himself on board.

He put the mag sled in gear and swung around to pick us up.

Seyal and I clambered onto the frame with some relief. Izan directed us to the last known position of *Nivala*.

Unfortunately, the Terran forces were now able to see us. And did. Their scanners were much better than anything the Vaers had. Almost as soon as we let go of the cruiser, a couple of missiles were lobbed at us. Both missed us, but one impacted on the cruiser.

There was a pause, then a blossoming rosette of white light as her engine room exploded, taking the whole of the back part of the ship with it.

We were buffeted by the resultant expanding ring of debris. One substantial piece of the ship flew between Seyal and me before shearing part of the frame right off. We stared at each other. There was absolutely no way we could have done anything to avoid being hit. One or two centimeters to either side and one of us would no longer have been there. It was a sobering thought.

Izan bullied the jet ski as much as he could, coaxing it up to top speed. Even so, I was aware that it wasn't going to be enough to escape the Terran forces. We were sitting ducks.

But I hadn't taken Mel and Neema into account. They had decided to break orders and come and get us, rather than wait for us to come to them. And I was very grateful that they had.

One moment we were hammering away from the stricken cruiser, in full sight of all of the Terran forces. The next we were through the invisible carbon cloud and *Nivala* materialized immediately in front of us, blocking our entire field of vision.

Mel was not hanging about, either. She reversed the open shuttle bay doors straight towards us, inhaling us together with several other pieces of debris. It was so fast that even Denaraz struggled to put us safely down on the metal ramp.

At the same time the doors of the shuttle bay started to close.

We stayed still while the rest of the debris that surrounded us succumbed to the false gravity. For a few moments things were rather hectic. Pieces of metal clattered from all around us to the metal floor in a shower of dangerous shards. We all put our hands and arms over our heads to try to protect ourselves. Seyal's EVA suit was slashed open by a lethal sliver of Vaer fuselage. Luckily, it was only the suit. It just grazed her skin. Finally, there was no further noise. *Nivala's* artificial gravity had annulled the danger.

We stumbled gratefully out of the sled, stepped out of our EVA suits and then hurried into the lift to the upper deck.

Mel and Neema were on the bridge. So was Segaton, who was calmly playing in his netted pen. His whole small face illuminated as he saw his mother again.

She rushed to him and lifted him to her, her own face misty with emotion.

I slid into the captain's station. "Take us over to *Aenysia*, Mel, please."

"Yes Captain."

It occurred to me that they all seemed to have accepted me at least as the person who gave the orders, even if following them was still an ongoing work in progress. I wondered when that had happened. So much had been going on in the last few months that it was difficult to pinpoint any exact moment.

The Terrans had turned their attention back to the Nepheal ships when they lost sight of the jet ski. Too late for the Vaer cruiser, though, which I saw had now completely exploded.

Sibby and Didjal came running onto the bridge.

"What happened, Mall?" My sister hugged me and mussed up my hair, which was sticking to my head even though I had divested myself of the helmet.

I pulled my head away. "Stop it!" Why do sisters always think they have a divine right to alter your appearance?

She pulled a face but put her arms behind her back. "Where is Zenzara?"

Didj's voice was quiet. "And my *faliif*?"

I couldn't help sighing. "You remember on Beznik, Didj? When you tried to reach Cunningham as he was pushing that arm band of his?"

The Enif straightened. "I do."

"Well, Eshaan did the same."

Didjal suddenly went absolutely still. "Only it succeeded?" it finished for me.

I nodded. "Only Eshaan succeeded."

"My *faliif* is on the Terran flagship? On *Chibuzo*?"

"Yes. With Zenzara."

Sibby was looking from one of us to the other with a very worried expression. "You lost both of them?"

I shifted feet. "Not exactly lost. We think we know where they are."

"You are telling me that now Didjal and I have found some tech that might help, we have to get it on board a Terran Flagship?" She put her hands on her hips.

Izan, whose crests had become rigid as soon as he saw her, took a step forwards. "Sibby—"

"No, Denaraz. Don't interrupt, please! I may love you, but this is something between my brother and I."

"You love me?"

She turned an expression of exasperation on him. "Yes, of course I love you."

"Why didn't you tell me so?"

Her whole face crinkled up in an 'are-you-kidding-me' sort of way. "Because I was waiting for you to say it first? Of course?"

He looked pole-axed. "You were waiting for me to say it?"

"Naturally."

"But my crests go up every time I see you!"

"And—?"

"And ... and that means I love you. Don't you know anything about Tyzarans?"

She narrowed her eyes. "Clearly not enough. Continue."

"You are my soul-mix. That only happens to a tiny percentage of Tyzarans. Of course I love you. I tell you every time I see you. My crests tell you. How can you not have understood that?"

"Because you never actually said the words?"

It was Izan's turn to look confused. "Tell you? In words? Why would I do that?"

She gave a sigh of frustration. "Never mind. I love you. There! It has been said. Is that enough for you now?"

He had gone white. "It is enough. We will marry as soon as this is over."

"Did I say we would marry?"

He swallowed. "You implied it. I think."

She was enjoying herself. "Did you ask my brother?"

"I am asking *you*. I don't want to marry your brother. No offence, Mallivan, but I like girls. I think you are aware of this, but ..."

Mel and Neema were both grinning all over their faces. I frowned at them. This was an extremely serious moment.

Sibby held up an imperial hand. "Stop!"

Izan stopped.

"I *will* marry you. After all this is sorted."

The indomitable Tyzaran warrior sank onto both knees in front of her. "It is a pledge."

Personally, I thought he looked pretty stupid, but both Mel and

Neema started to cry, so I was probably wrong. How can women do that? Change so quickly from one thing to another?

Didjal and Seyal looked to me for clarification.

"Sibby is to become Izan's *faliif*," I told the Enif.

Didjal strummed its antenna, creating a sort of crackling noise, rather like clapping. "Congratulations," it said.

Sibby gave it a tight hug. "Thank you Didj. But that is for much later. First we have to go rescue Zenzie and your Eshaan. Don't worry, we hadn't forgotten about them!"

Didjal's ebony carapace glinted in the light. "There is always time to find the right *faliif*," it said, with a faint bow.

Sibby leant up and kissed it just beside its right antenna. "Thank you. If my brother here marries us, will you and Eshaan be my best men ... err ... best Enif?"

The shiny black seemed to flush slightly. "It would be our honor."

Sibby gave a little dance. When she finished she fixed me with a long look.

"What are you waiting for, Mall?"

I sighed. She'd been making everything my fault since she was a baby. There was no point answering back. I knew I wouldn't win.

And, much as I might joke about Zenzara holding her own, I was worried sick about her. Our mission was severely compromised. Again.

Nivala sped on through the dark towards the waiting ships, but I wasn't optimistic.

11

We pulled up alongside *Aenysia* an hour later. The firefight had calmed down. There seemed to be a wary ceasefire in place. Both sets of ships were regarding each other across space.

As soon as we were close enough, I took myself across the short distance dividing us and let myself into *Aenysia's* immense shuttle bay.

Danaa was there to greet me.

So, to my immense surprise, was Scout.

He ran up to my ankles, snuffling with great excitement. I bent to my knees to greet the Geiga. "Hello, old chap. I hear you sensed we were in trouble. Thank you!"

He gave a few snorts of delight as I caressed his ears. Then he rolled over and exposed his hairy stomach for my approval. I patted it. "You miss me, my friend?"

"He did indeed."

I jumped to my feet. "Ouraali! I heard you had come to help us." I went up to her somewhat awkwardly and then stopped, unsure of whether I could give her a hug or not.

"Your pet insisted," she said dryly. "He stopped eating."

My jaw dropped. "Scout? Stopped eating?"

"Lost all interest in phyonwe trees."

"He has never done that before."

"I think he really does miss you. He was content at first to wallow in the excess of his favorite food, but it seems to have worn off. I mean, just look at him!"

I did.

He was lying with his snout on my shoe, as if telling me he would never allow me to leave him again.

"I'm sorry."

"Not your fault. You did what seemed best for him, but it seems that mere food is not enough. I'm afraid that his time with the Nepheal people has come to a close. If he sensed the danger you were in from half a galaxy away, I think his place is with you."

I moved my foot under Scout's head. He opened a baleful eye, staggered to his feet and shook himself all over. Then he regarded me with resentment, as if to say 'what now'?

I wasn't sure Ouraali was right. He might be my Geiga, but he was *such* a glutton for phyonwe trees. I found it hard to believe that I had been more of a draw than the best ripe fruit in the Major Shells.

She shrugged. "You will see. I doubt he will lose sight of you again."

I stepped to the side of the shuttle bay.

Scout trailed behind me.

"He doesn't want to let you out of his sight. He feels his place is with you." She crouched her huge frame down to tickle his neck. "We were very privileged to have him with us for so long. But he was never meant to stay with us forever."

"I'm sorry. I thought he would be happy."

"He was. Until he sensed you were in danger again. Then he made his feelings extremely clear."

"Good boy," I said automatically. I suddenly felt lighter, more optimistic about our situation. Geigas can be a lot of hard work, but they are very useful creatures. Having Scout around meant having an early warning system at my disposal.

And I was beginning to realize how important that could be to our mission.

I tapped him on the nose. "Alert, Hardhead!"

He stood immediately to attention, and began to move in a circle, testing the air by snuffling every few seconds. His little ears were pointed up hopefully and he looked extremely intelligent.

He completed the circle and then stood stiffly, his snout and his tail out, aligned away from the bundle of Vaer and Terran ships.

"The danger is from another quarter!" said Ouraali, surprised.

I looked back at the main visor. "No. *Chibuzo* has left. She must be shrouded by a carbon cloud, like *Nivala*, which is why we never saw her go. That explains those ships milling around so much. They are attempting to hide the fact that Admiral Ellison is no longer there."

I turned to Danaa, who was at the scanning station. She did a rapid check and then nodded. "The flagship is absent."

Ouraali raised her eyebrows. "And he detected that? He really does earn his keep. I shall make sure he is sent a plentiful supply of phyonwe fruit."

"He detected the direction of the threat. He can help us follow them."

"You were right; he is a tremendous asset."

"Mmm." I scratched a few of his scratchy hairs fondly. "He does his best." Which reminded me. "He seems in better shape. You have reduced his food intake?"

"I entrusted his feeding program to Jaaven. As soon as he heard we were coming with a fleet, he volunteered."

"Males are allowed on ships?"

She inclined her head. "There is little discrimination on board a ship. It is not really possible. Although the captains are always women, of course."

Of course. Funny how equality seemed to escape all races. There always seemed to be some discrimination. Males against females, Females against males, tall against small, intelligent against stupid, or on the base of religion, race, colour, appearance. The Shell races were all so much more advanced than the ancients, but there were similarities all the same.

"So Jaaven is on your ship?"

"He is tasked with caring for Scout. I will second him to you for the duration of this mission, if you like."

I nodded. "I would like that, thank you. Although he would find *Nivala* too constricting for his size, he would be very useful whilst I am on *Aenysia*."

Ouraali input a command on the nearest console. "He will be here shortly. What are your instructions?"

I raised one eyebrow. "I can hardly instruct you, or your fleet."

"We came to be of help. Not to interfere. We are at your disposal."

That flummoxed me. "Err ... thank you. I ... really appreciate that."

I did. Not only were these Nepheals, but they were female Nepheals. They were going against their principles.

"Are you sure?"

"I am. We are here now, and we are determined to help avenge Agraala. These people are a threat to all our worlds."

"They are. I am humbled by your help."

Ouraali gave me a sharp look. "I depend on you to keep my people as safe as they possibly can be kept. We will sacrifice our lives if necessary, but I expect you to protect them with your own life and judgement."

"I will get Sibby to bring carbon bubbles over for each of your ships. She will explain how to get them up and working too. You are going to need them."

"You have this technology?" Ouraali treated Danaa to a meaningful glare. Danaa looked stricken.

I answered for her. "*Aenysia* has just been fitted with this new technology. And I would remind you, Ouraali, that Danaa is one of my crew, and may not divulge anything about our missions, even to you."

The Nepheal woman straightened up. When she did that, she towered over me. I stared upwards at her long face and tried not to blink or flinch. It wasn't easy.

In the end her face relaxed. "I suppose that is true," she said.

Danaa breathed again. A little green crept back into her cheeks.

Proximity alerts went off as a Nepheal shuttle edged its way inside the shuttle bay. A surprised looking Jaaven came uncertainly down the hatch, peering around as if expecting something or somebody to bite him.

"Get down here, Jaaven!" boomed Ouraali.

He cringed and scuttled obediently down the ramp.

"Have you brought everything I told you?"

"Yes, Dialecta."

It was the first time I had heard the honorific title used. It suited Ouraali. She was certainly a force to be reckoned with.

She stared at the young Nepheal. "Hmmph. I am leaving you here, to look after Scout," she snapped. "Do a good job."

Jaaven's eyes almost popped out of his head. "Yes, Dialecta. Err ... thank you!"

"See I don't regret it!"

He swallowed and went three shades paler. "Yes. No. I will. You won't."

She rolled her eyes and turned her attention to me. "Where is this sister of yours?"

I attempted something more sophisticated than Jaaven's sheer terror of this imposing female. "She will be here shortly. Perhaps you would like an update before you go back to your ships with the carbon clouds?"

Jaaven gave me a look of sheer admiration.

Ouraali considered. "Yes. Thank you. That would be very nice."

I clipped Scout's lead on and handed him to Jaaven, but the Geiga was having none of it. Where I went, he went, he had decided. Jaaven did his best, but let's face it – a gangly young Nepheal is no match for the moving steamroller that is a well-fed adult Geiga. He was dragged along behind us.

When Sibby joined us, some twenty minutes later, there was a moment of silence as she walked in. Then there was a scuffle behind me and a cry of anguish from Jaaven as Scout pulled him over. Sibby's eyes opened in shock before a whirl of muscle launched itself at her from a distance.

She gave a thin gasp as all of the air was knocked out of her lungs. She sat down abruptly on the decking, just managing not to drop the three carbon cloud devices she was carrying.

I began to laugh.

She put the devices down and flung her arms around Scout's thick neck. His little tail was whirring around and around like a miniature helicopter.

"Hello boy! How did you get here?"

"He insisted that the Nepheals come."

"Good boy! Not lost your touch, then." She picked him up bodily – no mean feat – and gave him a big hug and a cuddle. His stumpy legs hung down from her arms, treading air as though he were running.

"This is Ouraali, the leader of the Ayaala Retreat on Nephealis."

Sibby set Scout aside and scrambled to her feet. "Nice to meet you. Please excuse my rudeness."

"I have become used to it." Ouraali glanced at me.

Ouch. And I thought I had been doing so well!

Sibby picked up Scout's lead and gave it back to a sheepish Jaaven. "Here. Don't worry. That happens all the time." She turned back to Ouraali and gave a sort of curtsey. "I have your carbon cloud technology with me. Would you like me to explain how it works?"

"Thank you. Yes."

They walked off towards the console that was used on *Aenysia* to activate the cloud, Sibby chattering away with all the technical data that I found hard to understand, but which Ouraali was soaking up like a sponge. They seemed to slot instantly into sudden understanding. I found myself staring. It only took about ten minutes, and then they were back. Ouraali was beaming all over her face.

"That will be very useful technology, Captain," she told me. "Thank you for allowing us to use it."

"Sibby has brought you three. If you need any more I'm afraid you will have to make them yourself."

"That should present no problem. We can break down one of the ones we have and reverse engineer it. Your sister has explained all of the physics behind the concept." Her long face twitched. "We may even be able to improve on it."

I felt offended on Sibby's behalf, but my sister wasn't. "I am sure you can," she said. "And I would be grateful if you could send me details. I was limited to what materials I had on board *Nivala*. I am quite sure my design can be vastly improved."

Ouraali bowed her head. It was the right thing to say. The Nepheals were scientists. Of course they would try to improve any technology. Science always builds on its past. It is the nature of the thing.

"I would like to invite you to the Ayaala Retreat," she told Sibby.

My eyes widened. My sister really had made a good impression.

Sibby glanced in my direction. I inclined my head almost imperceptibly. I would have to give her some background. "Err ... thank you very much. That would be an honor."

She had no idea how much of one.

We escorted Ouraali and three of the carbon cloud devices into the shuttle that Jaaven had arrived in. She asked us for six hours before we took any further action, saying that she needed that long in order to fit and test the devices in her three cruisers.

I agreed. I had the feeling we would need all the support we could get. And I needed to embed *Nivala* in *Aenysia's* hold again. Otherwise she would slow us down. The Nepheal ships were faster than anything the Flatlanders might have. A six-hour delay would not be a problem. We should still be able to overtake them before they reached their destination. I wondered where that was. Or would they simply disappear into the voids of space, now that they had *Chibuzo*?

I guessed that they would take the Omnistate cruiser back to the Local Shell. The whole point of opening a large wormhole must be to go through it. They would need Terran ships to do that. They would hardly give the Novan Vaers the honor, I thought. I suspected that the Vaers had outlived their usefulness. No; if I were Bull Cunningham, I would ditch the Novans and meet up with the rest of my own, well-armed fleet. *Then* I would build my first traversable wormhole.

Once *Nivala* was settled back in the belly of *Aenysia*, the rest of her crew joined me in *Aenysia's* conference room. This was interesting, because it allowed for virtual presence of the other Nepheal captains. Each was holo-represented in one of the ample chairs.

Ouraali also came to the virtual meeting. She introduced the captains of her three ships: Raseebi, Arialaana and Bulaan. All were young female Nepheals, all looked very intelligent. The young captains settled comfortably and prepared to take notes.

Danaa introduced us all and then turned to me with an expectant air.

I sighed. "We need to make sure that no macro wormhole is opened. If it is, we need to prevent passage through it."

Bulaan wrinkled her nostrils. "Where do the Terrans intend to go with such a thing?"

It was a very good question. But I had thought about this at some length. "I believe their intentions to be to seed the universe with unseen routes. They will gradually build up an empire. Each time they open a wormhole, they can map its destination. Each destination can be a new hub for further exploration. If they can reproduce the device that opens the wormhole, they could soon overrun the galaxy. And further, of course. If they open a wormhole they could potentially expand through the entire universe."

Even Ouraali seemed shocked. "These expansionist tendencies are highly aggressive."

I nodded. "They certainly are. I agree. Not only that, but the technology will threaten the Chakran environment. Quite apart from whatever negative energy that has been cloned or stolen." I looked slowly around the table. "We don't have any choice."

There was a silence. All those attending froze as they assimilated the meaning of this. Then there was a collective breathing out and many nods around the table. We were all in agreement."

"How do we find them?"

"Although sensors can be adapted to trace radian toxicity emissions, that won't work in this case. *Chibuzo* is too modern a ship to be emitting any measurable radian toxicity. We shall be using Scout."

There was a ripple of disbelief amongst the Nepheal women.

Ouraali voiced it. "I have seen that the Geiga can detect danger. I have no doubt whatsoever of his abilities in that direction. But to let the fate of our universe depend on the ability of a Geiga! It is ... unscientific."

Why did I have the feeling that was one of the worst things she could say about any plan?

"I am very much afraid it is," I agreed. "Nevertheless, the difference we have ... the only advantage we have over the Flatlanders ... is the Geiga. Scout directed you here, and he will direct us to the *Chibuzo*."

The Nepheal captains murmured. One of them turned to Ouraali. "If the animal is capable of that, Dialecta, it should be even more honored by our people."

"Indeed it should, Raseebi. Let us hope that the worst of our problems is figuring out how to do that in the best way!"

Raseebi's nose was scrunched up in doubt. "I do not see how an animal can detect the position of a spaceship many light years away. It is impossible! This is taking us back to the dark ages!"

I glared at her. "Just because we do not understand the mechanism is no reason to reject its validity."

"Scientific method is essential in all cultures!"

"I agree. However, an open mind is also a necessity."

Raseebi remained unconvinced. She was about to speak, but Danaa interrupted, earning herself a scowl. "The captain is right. Nothing should be rejected, particularly since your three ships were led here from Nephealis by the creature."

I saw Ouraali look down at the desk. So she hadn't told her captains what method she had used to find us? I found that fascinating. She should have, of course, but now I could see why she hadn't.

"We would be happy for your crews to work on different ways of tracking ships hidden in carbon clouds," I said. "Geigas do work, but it would be better to have alternative methods available to us."

The snort Raseebi gave indicated that she certainly agreed with that, but she said nothing more.

Danaa looked relieved. "So, Captain Mallivan, you believe that the Terrans will go back to the Local Shell to open the wormhole?"

"I think that they must, don't you? The Novan Vaers may have insisted on Ebyssia before for their experiments, but the Omnistate doesn't really need the Vaers any longer. In fact, I believe they will ditch that relationship and try to keep the wormholes within the Termination Shock of their own star. That has been agreed by the Alliance as the boundary of their rights."

The more I thought about it, the more convinced I was. Of course they would prefer not to share the technology. They might have gone along with the Vaers when they needed their help, but I bet they would never have opened a wormhole from anywhere outside their own territory. They would want to keep their claim to the wormhole watertight. They would not want the Alliance to get their hands on it. In fact, that might even be why they attempted to claim the whole Local Shell for themselves when they started this whole thing. It would have made the whole process much easier.

I thought back to my history lessons. We had been taught something about the geography of the Omnistate region. I screwed up my forehead. Mars, Jupiter ... there were more planets, I knew, but I couldn't really recollect their names.

"It is a long way to the Local Shell from Heisenberg's Halo." Denaraz was worried. "That means that they will probably be in a position to act as soon as they arrive. Chandrayanan will have had the time and the materials to create whatever is needed. We must try to get there before them."

The third Nepheal captain, Arialaana, looked even more skeptical. "You have just said that you didn't know where they were going. Even if we can use your Geiga to discover that, he can hardly know where to go before they get there!"

"I didn't say this would be easy."

She blew out air through her teeth. The Nepheals have a lot of teeth. It made a lot of noise.

"When we find *Chibuzo*, she cannot be merely destroyed," I went on. "That would be too risky. We have to board her and find a way to neutralize the threat."

"And what happens if we come up against the rest of the Omnistate Fleet? It seems entirely possible."

I had to agree with her there. "We fight."

Ouraali immediately turned to Denaraz. "We can only do that if your people will mobilize their fleet with us. As they promised to do when they signed the Statutes of the Interstellar Alliance."

Izan was clearly uncomfortable. He moved from side to side in his chair. "I hope they would mobilize for the Alliance."

"But you do not know for sure."

"I ... there is some history with Bull Cunningham ... I am afraid that ... No, I do not know for sure."

Ouraali nodded. "They did not back us up here. I do not think that they can be relied upon to confront the Terran Omnistate. I believe that some members of the Supreme Council on Tyzar are implicated with the Terrans." She tapped her foot on the plating. "That will complicate things. We will need to stop this by stealth rather than by sheer numbers."

"Do you have a plan?" I could tell she was mulling something over.

"No. It is clear to me, however, that Nepheals may not unilaterally attack the Omnistate ships. We were very careful only to return fire back at Heisenberg's Halo. We would need consensus from the Alliance to do anything else." She stroked her whiskers a moment and then made her decision. "Raseebi, Arialaana and Bulaan; I want you to go on maneuvers somewhere in the region of Berennis, in the Local Shell. My second in command will take over the cruiser I came in. I shall accompany you on *Aenysia*." She gave her captains a stern look. "Wait at Berennis until you hear from us."

Her captains all looked disappointed, but bowed their heads in deference to the orders.

"Then ... if we are all agreed ...?" I looked around the conference room. Everybody nodded. "This meeting is adjourned. We get underway within half an hour!"

Two ships. Two small ships against a whole civilization.

It wasn't much.

12

Scout, when he was brought onto the bridge of *Aenysia*, did not look as though he were about to save all civilization as we know it. He snuffled around everybody asking for treats and his little tail stopped doing cartwheels when he realized that there was no phyonwe fruit to be had. He fixed me with a baleful eye, turned his back on me, and sat down.

Jaaven was staring at Danaa with eyes the size of dinner plates. The Nepheal girl seemed irritated by his scrutiny. "Yes? What is it?"

He shuffled his feet and lowered his head. "Nothing."

I grinned. A bad case of hero worship, it seemed to me. It amused me that Danaa had no idea that her exploits had gone before her on her home planet. After all, she was only a young woman. She was probably clueless about how quickly gossip could travel. She certainly had no notion of just how exceptional she was.

Unfortunately, Jaaven was about ten years too young for her and time could never cure that disparity. I felt for him.

"Why don't you go for a jog around the shuttle bay, Jaaven," I suggested. "You can leave Scout with me for the time being. Get some exercise.”

"Thank you Captain." He gave Danaa one last longing look and left.

Mel and Sammy were exchanging grins. "Bit young for you, eh, Danaa?"

She was inputting data on her console. "Hmm. What?"

"Jaaven. Young for you."

She frowned. "Jaaven? He's only a boy. Whatever are you talking about?" She went back to her console.

The rest of us shook our heads. She had no idea. Literally, not a clue. As the only full-time Nepheal member of crew in the Interstellar Enforcement Agency she was a real trailblazer. Clearly, many young Nepheals thought what she was doing was world changing. From Jaaven's reaction, it was pretty obvious that she had become the new pin-up girl back on Nephealis.

But Danaa had no vanity. All she cared about was getting her friend Zenzie back. Of finding the young Tyzaran and the Enif that had gone with her. All of her concentration was on that. There was simply no room for anything else.

"Set a course for Waypoint," I told her.

She nodded, then passed the co-ordinates over to the other three members of our fleet. We turned and began to withdraw.

I had not ordered the Nepheal ships into their carbon clouds. Not yet. First, I wanted the remaining Vaer ships to think we were retreating. And I didn't want them to know that we, too, had the technology that had allowed the *Chibuzo* to slip away undetected.

So we made our escape in an orderly and highly visible fashion, keeping our speed pedestrian. It was only when we were hidden behind the southern arc of Heisenberg's Halo that we engaged the carbon bubbles and increased speed.

I was very uncertain about the course heading, so was pleased when Scout finally woke up and began to set towards the bows of the ship giving his characteristic high-pitched note of warning. It was a huge relief to know that I had been right in my guess. I could feel the tension draining away from my neck.

"I am going for a swim," I told the others.

Scout trailed along behind me.

"You don't swim," I reminded him.

He gave one grunt and barreled after me.

"All right, Hardhead. You will regret it. Last time I tried to get you in the water it looked like a Tsunami had hit the pool."

We took the elevator down to the middle deck and made our way into the central swimming pool.

The sight that met me brought me to a complete halt.

Izan Denaraz was sitting on the edge of the pool, dressed only in a pair of Bermuda shorts.

I blinked. I don't know if you have ever seen a Tyzaran in a pair of Bermuda shorts, but believe me, you don't want to.

"Rye," he greeted me with, "Sibby and I were just having a relaxing paddle around the pool."

My sister's head popped up out of the water on the other side of the water. "Mall! Come to join us?"

I thought my tongue was stuck to the ceiling of my mouth for a moment. I began to take a few steps backwards, but Scout soon scuppered all that.

He raised his head as he heard Sibby's voice. Then he squeaked. Then he began to sniff the air around him.

He couldn't see her for the high walls of the swimming pool cum water deposit, but he could smell her. His little legs skated on the slippery deck as he attempted to launch himself around the water.

I gave a shout of dismay and lunged for him.

He slipped right through my fingers and accelerated away.

I lost my footing and ended up prostrate on the floor.

On the other side of the pool I heard the frantic clatter of tiny hooves as the Geiga scrabbled to get up the wall that contained the pool. There was a terrific splash, a shriek from my sister and the squealing of an animal that was absolutely terrified.

I pulled myself back on my feet and peered over the edge.

Scout, finding himself out of his depth, began to paddle frantically. He churned over to Sibby and laid his front two legs on her shoulders. She went under, gulping water.

Denaraz, who had been laughing at the antics of the Geiga, realized that things were going wrong and jumped into the water. He was across the pool in a few seconds. Tyzarans are very tall and I discovered that they can swim extremely well.

He grabbed Scout by the scruff of his neck and tore him away from Sibby, who resurfaced gasping and spluttering.

Izan looked around and then hoisted the Geiga up, placing him on top of the wall, with his right hand legs hanging down on the outside and his inside legs on the inside. The Geiga struggled to get away from his restraining hand.

I ran around the outside of the pool and dragged the Geiga off the top of the wall, depositing him on the decking.

He shook himself, covering me with water.

When I was able to look back at the pool Denaraz was cuddling my sister and I had to look away.

"You know," I said. "I have gone off the idea of the swim. I think I will leave you two on your own." I grabbed Scout by his collar and clipped on his lead. We did a few laps around the corridors instead. It was safer.

That was the start of a week of shadowing the Terran ship. Scout had switched off his ability. The only thing we could do was continue on the same course until he indicated otherwise.

That took seven days. The Nepheal ships had peeled away to head for Berennis on the third day. We had long left Waypoint behind and were arrowing in on the Sol system itself when he signaled again.

I frowned. There was not a lot in the area he wanted us to go.

I checked in one of the consoles.

I had been right. It was part of the Sol system known as the Scattered Disc, on the far side of the Kuiper Cliff. It is an area of space which seeps out from the far edge of the Kuiper Belt into space. In fact it is only just inside the Terran Termination Shock, only just inside the Omnistate interstellar boundary. The Scattered Disc is really an extension of the Kuiper Belt, except that the objects found within it tend to have wild and sometimes random orbits whereas those of the Kuiper Belt are more stable. Many of the comets that periodically visited Earth were thought to have originated here.

I tried to find out more about this part of the solar outskirts, but there didn't seem to be very much more information. It appeared to be a relatively unexplored area of the Omnistate.

I checked Scout's indications.

He was urging us up off the ecliptic, towards a trans-Neptunian object that was in a semi-stable orbit around 60 Astronomical Units away from the sun. That is around half a trillion miles. Not a walk in the park. A ray of light from the sun would take around eight hours just to travel that distance. And it was empty. Relatively. There were a few large rocks and some small dwarf planetoids closer to the ecliptical, but not very much in the way of real estate where Scout was taking us.

Then the Geiga began to vary his directional indications. I took this to mean that we were actually overtaking the Terran ship at the time, so we had to be careful not to allow any of our emissions to be detected by them. When Scout had gone slowly through a full 180 degrees and was pointing due astern of our ships, I became reasonably confident that we were on the right heading. Their final destination definitely seemed to be the object that had come up on the console.

It was one of the strangest looking things I had ever seen. It was large – over 50 kilometers in length, but it consisted of three enormous flat three-sided rocky slabs fused together at their thickest points. If anything, it almost looked like half of a starfish feeling its way across space.

Flat is a relative term. Flattish is probably better. The legs of the starfish were vaguely rounded at the sides but presented a smooth aspect on the top.

I switched the scanners onto the highest resolution they could manage. Sure enough, they picked up installations and ships perched on the top side of the larger two of the starfish arms. The third, stubbier, arm seemed untouched.

I took a closer look at that third arm. It was more rounded on the top surface than the two larger arms, but there was still space on it for several ships to come down, near the join, at the thickest part.

I asked Danaa to aim *Aenysia* directly for the short third arm of the strangely sculpted object. But we decided to disembed the two ships first. We tucked ourselves behind an asteroid as we separated them.

Before I went I asked Danaa how she felt having Ouraali on board her ship.

"It is not my ship, Captain. It is Ouraali's while she is on board. She has far more experience than I do, and I still have much to learn. Her being here means I have the best possible mentor. I am just grateful for everything she is teaching me."

Once the ships were hidden behind their individual carbon bubbles, we approached the outpost with care. You don't just put down on any old asteroid or comet. They can be covered in a mixture of loose rocks and dust which is called regolith. The shock of a spaceship landing could cause avalanches or dry mudslides. At a very minimum clouds of particles could expand miles out to space. That was something we definitely didn't need. We needed to dock so lightly with the Starfish that we caused no disruption. Icy objects out this far in the Scattered Disc can contain water ice or methane ice, but our scanners were only picking up water ice, which actually would make this object technically a comet. That was lucky. It was probably what made this strange agglomeration of rock such a good staging point for the Omnistate Navy. Since water is the basis nowadays of all rocket fuel, they could easily take on supplies from the ice on the comet. Even so, we wanted to avoid any ice lakes or regolith and come down on solid rock of some sort.

It was like landing on the dark side of the moon. The ground was pock-marked and there were deep craters. What was a huge relief for the ships was the total lack of dust in the immediate vicinity.

Our sensors were detecting a rotational movement of the Starfish. That was what had given rise to the flattened aspect over the centuries, but it had also had the great advantage of precluding any dust settling on the surface.

At the last moment Danaa was forced to hop *Aenysia* some five hundred yards to starboard as our scans were showing deep ice directly beneath us. She did so with no panic. Nepheals learnt so quickly. As always, I was impressed by her aplomb. Because of the weak gravity she was able to skip horizontally quite easily.

I followed her lead and soon we were settled on the shortest arm of what I had decided to christen the Starfish. Settled is perhaps an exaggeration. The gravity was so weak that, although the vessels didn't float away into space, the best that could be said was that they were docked lightly against the planet. We left the carbon clouds in place but opened up the shuttle bays so that we could easily come and go from ship to ship via mag sleds.

"Jump out and fasten a rope to one of those rocks, will you, Mel?" I asked.

She gave me a now-I-have-heard-everything look.

"What? I don't want the ship to drift into space again. *Aenysia* should do the same. I expect they will when they see you out there. We could probably reach the escape velocity of this thing if I sneezed."

Mel didn't think that was funny. She left the bridge and we spotted her some time later, fastening the ship to a huge boulder. It took her some time. She was careful not to push off the Starfish as she walked. She looked like a man in chains as she shuffled one foot gingerly in front of the other. It was quite funny.

When she finally got back, I left Mel to track the arrival of the Terran cruiser and shuttled over to *Aenysia* in *Nivala's* largest shuttle, which was still equipped with a carbon bubble. Sibby, Denaraz and Didjal came with me.

Ouraali was harassed. She probably hadn't slept since Heisenberg's Halo, I decided. There were deep black circles under her enormous eyes, which themselves were red-rimmed.

She ushered us into her conference room. This time, because of the communications blackout, there were no virtual attendees. All those who needed to be present were physically sitting around the table.

She slapped a small black device onto the table. It fitted into her hand easily and was attached via a small ring to a chain. It had been designed to hang around a neck.

Sibby picked it up with interest and turned it over and over in her hands. "What does it do?" she asked.

"We have refined your own carbon cloud," said Ouraali.

Sibby's eyebrows went up. "Really? You have managed to shrink the components down to this? Wow! Impressive!"

Ouraali allowed herself to look just a tiny bit smug. She deserved it. I could tell from my sister's face that the achievement was noteworthy. Sibby was staring at her in awe.

"Put it over your head," Ouraali told her.

Sibby slid the chain over her head until the device was sitting comfortably in the space between her collar bones.

"Now twist the two parts against each other until the bottom part swivels 180 degrees with respect to the top part."

It took Sibby a few seconds to see that the device consisted in two halves and to twist the bottom half until the front part turned to the back. There was a small click.

Sibby disappeared.

We all gasped. There was a moment's shock, and then we all burst into applause.

Sibby's voice came from her chair. "You have been able to miniaturize it!" The voice began to move from the chair and walk around the large conference table, its orientation telling us exactly where my sister was at any moment. "What is its autonomy?"

"Not as long as we would like. Around eight hours."

There was a small click and Sibby reappeared in our midst, standing right behind Denaraz, who jumped.

"How do you power them for so long?" she asked.

Ouraali hesitated. "We have a way to transfer power across a hololink," she admitted with some reluctance.

Sibby's eyebrows almost reached her hairline.

Ouraali's face closed down. "I am not at liberty to say more."

Sibby accepted the Nepheal's reticence with a nod. She grinned. "We can use these to get aboard *Chibuzo*!"

"I hope so. At least they should allow a team a chance to rescue the Chyzar and your *faliif, Dialectis* Didjal." Ouraali bowed to the Enif, who inclined its own head in return. I was impressed by Ouraali's use of the honorific.

"We have three aims," I said. "One is to rescue Zenzara and Eshaan, one to apprehend Bull Cunningham and Ramesh Chandrayanan and one to safely destroy all the technology that can make macro wormholes, saving the remaining Chakran strand or strands if we possibly can."

Ouraali's face crinkled. "Unfortunately we only had enough parts to make three of them. The good news is that the smaller bubbles can cover two people at once, provided one is being carried by the other." There was a silence as we all worked out what that meant.

She elaborated. "I shall go, and I can carry Captain Mallivan on my back."

I caught my breath. She had carried me before, but it was a huge concession for her to offer. I lowered my head in recognition of that fact.

"Danaa can take Denaraz," she went on. "I know of his vow to protect the Chyzar."

Denaraz's face lightened. He also inclined his head in respect.

"Which will leave one device." Ouraali gave a sigh. "I am unsure of who should take it. What do you think, Captain Mallivan?"

"That will be for me," said Didjal with complete assurance. "I will carry Seyal."

There was a mutter. Most of those present knew neither the Enif nor Seyal.

My sister stood up quickly. "No! You must take me, Didjal. I *have* to go. I am the one with the most knowledge of nanotechnology!" Then she realized what she had said, and blushed. "Apart from Ouraali, that is."

I was already shaking my head to tell her she wasn't going to go, when Ouraali surprised us all.

"I definitely think this young Spacelander should go," she said, her face lined and very, very tired. "She is right. It will not be easy to identify and destroy the technology which has been created. We will need our brightest minds to go on this mission."

Sibby gave me a triumphant smirk and sat down.

Seyal managed to look impassive and disappointed at the same time.

Denaraz and I both bit our lips.

She was right, of course. But I hated – really hated – asking my sister to go on what was most probably a suicide mission.

Ouraali took our stunned silence as acceptance. "That is settled then," she said firmly. "We have a few hours until they land *Chibuzo* on one of the other arms. Until then, I intend to get some sleep. Wake me up half an hour before we are due to leave, please."

That was the end of the meeting.

Chibuzo came in about six hours after we did. We were able to track them in, because they switched off their carbon bubble before landing.

I guess they thought it was no longer necessary. It would certainly never have occurred to them that they could have been followed half way across the Major Shells.

At the same time there were scores of Omnistate ships coming towards the Starfish. Word must have got about that the wormhole technology was on the brink of being put into operation. Ships were popping up from all vectors. There were already a hundred or so in the immediate vicinity.

Some of those on the ground were taking off to join the gathering forces. It took very little energy. Gravity on the Starfish was so light that the engines needed only the slightest push to detach the vessel. I noticed that the Omnistate was being careful to preserve the Starfish as best they could. None of the vessels blasted off carelessly. All disengaged slowly and with the absolute minimum force necessary. They wanted to protect this environment, and I could understand why. It was a water refueling station that must save their fleet months of travel into the centre of the solar system. It was a base as yet unknown to the rest of the Major Shells. It was a place to set down and conserve fuel. It was a place to gather. It was, in fact, a secret weapon.

Except we had now found it.

I had called Jaaven to the bridge. He strolled in now, his eyes trailing automatically to the Captain's station, to see if Danaa was there. He seemed disappointed not to see her, but she was resting prior to what was going to be a very tense mission. I had been myself until Mel had called me to the bridge ten minutes ago.

"Take Scout and set up on *Nivala*, will you please? Seyal and Segaton will go with you. Seyal, you are now in command of *Nivala*."

Seyal nodded.

Neema and Anzany were the obvious choices to leave with *Aenysia*. They had already had plenty of practice with the Nepheal ship. I asked them to stay on her bridge for the duration. I had a feeling we would need fast action at some point.

That left Sammy and Mel. They had a very important part to play.

If we only had three of the portable carbon clouds, and each could only hide two people, there was no way we were going to be able to get Eshaan and Zenzara out of the complex without them being seen.

We were going to need an exit strategy.

I asked Sammy and Mel to take a shuttle each. *Nivala* had two shuttles. Although originally only the larger one of those had been fitted with one of Sibby's larger carbon cloud devices, more had now been made. We took one of *Aenysia's* spare devices and attached it to the smaller of *Nivala's* shuttles. We would settle one shuttle to either side of the *Chibuzo* and hope that we would be able to find Zenzara and Eshaan and evacuate all of us to them.

It was a good plan. Well, perhaps not good. Sufficient. Maybe. With a good headwind and on a lucky day.

It was all I had.

Mel had taken the larger shuttle, Sammy the smaller. They had made use of the time to stow as much equipment as they thought might be necessary.

We had docked some 40 kilometers from the *Chibuzo*, which gave me another good reason to use the shuttles. It turned out that the magnetic drive on the sleds was useless out here and it would take us forever to walk that distance across the flat frozen lakes and the icy craters. The shuttles could take us to 2 or 3 kilometers; we would do the rest on foot. The shuttles couldn't risk any closer approximation than that, even with the carbon clouds surrounding them. At least, with their help, our approach would be much quicker.

We gathered some time later in the shuttle bay of *Nivala*. We must have made quite a sight. Our boots were the most protective we could find. Nobody wanted their footwear to freeze off on what was basically the most inhospitable surface we had ever met. We were all festooned with tools and sensors. The Nepheals wore their own EVA suits, and these were enormous. They had to be, to accommodate their large bodies.

I had to smile when I saw Didjal. It had placed something that looked like thick diver's flippers over its feet. That is the first time I have seen an Enif use any sort of protection. It gave me a real sense of exactly how extreme this environment was going to be.

I sent Denaraz and Danaa off in the smaller shuttle. There was only room for one Nepheal in each shuttle, and I thought that Danaa would cope better with being squeezed into the smaller space. Ouraali was less used to having to fold her long body up into confined areas.

Sammy slipped past the larger shuttle and disappeared as he engaged the carbon bubble. I could trace his progress by a small disruption of the surface dust on the comet. Luckily, as we had already seen, there was very little of it.

The rest of us boarded the larger shuttle with Mel. We followed Sammy out. Neither of the shuttles was travelling very fast. We were trying to approach *Chibuzo* unseen, not blaze in throwing up a trail that could be seen a mile away.

The trip towards the Earth cruiser went off well. We were in position some twenty minutes later. It was relatively easy to coast to the fused base of the three triangular arms and then navigate the largest of these to where the majority of the Omnistate troops had settled. The shuttle lowered its rear ramp and we edged out. I waved to Mel and she raised the ramp again. She would detach the shuttle and allow it to hover some feet above the Starfish surface. Small corrections could keep it there for as long as we needed.

Sammy's shuttle had come alongside. We saw Danaa and Didjal as they descended to the surface. He then did the same as Sammy, except his shuttle flew away from us to take up his designated position on the other side of *Chibuzo*.

Once on the Starfish, I realized that walking presented quite a problem. There was gravity, but I felt like a feather. One jump, and I would be floating forever away from the ship I had come to think of as my only home. I found myself walking just like Mel had done – bending at the knee and sliding my feet along the surface.

That presented its own problems, as my sister soon found out to her cost. As soon as Sibby stepped off the ship, she turned to examine our surroundings with an expression of complete awe. I couldn't blame her. It was truly spectacular. There were a myriad pinpoints of light from distant stars and a tenuous light from the Sun that really didn't illuminate the ground at all. It was a timeless backdrop that made me feel insignificant.

Sibby spent a few moments admiring it all and then turned back to the rest of us to follow. She couldn't. Her feet were already frozen in place. Her face, through the protective visor, was a treat. Sheer panic.

Denaraz whipped back to her side and kicked at her feet, tugging at the same time. Eventually he managed to dislodge her from her ice trap. She shuffled very smartly behind him after that. We all did. No more dawdling. We had suddenly become extremely eager to get into the Omnistate Flagship.

As soon as the shuttle was clear of our position we got into our pairs. I scrambled up on Ouraali's back. Denaraz did the same with Danaa. In any case the Nepheals would have had to go down on all fours to traverse the difficult terrain. They needed to keep their centers of gravity as low as possible.

In Didjal's case, it simply hoisted Sibby onto its shoulders, She sat quite comfortably up there, perched between the two small humps of what were now vestigial wings and behind the thick black neck. She grinned at me, seemingly very happy not to have to walk any further across the frozen wasteland.

Didjal strode off toward the ships. The Enif covered the ground competently, but even so it took time. It was impossible to advance more than a few centimeters with each sliding foot. Neither the Nepheals nor the Enif had the same problem Sibby had experienced. I wondered if perhaps her boots had been damp or held some condensation. There must have been some difference, but I didn't know what that might have been. Shortly after that, they activated their personal carbon clouds and vanished. I did the same.

The distance to the *Chibuzo* seemed endless. I had plenty of time to stare out across the icy surface and into the dark beyond. With the strongest light coming from 500 billion miles away the whole panorama was ethereal and enthralling.

In comparison, the Omnistate ships were blazing light. At least, it felt like they were. For the first time in my life I saw their light as a contaminant. It was a strange sensation. I had a real impression of wild icy beauty that was being in some way diminished by our very presence. Even our footsteps across the ice were disturbing the landscape, waking this sleeping beauty in some way that ravaged it.

I shook my head to get rid of such thoughts. Thinking about the footsteps had made me realize that the marks we were leaving behind would be pretty clearly visible to any Terrans who happened to be looking out of their spaceport.

Then I decided that the darkness outside would mask our approach right up until the very end. The light only pooled in the area close up to the ships. We would have to be careful once we got close in.

We were. Ouraali and Danaa paused for a moment as we entered the light circle around the cruiser. Danaa extended her long neck so that it protruded from their carbon cloud and I could see her head.

I leaned forward out of our bubble and signaled a jumping motion.

Her eyes flashed. She thought it was too dangerous.

That might be, but there were guards stationed around the base of the ship, and they were most definitely not asleep. We needed to get past them without causing them to sound the alarm. In any case, Ouraali had me on her back and I weighed quite a lot. Surely that would help to bring her thrust down to below the escape velocity and not send her floating off into space?

The amount of white in her large eye told me that she was unconvinced, but she eventually nodded and withdrew back inside the safety of the bubble. I passed the signal on to the other two pairs.

We crept closer and closer until we were immediately opposite the guards. We all edged together so that our carbon clouds overlapped. When we could see each other, Ouraali assigned one guard to each pair, receiving small nods of understanding in reply. She counted down on the digits of one hand. Six, five, four, three, two, one.

We kicked off with such force that I almost screamed. Ouraali had tried to keep her trajectory as low as possible, but she had miscalculated slightly.

We flew over the head of our guard and impacted on the upper side of the shuttle bay doors. I felt the air woosh out of me as we were brought to a complete stop. Our feet clanged against the metal of the shuttle bay, making the guards all turn around and look upwards.

Ouraali was caught unprepared. Her hands scrabbled at the smooth metal as we slid down the fuselage. If she didn't do something quickly, we would drop straight on top of our guard. He could hardly miss us then, even if he survived the shock.

I felt frustrated. If I moved so much as an inch, I would probably throw her balance off. I froze in place and did my best to imitate a sphinx, my mind whirling.

We hung there for some moments. Gravity was light, but it still existed and we had no vertical velocity of escape. Then I noticed a spar just over my head. I was able to quickly stretch up and push off from it firmly in a downwards direction.

As Ouraali's grasp slipped down the metal, her fingers were waiting for an opportunity. She got it as we reached the edge of the shuttle bay door. There was a lip to the hatch, to make it sit flush with the bay and be truly airtight.

Her fingers latched onto that small lip and she was able to turn whatever little momentum was left from our slow slide down the metal to a horizontal vector. Then she let go.

We arched across the hold and landed on all fours way beyond the guard, who was still staring above him with a confused expression. Ouraali landed and quickly ducked down behind a mag sled that was stowed against the bulkhead. I slid off her and turned my attention to my scanner.

Denaraz and I had already spent quite a lot of time on this Terran flagship. So I knew where to look to find Zenzara and Eshaan. They were likely to be in one of the brigs. Those were situated about half way down the long ship. Finding Bull Cunningham and Ramesh Chandrayanan was going to be harder, and neutralizing the technology they had assembled even more of a challenge.

A thump nearby told me that one of the other pairs had landed safely on this side of the shuttle door. I looked around, trying to deduce who it must have been.

Then two thin hands slipped onto my shoulders and shook them. It could only be my sister. I didn't think anybody else on the mission would want to cuddle me. I smiled back through my helmet. Her hand and then the rest of her emerged from their bubble as Didjal bent forwards to enable her to slide over his head. I helped her down and then watched her disappear back into her own cloud. I retreated into mine, as well.

There was a sudden cry from in front of us. The middle guard had seen something. He was staring at a spot just between us and the shuttle bay opening. Water was pooling on the floor.

I hadn't thought of that. The shuttle bay was cold, but of course much, much warmer than it had been outside. The ice we had picked up on our travels was melting. And that meant that Didjal was standing exactly in the spot the guard was staring at. The Enif would be pinned there unless the guard could be persuaded to look somewhere else.

I picked up a small pebble I had picked up off the surface of the Starfish. I hadn't actually foreseen that I would need one ... I had picked it up because I wanted a memento of this strange place.

Anyway, I chucked it over the guard's head so that it landed outside the hold, on the ramp leading down to the icy ground outside. It landing with a sharp crack, and then skittered down the ramp leaving a rattle of rock against metal.

All of the guards looked back. The small patch of water disappeared as it was quickly mopped up and I saw other drops making their way towards the back of the hold, only to vanish almost as quickly as they were being made.

I grabbed a cloth from our own supplies and set to the area where we had been standing, then moving quickly to rub down Ouraali's feet. It took only a moment. She had not picked up much ice, but it would have been enough to give our position away.

Two of the guards were now examining the spot where the first one had seen water.

"You are seeing things. Like a mirage. It is this damned rock. It makes you imagine stuff."

"I wasn't seeing things, I tell you! There was water here. And what was that noise on the ramp just now?"

"Simple. That was just loose ice melting on the ramp and sliding down to the surface. What the krikk has got into you today?"

The first guard shivered. "It's this place. I don't like it."

"We won't be here for much longer, don't you worry. I hear that those two scientists are ready to open a bridge out of here. We will be gone by tomorrow. And then we won't be limited to the Major Shells."

"It's not natural. We weren't meant to travel through wormholes. No good will come of this, you mark my words."

"Bah! First you start seeing things and now you are prophesying doom and gloom!" The first guard turned away in disgust.

I let out the air I had been holding in my lungs. We edged backwards out of the shuttle bay, making sure to make absolutely no noise. We didn't want to push our luck.

Some fifteen minutes later the ship's warning siren sounded and there was a faint judder as *Chibuzo* was maneuvered carefully away from the Starfish. We were slipping out into space again. That was going to make getting away much, much more difficult.

13

I won't go into the journey through the battlecruiser's main central passageway. First we ducked into what looked to be a little-used storeroom to remove our EVA suits. Then we got underway. It was very uncomfortable. I had to walk under Ouraali's belly to keep within the personal carbon bubble, and that meant doubling over. Denaraz must have been doing the same with Danaa, and I think Sibby was draped over Didjal's shoulders as it walked almost in a crouch.

However, it was well worth it. I was amazed to see that the crew of the battlecruiser had no idea we were there. We ducked out of the way of any Flatlanders we saw, which was difficult sometimes. Especially for the Nepheals, who were so much larger than humans.

At last we came to the ship's brig. It brought back memories, none of which were particularly amenable.

I was hugely relieved to see Eshaan in one of the cells. At least he appeared unhurt.

Didjal or Sibby – I didn't know which, because they were both still invisible to me – pulled off the protective cover of the main door from the passageway into the brig area. A few sparks flew, and then the door slid open.

There were two guards on the other side. I moved in, edging to the right, and luckily Danaa must have moved to the left, for as I floored my guard, dropping him unconscious to the floor, the same thing happened to the other one.

Didjal must have already moved to the central console, because the door to Eshaan's cell opened after a couple of moments.

Eshaan peered out with a wary expression on its face, unable to see any of us.

"Hello?"

I heard the typical Enif thrumming. Eshaan did too. It's head came up joyously. "Didjal?"

There was a laugh. "Indeed. Were you expecting somebody else to come and rescue you?"

Eshaan raced in the direction of the sound and half of its head and all of its arm disappeared into the cloud for a short time.

I heard a small series of surprised clicks as it must have come across Sibby. "Are you up there for any particular reason, Miss Mallivan?" it asked.

Sibby giggled. "Sorry, Eshaan. This was the only way not to be seen." She must have slid down from Didjal's back because she appeared suddenly out of nowhere. "But I am very, very glad to see you."

"They have taken Zenzara away," it said, its tone worried. "Some hours ago. I am ... concerned about her welfare."

"Do you know where they took her?"

"No." It went up to the console and began to examine the memory. "But I am pretty sure there will be a record in here somewhere. The Omnistate is run with military precision. They take a note of everything."

The Enif was looking drained. I wondered if they had been feeding it. "Are you all right, Eshaan?"

An antenna gave a twitch. "I am a little stiff," it told us.

"Why?" Didjal sounded oddly hollow.

"It does not matter, my *faliif.* You are here now. It is of no consequence."

Although I couldn't see Didjal, I could feel its tension. "They have tortured you!"

Eshaan's carapace shone with a sickly grayish tint. "I told you. It no longer has any importance."

"Who did this to you?"

Eshaan refused to answer.

"Was it Cunningham himself? Or the Admiral?"

Silence.

A strange sound emanated from Didjal's bubble. It was a mechanical outpouring of clicks, so close together that they almost sounded like one note. I took it to mean Didjal was angry.

Then I heard Sibby's voice murmuring to the Enif, calming it down. She was right; this was no time to be demanding reparation. We had a very difficult task to try to perform.

"Got it!" Eshaan's black colour flashed back across its now dull gray body. "She was picked up from the Brig and her destination was … Cargo bay 18!" It looked over at me, pleased with itself.

"Will that thing tell you how to get to Cargo bay 18?" I asked.

It peered a little more, pushed a few more buttons, and then nodded. "Decks 32 through 37, right at the stern of the ship. Cargo bay 18 occupies the whole of the width of the vessel and has its own cargo doors to the exterior. It is the largest cargo bay the battlecruiser has."

I nodded. "They may already be trying to open another wormhole. They will have all they need, if the new cloning process is now operational. If not, they have the Chyzar. Still, I suspect they will prioritize divesting Zenzie of the rest of the Nexus in any case."

"I hope they have not hurt her." Eshaan sounded dejected.

"Not your fault."

"I came to protect her. I was unable to do so."

"I am quite sure that your being here helped her."

"We spoke about a lot of things," it admitted.

"She would have appreciated that. Last time they took her she was completely on her own. You couldn't have done more."

It went even paler than its sickly hue. "I did not come to talk to her. I came to stop harm coming to her. I was not able to do that."

"We don't know yet. She had not been harmed when they came for her?"

It shook its head. "They had concentrated on me. They wished me to tell them … things."

"What sort of things did they want to know?"

"He was very angry. He wanted to know how you found out about the Vaer space laboratory. He said you were getting too close for comfort."

"Did you tell him?"

Eshaan's carapace suddenly glinted with an angry darkness. "I did not!"

"Thank you."

"Enif do not give way to … pressure."

There was a sniff above me and to my left. Sibby was crying. I directed a cross look in her general direction. She muttered an apology.

Didjal was less circumspect. It gave out another burst of mechanical anger.

"All right. Enough. I think you *did* protect her, Eshaan. If you had not been there, they would have interrogated Zenzara. Think about it. She would have had to go through the same thing you did."

Eshaan was struck by that. "I had not considered that, Captain. Yes, you may be correct." It cheered up. "That is a comfort. Thank you."

"You're welcome. Now, can we get along to Cargo Bay 18 and put a stop to all of this? I think we might need to hurry. Your absence may be noticed soon."

I explained about the bubbles and why another person could not be hidden in one. Eshaan though for a moment and then a flash of yellow diffused its entire body. "I know! Captain, can you fit into one of those uniforms?"

I stared down at the two guards. The tallest was probably

approximately my size.

"This one ..." I touched him with my toe. "I think."

"We put them in a cell. You take his clothes." Eshaan turned back to the console. "I am changing the transferral order to read Enif instead of Tyzaran. "You can be the guard in charge of the prisoner."

I agreed straightaway. "If these two guards are discovered, we will have to fight our way there, but it will give us a head's start. Good idea."

We were soon on our way. I led the way, one hand on Eshaan's arm in a proprietary and pushy sort of way. We marched openly along the corridor, with many of the crew of the *Chibuzo* ducking to one side.

"Make way, please!" I love doing an officious tone. I find it easy, for some reason.

I had no idea if the others were keeping up in their carbon bubbles. It seemed unlikely, but I could only worry about one thing at a time.

We stepped into one of the elevators. It was a big risk, because the lifts would be paralyzed if Eshaan's escape and our presence were even suspected. However, the alternative ... over twenty-five decks of crawl tubing – was unthinkable. There simply wasn't time.

The elevator creaked ominously. We had been pushed over to the far corner by Danaa's carbon bubble.

"Is that you, Denaraz?" I hissed. I wasn't sure if the elevators were equipped with microphones and video cameras for surveillance.

"It is," came back the equally quiet answer. We fell silent. I tried to look like a guard going about his everyday business. A Flatlander guard.

That journey down through twenty-five decks dragged on forever. My nerve endings were jangling with unused adrenalin. I thought it endless.

Then the doors opened again and I shoved Eshaan in guard-like style out onto the corridor. I felt, rather than saw, Denaraz and Danaa step out behind me just before the door to the elevator swung shut.

Eshaan, who had memorized the route, turned sharply to the left. I pushed it along again to maintain the fiction that I was the one in charge. It stumbled and then led me along the central passageway. Here, it was still only one storey in height. It would open out into the five-deck high hold about a hundred meters further to the rear of the ship.

Chibuzo was now stationary, hanging some five hundred meters above the Starfish. That was increasing slowly, but I got the impression that the only objective was to find a quiet area where the stern doors on cargo bay 18 could be easily opened. If it were me, I would let the ship drift out on inertia to some ten kilometers. Maybe twenty. Then I would open the wormhole. That would be far enough out to allow for plenty of space to bring ships around, but still close to the Starfish for much needed refueling and easy vigilance.

I wondered what Sammy and Mel would do.

I hoped they would be tacked on, one on either side, like persistent fleas.

I would bet my life that they were.

I might have to.

We were starting to walk down the last section of corridor when they must have discovered the guards in the brig. Sirens started to sound around us and red flashing lights came up to each side of the overhead paneling.

I ran, grabbing Eshaan and dragging it along with me. The others were still invisible. My job was to get them inside Cargo Hold 18. And I had every intention of doing just that.

We thundered down the passageway as bewildered crew members peered out of their workspaces. One of them pulled out his pistol, but succumbed to a neatly delivered blow from somebody invisible on my right. Most simply ducked back inside again, looking even more confused. The fact that I was wearing the same uniform that they were made them loath to try to stop me.

The cargo bay had large doors, big enough for three people abreast to go inside. From about fifty feet away, I could see that there were two ratings about to close and lock the doors.

"Hold that!" I shouted. There was a word the Flatlanders used. What was it? Oh yes. "Belay that! Coming in!"

They both looked over their shoulders and hesitated just long enough for me to gallop along the remaining metres and push Eshaan through the doors. I did this so hard that it tripped and went sprawling inside. Everybody near enough to be in danger jumped out of the way.

I hoped that the two hidden pairs behind me had managed to sneak through those doors. I shouted back. "Close now. Close! Close! Close!" as I moved towards the prostrate Enif.

The ratings obeyed and within seconds the huge armored doors had shut behind us. That should keep the rest of the ship out nicely. I aimed my pulser at the mechanism and fired. The mechanism and part of the entire wall fused. Nobody was going to get through that in a hurry.

Unfortunately I came under fire at that point. I thought I had done rather well to get that far. I threw myself behind an iron column and began to take stock of my surroundings.

The whole space was about the size of *Aenysia's* shuttle bay. Because of the size of the Nepheals, that was big. Very big. So was this.

I looked past and up. We had come in at the lowest level. Looking straight ahead, all I could see was row upon row of shipping containers made for space, presumably full of provisions. The decking was flat, but there were indentations in it everywhere. Inside these indentations were cog-and-tooth mechanisms to move the space containers about the hold, to stow them in their correct places.

The containers were only stacked one storey in height, but each container was a rectangle of eight meters by four meters by four meters. There is no need for space containers to be smaller. There are fewer weight constraints. In the Omnistate fleet they are usually kept down to that size purely so that they can fit easily in through standard six meter cargo bay doors. The liquid containers are even smaller and cylindrical in shape.

Between the lines of containers were aisles of around two meters. These were also standard width, in order to fit the fork-lifts needed to load and unload freight from each container.

The files of containers were lining the central ramp. This was a steep metal incline with a hydraulic conveyor for the containers running along the center. It led up to the cargo bay doors and then beyond, out onto the rear freight dock behind the battlecruiser.

Right at this moment, it was not a container which was parked at the base of the ramp. It was a platform some six meters square. On this there were four corner console stations, and a central plinth. Balanced on top of this plinth was a large transparent sphere. There were people on the platform, and I noted idly that one of them was Bull Cunningham. It seemed to me that another had a shape very similar to the newly reappointed Admiral Ellison.

There wasn't time to stop and peer. My eyes swept over the platform and traveled upwards. On the left of the cargo bay doors, and with a two meter clearance above the tops of the containers, was a large mezzanine floor.

This had been taken over by a science laboratory. There were console stations dotted across it, and bank upon bank of high end computing memory against the back wall. Scientists were scurrying around up there. Their movement conveyed a sense of urgency. They were not ducking for cover. They were carrying on as if they couldn't hear any shots, as if they were immune to the pulser blasts in the hold space.

And there, right at the back of the mezzanine, in a break in the banks of computers, was Zenzara. She was contained in a metal cage that was set into the back wall of that level.

She had climbed up the cage and was waving down at me. I couldn't hear her over all the noise but I knew she was calling my name. I felt a huge wave of relief sweep over me. She was all right. So far.

Eshaan and I threw ourselves behind the nearest file of space containers. Nothing would get through those. I couldn't help feeling that fate had been kind to us. If you were going to get trapped with hostile forces in an enemy ship, then this was the place to do it. We could weave in and out of those containers all day without them pinning us down.

But I wasn't going to. I was going up. Up to the mezzanine floor. I was going to break Zenzara out of that cage.

Since Eshaan and I were the only ones of our group that were visible, we were logically attracting all the fire. We slid down an aisle between two rows of containers and Eshaan pointed upwards. I nodded, but looked at the towering metal box with respect. There was no way I could jump four meters, and apart from the door hinges and lock, the side was completely sheer. Impossible to get enough of a grip to scale it.

Eshaan clicked at me. The next thing I knew I had been chucked onto its back and the Enif was scaling one of the containers with consummate ease. I clung on for dear life, almost throttling my host in the process. Only a faint gurgle told me to loosen my grasp a little.

"Sorry, Eshaan. I didn't realize I was strangling you."

It shook its head, but forged on upwards. Within seconds we were both on top of the container.

At first we lay flat. We weren't sure if we could still be seen. Then I realized that we were out of sight of those on the lower level, and protected by the mezzanine platform from those on the top of the ramp. Our only danger came from the scientists who were actually on the mezzanine. Hopefully, they wouldn't be armed. Or, if they were, they shouldn't be quite so efficient with a weapon.

I signaled to Eshaan to make our way to the exterior wall of the mezzanine level. They would be expecting us to appear from the front part, where a metal staircase breached the height between the two levels. They would not be expecting us to appear from behind. That meant running across the tops of the containers and leaping across from one lane to the next.

I say running, but it was a peculiar bent-double sort of shuffle. There was only a meter or so of headroom between the tops of the containers and the underneath side of the mezzanine level. This was a steel platform on stilts, with girders welded together to form the base of another deck.

Jumping from one container to another while still doubled over wasn't easy either. Luckily they were only around eighty centimeters apart. Anything much more than that would have proved totally impossible. For me, at least.

As we came to the edge of the mezzanine, we both readied our weapons.

We grabbed the bottom of the safety railing and pulled ourselves over the lip of the decking. Once our feet were on the mezzanine it was an easy matter to vault over the top railing and start firing.

Zenzie was screaming at the top of her voice. I have no idea what she was screaming because all I could hear was an annoying high-pitched monotone. I guess she thought she was being helpful. In fact it almost made me want to turn around and leave her there. What a screech! It reverberated around all the metal and threatened to shatter my brain.

I shot at the scientist nearest to me and managed to get to his console without injury. Like all of the equipment on board, it was bolted to the floor and provided great cover.

"Shut up, will you?" I shouted up at Zenzie. "And get down from there. Stop providing them with a target."

She looked down and I saw her crest flicker. Then she dropped like a cat to the floor. There wasn't much in the round cell to give her cover but she obediently scuttled behind the toilet area, which at least was provided with a privacy barrier of metal that reached to her waist. She crouched down behind that and disappeared from sight.

The few guards on the mezzanine were slow to defend themselves, but I could hear heavy firing below me. I guessed that the others were targeting Bull Cunningham and the Admiral, with her security detail.

The scientists were beginning to feel exposed. It only took three more shots to neutralize the guards. As soon as we did that, the Terran researchers raised up their hands in defeat.

Zenzie crowed and walked to the front of her cage. I opened the lock by dint of burning through it with my pulser. She ran out and hugged me, taking me quite by surprise. Then she ran and hugged Eshaan.

I was really pleased to see the Indian amidst the scientists. "Chandrayanan. Nice to finally catch up with you again."

He grunted. "You will never stop the Omnistate. You Spacelanders have taken away our heritage. You have stolen our future."

I thought that was going a bit too far. "I don't quite see how you reached that conclusion."

"You are the ones that went out into space. But instead of bringing the profits back to Earth, you built your own society. You claimed the Landau Rift as your own!"

My jaw was sagging open. "You took away our citizen's rights! You said that anybody not born on Earth had no right to live there!"

"Of course we did! There wasn't room to take in all the people born in space!"

"What did you expect to happen?"

"You turned on us. We only want what is ours."

I gave him a look and he looked uncomfortable. Surely he was too intelligent to have fallen for all that populist rubbish? He was the leading Omnistate expert on the quantum microsciences. It felt strange to hear the same old cheap propaganda coming out of his well-educated mouth.

"You really think the Landau Rift is yours?" I walked over to him and tied his hands behind his back. "Do you think the whole universe is yours, as well? To invade at your will? Is that why you are planning to set up wormholes through it? What gives you the right to do that? You know how dangerous the technology is. The Chakrans have told you."

"We will not be constrained within our Termination Shock! Why should we care what the Chakrans say? Who is to say that they are right? Ethnarch Locke is the only person who can tell us what to do. Nobody else!"

I sighed. "Ramesh Chandrayanan, you are under arrest for use of illegal technology. Anything you say will be recorded and used as evidence against you."

He glowered. "I don't recognize your authority. This is illegal detention."

"You can tell that to the authorities when we get you to Ulon Prime. You will be tried for your part in all this."

"I am just a scientist. This is an outrage. You cannot stop the progress of science! I am within my rights!"

It was at this point that I gagged him. He was making so much noise that none of us could think. He was soon wrapped up in a nice quiet package that we could deliver anywhere we wanted.

I left him with Eshaan and moved over to the railing so that I could look down on the tracks below me, on the plinth and the round transparent sphere.

There was a lot of fighting going on.

Ellison and her detachment of marines had Danaa and the others pinned down behind a line of containers. I saw that Didjal and Denaraz had managed to scale the containers and were approaching silently from above. Bull Cunningham was behind Ellison at one of the consoles. He was busy at the controls.

The one thing I had to do was stop Bull Cunningham. I climbed onto the top of the railing and threw myself down onto the plinth below, landing right on top of the Flatlander. I vaguely heard a cry behind me and then something hurtled down from above to impact me.

Everything was on slow motion for quite a few seconds. Then the scene evolved to show me Zenzie's crest. It was rigidly perpendicular to her scalp, which turned out to be next to my chin. I then became aware of a wriggling figure beneath me, and of a pistol and an M596 nearby.

The red alert my neurons were trying to get past my stunned lungs finally penetrated the dull haze. I lurched for the closest of the guns and flung both myself and Zenzara away from the figure on the floor.

Bull and I came to our feet at exactly the same time. Our guns came up at exactly the same time. He had the old-school rifle. I had the pulser pistol. Unfortunately, I had part of Zenzara's body still blocking my aim.

He fired. I didn't.

Zenzara must have anticipated the move, because she was somehow between the bullet and my heart, which is where he was hoping to put it.

I felt her gasp as she was hit, then she slumped against me. I fired past her, rather wildly, but Bull was no longer in the same place. He took advantage of the melee to dive over to the other side of the plinth, behind the sphere.

I shot directly into the console, destroying as much of it as I could. The slight hum it had been emanating died immediately. The sphere, which had been slightly enveloped in white light, became quiescent again. They had been right at the start of the process, then.

Bull was gone.

I looked down at the Tyzaran girl. I wanted to shake her. But was it really her fault? I should have known that the Savior protocols would have made her follow me over that railing. She couldn't have done anything else. I should have tied her up along with Chandrayanan if I hadn't wanted her to follow me.

"Are you all right?" OK, I *did* give her a little shake. "Zenzie? Speak to me!"

The bullet had torn through her arm and into her chest. She slumped against me, a strangely heavy weight for such a light girl.

I had no idea what to do. My mind was in full-blown shock and panic. I just wanted to get her to safety. But that was going to be impossible.

Finally, some five seconds later, my brain realized where it was. In the middle of a fire fight, in the cargo hold of the *Chibuzo*. This was not the place to call for a couple of medics. Zenzie would have to wait.

I had to secure the surroundings, otherwise none of us would survive long enough to get her help.

I let Zenzara slide back to the ground and leapt towards the Admiral. At the same time I saw Denaraz and Didjal launching themselves down onto the marines.

I grappled with the Admiral. She was a tough old bird, but I had about thirty years advantage over her. This was one fight she couldn't win. I soon had her down on the plinth with her hands behind her back. She struggled feebly, but I got her tied up and handcuffed in short shrift. I gave her the new Enforcement Agency rights warning. She would have to face trial, too.

As I was doing this, and as Didjal and Denaraz were dealing with those of her detail who were actually on the plinth, Danaa and Ouraali cleaned up the rest of the resistance around the cargo hold. The Flatlander marines put up a good fight, but they were no match for two Nepheals that were twice their size. When the skirmish was over, three were dead, six wounded and the rest were huddling against a console with their hands up.

Some ten minutes later we were able to turn our attention to the sphere. I grabbed a couple of the captured M596s. There was nothing like solid projectiles for breaking stuff up. The sphere evaporated and all of the surrounding consoles were soon shattered into pieces too small for even Humpty Dumpty to put back together again.

I left Danaa tending to Zenzara, and Ouraali ensuring the marines were incapacitated. I had to drag myself away, because the sharp needle of worry about the girl who had just taken a bullet meant for me was still dulling my ability to think logically.

I needed to deal with any information in the computers on the mezzanine level. I gave Didjal a shout, and he kindly booted me up to the top of one of the containers. I spent a nice five minutes shooting up all the consoles on the upper floor. Eshaan was still watching over the rest of the scientists and Chandrayanan.

I was just getting around to considering whether to go after

Cunningham or not when the flashing red lights signaling full alert became twice as strident, and were accompanied by the worst sound you can hear on a spaceship. The decompression warning siren.

Then I knew what Cunningham had done. He had closed off Cargo Bay 18 and was about to open the doors out to space. He was going to write off Admiral Ellison, all of the marines, and his great friend Ramesh Chandrayanan. He was going to try to kill us all.

I gave a shout to Eshaan. "Bring the prisoner!" Then I leapt back over the railings and dropped down onto the plinth.

The others looked up at me. Only Denaraz had figured out what was about to happen. It was written all over his face.

I addressed him. "Izan. Get yourself into a Flatlander EVA suit. Get Zenzara and Sibby into a PSA as fast as you can. We don't have much time."

He nodded and leapt into action.

I grabbed at Eshaan. "Get your prisoner into a PSA! Take Admiral Ellison, as well."

The PSA, or Portable Safety Airbag, is one of the standards of all space travel, and used internationally. They are small cubes of space burlap, made to maintain integrity for small periods of time in the event of a catastrophic decompression in space. They are also ways of surviving a potential explosion, since a PSA will get you outside into the vacuum quickly, where of course, blast is not felt. The space burlap will not protect you from shrapnel, however.

The drawback is that they are small. They are designed to hold a maximum of three people, and measure just a tad over a meter in all three directions.

I wished we still had the specially made EVA suits that Ouraali and Danaa had come in. It wasn't going to be easy pushing a fully-grown Nepheal woman into a PSA. I wasn't even sure it was possible. But it was certainly the only way that they could survive this. And I wasn't going to leave them behind without trying to save them.

I grabbed Danaa's hand and tagged Ouraali at the same time,

indicating a bank of PSA's just by the main doors. They both looked terrified. They knew how hard it would be for them to fit into an airbag made for only three humans.

I got there first. I grabbed the small hammer that hung from one end of the red canister that was stored alongside the PSA. I struck the red seal firmly with the hammer and broke the seal.

I stepped back as the PS airbag deployed. It ballooned up into its cube within a couple of seconds.

I dragged the sides of the heavy duty zipper apart. The gas cylinder gives a positive pressure outwards for twenty seconds, before the safety valve releases the canister and the airbag can be deployed. The zipper needed to be closed by then. Twenty seconds is not long enough to stuff a large Nepheal into a small space.

I shoved Danaa into the first one. She curled herself up in a ball as she allowed herself to tumble inside. She was much smaller than Ouraali, so I was hopeful.

Sure enough, I was able to pull the emergency closure cords. I heard the typical metallic slithering as the vacuum zip sealed. Almost as soon as the light on top of the portable space airbag shone green, I had stepped onto the next one.

I broke the seal on the next PSA and stared at Ouraali. She knew what she had to do. I could tell, for the first time, that the leader of the Nepheals was apprehensive. She had enough courage for ten of her race, but she wasn't looking forward to this one little bit.

As the airbag expanded, the huge metal doors to the cargo bay began to open. I grimaced. I had been hoping for longer. I dragged one side of the space burlap towards me, leaving more room for Ouraali to get inside. She executed a strange sort of somersault which propelled her into the material.

It became a very different shape to the cube it was meant to be. Limbs were distorting the material all over the sack. There was a bulge where her head was and two others where her elbows wouldn't fit. Her legs were still outside the burlap, scrabbling uselessly to try to find a footing on the slippery metallic surface of the decking.

We were out of time. I pulled both of her feet against my chest and ran at the PSA.

It was touch and go, but finally I managed to slip each foot to the side of the zip, just within the airbag. Before she could move and part of her fell out again, I yanked at the emergency closure cords. To my great relief I heard the slithery sound that heralded the sealing of the vacuum zip.

But the hold was already decompressing. I might not have time to save myself. I was not sucked out to space because I had one arm curled around the cord that secured the hammer to the bulkhead, but I wasn't going to get to an EVA suit.

I had run out of time.

The two airbags were already being sucked out of the widening gap, along with anything else not tied down. To my dismay, I witnessed several of the bound marines being sucked out into space. Their bonds had stopped them being able to reach any of the suits or PSAs. I cursed myself for not foreseeing this. I had unwittingly condemned those men to a horrible death.

I wouldn't be far behind them. I had managed a last gasp of oxygenated air as it was siphoned out past me by the lack of pressure outside. That wouldn't last long.

Everything went into slow motion. I looked around me worried about the others. Izan had the two girls inside an airbag and was in the process of guiding it safely out of the cargo bay so that they were not injured as it was carried through the now almost completely open doors.

Eshaan was copying him, escorting the bag with the two prisoners inside it.

I felt my head begin to swim.

I wished I had been able to live longer.

I sent a mental goodbye to my sister.

Two strong black arms grabbed at my legs and pushed them inside an EVA suit. My eyes, which had been closing, jolted open again. Didjal was beside me, struggling to cram me into an EVA suit.

Maybe I wasn't going to die just yet.

Feebly, I attempted to help the Enif.

It ignored my attempts to help and fed my limbs inside the suit with great precision. It had to prise my hand from the hammer cord. Something in my head refused to let it go. Then the Enif slammed an EVA helmet over my head so hard that my brain seemed to shake. There was a rubbery squeak and then a sucking sound as the helmet sealed hermetically to the neck part of the suit. I felt fresh air running past my nose. I took a tentative breath. My lungs screamed for me to do it again. I did, this time taking in more. It was bliss. I think every part of my body tingled as I gulped down that first air. It went to my head, making me dizzy again.

Didjal pushed me out in front of it, trying to catch us up with the two PSAs that contained the Nepheal women. As I felt my senses coming back into a sharper focus, I nodded back. It looked very relieved.

Not as much as I felt.

We popped out of the open doors and floated out into the slate-gray space outside. It was dark, hostile, and extremely inhospitable.

14

Extravehicular Activity was meant to refer to gentle excursions around the fuselage of a spaceship. It was never meant to refer to being expelled into space at speed and being torn away from all air. EVA is something gentle. This was not at all gentle. It was violent and terrifying.

I saw some of the science technicians being dragged past us as the air in the cargo hold whistled out into space. Their mouths were open in utter horror. They knew that they had bare seconds to live. I even tried to grab the hand of one of them, but she was just too far away, and I don't know what I could have done with her if I had caught her. EVA helmets cannot be removed in a vacuum. Their failsafes come into play. I could not have protected her.

Didjal was tugging at me. It managed to spin me around and then directed me towards the airbag that contained Ouraali. I knew it was hers because it was so misshapen and distorted. Her appendages were straining at the seams of the space burlap and it seemed as though it could burst open at any moment.

I looked down at the Starfish. It wasn't far away from us. Perhaps a couple of kilometers. We might be able to get ourselves down onto the comet's gravity well before Ouraali's air ran out in the airbag. I just hoped she wasn't so scrunched up in there that she couldn't even breathe.

I nodded to Didjal and used the gas cylinder around my waist to boost myself toward the Starfish. All EVA suits are equipped with two small cylinders. These can be manipulated in case of detachment from a spaceship. They enable an astronaut to regain his footing quickly should he become separated. They are not meant to allow much autonomy, being tiny things that are only for use in a real emergency. Each canister is smaller than a cigar case. You simply point the green arrow in the direction you wish to travel and hold down the red button for two or three seconds, keeping it well away from your body.

In this case, with the airbag increasing my mass, it didn't move us very quickly. However, I could see, by comparing our vector with that of the *Chibuzo* as it swept past, that we were now heading down towards the surface of the comet.

I kicked my legs, as if I were diving in water. I don't know why ... my brain knew that I could make no difference in our speed. It was automatic.

I managed to take the time to look around. Didjal was falling behind me with Danaa, and on the other side of the cargo doors I could see Denaraz who was escorting the PSA containing Zenzie and Sibby, then Eshaan who had the prisoners locked in an airbag that it was clinging onto.

Denaraz had done the same as me, using his gas cylinder to impart a vector. We were both heading down to the surface of the Starfish. However, the two Enif had no way of propulsion. They didn't need EVA suits, of course, but at the same time they had no cylinders of gas. They were both drifting off, out away from the comet and into space.

My heart gave a tremendous thud of panic. Although the Enif may be able to survive for hours in open space, those in the PSAs had only a very limited air supply. And that was not their worst problem. The reinforced burlap kept the space chill at bay for minutes, rather than hours. They had to be rescued quickly. Really quickly.

I squinted towards the two PSAs that were now receding behind us. I did, for a moment, see something moving towards them. I could tell, because the debris around them was being blocked momentarily. I turned back to my own airbag, and let out a little more gas from my cylinder. I only needed to keep a last burst in case I required it for the landing.

I turned back. I was pretty sure that the shuttles were up there, trying to get to the two airbags that had been left behind. I hoped so.

Then three large Flatlander shuttles slid out of *Chibuzo's* forward shuttle bay. They almost hit me as they came past, and for a moment I wondered if they would. One of their back guns fired, almost in a desultory manner, at me. I ducked, another absolutely useless thing to do.

I think they could have turned to finish us off. In fact, I was rather expecting them to do so. On the other hand, they couldn't know if Admiral Ellison was in one of the airbags, nor which one. Surely they would not fire indiscriminately on their own admiral?

For whatever reason, there was just that one attempt to stop us. I guess they thought they could pick us up later, on the surface of the comet. We were certainly not going to be able to escape them at our speed. It must have been the slowest getaway in Spacelander history.

Even though our shuttles were encased in carbon clouds, they were now detectable. The shuttles from *Chibuzo* had clearly picked them up from the busy background, as I had done. That meant that the Flatlanders were going to leave Denaraz and me alone and swing around to deal with us later. We weren't going far. Their priority would be to deal with *Nivala's* shuttles.

I wondered if Bull was on one of the *Chibuzo* shuttles. I was willing to bet that he would be. He would enjoy the chase. I remembered how he was in his element under battle conditions. This would be a treat so far as he was concerned.

Izan and I drifted along behind our respective airbags, our necks swiveled around so that we could see what was happening behind us.

The Omnistate shuttles made no attempt to rescue any of their own crew. Perhaps it was too late by then, but there was little of the *Semper Fi* spirit, as far as I could see. They headed straight towards the floating PSAs and only the density of the debris field stopped them from pulling immediately alongside.

It was hard to see from our position, but we certainly spotted the moment when either Sammy or Mel, in one of our own *Nivala* shuttles, got close enough to reel it in. One of the cubic airbags began to disappear into the invisible carbon cloud. Both airbag and small accompanying figure drifted inside, and then disappeared as the carbon cloud encompassed them. It took a few moments more while they must have been opening the shuttle airlock and bringing the airbag in, then we were able to see the dark patch of sky moving out of the way of the rest of the debris.

One of *Chibuzo's* shuttles swirled after it. Guns were firing, and a pulser beam was rebounding off some of the larger pieces of debris. Most of the containers had been tied down, and had stayed in the hold, but perhaps ten of them must have been in transit and had been sucked past the main doors. The pulser beams bounced off one or two of the containers and scattered around the rest of the debris field. One of them hit another, loose PSA. My heart dropped for the people inside it. Some of the technicians had managed to get themselves into one of the safety bags, only to have it blown apart by friendly fire.

Our shuttle was not about to fire back. I hoped it had already got itself back to the main ships, back on the Starfish.

The Omnistate shuttle that had been firing on it made a couple of more passes before flouncing back towards the second shuttle.

This was now close to the other PSA. But it was surrounded. I saw the airbag beginning to vanish as it entered the shuttle's carbon cloud. Now there were several pulser beams criss-crossing the dark night sky. One impacted on the carbon cloud itself, and then vanished as it passed through the barrier. I crossed my fingers that it would not hit the shuttle directly.

The whole airbag and the tiny figure behind it disappeared.

I found myself holding my breath.

And counting.

How long was it going to take Mel or Sammy, whichever of them was left, to get the PSA on board and get themselves out of there?

Probably too long. I couldn't see what damage the shuttle was taking, because the carbon bubble was holding. But the shots were certainly finding their mark.

We had traveled too far by this time to see exactly what was happening behind us. With immense regret, I turned my attention back to my own trajectory and the PSA I was responsible for.

The space burlap was stiffening with the cold. I wondered if Ouraali was still all right inside it. If so, she wouldn't be for long.

We were now perhaps a kilometer above the surface of the Starfish comet. The three triangular legs, all attached at the thickest parts, were now quite clear beneath me.

I stretched out in space behind the PSA. It was time to think of how to save Ouraali. I certainly didn't want to come down in the center of the Omnistate space, which was concentrated on the largest of the arms. I needed to nudge our trajectory slightly so that we would come down on the stubby arm, the one *Aenysia* and *Nivala* were on. At least that way Ouraali would stand a chance of getting oxygen and warmth in time. I needed to land really, really close to the ships.

On the other hand, the Omnistate must know that we had the ships nearby, and it wasn't going to take them long to find us.

I waved across the expanse at Denaraz and made some signs towards the smaller of the arms. He waved back. He would have come to the same conclusions. Izan had a better brain than I did.

We both activated the last of the gas in our cylinders, gently adjusting the vector so as to bring us down as close to the ships as we could manage.

By that time the debris field above us was too far away for us to be able to make out what was happening. All we knew was that there was still some firing taking place.

Chibuzo herself had begun to descend to the Starfish herself. She was coming back into land.

I felt a thrill of triumph run through me. We may not have got Bull Cunningham, but the Admiral and Chandrayanan had been arrested and, more importantly, we had stopped their immediate plans to open a wormhole. That should be good news. Very good news.

I let my legs trail out behind me and looked around at my surroundings. The expanse of the Starfish was silhouetted against the Milky Way, which glittered magnificently right behind it, making a wonderful backdrop. Behind me, the Sun, though tiny, was just coming above the comet's horizon. Its weak rays were beginning to faintly illuminate the surface of the starfish.

And, where those dim rays touched the comet, I could see plumes of sublimated ice beginning to rise above the surface. They formed geysers that trailed up into space. Plumes of what looked just like smoke puffed up and began to reach towards me.

It was a stunning panorama, perhaps made more wild and savage because of the danger we were currently in. I think it was one of the most beautiful sights I had ever seen, though I was so worried that my mind was numb.

There was nothing I could do to change anything until we came into land. I was powerless. I felt almost as though the fall was happening to somebody else. I switched off and allowed my eyes to soak up what I was seeing.

It didn't last long, however.

The ground came up to meet us much faster than I had expected. Now the problem was going to be to adhere to the Starfish and avoid being bounced off to space at more than the tiny escape velocity. Then we had the slight detail of getting our charges out of the cold and into a breathable atmosphere. And there wasn't much time to do that. I had the feeling that Ouraali was running very low indeed on breathable air in her airbag. The tiny compression cylinder that was programmed to keep the oxygen levels stable was not going to last much longer.

As the ground barreled up to meet us, I gave the Nepheal woman a warning shout.

"Landing! Brace!"

The PSA smashed into a patch of ice on the Starfish and immediately skipped some ten feet away and rebounded again. I was dragged along behind it, quite unable to do anything to stop its momentum. So much for avoiding the bounce. I was quite incapable of influencing the PSA at all. It seemed to have a mind of its own.

We skipped along the ice, just like a flat pebble can be skimmed across water. Each bounce, thank goodness, was smaller. So long as we didn't hit a bump on the terrain, we should be all right.

No sooner had that thought occurred to me than I realized that we were heading straight for a small rocky outcrop.

I started to will the PSA enough height to clear it. Please. The jagged displacements of the billion-year-old crust could easily kill either Ouraali or me. Or both. It was only a small serration in the surface of the comet, but we certainly wouldn't come out of the collision unhurt.

The airbag was already in the air. I couldn't influence it.

The only thing I could influence was the rebound.

I gave a massive tug on one of the straps that ran around the outside of the Portable Safety Airbag and managed to propel myself up and over the top of the sack.

I hardly had any time to get myself into position before we came down on top of the barbed peaks.

I stared frantically at the spikes of rock, trying to place my feet on the smoothest part of them. I hardly had time to even look at them, let alone find the safest part.

Then we were down. I let my knees flex as the huge airbag and its contents smashed into me. Then I pushed downwards as hard as I could and ducked my back at the same time, trying to get some height on the PSA, trying to lift it just enough to slide over the outcrop without catching on any of the dangerous stone spears.

I shoved my whole strength behind the muscles of my legs.

For a moment I thought that I had not succeeded in changing anything.

Then the whole airbag began to somersault over itself in the air, dragging me around with it. I was clutching onto the straps for dear life.

We shot over the rocky heap and the whole package kept turning.

I remember swallowing.

If this thing kept cartwheeling over and over, chances were that on the next bounce I would be on the bottom side of the cube.

And that would not be good for my life expectancy.

However, it looked like I would have to wait quite some time before I found that out. We were sailing along at least ten meters off the ground. The impetus had pushed us quite a ways up off the surface.

The rotations were making me feel sick. I closed my eyes and when I opened them again I saw that the ground was much closer. We were about to hit.

I wondered if I should let go. But if I did, I could lose Ouraali altogether. I had no idea how far this cube would skitter across the surface before it finally stopped. If it did finally stop. She might hit another outcrop of rock. No, I would have to see this through to the end.

The only good thing was that we were actually traveling towards the ships, but I was far too terrified to be able to celebrate that.

The next bounce was upon us. I was lying flat against the bottom of the cube, watching the icy ground come up at me. I know I muttered a prayer. I have no idea who or what the prayer was addressed to. It just felt like a good idea at the time.

The ice got closer and closer until I could pick out the areas of roughness left by small parts of it melting and then refreezing. I wanted to close my eyes, but I was entranced by the approaching land.

Hanging upside down as I was, there was no longer anything at all I could do about it.

At the last minute I threw my head to one side and I am pretty sure my eyes turned white. I do know that it was out of the corner of my eye that I noticed things were changing. The angle of the terrain was no longer the same. The PSA was rotating onto its next facet.

It was only half way through the change when it hit the ground. The impact made it snap into the next face of the cube, accelerating the spin.

And that was where I lost any ability to see or sense anything. I think I passed out. I had wound my arms through the straps and when I became unconscious I was, miraculously, undislodged.

We tumbled over and over and over, completely at the will of the Starfish, until we finally came to a halt on a particularly icy patch of terrain.

My side of the cube was on top when it halted, and I lay there gasping as my brain reconnected with the outside world.

There was a tremendous crash just behind me and the sound of something heavy being stopped by the ground. It ground to a halt just behind me.

I was still unable to move when I heard footsteps approach.

Denaraz's admiring voice reached up to me. "That was quick thinking, Mallivan! We would never have got this close to the ships if you hadn't realized you could bounce the airbags across the terrain."

I began to laugh.

He had no idea why.

The fool had actually managed to follow my mad, careering passage across the surface of the planet. I didn't know whether to hit him or kiss him.

So I just laughed.

Finally, he joined in.

We were still clutching at each other when the crew from *Aenysia* arrived. We were only about a hundred meters away from the ships.

We got Ouraali and the girls inside and in the sick bay in record time. Both of the Nepheals were almost white instead of the lightish green they should be. Neither of them was able to walk unaided.

Zenzara went straight into a triage chamber. The Zeroth immediately pumped nanite mesh around her wound. Sibby gave me a hug. She was breathless and very pale, but she told me that she was fine.

I didn't stop any longer than that. I had to get to the bridge. One of my ankles was hurting like the devil, but I knew that it was something that a few hours in triage later would sort out.

I ran up to the bridge, hobbling as I did.

Both Anzany and Neema were on duty. They nodded to me as I came in and Anzany pointed to the viewscreen in front of us.

"They are still looking for the shuttles. I think both Sammy and Mel have managed to get away. So far. Unfortunately we can't move, because they might never find us if we do. We would have to disconnect the carbon cloud in order to hear what they were saying."

"I am taking *Aenysia's* last shuttle out."

Neema stared at me. "You can't do that! It isn't equipped with a carbon bubble! They will see you."

"That is the reason I am taking it out. Now, once I draw them away I want you to get both shuttles on board *Aenysia*. They should fit easily because I will have taken the second shuttle. I want you to get everybody back to Berennis."

Both girls stared at me. They didn't like their orders.

I went on, "Then please transfer the prisoners over to one of Ouraali's cruisers there and ask them to take them on to Ulon Prime. You will have to explain it all over ansible to the Macers. Some of you may be needed to give evidence, though I am hoping that you can bring *Aenysia* back here to find us."

"What about the rest of you?"

"I will take *Nivala*. Finding Cunningham again is essential. We know where he is now. We have no idea where he will go next. One of the ships *has* to trail him. Has to find out where his next base will be.

Denaraz will come with you on *Aenysia*."

"Scratch that. Denaraz will be on *Nivala*."

I swiveled around. The Tyzaran had come so quietly onto the bridge that I hadn't noticed him. "I thought you would stay with Zenzara?"

He shook his head. "Her injuries are serious, but not life-threatening. She won't leave unless I go with you."

I gave a harsh laugh. "She is hardly in a position to bargain. She is in a Zeroth machine!"

"True, but you know her. She is threatening to get out."

I rolled my eyes. That girl needed a serious talking to. Not that Denaraz wouldn't be useful. Otherwise Seyal and I would be alone. Well, we would have Segaton, of course, but a baby is pretty limited in its usefulness on a spaceship. "Fine. Glad to have you."

Neema looked at Anzany. She slid off her chair. "If you don't mind, Captain, I would like to volunteer as well."

I shook my head. "Sorry, Neema. I need both you and Anzany here on the bridge of *Aenysia*. Ouraali will take some time to recover. You have to somehow locate our two missing shuttles and retrieve them. You will need to be here. Both of you."

She was disappointed.

I tried to explain. "Look. The most important thing is that we have captured two of the three ringleaders. They must be taken back and tried. Be seen to be tried. That is the key to the future of the Major Shells and also to the Interstellar Enforcement Agency. Don't forget, we have also delayed the formation of the wormhole. We may even have stopped their plans altogether, although Bull obviously has access to all Chandrayanan's research. That is why *Nivala* has to continue to search for him. We cannot risk Cunningham rebuilding the facility someplace else."

"I see that. But taking a shuttle openly out there! They will just shoot you down."

I grinned. "They will have to catch us first. Don't worry. We can stay ahead of them. You just be ready. Once we have distracted the crew of the *Chibuzo*, you will have to act fast. They will soon realize that our ships have to be here on the Starfish. They will send out a whole flotilla to pin us down. We have to be out of here by then."

"Yes, Captain." Neither girl was looking particularly happy but I knew they would do their jobs.

"Thank you. If the worst happens and you leave now for Berennis, then as soon as the Macers clear you for another mission you can come and find us. What's left of us. Now, Anzany, can you come and help me clear that last shuttle for use?"

We left Neema on the bridge.

It didn't take long for us to clear the last shuttle of its tethers and have it ready for launch.

Denaraz and I swung out of the huge shuttle bay doors of *Aenysia* and swung up towards the debris cloud. I just hoped that we wouldn't be too late.

15

The debris cloud was still expanding out from where *Chibuzo* had been. We could see bodies in space, but it was far too late to save them. Even those in the PSAs would have perished by now. That made me angry. I hate wasted life.

I drove the shuttle at full throttle straight at the nearest container which was floating in space. When I got close enough I fired on it with the small pulse canon each Nepheal shuttle is equipped with. A hole blossomed out of one of its large flat sides, and a steam of what looked like loose grain rice or flour exploded soundlessly out into space. It looked like a white Rorschach test.

Chibuzo was putting down on the comet, but her shuttles, which had been carrying out a painstaking grid search for the hidden shuttles Mel and Sammy were driving, hurtled down onto our position.

"That got their attention," Denaraz said in a mild tone.

"Now all we have to do is keep it."

He grinned at me. "Shouldn't be difficult. Let me take a couple of pot shots directly at them. That will wake them up."

I hesitated. "That might start a war."

"Only a small one, surely?"

He looked so keen that in the end I was tempted to tell him to go ahead. But I couldn't. Even if they fired on us, it wouldn't allow me to fire directly back at them. Taking a couple of shots at a container floating in space was different. Who knows who owns containers floating in space? I had a good argument for removing a shipping danger.

I shook my head. "Only abandoned flotsam, Izan."

He huffed, but obediently slammed two more shots into floating containers. Both blew up with a satisfying flare and subsequent bleeding into space of the contents. One was some sort of liquid. We fired on it and were pleased to see that it was highly flammable. It went up with a satisfyingly big blaze of light, strong enough to reach all the way back to the Starfish and illuminate part of its extremities that the sun had not yet reached.

We leant forward and slapped palms.

I was looking for something interesting to shoot at when the lead Omnistate shuttle caught up with us. He fired directly at us.

"He doesn't seem to share your reticence about starting a war," said Izan in a bland tone.

I glared at my companion as I twisted the shuttle in a corkscrew to try to avoid being skewered by the pulse. "Very droll."

"Yes." He stretched. "I thought so too."

I managed to right the Nepheal shuttle after a bit of a battle with the helm. These things are bigger than Spacelander shuttles and a little more responsive. We whizzed over the heads of those in the Omnistate shuttle, straight at the nose of the second shuttle.

He hardly had time to react. I didn't.

Luckily, his instincts were fast. He threw himself and his spacecraft into a right turn, yawing away from the impact.

We almost touched skins as we passed in the sky. We were close enough to see the shapes of people on the small bridge.

Denaraz cursed and ducked.

"What good do you think ducking is going to do?"

He flushed. "I didn't duck."

"You definitely did."

He removed a fleck of non-existent fluff from his tunic. "I believe not."

"You're just lucky Zenzie didn't see you."

He paused and then gave a sheepish nod. "She would never have let me forget it."

"True."

"Will you?"

I began to laugh. "I shut my own eyes at one point, Izan. I couldn't swear to anything."

He looked ever so slightly relieved. Then his gaze tightened. "You may have overlooked it, but those two shuttles are both coming around for a second go at us. This could be a good time to retreat."

"Very good. I hope this thing can go as fast as the Nepheals say it can. We should be able to outrun them fairly easily if it can."

"Excellent. I was looking forward to a sightseeing trip around the local neighborhood. I have never been in a comet belt before."

"I am not sure you can really class the Starfish as a comet. It is in a fairly stable orbit around the sun."

"Asteroids don't have ice."

I shrugged. "No idea. We don't have many comets in the Landau Rift. I'm never sure how to classify all these space pebbles."

He clutched at his seat. "Incoming!"

I threw the shuttle straight down at the comet. We dipped under the incoming pulser beam, and shot past the firing shuttle.

I sighed. "I am going to have to come up with a solution. I can only do this so many times before they use both shuttles in combination. I won't be able to contort my way out of that."

"How long do we need to allow the others to get away?"

"Say they were still here in the debris cloud when we came up. Lying low. Then they would have run as soon as we opened fire. Half an hour to get into the shuttle bay of the *Aenysia*. Half an hour to get away." I checked my watch. "We need to keep them busy for another fifty minutes."

He looked extremely dubious. "Can't do it, Ryler, my friend. That is far too long. We will be surrounded by Omnistate vessels by then. We are going to have to go about this another way."

"There is no other way. We are dispensable. Our job is to buy the time for them to get clear."

Then he got a thoughtful expression on his face. I was surprised to see that his crests were up, but not completely. He was, as yet, unworried by the shuttle fire. Maybe he could come up with something.

He mulled it around in his head for several moments, then he turned back to me with a decided look about him.

"Do you think the Nepheals are particularly attached to this shuttle?"

Something inside of me lurched. "No-o-oo, I guess not. Why?"

"Well. I saw some research on comets like this one some years ago, and I believe that many of them contain a layer of micro particles underneath the surface. Miniature snowballs, if you like, made of a combination of ice and dust. They are around two to three millimeters, like the Styrofoam packing you get around fragile engine parts. And they are light like them too. Really light. If we can liberate a cloud of them from the surface they should coat the whole of the Starfish in a dense cloud that could take weeks to disperse. That would stop them finding their own mothers, let alone us."

Nothing he had said had alleviated my sense of doom. "And ...?"

"And all we have to do is cause a small explosion!" He sat back in his chair with a happy expression on his face, rather in the manner of a dog who has just dropped a juicy bone at his owner's feet.

"Is that why you asked me if the Nepheals are attached to this shuttle?"

"Of course. None of our pulse weapons is anything like strong enough. We will have to get up some serious speed and throw this whole thing at the comet."

I knew these Tyzarans were intelligent, but this was outstanding. It would never have occurred to me. I looked at him in awe.

"The only thing is," his face dropped and his crest stiffened. "We will have to abandon ship before it hits."

Even I could see the danger in that, and I didn't have any crests. "We can do that," I told him. I was actually quite cheerful about it. It was such a good idea. If we were lucky it might cause a bit of chaos with the bigger ships down on the surface of the Starfish. That would help. The fewer ships to follow us, the better. Especially the ones with the carbon cloud technology on board.

He spread his hands. "There might not be any of this aggregate below the surface, you know. It's just something I read."

"Whether there is or not, it is going to give them a nasty jolt and something except us to worry about." I wheeled us around and began to speed away from the comet. "What velocity do you need?"

He started to play with the console in front of him. "Hmm. This thing must weigh around between one and two thousand kilograms. We need to deliver something between four and six gigajoules of kinetic energy to carve out a crater big enough to release a big enough cloud of micro particles. So ..." he fiddled with some more numbers, "... I reckon that any speed over five thousand miles per hour should do it."

Now, I know that five thousand miles per hour doesn't sound much to anybody who travels in space, but you need to remember that we were currently at zero miles per hour, and we would be overrun by Omnistate shuttles pretty quickly.

I flashed him an irritated look. He wasn't asking much. Still, his idea was certainly better than mine, which had consisted in letting ourselves be blown out of the sky.

I pulled back on the throttle and laid on as much acceleration as I could, plotting an automatic course that would loop us out to pick up as much speed as possible and then take us back on a direct trajectory for the longest arm of the Starfish, well away from our two ships.

Then I nudged him towards the rear of the shuttle. "I think we need to get back into EVA suits."

We came up short some seconds later.

All of the EVA suits were designed for Nepheals.

I looked at him. He looked at me.

Then we both shrugged. At least they would be roomy. On the other hand, I wasn't sure they would work terribly well. Especially the helmets. The long faces of the Nepheals were about twice the size of a human face. I just hoped they would seal efficiently. In any case, we had committed to this course of action. We would slip out of the ship at the cusp of the curve, and watch everything from open space. Hopefully *Nivala* would be able to find us and pluck us out of the sky before we expired.

The Omnistate shuttles both piled on speed and tried to follow the shuttle. I found out that they had improved their ships in the last year. The Flatlander craft were easily able to pace the Nepheal shuttle. That was something to take into account in the future. Perhaps. If we had any future.

They shot at us as well. They were good at multitasking. Luckily, the speed was a disadvantage to their accuracy. We were only hit twice before we reached the cusp of the loop. I didn't think they would be able to alter the outcome once the ship was hurtling like an arrow at the Starfish. They would be getting too many screaming orders through their headphones. I didn't think the Terran command would take kindly to their nice shiny comet being dive-bombed.

We struggled to the hatch.

I knew there was a risk that the crew in one of the shuttles could peel off to grab us, but was hoping that at the speed we had all reached they would be past us before they could register that two lifeforms had left the craft.

We shot out of the back of the shuttle at a huge velocity. Even though the shuttle was only half way around its curve, it must have been travelling at several thousand miles per hour. Not that you would notice. There was only negligible gravity at that height and no air rushing past to denote speed.

We tucked a few flares into our tool belts. Then we clambered into the hatch. It opened out onto the blackness of space. I bent my knees and pushed off out of the opening. Izan followed within seconds.

We had roped ourselves together, loosely, so it felt to us as though we were hanging stationary above the starfish. We could see, looking down, the dots of ships on her longer leg. Our own shuttle was now changing course to flash down in a nose dive toward the comet.

Two Omnistate shuttles roared past us. They made no sound, but their engine flare illuminated our faces. We had to close our eyes as they crossed our line of sight.

One of the shuttles seemed to be slowing. Perhaps they had seen us, after all. But by then, it was becoming obvious that the intention was to ram the Starfish. The second ship seemed to stumble in space, then it accelerated after our shuttle again. The two Omnistate vehicles finally succeeded in closing in. They began to fire on our doomed shuttle, trying to evaporate it before there was any danger to the comet.

There were still other Flatlander ships in the area, though most of them had dispersed after the creation of the new wormhole had been aborted. We could see small streaks of light behind the engines of several that were on their way back to Earth. I could only spot three stationary ships in the area, now, and they were all far too far away to detect a couple of bodies out in space.

The shuttle had vanished into the night now. All we could see was the pinpoints of pulser fire that followed her on her journey down. Once there was a larger flare, as part of her fuselage was blown off when one of the Omnistate shots got through. It was enough to spin her slightly off course, but not enough to deviate the path far enough for her to miss the Starfish.

In the end she impacted right at the upper edge of the longest leg of the Starfish, some two miles from the Flatlander ships.

Izan and I stared down and waited. All I could hear was my own breathing in my ears.

The first flash was a small burst of yellow flame from the impact point of the comet as the shuttle was vaporized. The second flash saturated our retinas with a blazing white light that left us blinded.

My own eyes took over a minute to recover. Then I saw a plume of ejecta reaching out from the comet towards us, and another, larger, sphere of white blossoming outwards in all directions from the point of impact. It was like a snowstorm that blanketed out everything in its path. As I watched several of the large cruisers that were docked on the comet disappeared inside the white fog.

It looked as though Denaraz had been right. There had been a layer of micro particles under the surface of the comet, and the explosion had released a huge cloud of the loose aggregate. This was obediently obeying the laws of physics and bleeding out across the surface of the Starfish, as well as into space.

We couldn't see the stress wave that had been released into the rock, but we did see the result. Cracks were spreading out along the surface of the Starfish. We could see them because the ice was sublimating into clouds of steam. So, from above, it looked like trails of smoke were reaching across the surface in tendrils.

One Omnistate cruiser had been too close to the explosion. It teetered, before toppling gracefully to its side. I didn't think the resultant crash would be strong enough to kill its crew. The Starfish gravity was too small for that. In fact, it seemed to bounce benignly as it collapsed horizontally to the ground.

Just before the cloud of expanding micro particles shrouded it in anonymity, I thought I saw tiny figures struggle out of the hatches to examine the result. It must have been baffling to them.

The next thing we saw was that the three cruisers in the area had been called in to help with the effects of the blast. They moved carefully toward the comet, keeping their velocity down to a minimum.

The cloud had now enveloped all of the Omnistate leg of the Starfish and was slowly seeping over the joint to the other two legs. It reached almost half way out towards us, too, though it was dissipating much more rapidly out in space.

I started to stare at the place on the shortest leg where I knew our two ships were. It was hard to see anything, due to the brightness of the other side of the comet, but I did think I had spotted a small flare of engines.

I gave a tug to the rope that joined me to Izan, and pointed to his belt, gesturing five with my fingers. He nodded. We would give it five minutes and then set off the first of the flares. Hopefully, by then, the only ships in this particular area of space would be our own.

Taking a last look back down, the Starfish was almost completely engulfed in the white cloud, which obscured everything. The plumes of white dust now formed streaks in the sky, so that they almost looked like sunbeams creating a halo.

Then Denaraz pulled the ring on his first flare, and we had to turn our heads away and close our eyes.

We hung in space for what seemed like forever.

Nobody came for the first flare.

Or the second.

Or the third.

I was beginning to think that we were going to end our lives out here above the comet, tied together until the end of time. It sent a shiver down my spine.

I fumbled with the last flare and dropped it. Luckily, I was able to grab it back before it floated out of reach. I met Izan's gaze before pulling the ring on it.

I had expected his crests to be up, but they weren't. He looked quite calm and collected. I suppose the danger was past now. We were into the consequences, and he seemed resigned to accepting them philosophically.

I gave the flare a small push and watched as it edged away from our position, radiating light out to anybody watching. It was hugely bright to us, but barely a pinprick to anybody who was looking at this part of the sky.

When it began to die out, I could feel my spirits going with it. That was the last flare we had taken. Our suits were not equipped with any sort of communicator. We were so far out that we could travel on along this same vector forever, preserved for eternity by our EVA suits. It is not what I would have chosen, but as I thought about it I had to smile. It was not such a bad way for an astronaut to end his life. Even fitting, in a way.

I struggled to turn, to look one last time on the comet before my air ran out. It had been completely blanketed out by one large cloud of white powdery micro particles.

I looked over to Izan, and put my thumb up.

He nodded and did the same.

It was a pity he would never have a life with Sibby. They were so good together. They would have changed the Mallivan family, and it certainly needed it.

A large black shadow came between us and the white cloud.

I blinked, thinking that my body was already suffering from hypoxia.

A large doorway opened in the shadow. I thought I could see a shuttle bay inside it. It grew larger and larger until we were almost inside it.

I was having some difficulty figuring out what it was, until I saw a large figure who was brandishing, of all things, a boat hook.

The figure snagged the rope between Izan and myself and backed into the light, dragging us inside. It tethered us firmly to a railing and ducked behind us to close the gaping door.

I watched the shape as it pushed a large blue button.

It bustled around doing things until a blue light snapped on overhead. Artificial gravity engaged and we tumbled a foot or two to the deck plates. Then it removed its helmet.

I was still very groggy. I knew I recognized the figure, but I couldn't put a name to it. It was someone I knew very well. Somebody who I liked, I was sure.

The figure pulled my EVA helmet off. "Are you all right, Mallivan?"

I waved a hand, which is as much as I could do at that moment.

The figure moved to Denaraz and did the same thing. The Tyzaran seemed much more in control than I was. He said "Thank you, Seyal."

They both came over and peered at me. I could make out worried wrinkles across the Tyzaran's face. "His oxygen had run out. He needs a Zeroth chamber. Get him to a triage unit, will you?"

She picked me up and ran with me. I could see the overhead lights flicking past as she hurried along the corridor and into the lift. Then I closed my eyes.

I was safe. That much I knew. I thought I would go to sleep for a little while.

16

I woke up some time later. I was still in a Zeroth chamber. Seyal was sitting in a chair nearby with Segaton on her lap. She was crooning to him and the infant was smiling at his mother and babbling with pleasure.

When she realized that I was awake, she put her son down quickly and hurried over.

"Captain! How are you feeling?"

"Fine. I think. Can you get me out of this thing?"

She began to input the final cycle codes. "Of course. It was just a precaution. Denaraz said that you would be all right."

I was interested. "Were those his actual words?"

She blushed. "'Tough as an Avarak warrior's old boot,' was the expression used, I believe."

The door cycled open and I was able to step out. Nothing seemed to be broken. Even the ankle held up to my weight. I wondered how people had managed before Zeroth machines.

Seyal already had already turned away. She pointed behind her to some fresh clothes piled on a chair. "I got those from your cabin."

I couldn't help interrogating her as I got dressed. "Are we following *Chibuzo*? Did *Aenysia* manage to pick up the shuttles? Are the Enif safe? And Danaa? Did Chandrayanan and the admiral survive? Are Sammy and Mel safe? How is Zenzara?"

I would have gone on, but she already had one hand up and was counting off the answers on her fingers, still carefully not looking in my direction. "No, *Chibuzo* is still on the Starfish. She seems to have been damaged by the seismic activity after the explosion. We are at a safe distance, observing. Yes, *Aenysia* got away and has left for Berennis with all of them on board, as you instructed. Yes, the two prisoners were unharmed, if scared. All the others were relatively uninjured, just a few scratches and bruises. Your sister is looking after Zenzara, who is still in a Zeroth chamber, but will make a full recovery."

It seemed as though everything was under control. As I dragged the last of the clean clothes over my head I felt my shoulders relax. "Thank you, Seyal."

"You're welcome."

I walked past the pool and took the lift up to the upper deck. Denaraz was on the bridge. He raised his eyebrows when he saw me.

"That was quick."

"For an old boot."

His eyes twinkled. "We are to be family, are we not?"

"Oh, you can insult family, can you, if you are Tyzaran?"

"You can. It is a sign of affection."

"Hey! Wait a minute. Does that mean you want to marry my sister? Have you asked her yet?"

He nodded and shook his head, all at the same time. I interpreted that as yes to the first and no to the second.

I gave him a few slaps on the back and we exchanged a fist bump. "Congratulations!"

He stepped backwards. "I do not know if she will accept me."

"Of course she will. She is crazy about you!"

"But she is bound to a certain way of life. She may not feel she can marry."

That was true. I couldn't see my mother approving a marriage with an alien, as she would undoubtedly call Izan. "Hmm. Have you met Prime Mallivan?"

He shuddered. "I have not!"

I gave him a look. "I have seen you stand up to Vaer warriors, Denaraz! Are you telling me you are scared of one Spacelander woman?" Then I thought about my dear mother. "On the other hand, it would be wise to know what you are letting yourself in for."

"I can only *ask* Sibeal to marry me. I will understand if she cannot. I am bound by my promises to stay wherever the Chyzar goes. I cannot go to live with her on your family shipstation." His crests twitched.

"Sibby will find a way around that," I promised. "But it won't be easy. It won't exactly endear her to our mother either."

"I am aware."

"On the other hand, *I* have been exiled, and I am perfectly all right. It is hard to break with tradition, especially for a prospective prime, but it can happen."

He raised one eyebrow. "There may be some debate as to whether you are 'all right'."

I punched his shoulder and he pretended to stagger.

An amused voice behind us interrupted. "I can see you two are very busy, but you might like to look at the screens behind you."

We looked up at Seyal, who must have come in without us noticing, then at the screens. *Chibuzo* was lifting off the surface of the Starfish. Her unmistakable bow towers were just appearing out of the drifting white clouds of micro particles that still enveloped the comet.

We settled into our stations. Denaraz fired up the engines, but kept them at the lowest levels he could. We didn't want them to notice any emissions from this vector.

"Is our carbon cloud still working well?" I asked.

Seyal nodded. "Sibby told me that it could run as long as the ship did. She and Didjal figured out a way to plug it into the main engine frame.

It needs maintenance, though, so we will just have to pray that nothing goes wrong with it. Though Denaraz can probably troubleshoot small problems."

Izan looked up. His brow creased. "I worked a little on it, but I will only be able to manage quick repairs. I hope we can get the others on *Aenysia* back soon. How will they find us if we can't get to the rendezvous point?"

"We will leave them a trail of breadcrumbs," I told them. "We can't use any of the transmitters on the ship, and that includes the ansibles. Their emissions could be picked up, and we really need to find out where Cunningham will put his next hub of operations. I think they will abandon the Starfish. They know that it has been compromised, after all. They would be stupid to rebuild the facilities here. And one thing Cunningham is not, is stupid."

From the dumb expressions they gave me, I gathered that they had no idea why I was talking about breadcrumbs. "Never mind. You will see."

We let *Chibuzo* edge out away from the comet. She engaged her carbon bubble as soon as she cleared the remnants of the explosion. They were naturally taking no chances. Though they must have realized that we had a way to trace them even with the carbon cloud on.

I nodded to Seyal, and she slipped out of her chair. We were going to need our secret weapon again.

Scout trotted up onto the bridge looked exceptionally pleased with himself, Jaaven jogging behind him.

I bent to scratch behind the Geiga's ear. "Hello, hardhead. Did you miss me?"

His little tail performed endless circles in the air, so I supposed that he had. "Good boy! Did you behave yourself?"

Scout snuffled happily. I checked with Jaaven.

"He was ... reasonably quiet," he told me.

"Well done. OK. We are going to need him again. The Terran ship is on the move and has its carbon cover engaged. Their emissions level is so low that we can't follow them by checking their radian toxicity. It is below the threshold of the machine."

The Nepheal boy nodded. Then he looked around. "Where are the others?"

Of course. He had been in hiding with Scout. He had no idea of anything that had just happened.

"*Aenysia* has left to rendezvous with your cruisers."

The boy was still looking around. "And Danaa? Ouraali? How are they?"

"They are also recuperating well."

He nodded, relieved. He probably felt that he should have stayed with them. I hadn't even considered the boy. Oh well, too late now. Not that I could have done very much about it in any case. But I hoped that I hadn't put him into too much danger. He was only a boy.

Scout had decided to run after his tail. He was galloping around and around in a circle, making little squeaky noises. I put my hand down on the scruff of his neck and exerted a small amount of gentle pressure. He began to slow, and then came to a stop.

"Scout, stop it! We need you to lead us to Cunningham."

But the Geiga ignored me. He must feel that Cunningham was no longer a threat to us. I was not sure whether to be pleased about that or sorry that we couldn't follow *Chibuzo* directly. I found myself simply staring down, with no idea of which path to take.

"I have the vector!" It was Denaraz.

"How the krikk did you manage that?"

He grinned back at me from the Navigator's station. "They are suspicious. They are using quantum radar to try to detect any cloaked ships."

That didn't help me join the dots. He must have seen the question mark over my head. "Remember back on Vaer Nova? When Sibby managed to disable the field?"

"Yes. She used that drone."

"She could do that because the drone interfered with the DEX repeaters. She showed me how. So I knew that any technology using quantum radar would be amplified in the same way. And that, it turns out, is trackable. We have to be very close, like now, and we need to pick up various sightings so that I can triangulate a position and a vector." He smirked. "And we are, and I have!"

"Well? Where are they heading? Earth? The Moon? Mars?"

His smile slipped a little. "Err … no. Actually they are heading out on a tangent to the ecliptic. They are heading as far away from all the planets as they can."

That didn't sound right. "In the opposite direction?"

"Completely. If they go on as they are, they will come to a position high above the planets, looking down on their orbits."

"There is nothing in that area?"

"Nothing at all. Not even a stray comet penetrates that far off the main planetary plane. You'd be lucky to find a loose asteroid up there. I mean, to get deviated that far away from their original orbit they would have to have undergone a catastrophic collision. And that would have been more likely to destroy them rather than send them so far off course."

I thought.

Actually it was a very good idea. If they stayed away from the busy parts of the solar system, which is basically all of the ecliptic —where you can find the planets and asteroids—it would be virtually impossible to find them. The only material crossing such a position would be an occasional long period comet coming in from the outer Oort cloud, way beyond the Omnistate Termination Shock. They would be safe from discovery. The nearest planet would be seven billion miles away. And, let me tell you, you can't detect much at seven billion miles. It would be like looking for a neutrino in a void.

I set a course to copy their heading and we began to trail them slowly. Denaraz warned me that their quantum radar would mean that they might detect *Nivala's* presence at anything less than ten thousand miles.

I looked down at Scout. The Geiga had fallen asleep, his back legs sprawled out behind him, his snout on his two front legs. He looked cute. I was tempted to shake him awake, but it really wasn't his fault. Denaraz had given us a heading to follow. The only thing we could do was to follow that lead and hope that the Omnistate wouldn't deviate too much from it.

I knew what I had to do. I left Denaraz in charge of the bridge and went down to the waste containers, way down in the belly of the ship. These were situated right at the back, at the rear of two small holds to the side of the engines. This is where our toxic waste was stored until it could be dumped planet-side in special recycling facilities.

I dumped part of the starboard size radian toxicity surplus as soon as I got down there. Then I waited another fifteen minutes to dump about a quarter of the port surplus. That should give the others a pretty good idea of the direction we had taken. I knew that they would be back as soon as they could. I doubted *Aenysia* would accompany the prisoners to Ulon Prime, despite my instructions. I couldn't blame them; in their shoes I would do the same. They would soon be back in the Sol system, if Ouraali had any say in the matter, and I thought that they would be monitoring for radian toxicity. These two dumps would show up from light years away. I had, effectively left them a beacon that would point them in the right direction. And the beauty of it was that nobody else would see the significance, because only the Enforcement Agency had realized that ships could be traced by their toxicity reading. The scanners were not standard issue on Omnistate vessels, so the idea of their adaptation for detection purposes was unlikely.

I went back up the bridge, feeling pleased with myself.

Denaraz was looking impressed. "Were those your 'breadcrumbs'?" he asked.

I nodded.

"More like fireworks!" He showed me his visor. The two dumps were shining like spotlights in an otherwise dark sky around us. "How did you get them to stop like that?"

"I just programmed the scows to decelerate to null velocity when jettisoned. Those scows have a small engine attached to enable easy maneuverability near recycling stations. They aren't powerful, but they were enough to negate the residual momentum." Scows are space containers for waste. It is illegal to dump such things in open space. I'm afraid, for once, that didn't concern me.

"Danaa won't miss them. When she sees those sparkles on the scanner she'll think it's her birthday."

"Do you think they are heading for Eris or Pallas?" asked Seyal, who had been pouring over a map of the solar system. "Those seem to be the only large bodies that orbit the sun with a high orbital inclination."

I checked on the astrogation plotter. "Nope. Eris is over on the other side of the solar system right now and the angle they are taking is much too tangential for Pallas. They appear to be heading to a position directly over the sun, as far away from the planets as they can possibly get. I can't even find any comets passing through there at the moment." I checked again. "Halley's is due through in twenty years."

"Looks like Cunningham plans to set up shop in the middle of nowhere."

"We are lucky he hasn't spotted us so far. Let's hope he never does."

"What do you think they will use as fuel?"

"A water source? No idea. Maybe they will lasso a passing comet?"

Seyal gave me a look.

"What? It's not such a stupid idea as all that. If it's a small one. All you would have to do is push in the opposite vector to its direction. Should be easy to slow it down. Then it would just slip into a solar orbit and Bob's your uncle."

She rolled her eyes, which I took to be doubt as to my sanity. I thought it was a very good idea. It would give them a base, just like the Starfish, but in an area where nobody would ever find them.

"They will set up a supply line," suggested Denaraz. "That shouldn't be too difficult."

"I don't know. Traveling outside the ecliptic uses much more fuel. You are going against the lowest energy trajectory." Ships always try to travel in the plane of the planets, and in the direction of their motion. Otherwise you are struggling against that initial velocity. It also means that you can't slingshot around any stellar bodies to aid your acceleration at no fuel cost.

"All right. At that snail's pace they are going, it is going to take them four days to get towards the edge of the solar system over the sun, so we might as well drop to one on, two off shifts. We all could use some sleep and relaxation. I will take the first shift. Denaraz, you take the second, and Seyal can come up for the third. It is time Jaaven had a break from Scout, so I will spell him with the Geiga for my relaxation hours."

The Nepheal boy looked pleased. He had been taking his pet-sitting duties extremely seriously and his small face was strained. "Please, Captain, will you teach me how to swim?"

I stared. "Don't you do that on Nephealis?"

"No, Sir. None of my race knows how to swim. I should like to try."

Hmm. He was a bit big already for our small pool, but that would help rather than hinder at an early stage. "Sure. Why not?"

His face split into smiles and he almost ran off the bridge with Scout. "Thank you, Mr Mallivan. Thank you very much!"

It took me all of three seconds to realize who Mr. Mallivan was. I really was getting old.

"You're welcome!"

It was three days later, after some pleasant days of recuperation, that Scout suddenly showed signs of picking up danger again.

I was in the pool, fruitlessly trying to show a four-legged Nepheal how to swim.

The water was a dangerous place to be. Jaaven, though still young, was twice my height and totally unable to dominate his legs in a watery environment. I had already been kicked twice, and was regretting agreeing to teach him. It had not occurred to me that Nepheals might lack the coordination to swim.

This was complicated by Scout's having decided that if we were both in the water, his place was beside us. The Geiga was paddling around generally getting in the way, having finally overcome his aversion to the pool.

Jaaven went under the water for about the tenth time and came up choking and coughing. "I will *never* learn," he wailed.

"Of course you will!" I backed up a little, having just received another blow to my stomach. Nepheals are strong; I was finding breathing a little difficult.

"Sorry! Did I kick you again?"

"No, no. Keep going. Now, why don't you try to copy what Scout is doing? He has four legs too. Maybe your style of swimming will be less like mine and more like his?"

Jaaven's face fell, though he did study the movements Scout was making in the water. When he attempted to emulate them, he made some progress.

"There! That is the way to start, then. You need to practice that for the time being. Once you can keep yourself up on the surface like that we can attempt something a little more sophisticated. We are going to have to come up with a new way of swimming. One more suited to your physiology."

Scout suddenly gave his high pitched note of warning. He stopped paddling and tried to point in the direction of the danger. This put him under the water. He panicked and gave to the surface squealing in terror.

I swam over, hoiked him out by the scruff of his neck and deposited him on top of the wall of the pool. His front and back legs draped down on different sides. All were moving futilely in a sort of feeble attempt to gallop.

I sighed, swam to the ladder and got out of the water. It only took a moment to fish Scout off the top of the wall and deposit him on the floor.

He shook himself all over, spraying me with streams of water. Then he turned round and around several times, trying to pick up the direction of the danger he was sensing.

Within seconds he was determinedly pointing towards the saloon.

"They have changed course. Drat!" I quickly toweled myself dry.

Jaaven's long face was peering over the top of the pool. "What is happening?"

"Cunningham must have managed to piece together all the data again. The threat is back, and they have changed course. I have to get to the bridge."

The water streaming down his face made it look even longer. "Do you need me?"

"Not just yet. Why don't you practice a little more on your own? I will have to keep Scout on the bridge for the time being. You can bring his basket up when you are done here."

"Of course."

I grabbed Scout in my arms and padded out of the pool and up in the lift.

Denaraz, whose turn it was on the bridge, raised his eyebrows at the sight of two bedraggled creatures arriving, still dripping water.

Then he noticed that Scout's tail and snout were pointing directly backwards and forwards, respectively.

"He senses them?"

I nodded and plonked the Geiga on the decking. He didn't hesitate this time, settling straight away into an arrow indicating the starboard side of the ship.

His bristles were also at right angles to his skin, so he looked much bigger than he usually did. This was a defense mechanism that the

Geigas use to try to dissuade their attackers.

I realized he must have been like that as I carried him up. His bristly hair had pricked into my skin, which was now coming up in angry red bumps. I swore. I hadn't even felt a thing in my haste to get him to the bridge.

"You look like a cross between a lobster and a pincushion," said Denaraz, enjoying my discomfort.

"Yeah, whatever. Just change course, will you?"

He finished inputting the change. As we watched, Scout shuffled to the left so that he was pointing directly almost directly ahead. Both Denaraz and I studied the angles.

"About five degrees to port, I would say. Wouldn't you?"

He nodded and programmed the course correction. This time, Scout was as near as krikk exactly facing the bows of *Nivala*.

"Slow us down, as well, will you Izan? I don't want to run the risk of being spotted. How far are we now from the Termination Shock exactly perpendicular to the Ecliptic?"

He peered at the screen in front of him. "Half a million miles. Give or take."

"Near enough to take it very slowly from now on. We need to find them without being seen. It doesn't matter if it takes a few days longer. Cunningham isn't going to be able to reproduce that wormhole immediately."

"There is one problem."

"What?"

"If they do the same as last time, many other ships will arrive at the same coordinates. There is, after all, little point opening a wormhole if there are no ships to go through it."

He had a point. I thought about it. Then I shook my head. "I don't think they will go about it the same way this time. I think his priority will be to open a traversable macro wormhole as quickly and as quietly as possible. Once it is open, we would be unable to close it down again. We would have lost all chance of preventing them from using it to get to other galaxies."

"You're right. It was the Alliance that determined the Termination Shock as being the limit of their system. As long as they are inside that, we can do nothing about it. Once the ER bridge is up and running, we would be completely helpless to change anything."

"I think," I said slowly, "that the Omnistate has some sort of a hidden depot up here in the middle of the black. Somewhere they know they can fall back to if attacked. I think they will have constructed some sort of small space station in space. Here, where no self-respecting astronaut would even think of going. And that is why Cunningham is heading so far off the beaten track."

"Makes sense. That is good. If there is flotsam in space we should be able to pick it up."

"Yes. Let's cruise on for the next twenty-four hours like this, and then we will search for anything in the near surroundings. Can you carry on here? I need to add another breadcrumb to our trail."

"You do that. I have the feeling that we are going to need *Aenysia*. We may have to go in with all guns blazing this time."

"For sure. This is going to be our last chance at stopping the Omnistate. I just hope we can."

"One good thing, at least. There have been no communications from them since the Starfish. And Seyal was monitoring them there. They have not passed this technology on."

I was sure about that. "Bull Cunningham would never pass this technology on. It would mean he would lose control. This whole thing is all about giving himself power. He will keep it to himself, even if the discovery is lost to the Omnistate. This never was about his loyalty to them, however much he claimed it was. This was an ego trip to empower one person, and one person only."

"You think he is aiming for Ethnarch Locke's job?"

"Of course he is. He wants to prise open the rest of the universe via the wormholes. He will then control so much of space that they will have no choice but to elevate him. I wouldn't give two credits for

Locke's chances. Would you?"

"No. You are right. Cunningham must have had a subagenda all this time."

"It has to end here, Izan. Otherwise he will have so much traction that we will never be able to stop him."

His crests were up. "Agreed."

We exchanged a long look. I would do my very best to arrest Cunningham and take him for trial. But I simply could not afford to let him escape again. He was getting closer and closer to opening a traversable wormhole and there would be no holding him back when he did. I had hoped that arresting Chandrayanan would delay his plans, but from Scout's recent reaction it looked as though that was not going to happen.

About six hours later, Seyal held up her hand. "I have something on the scanner."

I joined her at her station. "What?"

"See?" She pointed at a small dark clump, right on the edge of the scan. "Here."

"What could that be?"

Denaraz had come over too. His face wrinkled as he tried to make sense of the images. "I think it must be some sort of asset dump," he said finally. "It isn't dense enough for a ship or a space station."

"An asset dump?" I had never heard of such a thing.

"Sure. My government has a few of them scattered around the Major Shells."

That was news to me. And, I suspect, everybody outside the Tyzaran fleet.

I must have blinked, because he looked taken aback. "Don't the Spacelanders have them?"

"Not as far as I know." Then I thought about it. "Which isn't really saying much because I suppose I wouldn't know anyway. They might. Can you tell me what exactly they are?"

He gave a sigh. "They are places where a large quantity of water and other essential supplies are held in silos or containers. They are meant to enable a fleet to be autonomous for long periods, if there is a war or some sort of natural catastrophe. Usually stocks are replenished and refreshed every few years by a small convoy which changes out the old for the new."

"Are they manned?"

"Oh yes. A skeleton crew only, of course. All asset dumps are fitted with explosives so that they can be destroyed if alien fleets attempt to use them for resupplying."

"That must be a popular posting."

He grinned. "Usually you have to do something really stupid to get posted out to one of the asset dumps."

"How many do you have?"

He pressed his lips together. "I like you very much and we are about to be brothers-in-law, but I don't think I should answer that question. I have probably already said too much."

I could understand his reticence. I didn't think that the Supreme Council would appreciate his talking about their secret stashes of food. Something else occurred to me. "Do they include ammunition?"

"Usually. Yes."

"Hmm. Interesting." I turned to Seyal, who had Segaton perched on one hip. He was getting big now that he was a toddler; she could hardly carry him. "Does that fit with the image?"

She nodded. "Yes, that fits well. What I am seeing on one of the arms could well be large cylindrical silos all attached to some sort of central docking arm. It is quite a large installation. If that is what it is, it could probably feed and fuel a whole Omnistate division for a couple of years."

"That is their destination, then. Can we get there first?"

She leant over the screen to do the calculations. "Yes. Easily."

"Do it. We don't know how many other ships will be arriving there soon, and if we want to get in close to *Chibuzo* this may be our only chance. Oh, hang on a minute. I will just drop off another breadcrumb."

She nodded, waiting until I gave her the signal. *Nivala* shot forward. We covered the remaining distance to the asset dump in record time. She brought us to within a kilometer and then stopped the ship so that we could examine our new destination.

It was hard to see well. This far out in the solar system there was only a trace of light from the sun, and there was nothing for it to reflect off in millions of miles. There was no artificial lighting on the installation, either, so it loomed a little gloomily in the dark star-studded sky.

The containers seemed to consist of two types, rectangular and round. The rectangular were the normal space containers for general provisions and loose grain; the cylindrical ones were for water, oil and other liquids. Mainly water, of course. In actual fact the asset dump consisted of many long rectangular beams of about a hundred meters, all of which spiked outwards from a central hub. Containers were attached to each of the four sides of the beams at regular intervals. The beams were hollow so that staff could patrol the installations, and the very front and the very back of each beam had been left free to house a small control box. It didn't look very comfortable. There might just about be room for a desk and a chair, I thought.

Each rectangular beam measured about three meters in width and was the same height as the containers. The rectangular storage containers were half pots, as they were known in the trade. Instead of the eight meter by eight meter giants used by the Tyzarans and the Nepheals, they were eight by four by four. There was space for twenty five of them along each side of the rectangular beam, making a capacity of a hundred in total.

Other beams that protruded from the hub had the long rounded cylinders for liquids attached to all four of their sides, so that they resembled more crossed dumbbells than anything else. Unlike the containers, which were attached by their shorter cross-section to the beams, these liquid tanks were set lengthways along the spokes of the hub.

All of these platforms had been loosely joined together in a most unusual way. They were tethered to a large round metallic structure that almost reminded me of a supersized crown such as the ones that ancient kings used to wear on Earth. It was like a large ladder on its side that had been curved into a circle. The rungs and sides of the ladder were fashioned out of hollow tube around two meters in diameter. Every twenty-five meters one of the rectangular beams was joined rigidly to it by socket flanges so large they made my eyes open wide.

The hollow tubing then continued in beyond the circle to a larger control room right in the center of the circular ladder. This was much larger than the boxes to the front and rear of each rectangular beam. It was clearly where the staff of this asset dump would be living.

The whole circular structure contained ten spokes leading to ten rectangular beams. The width of the whole thing was two hundred meters, so that the spokes were each around a hundred meters. Then they passed into the rectangular beams that stretched another hundred meters out into space. The entire thing was a huge wheel that hung stationary in the darkness.

I peered towards it. "Are those engines in the central hub?"

Denaraz copied me. "I would imagine so. Each beam will be detachable and will have small positional engines, but the central hub will be maneuverable. It has to be."

"Will it not be in a stable orbit? Or is it too far out from the sun?"

He shrugged. "Anything within the Termination shock is inside the Sun's gravity well. That attraction probably extends half way to Alpha Centauri. But the forces this far out are extenuated. A small particle collision can alter an orbit. They will be continually monitoring in case micro-corrections are necessary."

I nodded. "That is why those containers are so thick."

"Of course. And I would guess that it is also why they have chosen a position so far away from the planetary orbits. Out here there is very little chance of a random collision with anything left over from the protoplanetary disc."

I liked the look of the thing. "Are all those tubes and beams hollow?"

"They must be. They will be at normal air pressure so that the containers can be hand-checked at regular intervals."

I smiled. "And *Chibuzo* will be taking on fuel and provisions, right?"

"I should think so."

"Then I guess it's time you and I went for a walk. They will be leaving their back door open."

Seyal opened her mouth to protest, but we both gave her such a look that she closed it again with a snap that surprised Segaton, who burst into loud tears.

"You will stay with *Nivala*, Seyal. Your job is to hover just off that water line." I pointed to the one line that had only the first six cylinder slots occupied out of the ten possible. "That should be the one with the least daily movement. I want you to keep the ship stationary with regards to the asset dump and about fifty meters out. Nothing else will come that close to this hub, and we can always eject out of the rear control box if we have to. Keep your eyes peeled, will you?"

She nodded and put the squalling infant down on the floor, where he lay full length on the floor and began kicking the deck with both his hands and his little feet.

Denaraz bent down and touched the little fellow's arm. "Desist!" he commanded.

Segaton rolled onto his back to see who had touched him. He saw the large Tyzaran towering over him and stopped crying immediately.

Denaraz glared at Seyal. "You are spoiling the child," he said, before stalking back to his station.

The Avarak muttered something in her own language. I only know a few words of Avarak so was not able to translate fully. I think the gist was that she didn't need pointy-headed double-crests telling her how to bring up her own child.

Denaraz wisely refrained from answering.

There was a deferent cough from the corner. I swung around. Jaaven was looking at me, hope in his eyes.

"May I come with you, Captain?"

He was so eager that I was almost tempted, but this was not going to be a place for an adolescent Nepheal. I shook my head. "I need you to stay here with Scout," I told him.

His face dropped. He gave a lethargic kick to the deck. "I have done nothing since I got here."

"Your time will come, Jaaven. Keep alert and be prepared to defend the ship and act when necessary."

He straightened slightly. "Yes, Sir."

I almost peered behind me to see if Captain Tevis was standing eerily behind me. It felt so wrong to be addressed by that three-letter word. I gave the boy a nod and he escorted Scout off the bridge. Both Scout and the boy gave me the exact same accusing look as they went. I sighed.

Once Seyal had brought the ship around to the beam that had been half emptied of its containers, Denaraz and I began to suit up. We would stash the EVA suits somewhere in the rear control room, so that they would be there if we needed them. We decided to take some spares along with us, in the hope that we would be able to bring Cunningham back with us, firmly under arrest.

Getting inside the facility provided us with a bit of a challenge. Until we saw the vent stacks above each cylindrical container. That gave us the clue.

You can't pump water out of a tank without air coming in. All deposits of water are provided with air vents. In the case of this facility, they were using the same air that was pumped into all of the corridors.

Each cylindrical tank had an exterior nozzle where the ship would dock, and an overhead vent pipe that curved out of the top of the tank and over into the central passageway of the rectangular beams. There would undoubtedly be alarms set on all emergency hatches and on the container hatches themselves. I doubted very much that there would be any such thing on the vent piping as it curved overhead. All we had to do was replace a section of the piping with a hatch.

In the event, it took us hours to cut through the piping on the side furthest away from the central hub. We took it in turns to cut until, finally, Denaraz got through.

He battened himself over the now loose piece of metal as I wrestled with a deployable hull patch.

All ships carry such patches for temporary repairs. They are made of a rigid material which cannot be bent but can be cut. We know it as spaceplate. Since the pressure in a hull breach is from inside to out, if you can open a piece of spaceplate big enough to cover the breach, it will seal the hole and prevent total loss of oxygen while you attempt to sort out a more permanent solution.

It sounds easy, but in fact these things are extremely difficult to get correctly in place. You have to be pretty quick or the air is already gone.

In this case, we needed to be very speedy indeed. We knew that the caretaker or caretakers of the installation would be monitoring the air pressure, so we needed to get ourselves in through the hole, and the hole tapped, before the air pressure monitor in the main control room was triggered.

Izan was giving me frantic rolls of his eyes. I gathered that he couldn't hang on for much longer. I positioned myself to one side of the hole and waved him to the other. Then I began to count down on my fingers, starting with five and then bending one out of the way each second. Four, three, two, one ...

Izan threw himself to one side.

The loose piece of metal shot away from the vent tube and set off on a long voyage to an unknown destination.

We dragged ourselves through the hole against the escape wind. I slapped the patch in the center of the hole and then deployed the two sides. It bulged out towards open space in the center and then decided to hold.

We braced our legs against the sides of the air vent and stayed absolutely quiet for some time, waiting to see if the air pressure gauge had been triggered.

It hadn't.

We were in.

17

The first thing we did after dropping out of the vent tubing in the ceiling of the rectangular beam was edge our way along the main corridor towards the small control box at the rear of the module.

There was little room to hide anything, but we did find a storage space under the bench that was presumably used for seating and sleeping, if necessary. The thing had been built into the deck plating, and the area underneath the seat was divided into metal bins. They were not currently in use.

We pulled our own EVA suits off and stashed them, together with the spares, under the bench. Then we stared at each other. I still had no fixed plan, but it was clear that if we wanted to have a chance to board *Chibuzo* we were going to have to get inside one of the containers. We no longer had individual carbon clouds that worked, so we couldn't hide in open sight any more. And there were too many containers. Unless we were in charge of which ones were transferred, we would never have enough time to get a stowaway inside. No, we would have to take over this asset dump and hope that the caretakers were not recognizable figures. That meant that one of us would have to stay to operate the machinery, and only one would be able to enter the Omnistate vessel. I just hoped that the others would find their way here before the assets were transferred. It was hoping for a lot.

Along this particular arm of the asset dump four of the ten cylinders were missing on all sides of the rectangular beam. So instead of its total 40 silos, there were only 24. The last part of the beam had been denuded and jutted out of the background like a stripped antenna. I couldn't see why any of the caretakers would bother to tramp all this way out. Of course, there might be some bright spark who believed in jogging around all ten spikes to do his full kilometer. Based on what Denaraz had told me about the staff on this kind of installation, I rather doubted that. I thought they were more likely to be huddled together in the central command module drinking coffee and talking about their retirement. At least, that is what I hoped.

I signaled to Denaraz to follow me and we crept along the rectangular beam towards the central hub. Gravity was artificial, and seemed to be around three-quarters Earth standard.

We skulked down the passageway, making no sound. The metallic tubing on a thing like this would reverberate for many hundreds of meters, and the slightest noise could alert the caretakers to our presence.

We were soon at the end of the rectangular beam, at the point where it joined the fixed platform of circular tubing. There was a hatch through into the inner ring.

We exchanged a glance. Then Izan shrugged. We had only one option ... to go forwards. If it was set with an alarm, then that was simply too bad. We agreed to duck through and separate if there was any noise. We would play it by ear from that point on.

I turned the wheel on the hatch, and pushed. For a few moments I thought that we were safe, then a dim ringing sound started up in the center of the platform and I heard a muffled curse and footsteps coming our way at a run.

There were only three ways to go. Left, right or straight on. Straight on was not an option; that way led to the command center and the footsteps were coming from there. Denaraz ducked to the left, and I took the right tube.

Now we were in a much smaller environment. Each tube was a little over two meters in diameter – just large enough to allow a grown man to stand up straight. The walkway was made of steel mesh and rattled as you walked. It would be hard to go unheard on it.

I made up my mind quickly. I ducked along the outside perimeter tube and then down the next spoke that led into the center. Taking advantage of the noise that the Caretaker was making in his tube, I sprinted as lightly as I could along the spoke until I came to the central command module.

There was only one man left on duty. He was wearing a headset and had his back to me. It took only a moment to race up to him and disarm him. I already had him gagged when Denaraz appeared at my side. We quickly bound him to the chair and tried to intimidate him into absolute silence. It wasn't particularly difficult. His heart was pumping so fast that it seemed to be trying to clamber out of his chest. The poor man had nearly had a heart attack.

We could hear the footsteps returning from the hatch now.

A voice thundered down the pipe. "You flat fool! You forgot to turn the wheel on number four hatch again! I don't know why I put up with you! I am going to ration your sugar intake for this! What if somebody had come to steal all our supplies, eh? Then what would you have done?"

Our prisoner rolled his eyes until I could see only white. He slumped in his chair. The strain had been too much. He had passed out.

A large bear of a man rolled down the last section of tubing and appeared at the joint with the command center. He stopped, staring in disbelief at the sight of his coworker bound to his chair.

He was far, far too slow for Denaraz. The caretaker had barely begun to move his hand towards his pulser when the Tyzaran flung the male variation of the thoria at his throat. It wrapped round and round his neck with no sound and he dropped onto the plating with an enormous crash. The loose mesh clattered and then the plating bent under his weight.

Denaraz ducked down and tied the man up carefully before removing the thoria which was threatening to throttle him. The Tyzaran carefully unwound it and slipped it around his waist again, where it served as a prosaic belt when not needed for more aggressive purposes. The whole process can't have taken more than a minute. I was impressed.

He shrugged. "They teach us stuff like that when we are small."

I wondered what they taught them when they were big.

The large man was thrashing about and threatening us with all sorts of dire consequences. I decided that the priority was gagging him. No wonder he had been put out here in the middle of nowhere. I pitied the poor soul who had been sequestered out here with him.

"You'll be sorry!" he was shouting. "They will space you as soon as they arrive! They will know you aren't caretakers!"

"Now how will they know that?" I asked, bending over him.

He slammed his mouth shut and glowered at me.

"Is there some kind of password? Now, that's interesting."

He blanched. He couldn't hide his physical reaction. I bound his mouth securely.

"Izan, find somewhere to stash these two Flatlanders, will you?" He nodded. "And then see if they have any recordings of recent arrivals here, will you?"

"We are going to take their places?"

"We are."

"How are you going to hide my crests?" He seemed quite eager, just mildly interested to know the logistics.

"I haven't got that far yet."

I sat down at the consoles and tried to figure out exactly how the asset dump worked. I heard Izan stomping around and then he came back and began dragging the thinner of the two caretakers out by his shoulders. "They have two Zeroth chambers. I think a long nap is indicated."

Perfect. That would keep both of them quiet for as long as needed. I looked at the now-prone giant, who was glaring at us balefully. "Sweet dreams."

It took Denaraz more energy to drag the heavier caretaker out of the room, but he was back soon, whistling happily between his teeth. "Does your sister want more children?"

"What?"

"I don't know what the protocols are for Spacelanders."

"She already has her standard six."

He smiled. "But they are not mine."

"Do you want your own?"

"Naturally. Will that be possible?"

"I … I guess. I don't know what the rules are about mixed marriages between the Major Shell races. Would that be a problem on Tyzar?"

He shook his head. "I am allowed two progeny. If the Supreme permits it, that might be amplified to three or even four. I only have one so far. I would wish to use up my quota with your sister."

It wasn't the most romantic thing I had heard, but we Spacelanders don't do romance. "You don't expect her to carry them herself do you?"

He was horrified. "No, of course not!"

"Go for it, then!" It would mainly be a bureaucratic decision. Whether stores on Zenubi would be transferred to stores on Tyzar or not. Whether such a transfer would be approved. The actual progeny would be generated artificially and incubated until they could be removed to their parents.

"Thank you, Mallivan. I appreciate your encouragement."

"Not at all. Now get to those recordings, will you? I think there is some sort of password used between the ships and this asset dump."

He dipped his head and began to trace back through all of the archives he could find. I heard him give a grunt of satisfaction as he found something worth watching and then he fell silent.

Chibuzo arrived at the asset dump about an hour later. I had had time to practice how to be a caretaker. The archives had shown us what was required by us in order to supply the ships that were coming in and we were ready and very willing to be of service to them.

The Omnistate battlecruiser came to a full stop in space some two miles out from the platform. Her lights went on and off and a bored bridge officer contacted us.

"*Chibuzo* to Platform Six."

I pushed the comlink. "Platform Six here."

"Code ER 1/14"

"Accept code ER 1/14." I frantically looked down at the notes I had taken. "Return code BX 9/11"

There was a brief hesitation, before the comlink crackled again. "Confirm code BX 9/11. Stand by for asset list."

"Standing by." I crossed my fingers. We needed them to requisition fuel supplies. Using a loose grain transfer to enter their ship would be impossible.

I was able to breathe a sigh of relief a few moments later. They wanted eight containers: one of bulk flour, one of bulk grain and six of water. The water would be perfect.

I had already practiced the way that containers were loaded into the visiting ships. It was quite basic. Each container was released by the command center, then scooped up by one of the asset dump haulers and deposited on the outer platform of the visiting ship. Once there, it would automatically latch on to the space conveyor and be transferred inside the ship. The hauler would wait where it was for one of the empty containers to be hitched onto the space conveyor and transferred outside the ship and back to the asset dump, where it would eventually be exchanged for new stores. All this was done by remote control.

I was just in the process of acknowledging the requisition order when I heard the metal mesh walkway in one of the access tubes give a suspicious rattle. Both Denaraz and I leapt away from the center consoles and towards the passageway in question.

There was a shimmer of movement in front of me and Sammy appeared at the entrance. He looked very disheveled.

"Captain," he said, extricating his gear from the tube with some difficulty. "Lucky I haven't been eating very much recently."

I gave him a hug. "You found us then? How is Zenzie?"

Mel pushed past Sammy and grinned over at me, answering my question herself. "Cross that we wouldn't let her come. The Zeroth was able to stabilize her. She is up and about and back to complaining."

I felt a wash of relief. "Thank krikk for that. Are the others with you?"

She nodded and stood aside as others moved inside the command hub. "I have brought the two Enif, together with Sibby. Neema is here too, but Anzany is back on *Aenysia*."

As she spoke, they began to enter the command center, one at a time. "Oh," she finished, "and Danaa is sitting on top of one of the containers, with Ouraali and Jaaven, who came over to show us the point of ingress, as you had ordered. They are enclosed in carbon clouds, so should escape notice."

If I had had Jaaven in front of me I would have had something to say about his inventing orders from me in order to volunteer as their guide. I might have said 'act when necessary', but I was pretty sure I hadn't authorized him to tag along on the mission, and I was certain Seyal must have found out about it after the event too. However, he was here now, and under the orders of the leader of his race. I no longer felt it was my place to forbid or allow his participation. Ouraali would take care of him. I did wonder fleetingly what he had done with Scout. I didn't think Seyal would be very pleased to have to add babysitting a Geiga to her responsibilities. She might have something to say to him when we got back.

"I don't suppose you have any more individual carbon clouds?"

Sibby looked pleased with herself. "I borrowed three from Arialaana after ours were all damaged beyond repair in the incident over the Starfish."

They had turned out to be pretty fragile, which is why I hadn't been able to use them to board *Chibuzo* directly.

"Will the Nepheals know what to do?"

Sammy nodded. "We agreed that they would stay there as long as they could. If the containers go into *Chibuzo* they will clamber on board one of them. Otherwise, they will head back to the *Aenysia* when their EVA suits begin to show signs of depletion."

"Right. Then the rest of us will go in via the water containers." I looked around, feeling much more optimistic now that the others were here. I had not been looking forward to trying to do this on my own. "One of us must stay here and take charge of the haulers."

They all tried to shrink into the sides of the command center. Nobody wanted to be left behind. I thought about who to leave.

"Sammy, I am very sorry. It really ought to be a human-ancestry male voice."

He was disappointed, but too well-trained to admit it. "Yes, Captain."

I went into a huddle with him to explain the workings of the consoles and the codes they were using. By the time I had finished, *Chibuzo's* officer was getting irritated at the delay.

"Are you planning on doing anything about our order today or have you decided to take a siesta?" asked a clearly irritated voice.

Sammy snapped the toggle. "We are going as fast as we can, *Chibuzo*," he said in a whiny, lackadaisical voice. "Keep your hair on."

I gave him an admiring nod. He really sounded the epitome of an unmotivated worker who had been left for years in the back of beyond. He nodded back and then gave me a weary and rather sarcastic salute. "Go on with you all, now," he said. "I have work to do."

I hurriedly explained about where he would find the real caretakers and he hurried us off. "Get yourselves into the end containers on the first arm," he told me. "I'll take the last four, one from each facet. And let's hope they don't scan them."

"They won't. Containers are scanned at the first point of pick up. These would have been scanned before they were brought here. They have been here in the middle of nowhere for years, some of them. There is no reason for them to apply additional measures of security."

"Let's hope you are right."

"Once we are aboard, you should make your way back to the *Nivala*," I said. "As soon as they close up the cargo bay doors and you are sure we are inside. Then be ready to pick us up."

"We'll be there."

I gave him a pat on his back. "Thanks, Sammy. Sorry it had to be you."

"That's OK, Rye. Now, get going."

We ran along the corridors of the asset dump as fast as we could. Now it was time to get ourselves inside a container. Without being seen. And there was only one way that was going to happen.

We scurried along number one rectangular beam to the very end. This was one of the spokes of the asset dump that only carried water cylinders. There were ten cylinders attached to each facet of this arm. We needed to get ourselves inside the last cylinders before open space.

I pointed up to the air vents. That was why we had to use the water containers. The vents to the containers were far too small for anybody to crawl through. The vents to the water tanks were just large enough, providing we weren't in protective suits. There were seven of us. Two to each and I would take one on my own.

"Are we sure that these things have gravity applied to them?" asked Neema in a wary sort of voice.

I could see her point. If they didn't there wouldn't be a layer of air sitting on top of the water. We would have nothing to breathe.

"They must have." Sibby's large intellect was still working, thankfully. "Otherwise the air vents wouldn't work. They can only be here if gravity holds the water down and if there is a small clearance of air in the tank." She glanced at Denaraz, and I think she gulped. "It might be very small."

I nodded to Eshan and Didjal. The corridors were only two meters high, so it was an easy matter for them to hoist the others of us up and inside the air vents.

I went last, except for the two Enif. I found my heart sinking as I crawled along my air vent. It was dark and frightening, and I wasn't sure I would be able to breathe above the water level. I had no idea how high it would reach up the container.

Finally I got to the point of no return, where the inclination was so steep that I had to either let go and drop into the water silo, or try to scrabble back along the vent.

I had gone into the vent head first, and there wasn't enough room for me to turn around.

I swallowed.

The feeling of panic took hold of me, to such an extent that I began to hyperventilate. I was sure there was not enough air to breathe, that I was about to die. I felt ashamed of myself. I had sent the others on this mission. Had I sent them all to their death? Were they even now struggling to get sufficient oxygen into their lungs. Had any of them already suffocated?

I began to thresh out at the sides of the vent, which were slightly damp and were coated in a thin black slime. I could feel beads of sweat breaking out all over my face. They prickled slightly as they appeared.

My heart was thumping in my throat.

Then, suddenly, an image of Zenzara came into my head. She was calm, and was surveying me with her neck tilted to one side. Then she smiled and held out her hand.

In the tube, I reached forwards towards her. That broke my death grip on the sides of the vent. I fell into the tank.

The water was so cold that it felt as though I would freeze, but it did have the effect of snapping me out of the anxiety attack.

I was carried down some distance before my brain began to function properly, telling me that I needed to swim upwards. I jackknifed under the water and began to drag myself upwards.

My head hit the top of the tank. At first I thought that Sibby must have been wrong, because I hadn't broken clear of the surface. Then I realized that I had about a six inch clearance of air. I floated on the top of the water, face up, breathing pretty erratically. Still, it was mildly better than blind hysteria.

I had surfaced close to the air vent, so I heard the automatic hatch close as Sammy prepared my silo for transfer.

It was at that exact moment I realized that gravity would disappear for the duration of the journey.

My state of anxiety soared again. What would happen to the bubble of air I was currently breathing? Would I be able to find it? Would it stick together cohesively?

I was glad I had sent the others in pairs. At least they would not be alone.

I found myself involuntarily taking great gulps of air and had to stop it by sheer will. I wasn't helping myself.

There was a jerk as the automatic hauler grabbed hold of my cylinder, disengaged it from the installation, and accelerated away from the rectangular beam. The air I was breathing started to move slowly down through the water, forming a solid bubble which began to transform into a sphere – a bubble that was loose floating and moving towards the back of the water.

It was terrifying, but I managed to follow the bubble. I poked my head through the sides of the air bubble until my whole head was clear. Now I found I could breathe much more easily. Another wave of relief flooded through me.

We were soon at the docking platform on the back of the battlecruiser. I knew when we had arrived, because gravity kicked in and my nice large bubble once again became a small thin layer at the top of the tank. As the silo was edged on board, it had to travel down the ramp into the cargo hold, which then tilted the air clearance that was left. I trod water frantically as I attempted to follow it.

The air was becoming stale. I just hoped that somebody would open the hatch shortly. Otherwise the operation was going to be over before it even began.

Thankfully, the cargo bay staff were quite competent. As my tank came down and was shunted to its final resting place amongst the rest of the water silos, the hatch was opened from above.

I ducked quickly out of the way, although I doubted that anybody would be looking down at just that moment.

There were some sounds of metal against metal as the air vent tubing was attached. Immediately the quality of the little air I was getting improved, though what was coming in had the hard smell of having been scrubbed and recycled many times. I lay on my back and wondered how long to wait before trying to get out.

Then I remembered that the Nepheals were already somewhere in this hold, free agents. They would come and get me when it was safe. I had only to wait it out.

By the time they did come, my legs were tiring and I was beginning to feel exhausted. Keeping myself afloat in the water had taken a higher toll on me than I had expected.

I had become very cold too. My blood was moving only sluggishly around my body, and it had dulled my brain. I was almost comatose.

Then I heard the air vent above me being cut away.

Ouraali's long face peered down at me from behind her IEVA suit. She proffered one extended arm and I grasped it gratefully. With a long fluid movement, she pulled me out of the tank and settled me on top of the cylinder beside her.

I was shivering too much to thank her, but she seemed to know. She wrapped me in a piece of cloth she had found somewhere and rubbed me down as if I had been a tired carthorse. It was wonderful.

After about ten minutes I found myself able to speak. "Do you know where they are building the wormhole?"

Her eyes sparkled. "And here I was thinking you would thank me for coming to your rescue."

I may have blushed. "Sorry. Thank you very much. Now, do you know where they are building the wormhole?"

She laughed. "Jaaven has been proving an invaluable spy. He is small enough to cope easily with your small corridors. He has found the place they are using, yes."

My shoulders relaxed a little. "And the others? Are they all right?"

"They are. A little waterlogged, like you, and Mel had a panic attack inside the silo. She is recovering now."

I looked across and saw poor old Mel. I had not considered her claustronetia. That must have literally been her worst nightmare. I stumbled across to her and held my arms out.

"I am so sorry! That was one of the worst experiences I have ever had. You must have found it unbearable."

She clutched at me. Her eyes were bleary with tears. "I didn't think I would make it out."

"No. I apologize. I should never have asked you to do that."

She shrugged. "You can't always be considering my weaknesses. I have to perform in the same conditions as the others. I have always known that." Her chest was heaving still and her breath was coming out in fits and gasps.

I gave her a pat on the shoulders. "Well done. You made it."

She gave me a grin. "What doesn't kill you ..."

"The day is young. Don't get too cocky."

"And to think, Sammy had to miss all the fun."

"Are you good to go?"

Her chin came up. "Raring to go, Captain!"

Danaa led us across the cargo hold. She leapt nimbly from the top of one container to another. She was followed by a euphoric Jaaven, who had come into his own. He was so pleased to be on this mission that his face glowed with excitement.

Ouraali was just in front of the rest of us.

The cargo bay and surrounding areas were completely deserted. It must be the night watch on the ship. There was no need to use the three carbon clouds. They had switched them off to save battery. They might be needed to help in our escape. If we ever got as far as that part of the plan.

Sibby ran beside me. "Would you mind terribly if I married Denaraz," she asked, puffing slightly as we hurried along.

I gave a sigh. This was clearly a major theme for the two of them, but I was trying to get my head around other topics just at the moment. "Sure. Marry him. Have a few kids with him. Great guy."

She shot me a look of the sort women give you when you have said the wrong thing, and pulled me to a stop. "What do you mean, have a few kids with him?"

"I didn't mean anything. Come on, we are falling behind." I tried to tug her forward again.

"Yes, you did. You always mean something. I said 'marry'. I didn't say anything about children."

"Sibs, we are in the middle of an operation. Do you think this could wait a little until we see if we can manage to get through it in one piece?"

She was blowing little puffs of air through her nostrils. It reminded me of a vid I had once seen of an animal called a bull. Why could women think of so many things at the same time? I knew I couldn't. I was at full capacity just trying to stay focused on the mission.

"No it can't wait," she informed me in a clipped tone I recognized all too well.

I knew from experience that I should give in now or face dire consequences. "Oh, all right. If you must know, Izan asked me if I thought you would be open to having a couple of children with him."

"Really?" Her face melted.

"Yes, really." I felt so relieved I stumbled and nearly fell.

"Aw. Bless him." She looked pleased.

"All right, then. Now can we get on with the mission?"

"Of course we can. It was your fault for not explaining quicker."

I have had a sister for all of my life. I was not at all surprised to be blamed for the delay. I had been expecting it.

"Great. After you." I let her sprint ahead.

We finally reached the hold that Bull Cunningham had taken over after many minutes of turning up and down corridors. We were very lucky not to be spotted. Eventually Jaaven flagged us down and pointed ahead. We paused to take stock.

The young Nepheal had done a good job. This hangar was tucked several decks down from the main cargo bays, and a little to the rear, since it was smaller.

I didn't think I would have been able to pinpoint it so quickly. He must have spent all the time he had been on the ship scouting. He was turning into a great asset himself.

He tweaked the door to the hold so that he could estimate how many Flatlanders were inside. I expected there to be many. This was one part of *Chibuzo* that would not be winding down during the night shift. Though I doubted Bull Cunningham would be present. Even he had to sleep some part of each day.

Jaaven turned to tell us that there were over fifty people in the hold.

Everyone looked at me. I nodded to the three with carbon clouds, to indicate that they should turn them back on and enter first, to give them time to get themselves out of the line of fire. Then we put them in front of us and clustered around the doorway, ready to burst in.

When I nodded, the door was flung open and we ran in, arms at the ready.

We found ourselves in rather a run-down abandoned hold. It must have been designed for one of the elite forces of Omnistate stealth fighters, because it had one of their logos stamped across the decking, but had clearly been empty for a long time. Perhaps the *Chibuzo* no longer had such an elite force. There was just one lone plane pointing up to the ceiling from one of the moveable hoists.

The hold was relatively small, so the ceiling was only around six or seven floors above us. There was a network of walking platforms criss-crossing the area between the deck and the ceiling, where once upon a time dozens of flight engineers would attend to their planes. Now there was just one round platform in use. This had been constructed right in the center of the space. It was roughly designed, clearly disposable. On this, an iridescent sphere shone in a faint green light. It was big enough to fly a shuttle through, but not a cruiser. It glistened in the semi-darkness of the hold. The doors of the hold were closed.

Surrounding the sphere, which seemed almost ready to go to me, were around thirty Omnistate guards, who had been positioned at regular intervals and were all facing outwards.

Close up underneath the sphere was a console. I groaned when I saw that Bull Cunningham was standing behind it. I had hoped he would be sleeping.

He looked up quickly, saw me and snapped an order out. All of the guards swept forwards and brought their weapons to bear on us. Bull seemed more irritated by my presence than actually worried. He gave me a large smile that I took to be one of triumph and deliberately pressed his finger down on a large red switch in front of him, removing the safety guard with his other hand first.

I leapt forwards, but met with a storm of fire that pushed those of us who were visible to the guards straight to the sides of the fighter bay, where there were huge supporting stanchions set into the bulkhead at regular intervals. These girders must have been about three feet in diameter, so they were just enough cover for us. They wouldn't have protected a Nepheal; I was glad our larger members were still hidden by their carbon clouds. Everyone else had emerged from their cover as they separated from their partners.

Unfortunately, there was not enough time to save the entire group from injury. I saw, as I dived for safety, that Denaraz had thrown himself in front of Sibby. He took a pulser to the arm for his trouble. If he hadn't interposed himself, the same pulser would have gone through Sibby's head. She was looking up at him in astonishment as he winced and tried to stem the blood that was welling up above his elbow.

Neema was unlucky, too. One of the pulses rebounded off the pillar she was heading for and hit the upper part of her thigh. She collapsed, but was able to fit herself behind the stanchion as she did. Then she grit her teeth and fired back from around the beam.

I heard two pulsers rebounding off an Enif carapace. Eshaan and Didjal had not bothered to find cover. They were drawing the fire. They moved so quickly towards the line of guards that all of the Omnistate weapons turned in their direction to stop their advance. That gave the rest of us a chance.

We took it. There was a massive outburst of fire, and then we came out from behind our metal plating and advanced on the Ethnarch's forces. There were few of them left unhurt. After all, they had advanced in a straight line, declining to seek cover. I thought it was rather short-sighted of them, but the Omnistate had very strict protocols for their fighting troops. Attack, rather than defense, seemed the order of the day. Of course, they couldn't know that we had invisible troops behind them as well. They were in an impossible position.

All this had happened in scant seconds. But those seconds had removed our attention from Cunningham, from the rest of this small elite fighter bay.

Because the bay doors were opening. It had taken some time for the huge metal weights to obey the now unaccustomed order to separate. The doors were protesting as they finally dragged their huge metal frames apart.

I felt a flare of panic run through me. Again, most of us were without EVA suits. And the air was already being sucked out into the vacuum.

I couldn't help it. I looked directly at Bull Cunningham.

He had the same reckless tilt of his head that I had seen when we were fighting the Avaraks on *Commorancy*. Only now he met my gaze.

"You're too late," he shouted. "It has already begun." He tipped his right hand to his forehead in a jeering salute to my incompetence.

Then he pushed another button and the hydraulic platform began to lift the green ball of energy towards the opening doors. At the same time the cables leading to it disengaged, snapping free and snaking around the decking as the momentum dissipated.

I was still staring at Cunningham. It must have taken me five seconds to raise my ZR up and point it at him. It was an age too long. His hand had already gone to the bracelet he was wearing and he disappeared just as my pulse beam flashed through the space between us. I swear he was laughing as he vanished, though I did notice his smile slip as he transported away. It seemed to me that he flung himself suddenly sideways, though I couldn't be sure.

Ouraali came into view as he went. Her face was shocked and she moved as if in pain. She bent down to deactivate another carbon cloud. I saw that Jaaven was lying at her feet. He didn't move.

I left the two Enif and Denaraz to disarm and neutralize any of the remaining guards, though there were none that were still uninjured. I ran across the hold and knelt down beside the boy.

He wasn't breathing. His long narrow face was relaxed in death. He looked even younger than he really was. A pulser had penetrated his heart. He must have died instantly. His expression was one of satisfaction. He must have felt pleased to have been a part of this mission, to have done his duty.

I pressed my lips together, and then touched Ouraali lightly on the shoulder. "Where is Danaa?"

Her eyes, which had been staring into the distance, suddenly focussed. She swung around the hold. "Danaa? DANAA?"

Only a silence greeted us. Then I knew what had taken that smile off Bull Cunningham's face. The Nepheal girl had thrown herself at him just as he had transported out of danger. She had been taken with him. And we had no idea where they could have gone.

There was no time for pity. No time to do anything for Jaaven. His eyes were staring wide at us; there could be no doubt that he was dead.

I pulled the carbon cloud mechanism from his neck, sliding it gently over his head and then closed his eyes. "I am sorry, Jaaven. You were far too young to die."

Ouraali's large eyes were pools of guilt as they met mine. "I shouldn't have let him come," she said.

I smiled down at the dead boy. "I don't think you could have stopped him. This is what he felt he had to do."

Then we couldn't say any more because the sensors detected a dangerous lack of oxygen in the air and Ouraali's helmet automatically deployed. That gave her only a limited time to get herself to a safer environment. The rest of us had no protection at all. And we had to disarm that green ball of energy before it became a true wormhole.

The others had come up and were staring down at Jaaven's inert body. I saw tears in Mel's eyes. Eshaan had gone to assist Neema and now they both approached. I slipped the chain I was holding around her neck. "Here. You are the one who needs this the most. Eshaan, try to get her back to *Nivala*."

It nodded and picked her up in its forearms. They both disappeared inside the carbon cloud. I saw one of the emergency jet packs disappear from a case of them lining the wall, together with an EVA suit.

If anybody was equipped to deal with the vacuum, that would be an Enif. Neema stood her best chance with Eshaan.

That left Denaraz, Sibby, Mel, Didjal, Ouraali and myself. Six of us, and only one carbon cloud. Whatever we did next, we would be highly visible.

I turned my attention to the Tyzaran.

"How bad is it?" I asked Denaraz. At least, I tried to convey that question to him without words.

He was submitting to Sibby's idea of first aid. I pitied him. My sister had a brain that outshone my own by fifty IQ points, but she had never been particularly gentle when curing wounds. This time she was applying a rough and ready bandage-tourniquet. I could tell that he was suffering because his crests were drooping. He was no good to us any more here.

However, he managed a faint grin and a thumbs up. Then he moved his fingers as if they were walking and gave me another thumbs up. I took that to mean that he thought he would be able to continue. I knew that wasn't true. Just the colour of his face told me that he needed immediate evacuation.

It was absolutely clear to me who had to go. I hated keeping Sibby with me, but if anybody was capable of stopping Cunningham, it would be her. And possibly Didjal. Denaraz's specialty was computer systems. He would be better placed to utilize that back on *Aenysia* or *Nivala*.

I touched both Izan and Ouraali then placed the chain over the Nepheal woman's long neck. It only dropped a few inches down before becoming stuck. The sheer size of the Nepheals never failed to amaze me. Then I pointed to Izan and drew a ship in the vacuum in front of me.

Ouraali's large eyes opened and she shook her head. She didn't want to go.

Denaraz gave a sigh and hugged Sibby. He knew he was only a brake on us down here. He bent down and when he straightened up again he was holding the broken body of Jaaven in his long arms, ignoring the tourniquet around one of them. He stood there, meekly waiting for Ouraali to take them both back to our ships, to take Jaaven back to Scout for the final time.

Ouraali held her position for some long seconds. I could see that she was

considering all her options. She wanted revenge. I was sorry to have to ask her to forgo it temporarily.

At last the fight went out of her. She walked up to Denaraz and bent her shoulder down to the ground. He laid Jaaven across her back and then allowed me to give him a leg up behind the young Nepheal's body.

Ouraali followed Eshaan's example. She moved over to the wall and took down one of the small jet packs. Then she fiddled with the mechanism around her neck. The carbon cloud did not have enough energy to completely hide them, but it did camouflage their presence pretty well.

I watched as they moved out through the cargo hold doors. You could see part of Ouraali and a faint flickering of the jet pack, but as soon as they got to the outside of the ship, those tell-tale signs were completely swamped by the huge radiance coming from the expanding sphere of energy.

The green ball of light was already outside the ship, free floating in space, and it was getting bigger by the moment. It would no longer have fit into the reduced space that the fighter hold had on offer. If it continued at this rate it would soon be bigger than *Chibuzo* herself. I thought that Cunningham had been telling the truth.

It was too late.

There was nothing we could do.

We all watched sadly as the small ripple of disturbance that was Ouraali and her heavy burden gradually passed in front of the massing energy ball.

Then there was a rush to the racks. We were going to need the EVA suits. Luckily, those of us left were all of human proportions. *Chibuzo* would have something in our size.

Sibby, Mel and I hurried over to the nearest EVA cage. It had unlocked automatically when the pressure had dropped. Within a minute, all three of us were kitted out.

18

As soon as I had donned a full EVA suit, I turned to see what the situation was in the hold.

Many of *Chibuzo's* crew were still prone on the floor.

Some of the others had managed to reach EVA suits and were now kitted out. I saw three of the ship's complement heading for the controls that would close the large bay doors again. I was doubtful that they would be in time to save the crew that had taken casualties in the last few minutes; the hold was now airless. Many of those present had been caught in fatigues only. They had nothing to protect them from the vacuum.

My eyes darted around the area. We needed to defend ourselves. Already I could hear the murmur of repair and rescue crews on the other side of the door leading to the passageways. We were going to be caught here with no escape, if we weren't careful.

There was only one place to go. Out.

I pointed to the jet packs and the girls nodded. We took an extra one each, in case the EVA packs would not last long enough for our needs. That ball of energy was already quite a long way out.

We headed directly out of the bay doors that were still standing open. I passed two heavily suited figures going into the fighter hangar. Someone on *Chibuzo's* main bridge had ordered them to try to secure the area. I was glad. It would give some of the downed crew at least a chance.

As they crossed paths with us they examined us cursorily, but they didn't stop. We could have been part of *Chibuzo's* crew. That was the advantage of the common ancestry between the Flatlanders and the Spacelanders. We blended in. They decided to leave us in peace and save their companions.

We jetted away from the enormous ship, only too aware of its size as we began to distance ourselves from her. She took up the whole of one side of the sky. I felt very vulnerable. There must have been nearly a thousand crew members on board the Omnistate battlecruiser and any one of them would be delighted to put an end to our lives. That gives you a sense of fragility, believe me.

I turned to look towards the blazing light in front of us. It took up the other side of the sky, because it shone so brightly that everything else disappeared into the light it was giving out.

I felt gutted. The sphere was already too far advanced for us to hope to stop the process. In any case, what could we do when we got there? We had no idea where Cunningham might have gone. Our plans were in shreds. We had failed completely.

I contemplated, just for a second, breaking radio silence and asking the ships to fire directly into the shining sphere. But I couldn't be sure that something like that would not catalyze it further, would not actually be the cause of a cascade reaction at the quantum vacuum level. It was a risk that we couldn't take.

Then the darkness exploded with light. The two crew members had been informed of who we were, and they were armed. I had been wrong. We were apparently more important than the rescue of their fellow shipmates.

Didjal and I had forged slightly ahead of the girls. We both turned as soon as the first shots sped past us, luckily missing the girls too. We jetted back past them and headed directly for the two bulky figures. One of my pulse beams snagged a partial hit on the left man, who was propelled into his compatriot. That was a real piece of luck.

They were so busy trying to disentangle themselves that the one on the left never saw me coming. I slammed into his back and we were both carried on towards the energy sphere.

He tried to twist in mid air, but I clamped my arms around his body and held him immobile. He was in one of the newer models of EVA suit, so I was able to see all of his facial expressions through the thick helmet. He was furious.

We went into a slow somersault, curving over and over, dangerously close to the boiling light inside the sphere.

The Flatlander suddenly jackknifed in my hold. His head slammed into mine; my neck snapped backwards on my vertebrae. It made me lose my grip. I saw his eyes glitter with black complacency. I wanted to wipe that satisfaction off his face, but I was turning over in space, as helpless at that moment as a baby would have been.

Then a pulser beam cut through the gap between us. His eyes shifted hurriedly away from me. The enjoyment he was feeling at having bested me disappeared. The expression changed to one of alarm.

I smiled.

I used my own jet to stop the angular momentum.

Then I used it to vector in on him again.

Things in space are so much slower than you would think. It takes a long time to do anything. You can throw yourself towards somebody, but it may be minutes before you get there. And the Flatlander had a jetpack attached to his own suit. He moved, I corrected. He moved again, I corrected again. It was a macabre dance in space as I attempted to choreograph our encounter and he attempted to make his escape.

But there were two of us against two of them. As we wove up and down, Didjal was also closing in on his man.

The Enif had been able to shoot at him, but that very action had pushed Didj out of alignment. The *Enif* was now between the *Chibuzo* crewmember and the energy ball, which meant that the *Chibuzo* guard could no longer fire directly at his objective. Didjal was attempting to use the pulser for some small amount of directional impulse, firing it in the opposite direction from the one it wanted to go in, but careful not to fire into the light.

Mel came to help me. She had already got her ZR up and aimed at my crewmember, but he reached down to his second jetpack and jetted straight at Sibby. Sibby fired, but that knocked her backwards off track. She began to cartwheel slowly over and over, struggling to get herself on an even keel again.

I saw a swarm of figures in EVA suits leave one of the EVA exits of *Chibuzo*. They knew we were here. We were about to be just as trapped here as we had been inside the hold. I bit my lip. I had apparently made the wrong decision.

I suppose we were lucky that they couldn't fire on us from such a distance, for fear of damaging the glowing sphere. But there was no way we were going to be able to avoid them. Hundreds of black-suited shapes were pouring out of the hull of the battleship. One small group was heading to the asset dump, the rest were coming our way.

The figures jetting out of *Chibuzo* would be on our position within a couple more minutes. Already some of them were beginning to fire on us. At the moment it was only those whose sight line was not backed by the hypersphere. That could and would change in the very near future.

I put my pistol directly over my head and fired upwards in a continual stream of pulser fire. The others did the same. It rocketed us downwards, but that didn't matter. It would temporarily put us out of the line of fire.

Almost as soon as I had done that, a huge invisible something drew up between us and the line of suited Flatlanders heading for our position. Suddenly they were all blocked from my view. I couldn't see what was causing the light to cut out, but there was a *Nivala* size hole in space between them and us.

I saw a window of light open up in the darkness. A couple of space skis sped out of the gap. One headed to Didjal then Mel, the other came for Sibby and for then for me. The angle of my shots above my head had drawn me closer to her.

Sammy was driving one of the skis, but Zenzara was driving the one that came towards me, wearing only an IEVA suit and helmet. She had collared Sibby and dragged her onto the platform, but when it was my turn she simply leaned over and grabbed me by one arm as she accelerated past. I dangled after her as she raced the space ski back to the ship, driving with only one hand on the handlebars.

We shot into the shuttle bay and inside the ship. *Nivala* was already shuddering from rail gun fire that was coming our way from the battleship. Someone was trying to hurt us without affecting the sphere. I couldn't blame them. I thought it had taken them rather a long time to establish that we must have ships in the neighborhood. Now we would be standing out to them like a moon eclipsing a sun. Even they could hardly have missed that.

I dragged off my helmet. "What the Shells are you doing out of your Zeroth tank, Zenzara Zylarian? You need another three days! And don't ever go outside the ship in only IEVA again! It is far too dangerous!"

"De nada." She gave me a cheeky grin. "You know I couldn't leave you for the Flatlanders to mop up, and I feel fine. Those triage units always err on the side of conservative treatment. I am young. I don't need all their cosseting."

She certainly looked all right. Her young face was pink with exertion and I could see that she had full use of both arms.

I leant over suddenly and gave her a hug. She squealed and pulled away. "Ouch! Don't go around hugging people when you are in EVA. It hurts!" Her crest flared up and her claws peeped out of her fingers. But I could tell she was pleased. A small pink flush had colored her crinkled cheeks.

"Sorry." I dropped her again and she almost fell. "Just glad to see you better. You saved my life back on the Starfish."

"Well, of course I did. That is what saviors are for."

"Thank you."

She sniffed. "You don't make it very easy. I have to have eyes in the back of my crest."

"Don't exaggerate. You know you love a bit of excitement. If it weren't for me you would be shut up in some Tyzaran laboratory with a host of scientists running experiments on you."

She shuddered. "Don't remind me."

As soon as the atmosphere inside the shuttle bay stabilized, Sibby pulled her own helmet off. Her hair was sticking out at right angles. "Is Denaraz all right?"

Zenzara opened her eyes wide. "Was he hurt?" At Sibby's nod, she shrugged. "We have been under tight-beam silence. I had no idea. I am sorry."

Mel brought her up to date as we stripped the hefty EVA suits off and then hurried up in the lift and along to the bridge.

Seyal and Eshaan were together at the controls. They looked up hopefully as we all strode in. Eshaan saw its *faliif* and ran up to it. The two Enif chattered together for several moments. Neema was in the sick bay in a triage chamber. Eshaan indicated that she would be fine, but that she needed several days in a Zeroth.

When I asked about Denaraz, they shook their heads. "Ouraali must have taken Jaaven back to *Aenysia*," Seyal told me. "Denaraz will be there too." The Avarak woman looked around. "Is Danaa with them too?"

There was an awkward silence. Then Mel told the others what had happened to her.

Zenzie looked sick. "You mean she is with that Cunningham?" Her crest drooped.

"I am afraid she is. And the worst is that we have no idea where Cunningham transported to."

Mel cleared her throat. We all looked at her. "Oh," she said. "I think we do. I think we know exactly where Cunningham is."

I wasn't the only one of us to swivel quickly around. Mel was staring at a small quadruped who was pointing fixedly to starboard, his little tail held stiffly out from his body at the horizontal.

Zenzara frowned. All her creases along her forehead joined together into one big furrow. "I don't understand. There is nothing out in that direction. Is there?" She looked around at the rest of us.

Then I clicked. "*Aenysia* is out there! He is on *Aenysia!* "

I pushed a button for a tight-beam. The Omnistate would probably be able to hear us, but I *had* to talk to them.

Ouraali was on the bridge of *Aenysia*. "Captain," she said. "What do you need?"

I felt a rush of relief. "They picked you up, then. I'm glad to see that."

"I floated quite close to their position," she explained. "Anzany took pity on me."

"Are you all right?"

She nodded. "We all are." Then her tone dropped. "Except Jaaven."

"We think Cunningham transported to your ship. Danaa must somehow have managed to manipulate his destination. We are coming over. Please remove your carbon cloud cover briefly in ten minutes' time."

She acknowledged and then closed the channel. Hopefully the *Chibuzo* technicians would not have been able to get a fix on her position in such a short time.

I nodded at Seyal and Eshaan. The others glared at me.

"We want to go too," said Mel, her tone frigid.

"I know you do. But you are exhausted. Stay on the bridge, get some food and a modicum of rest. This isn't over yet. That ... thing ... out there is not about to go away on its own." I pointed to the sphere. "If that amount of energy is suddenly released, it will evaporate both our ships and the asset dump as well."

Sibby's face took on the arrested sort of expression that meant she was thinking up one of her scientific inventions. "We would have to stop a lot of light," she murmured to herself. "Stopped light. Mmmm.

Maybe it would work. But to deflect so much energy?"

I turned to stare at her. "Say again?"

Her eyes came back into focus and she realized that we were all gaping at her. "Sorry. Thinking." She screwed up her eyes. "Actually, Mall, I think I *had* better stay here. You are right. I would be of more use trying to increase our shield potential. And I am going to need Didjal too." Then her face dropped. "But Izan is on *Aenysia*. I have to go to him."

Eshaan stepped forwards before I could say anything. "I will undertake to protect him," it said in a somber tone. "You will stay and do what you must to protect the ship. This is as your *faliif* would wish it."

Sibby considered what the Enif had said for several long moments. Then she gave a decided nod. "Thank you. You are right; I should stay. Didjal, will you help me, please? I am thinking that we could modify the carbon cloud to allow coalescence of frequencies and eigenvalues?"

The Enif engineer thrummed its antennae with interest. "You are thinking of creating a macro Exceptional Point?"

She nodded. As they began to walk away, I saw that they were already lost in the science. Sibby lowered her voice excitedly. "Yes, because a network of exceptional points would stop light pulses, which could then be deviated around the cloud. What do you think? Could we do it? Would such a thing work for such high energies?"

"It *is* a radical suggestion. And as far as I know, it has never been attempted before on such a scale. However, I do know a little about PT-symmetric waveguides. That knowledge may be of some use to us here."

They disappeared, still talking about the physics. I was glad. It was not likely to be a conversation I could follow.

"Right. Eshaan, Seyal, ready?"

They nodded. "We will take a space ski over to *Aenysia*. We will go over with IEVA suits, but will tether an EVA suit for each of us to the platform."

"I am coming too." Zenzie's crest was up. She was standing next to Scout. I am not sure which of them looked more obstinate.

I smothered a sigh. Of course she was.

I nodded. She did a little dance on the spot, which made Scout look up at her.

On a spur of the moment whim, I decided to take the Geiga with us as well. He had proved himself invaluable in detecting danger; he could well help to find out where Cunningham had hidden himself on board *Aenysia*.

Zenzie had a fixed, angry look on her small face. She knew what Cunningham was capable of and she was worried because her friend was in danger. I hoped he wouldn't have harmed Danaa, but I wouldn't put anything past him. He had already caused the extinction of so many lives that I feared one more would not present a problem for him.

The opening of the transit bay doors showed us where the ship was. The shaft of light was small because the transit bay is only used for private space yachts, but even so it must have been visible at tens of kilometers out here in the deep dark. It was certainly enough for both us and the *Chibuzo* to get a fix on her.

The Flatlanders did not hang about. Just as we swept inside the Nepheal ship, she was hit by railgun fire. The whole of her structure trembled, but the doors luckily closed smoothly behind us.

I guess the carbon cloud had gone back up and that Ouraali had moved the ship, for that was the last impact. I could hear a barrage of detonations nearby, but they failed to find us again.

I snapped on one of the onboard comlinks. "Have you seen Danaa, Ouraali?"

Her voice was calm. You wouldn't think she had just risked her life and her ship to pick us up. "No. I'm sorry. We are still looking for her. We started from the top down. Can you take it from the bottom up?"

"Of course." I pulled my finger off the button again.

We checked the transit bay and then headed along the corridor towards the rear of the vessel. The passageways of the Nepheal ship were so large that we felt almost like children as we hurried along them. Zenzie, in particular, almost disappeared in their enormity.

I could hear the sound of Scout's four trotters as they clattered along the deck plating, but when something was suddenly missing it took my mind several seconds to trace what that was.

When it did, I skidded to a halt. The Geiga had stopped.

We turned around to the sight of Scout frozen in place. His tail and his snout were horizontal and all of his bristles were sticking out of his skin at right angles.

Zenzie took one look and her crest stood up from her head. She stilled as well, in the automatic Tyzaran response to threat.

Eshaan and I looked at each other. Clearly, the Flatlander *was* on board. From Scout's indication, he would seem to be inside the main shuttle bay.

And that was a huge space.

We began to approach the nearest door to the shuttle bay. It was closed, but not battened down. We eased ourselves through the smallest gap that would allow us to pass.

Zenzie immediately slid off to the right. One minute she was there, fingering the thoria around her neck, the next she had vanished. I grinned to myself. She no longer interpreted her remit to shadow me so literally. I approved.

Eshaan moved slowly out to my right, and I advanced towards the center of the huge shuttle bay, towards the only vessels currently inside it – two Nepheal standard runabouts.

"I see you brought that filthy animal, Ryler." The voice came from above me.

I tried not to show him that he had startled me. "He's just a pet, Bull."

There was the flash of a jet and a squeak of pain from Scout as he was hit. He gave a high-pitched scream and then started to keen on a lower tone. I reached out with one foot and gently kicked the poor animal to safety behind a large metal box, hoping that I hadn't damaged him any further. He snuffled his objection to such treatment and then fell silent. I wasn't sure if he was dead or simply unconscious. I felt a burning sensation in my chest.

"Scout was just an animal, Bull. You didn't have to kill him."

"Where is Chandrayanan? And the Admiral?"

"Not on this ship, but I am not going to tell you where they are." I was peering up towards the roof. All of the hanging platforms that were used to repair the upper inner skin of the shuttle bay were back in place. Cunningham must be perched up on one of them.

To my left I saw that the closest hanging platform was swinging backwards and forwards. Somebody had used it to climb up to the next plinth along. I knew who that would be. I looked away quickly. There was no point letting the Flatlander know Zenzara was there.

"Am I going to have to come up and get you, Bull?" The right-hand platform was swinging from side to side as well. The Enif had followed Zenzara's lead. I realized that it was my job to keep him busy, keep him talking.

"Not unless you want this young Nepheal girl to drop on your head," he replied, in a pleasant, communicative voice.

"Are you all right, Danaa?" I shouted up.

A faint cry of pain gave me some sort of an answer to that.

"Give it up, Bull. Do you really think you can escape us now?" In fact, I was wondering why he hadn't used his wrist device again.

"That is for me to know and for you to question, as they say."

I pulled myself onto the lowest platform in front of me. My heart had shrunk; I remembered how hard I had found it last time I tried to scale this improvised staircase up to the top of the shuttle bay roof. I had completely humiliated myself. I had been out of form then. Now I was in an even worse state.

Still, I would have to try. I leaped for the plinth and then struggled to bring my body up from a hanging position. Yes, I know it sounds easy, but believe me, it isn't. IEVA suits may only be halfway to a full EVA protection, but they still weigh a lot and impede movement.

A laugh came from above my head. "Call yourself a Spacelander? A six-year-old could scale that thing faster than you. You have let yourself go to pot, Ryler."

"Yes. Chasing around the Major Shells after you has not helped."

I still couldn't see him; he was too far up towards the roof, but I had zeroed in on where he had to be. He was about half way in to the center of the space.

I scrambled onto the first platform and grabbed one of the four hanging cables to help myself up. The next plinth was slightly towards the middle of the shuttle bay, and a little more than my own height above me. I sighed.

But I had to give the others the time they might need. I leapt for the second platform.

For a second I dangled uselessly.

"Having fun? You look like you wilted. You're all limp."

"Ha ha, very droll!" I may have glared up at him. I think I heard a smothered giggle from my left.

"No, seriously. You need to exercise more."

"And how is it you ended up on one of these hanging platforms, Bull? It can't have been your intention?"

"This stupid Nepheal!" I heard a muffled whimper as he must have shaken Danaa. "As she grabbed me our hololink data crossed and we ended up on a platform at the very top of this fritzing amphitheater. It is all her fault!"

"Can't you get down, Bull?" How clever of Danaa. I didn't think they had ended up here by mistake.

His voice was irritated. "This asinine female is too scared of heights to move."

That was another bright move on Danaa's part. "How unfortunate for you. Never mind. I will come and get you."

"At the rate you are going you will expire before you make it up here."

"You underestimate me." I was on the third platform now, but it was, admittedly, getting much more difficult. I hoped that the others would get to him soon. If not, I was going to lose some serious face.

At that moment a pulser beam shot out through the dimly lit rooftop space above me. There was a small sigh as it hit a shiny black carapace to my right, but it was followed immediately by return fire. Bull had spotted Eshaan. Or Eshaan had deliberately let Bull spot him. I thought the second option was the most likely.

The return fire was high, and must have served to make the Flatlander drop down onto the platform, presumably on top of the supposedly cowering Danaa.

Then I heard a blood-curdling shriek from my left. There was a shine of cables jolting in the gloom and then three loud cries.

Shots flashed out. One sliced right through the platform I was standing on, leaving a hole in the metal which smoked slightly.

I heard a terrific scraping as platforms and hanging cables jostled each other. There was a shout of triumph, then one of disappointment.

A supple figure dropped down platform after platform, way off to my right. Another, slimmer black one matched its progress. To the left, the cables were also vibrating as the platforms were used.

I began to let myself down to the floor again. I was much closer, but still thought it would take me longer. Especially if Danaa was all right. She was so at home on these things that she could scramble up or down them in seconds.

I still couldn't think why he hadn't transported away. It wasn't until later that I found out Danaa had made a grab at the bracelet as they transported, loosening it on his wrist. When they landed on the platform, it swung and jostled so much that Cunningham had lost the mechanism over the edge. It was somewhere on the floor of the shuttle bay. When they ended up on the platform, Danaa had been on top of him. She had refused to move, pleading panic. It had been a great move on her part. He hadn't dared shoot her in case he would never get out from under the dead weight. It had taken him so long to struggle free from under her large body that he simply hadn't had time to retrieve the wrist device.

Nor did he now.

He swung down onto the deck plating at floor level when I was still letting myself over the last plinth. But Danaa and Eshaan were way before him.

The Nepheal girl came down like an avenging angel. She barreled into the Flatlander without giving him time to target her with his ZR pistol. He had been obliged to holster it for the trip down the hanging platforms.

Eshaan was upon him at almost the same time. Between them, they had him subjugated and restrained within a minute.

"Having fun up there?" Zenzie's dulcet voice rang in my ears.

I looked down. I was hanging off the last platform, about to make the jump to ground level. "Don't mock; it isn't nice of you."

She made a rude sound and shook her head. "The Flatlander is under arrest." The unspoken 'no thanks to you' rattled around in the air between us.

I dropped down to the ground and slapped my hands together. "Well done, all of you."

Zenzie shook her head. Then she ran up to Danaa and gave her a big hug. Considering her relative size against the statuesque Nepheal, it looked very strange, but Danaa responded, gently returning the gesture.

"Well done, Danaa!" said the Tyzaran girl. "You took him to the one place on the *Aenysia* that he couldn't just shoot you and walk away."

"I thought about shooting her, but she felt like a ton of bricks." Bull was not best pleased. "A dead body would have anchored me even more firmly to the plinth." He paused for a moment and then went on bitterly, "If I had realized she was doing it on purpose I *would* have shot her." He gave her an accusing stare. "You *said* you were scared of the platforms."

In one fluid movement Danaa leapt up two of the hanging plinths in one jump, sideways to another, and then launched herself back down to the floor, where she landed with the grace of one of the big cats.

She stared Cunningham straight in the face. "I lied."

Eshaan had removed Cunningham's pistol and everything he was carrying. I looked idly through the contents of his pockets. The Flatlander noticed.

"You are too late to stop the process," he jeered. "You managed to interrupt the last one, but this time I left instruction for the canister to be deposited right at the center of the hypersphere, just after full eversion. A nicely modified torpedo will do the job. They know exactly when to fire. And there is nothing you can do to stop that now. The *Chibuzo* outmans you and outguns you." His head came up proudly. "You may have captured me, but I have beaten you in the end. It will be a very bitter victory for you. You will soon have to hand me over again to the Omnistate. I am important to them. As soon as the wormhole is established they will make you exchange me."

I gestured to Eshaan, who began to drag the shackled man out of the shuttle bay.

Cunningham seemed to be looking for something on the floor. Danaa noticed and held up her hand for Eshaan to stop. The Nepheal girl looked around until she spotted something dark on the deck plating by the runabouts. She darted over and picked it up.

"Looking for this?" She saw our expressions and explained about the bracelet.

Bull's shoulders slumped. I think that had been his last hope at escaping his current situation.

I waited to feel some sense of closure, of a job finished. It didn't come. If the wormhole was going to open anyway, then Cunningham's detention was definitely an anticlimax. It was too small a win to offset against a giant loss. I felt only deflation and a sense of failure. My shoulders slumped too.

Eshaan marched Cunningham off to put him with the other detainees.

Zenzie looked after them, and I felt a small hand take mine and squeeze it once.

"It isn't over yet, Mallivan," she whispered.

Danaa agreed with her. "There is still time." Her face took on a strange sadness. "Zenzie has told me about Jaaven. We can't give up. Not yet. Not while we can still make Jaaven's death count for something."

I felt the dream-like state of lethargy loosen its grip on me. She was right. We had to make that poor boy's sacrifice count for something. It wasn't yet time to give up. I scooped Scout up in my arms. The Geiga had been able to drag himself over to me, I was thankful to see. I scratched his ear, hugely relieved to see that he had not been killed. We would simply have to fight on. Until there was nothing else we could do to stop the wormhole and save the Chakran strands.

19

Back on the bridge, I pressed the tight-beam to speak to Eshaan. "How is our latest captive looking now?"

There was a short silence. "Angry."

"Good. That makes me feel better. Please make sure he is completely secured."

"Yes, Captain."

I took my finger off the comlink and gazed through the viewport at the hypersphere.

It had stopped growing while we had been in the shuttle bay. Now what had before seemed only diffuse light had begun to settle into the spars of a huge hypersphere similar to the one we had seen in the Aschasi nebulae. It was spinning rapidly in space, cutting through the darkness as if it was slicing pieces out of it.

I turned to Ouraali. "I need to get back to *Nivala*. We can't risk *Aenysia*, not now that you have Cunningham detained on board."

"What are you thinking, Mallivan?"

Zenzara stepped forwards. "I have to go into the hypersphere. If the canister is deployed there I am the only one who can stop this."

I raised my eyebrows. "You think that you can absorb the Chakran strands into your Nexus again before they are destroyed in the creation of a wormhole?" It seemed unlikely to me. "Those strands might even be clones."

Her head came up. "I know I can."

I continued to stare at her. Her crest deflated a tiny bit. "At least," she amended, "I think I can. I have had more time with the Nexus myself. My link with the Chakrans is coming back stronger than it ever was." Her chin came up, challenging me to gainsay her.

"We have to let her try." It was Denaraz. He had been standing on one side of the bridge, a pale imitation of himself.

I walked over to thump him on the back.

He winced.

I thumped him again. "I thought we might lose you that time."

He gave a huff. "I hope I am harder to kill than that!"

"You look like death."

"So would you if you had taken a full pulser through your arm."

"You saved my sister. Thank you."

He met my gaze. His own eyes were steady. "I told you I would put her life above my own."

I put my arm around his neck and squeezed. "Now I believe you."

"Ouch!" He twisted away. "Do you mind? That is still very painful. Where is Sibby? Is she all right?"

"She is. She is busy trying to manufacture some sort of miracle shield. She and Didjal went to engineering on *Nivala*."

"I need to get over there, then. I am no use to you like this. I can't even get into an EVA suit."

Zenzie had moved close to him, as if the heat in her small body could help to make him better. "We will take you over there now."

He smiled down at her. "My job is to take care of you, Chy Zenzara. I am sorry that I will be unable to protect you this time."

"It is by no means certain that she will go anywhere," I pointed out. "We may be able to stop the torpedo before it reaches the hypersphere."

"How?" Zenzie put her hands on her hips.

"Err…we could put ourselves between *Chibuzo* and the hypersphere?"

"So they could see us and pound us to pulp?" Denaraz spread his arms. "We would be clearly visible against the light. *Chibuzo* still has some serious armament. We wouldn't stand a chance. They would simply blow us to smithereens and then fire the torpedo. Even with both of our ships, that isn't a viable option."

He was right. It would be suicide and it would not stop them finishing the wormhole. My teeth ground together. "Anybody?"

Sammy was looking thoughtful. "How about the asset dump? Is there any way we could use that? Could we interpose it between the Omnistate ship and the hypersphere?"

I liked the idea, but I knew at once that it wouldn't work. "It is too slow. They would simply maneuver around the dump."

"I have the solution."

We all turned to see where the quiet voice had come from. It was Danaa. She was holding up the bracelet she had retrieved from the floor of the shuttle bay. It glittered in the dimmed lighting on the bridge.

"I will use it to go back to *Chibuzo*," she said. "Our only chance is to sabotage that torpedo before it is sent into the sphere."

Sometimes there is a silence that tells you of a solution.

This was one.

Because it was a solution nobody liked. It was very probably a one-way trip for whoever transported.

I stepped forwards. "I will go."

Denaraz stepped in front of me. "You can't. You have to go with Chy Zenzara."

"She will not have to go if somebody stops the torpedo."

Izan was giving me a pitying look. He could tell this was very difficult for me. "She will have to go in any case. If the torpedo gets through to successfully deposit the canister containing the negative energy, she is our very last hope of aborting the wormhole. And she will not go unless you do. The Savior protocols won't let her."

Eshaan had arrived on the bridge in time to hear the latest arguments.

"I'll go."

I stared at it. "You are likely to be killed."

It shrugged. "I have evaded it once. I am not looking to circumvent fate again."

"But you would condemn Didjal to the state of enlightenment too."

It thrummed its wings. "Didjal feels as I do. We know that our time is close. My *faliif* would only be happy I acted as I should. That is what is important."

I shook my head and blew air out of my mouth. I couldn't see myself sending *any* of my crew. It was an impossible choice.

Denaraz was right. Zenzie and I would have to be the last barrier to their success. That meant that neither of us could go back over to *Chibuzo*. Seyal had a child on *Nivala*. I could not send her. Denaraz was injured. He had to stay here. I made a list in my head of who was left. Ouraali and Danaa. Sammy and Mel. Anzany and Neema. Didjal and Eshaan. Sibby.

Sibby and Didjal were needed to work on the protective shield, in case things went really wrong. Both Ouraali and Danaa were too big. They might not even fit in some of the ordnance compartments on *Chibuzo*.

So it was Eshaan, Sammy, Mel , Anzany or Neema.

I couldn't send either Anzany or Neema. Neema was injured, and although Anzany had weapons training, it had to be somebody who could disarm a torpedo.

So it was Sammy.

In the end, there was really no choice whatsoever. Mel's claustronetia had to be an impediment, and Sammy would have taken her place even if I *had* sent her. I knew him well enough to be sure of that.

The strange thing is, he knew at the same time I knew. His eyes met mine and he gave me a smile. It told me everything I needed to know.

I gave a sort of grimace back. He nodded. He knew that it had not been an easy decision.

"Are you up to it, Sammy?"

Mel sucked in air. "No!"

Then she thought better of her comment and subsided into a slightly smaller woman than she had been a few seconds before.

I hated sending him. He had already been through so much. Injured so many times.

His head came up. "Yes Captain!"

Eshaan stepped up to his shoulder. "I shall accompany him. We know that the wrist device can take two. Two of us will stand a much better chance of success."

There was no denying that statement, either. And Eshaan, though an artist, had proved itself so many times that I had no justification for not sending it out there with Sammy.

I looked around the room for Danaa. "How does that thing work?" I asked. "Can you tell them how to get to the Omnistate vessel?"

"I think so." She went into a huddle with them, explaining what she had experienced with Cunningham, and how she thought the device worked. The two males were nodding, so it seemed that they understood.

I turned to Zenzara. "They will go first, from here. Then we will take Denaraz to *Nivala*. Seyal will then take us in as close as she can to the sphere. We need to be in position if Sammy and Eshaan fail. If they succeed, we can simply make our way back out again."

Although her crest was rigidly upright, she nodded with a certain amount of calm. "We will need EVA suits and a couple of the space skis."

Space skis were the Nepheal equivalent of jet skis. "Yes. We will take a couple of them over from here. Denaraz, can you meet Zenzie and me in ten minutes in the transit bay?"

He nodded.

Ouraali's eyes were soft. "What do you require of me, Captain

Mallivan?"

"I am sorry, but I need you to abandon this space as quickly as you can."

She seemed taken aback. "Leave you behind?"

"I am afraid so. One of our priorities was to capture the main players in this lethal game, and we have done that. Whatever the outcome, we need to ensure that they are taken to Ulon Prime, that they are tried according to Alliance statutes. You can do nothing to assist us now. Your job is to place this ship out of danger should anything happen here, and return with Cunningham to Ulon Prime. Your other ship should have already arrived there with Chandrayanan and the Admiral."

She gave a solemn nod. "Then that will be our path."

"Thank you. I am very sorry for the loss of Jaaven."

"He represented the Nepheals in one of the most dangerous situations that our people have experienced in centuries. He will not be forgotten."

"I am glad. He deserves our remembrance. He and Agraala both do."

We both inclined our heads. Danaa opened her mouth to speak, but Ouraali anticipated both her question and my wishes on the matter.

"You will stay with me, on *Aenysia*. Your presence is necessary."

Danaa shot an anguished look at Zenzie but said no more. Zenzie ran over and hugged her, before coming back to me.

A small snuffling sound brought my attention down to the deck. Scout was pushing at my ankles. His wound was ugly, but he would get better.

"Can I leave the Geiga with you?" I asked.

"Of course. We will take good care of him for you." I wanted him to be safe. I could, at least, do that for the creature. He deserved it. He had found *Chibuzo* and Cunningham across vast tracts of space. I wanted him to live.

There was nothing more to say. I gave them all a smile of thanks. "Please leave as soon as we are out of the transit bay, and use your full engine speed to get as far away as you can, as fast as you can."

Danaa's eyes were wet as she watched us go.

I noticed Zenzara peeking back at her friend several times.

I wondered if they would ever see each other again.

20

We dropped Denaraz off in *Nivala's* shuttle bay. His arm was tightly bandaged and he was paler than usual, but his eyes were strong.

"Where is Sibby?" he demanded of Seyal, who had come down to meet us.

"She is in engineering and needs you to go down there."

I was about to tell him to take good care of her, but Denaraz had already disappeared.

I told Seyal of our plans and asked her to take us as close into the hypersphere as she could, approaching from the rear so that we would not be visible to scrutiny from *Chibuzo*.

She didn't look happy about it, and her face got even longer when she heard about Sammy and Eshaan. She shook her head. "That Flatlander has much to answer for."

"Yes, but at least we have him in custody now."

Her mouth turned down. "It is my experience that people like him do not stay in prisons forever," she said sadly. "There is always somebody who has a use for them."

"I hope you are wrong. People have died to see him locked up."

She gave a small sigh. "Dying is not the worst thing that can happen to you."

Zenzara touched the Avarak on her shoulder. "We will make sure he stays in jail," she promised.

Seyal stepped away rather uncomfortably. "We have a saying on Rhyveka," she said with a small sniff. "The only certainty is that we will die."

Zenzie dropped her arm. "It can still be a good day," she insisted. "We can still save the Chakran Nexus. We can still stop the wormhole from forming."

"I wish you good fortune. *Avarak Karax!*"

Both Zenzara and I returned the salute.

"*Avarak Karax!*"

"*Avarak Karax!*"

As soon as I moved into the pilot's position on the space ski I realized that it had been built for Nepheals. The platforms are just big enough for a Nepheal to kneel on. Although they are similar to our own jet skis, they are not identical. The platforms have a steering system at the front and three jet pack engines at the back. The platforms themselves are hollow, so as to be able to carry a reasonable amount of fuel. They are very useful on extravehicular trips, although they are hard to steer and not particularly quick on a turn. I was used to Spacelander ones, which are easy to steer. The Nepheal space frames are more complicated, with arrow-shaped handlebars. You have to depress the handlebar on the side you wish to follow, and there are two hand levers for forward and fast. There is no reverse, of course, which also makes them limited in their use.

However, right here and now they were the perfect thing to take out of the ship. Mag sleds would not work out here in the middle of nowhere, and taking only individual jet packs would sentence us to a snail's pace.

I wobbled quite a lot at first. I had only been on one of these things once before, when Ouraali had been showing them to me and offering to give us a couple. It had been hard then, and I saw that it hadn't got any easier.

Zenzie had dominated her space ski almost immediately and was sitting quietly in front of me waiting for me to stop the bucking and weaving that was making me feel nauseous. She was staring at me as if rather unsure of my motives. Perhaps she thought that I was doing this for amusement.

I finally got the hang of the weird handlebar commands and fell in behind the Tyzaran girl. She led the way out of *Nivala* and we headed straight for the hypersphere.

The thing was enormous now. It was circling in the sky. We were on the other side from the small figures that had come out of the *Chibuzo* to protect Cunningham. They would have to go around this thing to get at us, and I didn't think they had enough time. Already I could see signs of sphere eversion. There were ridges forming along the sides of the hypersphere. When it had finally turned itself inside out was the moment that *Chibuzo* would release the canister, dumping the strands of the Chakran entity into the center of the seething mass of energy.

I ignored the spinning ridges that were scything past our position. I closed my eyes, pointed the space ski straight between two of the ridges and muttered a small prayer to my ancestors.

Zenzara matched my impetus and, side by side, we accelerated into the side of the huge hypersphere. I opened my eyes again to find that we were now just above the gulley between two of the ridges, which were bulging further and further apart.

I signaled to Zenzie to hold position flat up against the gulley, as close as we could get to the side of the sphere after matching its speed. Although the ridges were formed of what looked like light, they were now semi-solid, and we had been buffeted about as we cranked up to the speed of the outer part of the hypersphere.

Zenzie's face glistened in the reflected glow. Her body was flattened against the false surface, but she was looking up at the ridges as they blossomed out so much that we were being engulfed by them. Everything around us was hardening, passing through gel to a rubbery-like consistency.

I wondered if she knew what this was, if the studies of a Tyzaran child included abstract mathematics such as sphere eversion. If not, she could have no idea of what was happening. You wouldn't, unless you had seen models in Topology. Luckily, I knew what to expect.

First the two polar caps would press down towards each other, then pass through so that the outsides became the insides. Then the poles would go through a series of twists, to place the outside of the gulleys on the inside, then the gulleys would pass through each other and become the inside of the new eversion. After that, the ridges would slowly disappear.

I don't think I have ever been so frightened by light. Of course, I already knew from pulser theory that light can kill you. But I had never been compressed by it. It was a strange and extremely unpleasant feeling. No wonder making a wormhole had escaped the most educated minds for all these centuries.

I could well believe that scientists had considered this to be only a hypothetical construct. I don't think anybody had ever thought eversion could actually exist in the physical world. My mind was struggling even now to accept the evidence of my eyes.

The ridges were now so large that they had cut off the light from outside the structure. I was pressed against the gulley and could see nothing outside of the hypersphere. I was ensheathed in its wall. My space ski had been ejected by the closing folds. It had disappeared.

I could hear my own ragged breathing in the helmet as fear kicked in. The unknown is always terrifying, I find. This was particularly so. To be trapped and squeezed by spinning light gives you a sense of impotence that transcends daily problems.

I began to shake.

I couldn't even see Zenzara, who was right next to me.

I felt as though the air supply had been cut off, as though I couldn't breathe, although I was aware that this could not possibly be true. I started to hyperventilate. My heart was pounding in my chest.

Then the two polar caps of the sphere pressed down towards us, and the sphere became oblate as they descended.

I was thrust over and over and the small space I was trapped in became a cage, about six inches wider than my EVA suit. The sides of the wall of the hypersphere were oppressing.

Then we began to suffer torque as well as the poles reached their new positions and twisted to transpose the outside of the gullies to the inside of the newly forming eversion. I felt the pressure intensify before it released again. I clung onto the small area that had become mine.

Suddenly the strip of gully detached from its side ridges and we left them behind as we travelled right across the hypersphere. Now, almost miraculously, we were on the inside of the inside-out sphere. I felt huge relief as the spaces surrounding me became bigger and bigger. I was able to see further, able to judge more easily what part of the process we had reached.

And I could see Zenzara again. She had come through the transition in better shape than I had. She had already kicked off from the inside wall of the newly everted sphere, and was coasting down into its center.

I saw that her space ski was still visible. It was penetrating the sides of the hypersphere. Half was protruding through on the inside. I couldn't see the rest. I tried to drag it out of the wall of the hypersphere. It was stuck. I had to shake it up and down several times before the platform came free of the wall.

I turned it around to face Zenzie. She was ahead, but she was using inertia. It would take her much, much longer to get to the middle of the new structure. I pushed hard down on the handlebars and was almost catapulted off the platform in my haste to get the thing started and going in her direction. I had the feeling we might need the space ski before this ended.

Inside the eversion, we could see nothing of real space. That was now blocked off by the semi-solid walls. Light and energy were playing off the walls, bouncing and rebounding with flashes of color that almost blinded us. I switched the sun filter on my visor to the maximum.

It was very beautiful. Perhaps, if I hadn't been so worried about the outcome we were facing, I would have admired it. I think an artist would have been transfixed by the display of energy inside. Certainly Eshaan would have been able to make a masterpiece of the intertwining wisps of energy.

And it was Eshaan and Sammy I was thinking of as I drew level with Zenzara and pulled her onto the platform with me. As we closed on the center of the sphere, I wondered what was happening to them, whether they had got as far as the torpedo that the Omnistate were about to send our way.

We wouldn't know until it deposited its charge inside the everted hypersphere. There was nothing more we could do except wait.

We had been hovering at the center of the convoluted hypersphere for perhaps an hour when we found out the answer to that question. They hadn't.

At least, they hadn't been able to stop it.

We knew that because we saw the torpedo appear and detonate.

I lurched towards Zenzara and grabbed her hand, pulling her in behind the space ski as some protection against the fragmentation of the torpedo casing. She ducked down behind the tank with me, but the nearest piece of metal clipped past us a good three feet to our right.

Then she was gone. She shot past me, towards a small sliver of light that was flashing in the epicenter of the energy surrounding us. This is what the torpedo had delivered.

I pushed down on the handlebars of the space ski and raced after her. I had no idea what she was about to do.

The sliver of light was turning around and around on itself now, forming a small diamond shape in the sky. The facets gave off an opaline glow, almost like a pearl.

As I stared at it, it began to heat up and expand. Part of the energy that had been iridescing inside the hypersphere approached it. There was a moment of doubt, it seemed like, and then the rainbow light from the everted sphere pushed against the shining facets of the Chakran strands.

Zenzara arrived at the diamond. She seemed to be shouting something, but I couldn't hear anything through space and these EVA suits were not synched. She hurtled right up to the rhombus and seemed to me to be trying to hug it. Her arms went through the walls.

The glittering light from the hypersphere was momentarily pushed back, but then it crowded down again onto the sides of the diamond. Parts of the diamond seemed to be dissolving towards the surrounding light.

Zenzara put her head and her arms and legs back, as if opening her soul to the surrounding aura. She hung there in space, frozen. I was terrified for her.

A flash so bright that it blinded me traveled outwards. Then another. Then another. I had to cover my visor with both arms, despite having had the highest dark filter automatically deploy.

She would never survive this.

I pushed forwards to reach her, to pull her away from the geometric shape that had emerged from the torpedo.

A shock ran from her to my suit, electrifying every single cell in my body. My hair stood on end and my muscles spasmed. My hands dropped off the handlebars of the ski. Only inertia kept me on the platform. For one second my heart stuttered, and seemed about to stop.

Then it thumped on again with a jolt. I found myself covered in an icy sweat, from head to toe. The whole experience was most unpleasant.

I manually lightened my visor block until I could just detect what was going on around me.

Zenzara had not moved. She had kept the strange position and her limbs were quite still. I could not see her face any more because her helmet was now on a full blackout.

I sighed. I knew enough not to attempt to touch her again. My body would simply not take it, and I doubted that hers could.

Whatever was happening, I could only wait.

As another flare pulsed out from this central spot, I let the helmet take me back to full blackout. I was blinded. And utterly, utterly useless.

Ten minutes passed.

Twenty minutes passed.

I overrode the blackout again to check on my surroundings, but there was no change to anything. I had no idea whether or not Zenzie's presence was having an effect on the wormhole formation. I had no way of knowing.

But she was alive. That much I knew. Her muscles were twitching from time to time, causing her arms and legs to jerk slightly.

I let my visor take me back into the darkness.

Another ten minutes passed.

Another twenty.

I checked again. No difference. The outward pulses of light were still flowing away in concentric circles about every five seconds. One caught me, and even though I had only attenuated the visor's opacity slightly, it still hurt my eyes. I winced. Then I followed the pulse outwards towards the walls of the hypersphere, which is when I saw them.

Eshaan and Sammy were floating just inside the edge of the huge sphere. Neither of them was conscious, I thought. I could see no movement and their arms and legs were spread out as if they had been flattened by some giant foot.

I turned the space ski around as best I could. It was obvious that I could do nothing to help Zenzara; she would succeed or fail on her own. But I *could* do something for the other two.

I engaged the jets and, with my visor opacity only a tiny bit short of totally opaque, set the space ski for their position.

At first I couldn't imagine how they had got there, but then I saw the bracelet on Sammy's wrist. It was smoking. Nobody would be using that again. The whole thing was blackened and the parts had all fused together. The strand powering it had to have perished too.

I reached Eshaan first.

The Enif was without protection. The amount of radiation in this hypersphere had to be over even its limit. But I didn't think that would matter. Eshaan was not likely to live for very long. Its carapace had been torn apart by an explosion. Threads of body fluids were trailing out of the opening and it seemed to me to be in a coma.

I grabbed the inert body and lashed it to the platform. Then I turned to Sammy.

Sammy's eyes were open and the glare wasn't going to bother him anymore. Nothing was going to hurt him anymore. One shoulder had been blown away and his left leg was gone.

I felt the tears come to my own eyes. I remembered Sammy as a young boy, eager and good-tempered. I remembered him on *Commorancy*, just before all this nightmare had started, drinking a couple of beers with Bull and myself, joking about life and girls.

I took hold of the arm that still bore the fused bracelet. He must have been dying when he transported out of the ship. The bracelet had brought them to the sphere. I was carrying a portable hololink. His last act had been to lock onto it. He had wanted to save Eshaan. The least I could do was take both of them back to *Nivala*.

But I couldn't leave Zenzara alone. All three of us would have to wait here with her.

I tethered Sammy's corpse to the back of the platform. Then I approached the center of the hypersphere again. I did it slowly; nothing seemed to have changed. Zenzara had not moved.

I hugged Eshaan's broken body to me, trying to give it some small protection from the radiation. It moved once, weakly. I thought it might stand a very small chance, if I could get it to a Zeroth chamber quickly enough.

Then the outgoing pulses of light suddenly finished. I was able to reduce the block to my visor.

Zenzie was still in the same position as before, but there was a glow around her. The molecules of her body were growing, pulsing outwards. She was bloating up into the surrounding light.

At the same time the diamond shape was becoming more and more diaphanous. It too seemed to be expanding. As it did, it was mixing with the Tyzaran girl, swirling inside her inflated EVA suit.

I stared, mesmerized.

The whole of the diamond shape gradually evaporated, its wisps mixing slowly inside Zenzie's body. Her body began to collapse back to its normal size. The glow around her intensified until it was a blazing gold. The aura seemed to be pushing back against the phosphorescent light of the everted hypersphere.

The Tyzaran girl suddenly jerked back into consciousness. Her visor cleared as she overrode the opacity control. I saw her eyes open.

There were a few moments of complete disassociation. Her pupils were black, void of consciousness.

I left Eshaan briefly to reach over to Zenzara. She saw me, and, after a couple of seconds, recognition came into her face. She smiled at me and reached out to me as well, just before her eyes tipped upwards to show their whites and she slid into unconsciousness.

I dragged her onto the platform and tucked her under one arm. Then I pulled Eshaan under the other.

It was hard to maneuver the small space ski like that, but I managed to get us out to the edge of the hypersphere, on the side opposite the *Chibuzo*.

The radiance inside the sphere was twisting faster and faster as we approached the walls. It was as if the thing was angry with Zenzie for taking away the Chakran strands. The energy levels were spiking.

I was too tired to think. Eshaan was heavy on my arm, and the knowledge that Sammy was being ignominiously tugged along behind us was even heavier.

I pushed the space ski to the barrier and then tried to push it through.

At first nothing happened. The ski came to a halt. The barrier resisted.

I did the only thing I could. I pushed back against the barrier and put my whole weight down on the handlebars. There was no other way out of this place. We had to break through or we would be submitted to whatever the hypersphere's fate was going to be. I didn't know what that was, now that it couldn't become a wormhole, but the build-up of energy was not giving me a good sensation about it.

Just when I thought we would be condemned to share the sphere's fate, the corner edge of the ski began to slide through the wall of the sphere. First only one corner, then a little more.

With something like a sob of relief, I let my whole torso slump on top of the control. There was a long moment of tension, then the hypersphere ceded and let us through the barrier.

We slipped out of the other side and the jets stopped. I checked the gauges. We had used up all of our fuel. We were now freefloating slightly outside the Hypersphere.

I grabbed my ZR pistol and aimed it directly at the sphere. I kept my finger on the trigger for as long as I could. I hoped that it would take us away from those rubbery walls and I also hoped that Nivala would see the track of the pulser beam and come to get us. I no longer cared about its effect on the inverted hypersphere.

When the pistol overheated I threw it into the void. I bent my body over Eshaan and Zenzie. I didn't think there was anything else I could do for them.

$$21$$

The circle of light broke through my haze of exhaustion. It was *Nivala's* aft airlock. Seyal had twisted the ship to present it to us.

As soon as I saw the light I also saw figures attached to lifelines. They were jetting their way over to me. I couldn't bear even to look at them. I felt as though the world had ended. There was absolutely no pleasure in removing the negative energy. There should have been. It seemed that Zenzie had saved the remaining Chakran strand, along with any clones. I should have been pleased for that. I wasn't. I was numb and sick and exhausted.

Didjal was the first to reach us. It came up to me and gently extracted Eshaan from my death grasp on the Enif. I didn't want to let go. Didjal knocked on my helmet and signaled to me. I knew I had to let it take its *faliif.* I managed to loosen my grasp.

Didjal pulled them towards the airlock.

Another tap on my helmet. Denaraz had arrived, despite his injury. He extricated Zenzara from under my arm and then floated back to the airlock with her.

The patch of light closed. They were recycling the air. They were right. Sammy was in no hurry, and really, neither was I. I found myself coming more to my senses and looked back at the hypersphere.

Although Zenzara had managed to absorb the Chakran strands, the sphere was still ablaze with energy. In fact, it seemed to be pulsating even more. Little blue sparks of light were rippling through it, and I could see bolts of lightning building up inside it. They were jagged firebolts the size of the space ski platform. They tore through the orb, almost shattering the walls as they dissipated. The outside of the sphere had an electric blue halo.

The circle of light appeared again, with the same two figures attached to lifelines. They came for me now, detaching me with care from the space ski and reeling in Sammy's body at the end of the line.

I tried to say I could pull myself along the rope, but I realized I couldn't. My mind simply wasn't working. I needed a reset if I was to function.

I was aware of the hatch closing behind us, of the space ski being abandoned to its fate. There was a moment's darkness as the vacuum was replaced with air, and then the internal lock rolled clear.

I met Mel's eyes just before they lost all hope.

She looked through my visor to identify me, and then her gaze slid down to the decking at my feet, to the cadaver that was lying there.

She stopped breathing.

Even if his injuries hadn't been fatal, his space suit had been compromised. The ends of Sammy's leg were grossly distorted by swelling. So was the arm where it had been amputated. The vacuum had attacked the stumps and they had swollen up until the opening in the suits had been plugged. Poor Sammy was disfigured and grey.

Mel sank to her knees next to him. Tears began to course down her cheeks.

Izan pulled off my helmet.

I leaned in to Mel, to touch her on the shoulder. "I am sorry, Mel."

She shrugged off my hand. "Keep away from me! You sent him out there. This is your fault."

I closed my eyes. "I know."

I turned to Didjal. "I am so sorry. How is Eshaan?"

Didjal shook its head. "My *faliif* has entered the state of enlightenment. Thank you for keeping Eshaan alive long enough to die with me. We are very grateful to you."

Now it was my eyes that were damp. "Is there no other alternative?"

It shook its head. "Do not be sad for us. This was overdue. We are lucky. You brought Eshaan back to me. I may complete the state of enlightenment with my *faliif*. It is all that either of us have ever wanted. We are blessed indeed." It looked around at us. "We would be honored if you would be present. We have come to think of all of you as friends."

I bowed slightly. "The honor will be ours. There are just ... one or two things we must see to first."

"I understand. Thank you, Captain Mallivan. It has been a privilege to spend our last months with you."

"I wish this weren't happening."

The grey Enif gave his race's equivalent of a smile. "Nobody can pick the moment of their death, Captain. I am very grateful to die with Eshaan. I have never wished for anything else."

"We shall miss you both."

"The Enif believe that we all live on in our artwork. You will find us there."

"Yes. I regret that I will not be able to find a *Belofiin* out here to join with you."

"That does not matter, Captain. We have left all that we wanted to leave in our artwork. Neither of us have anything more to say. Now, if you would excuse me, I must join Eshaan. Our time is very limited. May we use the bridge for our enlightenment? We would like to be amongst you. Normally a state of enlightenment is attended by the two *faliifs'* friends and I know that you will not be able to leave the bridge at this time."

"Of course. We will join you as soon as we can."

"We will know that you are there, although we will not be able to tell you so."

"Thank you for everything. I ... I ..." I was unable to finish the sentence.

"We also, Captain." Didjal gave us all a deep bow and then picked Eshaan's broken body up in its arms. It nodded again and then strode off towards the lift.

Denaraz looked shaken too. "I will take Zenzara to Sickbay," he said, "and then I will join you on the bridge."

Zenzie was coming around. "I am all right," she told us in a shaken voice. "I saved the Chakrans!" She sounded proud.

"Yes. Well done. Go with Denaraz. This is not over yet. Get yourself checked out by the portable triage unit and consider giving yourself one of those injections the Tyzar doctors gave you."

She nodded, still woozy. Just as her eyes settled on Sammy's prone body, Denaraz hoisted her into his arms. "Is ... Is that ...?"

"Izan will tell you everything. Please go with him."

They disappeared slowly towards the second lift.

Mel and I stared at each other. Her anger had dulled. Now she just looked like a broken bird.

I lowered my head. "We have to go to the bridge."

She nodded and stood up. "Sammy will not mind waiting," she said sadly.

"Are you up to it?"

"Are you?"

I opened my arms and she walked into them. We hugged each other. "I don't know."

"It wasn't really your fault. I am sorry I said that."

"It *was* my fault. It was me that sent them over to *Chibuzo*."

She dragged shaky air in through reluctant lungs. "Somebody had to go."

"In the end they were not able to stop the torpedo. It was Zenzara who saved the Chakrans."

"Yes. But you couldn't know she would. I am sorry I spoke to you like that.”

I felt her whole body tremble and gave her a final hug. Then I stood back more formally. “The responsibility is mine. It always will be. Please accompany me to the bridge.”

“Yes Captain.”

The scene from the bridge was not reassuring. For some reason, the hypersphere was not dissipating. In fact, it seemed to be exponentially increasing in energy.

Seyal’s face cleared as she saw me, then fell again as she saw the expression on our faces. I could tell that she wanted to ask us questions, but she had grown up on a planet where some questions were best left unasked.

“The sphere is growing again, Mallivan.”

“Can it form a wormhole? Even without the Chakran?”

She shrugged.

“Get Sibby up here. At the double!”

Seyal leapt to obey.

Mel slid into the scanning station.

“What have you got, Mel?”

My friend blinked several times, trying to clear the tears from her eyes. She peered at the instrument panel in front of her. “These energy levels are tremendous. That thing is either going to explode or implode. Neither would be good for us. *Nivala* couldn’t take such an energy blast.”

So perhaps blame would all be moot. If we were vaporized I suppose none of it would matter anyway. That actually cheered me up, so I guess my emotional state was still compromised.

Sibby came racing in and threw me a welcoming smile of relief. “You are back, then.” She must have heard something about what had happened, because she just looked at Mel, her expression saying how sorry she was.

"Tell me what is going to happen to the hypersphere." I pointed at the viewport.

Sibby nodded. "I was monitoring it from the engine room. The Chakran strands have been removed, I believe?"

"Yes. They were reabsorbed inside Zenzara's Nexus."

"Then I think what is happening is that the hypersphere is in a runaway build up. The shell that contains it is, at some stage, going to bounce through the surrounding shell of normal space and there will be an explosion. A white hole, if you like."

I gulped. "A white hole?"

"Possibly."

"Won't that fry us?"

"It would, except I think we can establish a shell of our own that will provoke a stable Exceptional Point in its interior. And I'm saying that with capital letters, because it will be nothing like what we generally know as an exceptional point. This will protect everything inside the shell. All shock waves will be rerouted around us and our ships should be able to ride out the conflagration safely inside."

"What about anything outside the shell?"

"It will be instantly incinerated."

"*Chibuzo* too?"

Sibby nodded. "Our calculations show that a hole will be punched in the surrounding space. It could have a radius as big as a hundred thousand miles. And it is going to happen soon. None of us are going to have enough time to get away."

"So we just sit it out? What about *Aenysia*? Will she be beyond its influence?"

"She left two hours ago. She will be long gone. They won't even notice the commotion behind them."

"And is this ... 'Exceptional Point' ... already up?"

"It is. We finished the preparations half an hour ago."

"So that thing is going to explode, rather than implode?"

"I think so. That was, after all, the function of the Chakran negative energy. To introduce the specific exotic material that would permit implosion to a wormhole. Without that, there is nowhere for the escalation to drain. Eventually it will simply explode outwards. Err ... there is one other small problem."

I didn't like her tone. "What now ...?"

"Well, this is the first time that exceptional point theory has been applied to a macro situation like this. Even if it does work, and *Nivala* is protected, there might be ... well, side effects."

Her tone was calm, but I know my sister well. This was her calamity voice. "What sort of side effects?"

She pulled a face. "Light sometimes stops at exceptional points. We don't know what will happen inside ours. Light and time could stop. We might be frozen, or it could be that time passes normally inside and it appears that time is frozen on the outside. We won't know until we are inside."

I looked over at Mel. She looked like she didn't care which of those happened. I had some sympathy with her.

"Is there anything we need to do with the ship?"

"We have already done it. We have shut down all engine systems. We need to stay as stationary as we can, right in the middle of the modified carbon bubble. We have left life support on minimum. Denaraz has gone to fetch Segaton. We will all come to the bridge. That way we can be present for the Enif state of enlightenment, but we can monitor the situation outside through the large viewport there."

"All right. Tell everybody to make their way here."

Shortly after that, we were all congregated on the bridge.

Eshaan had been laid gently and lovingly on a beautiful tapestry that

Didjal had apparently been keeping for just this occasion. The dying Enif was so pale that its black shiny carapace was streaked with white. It was clear that Eshaan would not recuperate consciousness.

We stood in two small rows on either side of the tapestry as Didjal lay down beside his *faliif*.

"This is a happy day," it said sternly to us. "Please rejoice with us as our souls become one forever."

I nodded, though it was hard to contemplate the broken body in front of us and rejoice.

Didjal looked past me to Sibby and I saw some silent exchange between then. She also nodded. I think the Enif was giving instructions about their last joint invention, the Exceptional Point.

Then it curled up next to Eshaan, touching its partner with as much of its body as was possible. The next few minutes or hours would be spent communing together and should never be interrupted, unless it was by a *Belofiin*.

I had read up a little on the process, after the last time when the pair almost became enlightened. There is a physical change to their cordotonal organs – a heightening and intensifying. This provides the moments that for the Enif are sacred.

Normally a state of enlightenment would last for many hours, perhaps even days. I was sorry that our friends would not have so long. It was clear to me that Eshaan's life was hanging by a meager thread.

Yet, as I looked at them, I realized that there really was a reason here to be happy for them. They were dying together. Neither of them would have to face their last moments in the Shells alone. They were warmed by each other's souls and love. I had been close to dying many times, and it had always given me a sense of isolation. These *faliif* would never be alone again. Their consciousnesses would, according to Enif lore, merge and become one. They were at the start of the journey they had been waiting for ever since the *faliifa* ceremony when they found each other.

Didjal was also losing its color now as they lay clasped together.

Their forearms were touching all along the length of their limbs. They would be communicating with each other, even if only on a cellular level.

The streaks of white were extending across the injured Enif's body and onto Didjal's. They deepened and extended until both bodies were coated in an aura of white. The air around their carapaces began to shine with this bright light.

We all bowed our heads, aware that the moment of their death, or their birth, or whatever this was, was almost upon us.

Both Enif gave a small sigh that seemed to come from their very bones. It was a sigh of contentment, of fulfillment.

Then they fell silent.

The intense white aura hovered for a moment longer and then dissipated slowly out into the surrounding air.

Sibby let out a ragged sigh.

Mel was standing quietly but she was crying.

I looked up as I heard small footsteps approaching. It was Zenzara. She had arrived on the bridge just before the state of enlightenment had culminated. Her eyes were bright, too.

She was looking better. Her crest was rigid, but apart from that she seemed calm. The triage unit must have administered the injection that she needed. I knew that the Tyzaran doctors had insisted in updating the unit with all the latest knowledge of the physiological changes a Chyzar host might undergo.

She knelt down beside the two bodies.

For a moment nothing happened. None of us moved.

Both bodies began to ripple and unravel outwards slowly. Molecules from both bodies flowed together as what had been Enif flesh became motes of dust that intertwined upwards and outwards, coalescing in one whirling mass of particles that formed a flurry in the air above the vanishing bodies.

As we watched, the disintegration accelerated and the dust also transformed until all that was left of the bodies were curling waves of energy that dipped and soared, curving through and past each other.

Zenzie lifted her hands and the energy became a blazing light that flared and then passed straight through the ceiling of the bridge and out into the vacuum of space.

"Now they will never be apart," she said.

Mel was staring at the Tyzaran girl. "Can you do that for Sammy?" she whispered. "Can you set him free in space, too?"

Zenzie blinked. "I ... I think so."

"Then come." Mel stood and offered her hand to Zenzara. "I want him to fly out there as pure energy. I want him to transcend his poor broken body, too."

The two of them looked at me, but I couldn't leave the bridge. They understood. This was a fight for the survival of the rest of us. Mel nodded. I think she gave me her permission not to attend. Then she extended her hand to Zenzie and the two girls walked slowly out. Mel's thin shoulders already seemed lightened. The thought of Sammy's body being enclosed in a metal box forever was something she must have been finding hard to reconcile with her claustronetia.

The rest of us stared at the screens. The hypersphere had been cranking up its energy exponentially. I think that, had we been outside then, our bodies would have been damaged without repair.

The whole thing was beating. Pulsating in and out as if it were breathing.

Seyal's eyes were round. "It can't last much longer!"

I had to agree with her. Something that was building up so fast could not maintain its integrity for much time. I checked to see that the ship was as protected as we could possibly make her. Not that it's easy to leave a back door open on a spaceship, but it never hurts to triple check things.

It's just as well I did. We had forgotten all those helmeted figures that had poured out of *Chibuzo*. Some of them had found us. I picked up around twenty of them clinging to our hull as soon as I scrutinized the aft cameras. They were trying to get through the airlock there.

There was an industrious buzz about them. They meant business.

"What the krikk ...!"

The girls looked around enquiringly. I pointed to the dark figures that were attaching themselves to our hull in increasing numbers.

"I will be back soon," I told them grimly.

Denaraz nodded with me. "You will need back-up!"

Sibby gave a cry. "No!" She ran over to Izan and pulled back on his arm. Then she grabbed one of mine. "Stop! You can't go outside now, either of you! You will be subjected to far too much radiation. All those men are dead. They just don't know it yet."

I began to calm down. She was right. Attacking them outside the ship was pointless. We simply had to make sure that they couldn't get through the airlock.

Before I could move, Zenzara stiffened. All the Tyzaran crests peaked higher than I had ever seen them before. Mel gave a gasp. We all turned around to peer at the viewport.

I whistled. "I hope that protective screen of yours is ready, Sibby."

My sister was staring at the spectacle in front of us. "So do I."

The hairs along my arms stood on end.

The sphere was now rippling in the sky at the center of what looked like a radiant aura. Light beams from the halo had started to surge across the vacuum in a three hundred and sixty degree circle. They reached almost to our ship, illuminating the surroundings like sunbeams stretching through dust in an abandoned room.

There was a deep rumbling sound. The deck tilted ominously. The whole ship began to shake. We all grabbed hold of something that would help us to stay on our feet. The outer casing was trembling and the deck plating was screeching as it twisted underneath our feet.

Sibby peered out towards the sphere. She gave a sort of strangled groan.

I turned on her. "What?"

She pointed. "Look!"

I shrugged. "What? What is it?"

"The E.P. receptors. Those pointy things that stick out of the front of the ship, you know?"

"I know what E.P. receptors are. They are necessary for the ZEPH drive, right?"

She nodded. "Yes, but ..." she tilted her head on one side and considered, looking a little bit like a bird, "... I hope those two booms don't act as collectors."

Now we were all staring at her. Her face had gone pale; she clearly didn't like what she was thinking.

I tried to make out what was happening on the outside of the ship. As far as I could see, the aura was getting stronger by the second and the center of the sphere, if anything, seemed to be slightly smaller and denser than before. I could just make out blue lightning undulating across the walls.

The E.P. receptors – the two long metallic poles that jutted out in front of the ship – were beginning to heat up. They were glowing with white-hot tips. The ship convulsed with shudders. Zenzie slammed into me, and I only just managed to stop her from being impacted into the corner of the console. She was almost jerked out of my grasp as I tried to position her behind the pilot's chair, where she would have a better chance of staying upright.

The beams of light that were blazing across the expanse to the receptors intensified. Then there was a ripping flash of white light so bright that it seared my retina, even through the treated and reactive glass of the viewport. We were all left blind for several moments as the high-tech finish prevented any more radiation from coming through.

The instrument panel in front of me died. All the lights went out. We were blind inside and out, but the vibrations didn't stop.

I gave my sister an accusing glare which asked her why she hadn't foreseen this.

Her shoulders slumped. "I am sorry, Mall. It never even occurred to me. And I don't think it did to Didjal, either."

I sighed. "All right. Just tell me what you think is happening."

"I think ... I am very much afraid ... that the sharp points at the bows of *Nivala* have acted to create a plasma bridge from the hypersphere to the ship." She looked around at us all to see if she had our attention. She did, so she went on, "That means that the large potential relative to the spacecraft would discharge in an arc."

"An electric current? Like lightning?"

She nodded. "And possibly a sustained arc, I am afraid."

There were some small explosions. They seemed to be outside, on the hull of the ship. She looked resigned. "That will be the PCUs burning out."

Zenzie asked her what PCUs were.

"They are mechanisms put on all spaceship hulls to prevent potentials building up. Plasma contactor units. They mainly target negative potentials. In this case, with positive potential, I am afraid they might have been an exacerbating factor. It is probably just as well they are gone." Her face fell, "though if the *Chibuzo* crew had any metal on them, they will have been exposed to a high energy discharge."

Seyal, who had been busy at the controls, sat back at her station with a sigh of relief. "Got it!"

The lights started to come back up and then the consoles rebooted, each at its own speed.

As soon as my station was back online, I glanced on the posterior vid-screen at the small figures clustered about the airlock. They were there no more. They were all floating off the side of *Nivala*, small, broken matchstick figures that no longer held any signs of life. Their arms and legs were open, as though they had been set in space to telegraph a static distress signal to us.

Sibby shook her head and looked sick. "The kind of current they have been exposed to will have fried them inside their suits. There is nothing that can be done for them now."

The reactive glass decided to allow a small amount of light through again. We stared out.

The plasma bridge was visible. It was a shaft of light that traveled from the walls of the everted hypersphere and curved across intervening space until it terminated at the ZEPH booms at the front of the ship. The aura shone so brightly that it almost blocked out the hypersphere.

"So how do we stop it?" This time it was Izan who spoke. "And why didn't the carbon cloud block it?"

Sibby bit her lip. "The carbon cloud didn't block it because we have modified it to create an Exceptional Point. Exceptional points create a sort of stasis at the centre of waveguides, if you like, but that was not a waveguide. That was basically a stream of electrons, which is why it penetrated the modified barrier. And the only way we can stop it is to fire directly at the hypersphere, which will possibly break the plasma bridge, but will also serve to precipitate the final explosion. On the other hand, if we don't do that, the barrier will not be effective, because the plasma bridge breaches it and the exceptional point will not protect us from an explosion which can only be minutes away, at best." She wiped sweat away from her brow.

The shuddering of the whole ship made it hard to understand what she was trying to say. It seemed to me that *Nivala* couldn't and wouldn't last very much longer.

Denaraz and I exchanged a look.

Whatever the result, our choice was clear.

We had no option but to fire on the hypersphere. It was our only chance. *Chibuzo* and the asset dump were already condemned to disappear. *Nivala* was the only thing that might survive, and my job was to make as sure as I could that she would.

Denaraz was in no state to run.

I threw myself off the bridge towards the crawl ladder. I needed to be one deck down and I needed to be there fast.

I had never seen my sister sweat like that before. It galvanized me into action like nothing else could have done.

I slid to a stop in front of the weapons console one deck down and forced my fingers as fast as I could across the controls. I didn't have to think much. I was simply going to detonate the biggest missile we had in the centre of the hypersphere.

The automatic targeting and range presented me with a list of all possible objectives in the area. There were only three: *Chibuzo* herself, the asset dump and the hypersphere.

I arrowed in on the hypersphere, allowed a three dimensional plan to show me the exact center of the phenomenon, zoomed in again, chose our biggest torpedo, pushed the arm button and safety coded it, then pushed the button.

I didn't wait to hear the result. I raced back to the main bridge, flinging myself back up the crawl tubing to the deck above.

The torpedo exploded before I was half way to the upper floor. There was a tremendous *CRUMP* and the whole of the tube I was in rattled, shaking me until I nearly lost my hold on the iron bars set into the crawl shaft.

I was slammed against the vertical stanchions set into the shaft. I yelped and closed my eyes. Not again! It reminded me of *Commorancy*, when my comfortable status quo had dissolved forever.

I couldn't move for some long seconds. The whole of the shaft was juddering as if it were the end chisel in a jackhammer. I clenched my jaw and desperately hung on.

Finally the vibrations settled and I managed to propel myself to the top of the shaft and out into the wall of the main bridge. I punched at the service hatch and tumbled out onto the bridge, where the others were still staring at the viewport in front of them.

It seemed as if they had not moved at all. Sibby's mouth was slightly open, illuminated by the blast that was still washing over the *Nivala*.

I turned to the window in front of them. What I could see was a wall of fire that completely surrounded us. But it was more than fire. It was the white heat of a thermonuclear detonation, it was the utter destruction of a fission warhead. It was like looking at the frozen result of a RAMP missile strike.

The plasma bridge had collapsed. The E.P. poles were clear of any plasma. The modified carbon cloud had snapped back into place. We were left in total isolation.

The Exceptional Point that Sibby had created was diverting the blast around us. Over and under us. We were sitting in the middle of a huge quantity of light. There was no colour to it; it was a brilliant, blazing white. It clung to the boundaries of the carbon bubble, encasing us in a dazzling sheath of energy.

The automated reactive glass was dosing out the amount of light we were allowed to perceive, but even so it was like being in heaven. Pure, brilliant, silver light in a glittering canopy cocooned us from the rest of existence. It was not an amorphous lump. Strands and threads shimmered inside it, forming a lattice of filigree that was one of the most beautiful things I have ever seen. It was almost a metaphysical experience to see the delicate tracery of the tendrils of energy.

I managed to stand up and hobbled over to Sibby. "Well done!"

She smiled back at me. She was holding hands with Izan as they stared out at the phenomenon. "I have never seen anything like it."

"Nobody has. Why is it lasting such a long time?"

She looked down at me for a moment, but could hardly bear to tear her eyes from the display outside. "I think time has been slowed down for us. That whole explosion should have consumed us and moved on in a fraction of a second. The Exceptional Point has left us in ... in limbo, if you like."

I glanced at Zenzie's crest. It was relaxed. So was Izan's. "Err ... how long are we going to be caught in this limbo? We aren't going to be stranded here forever, are we?"

She shook her head and then lifted her shoulders. "I have no idea. I don't think anybody has ever been inside stopped time before."

I realized that the ship was now completely still and quiet. The vibrations had died away. It was eerily silent, as if in a trance-like state.

Sibby shook her head, trying to free herself of the almost mesmeric quality of the surrounding energy. "I ... I will get myself down to engineering. I need to do some calculations."

Denaraz tore his own eyes from the panorama. "I will come with you."

I nodded. I was going nowhere. I knew that the explosion we were currently gazing at had vaporized thousands of Flatlanders. It was a violent, brutal explosion. But, from this angle, it was magnificent.

Zenzie came up beside me and touched my arm. "This must be what the universe is like all the time for the Chakrans. It must be full of a brilliance we can never hope to experience."

I clawed my way over to my chair. I needed to sit down.

"I wish Eshaan had lived to see this," I said sadly. "Think of the picture it would have made!"

Zenzie nodded. "Yes, but maybe something like this is not meant to be seen by beings like us. We have transient lives. This sort of enormity is meant for beings that can live forever."

I had to glance down at that. "Maybe this time-freeze we are in will last forever. Would that mean we were immortal?"

She thought about it and then shook her head. "I don't think so. I think we would live our normal lifespan inside this bubble. Then we would mummify."

That was enough to break the spell. "Fine," I told her. "I need some sleep. I am going to my cabin, and you should get yourself back into a Zeroth chamber. We may as well use this gifted time to recover."

She hesitated, so I pressed on. "When *will* it be all right to leave the bridge? In one day, one week, one year?"

She giggled. "Put like that ..."

I called down to Sibby, in engineering. "Let us know when you figure it out, Sibs."

Her voice, when it came back, was happy. "Don't sleep too long, Mall. Izan and I want you to marry us on the bridge, with that backdrop. We want our ceremony to be truly unique."

I turned automatically to Mel, who had stopped breathing. Then her face lightened. She turned towards the canopy of light around us. Sammy was a part of that now. He was out there too. She gave me an almost imperceptible nod. I pushed down on the tight-beam. "Copy that, Sibby. Whenever you like."

I looked back out of the viewport again. The Landau Rift, the family ship and my mother seemed a million light years away. I looked at the astounding network of energy that was surrounding us and I felt insignificant.

The bridge was illuminated only by the wonderful light from the Exceptional Point. It served as a backdrop to the strangest wedding you could imagine. There, in the outer reaches of the Sol system, surrounded by the vaporized remnants of an Omnistate battle cruiser, an asset dump, two Enif friends and Sammy, Sibby and Denaraz made their relationship official.

Captains of ships have always been able to officiate at weddings. I was no exception. But weddings were now so rare that Mel had had to look up the protocols for me in the data banks. I had never even attended a wedding. Spacelanders rarely marry, since children are created mechanically at the Genetic Institute on Zenubi.

Mel was generous with her spirit. She was mourning Sammy deeply. The last thing she could be feeling like was a wedding. Yet she threw herself into the organization with a selflessness that I found admirable. There were no grumblings, no envious glances. She was genuinely happy that her friend had found someone to share her life with.

And here we were. Music of some sort was playing through the consoles. I couldn't have told you what it was, but Mel had assured me that it was most appropriate.

Personally, I wouldn't have bothered with music. The backdrop was so special and so stunning that I didn't think anything else would be needed.

However, apparently music was key to a wedding ceremony, so I kept my own counsel and waited for Mel to nod me in to say my piece.

Sibby was not dressed in a wedding dress. She would have looked most peculiar if she had been. Mel showed me the sort of thing that was generally used, and I burst out laughing. It looked like something an ancient queen might have sported. It certainly wasn't something I could see Sibby putting on. She would have been lost in it.

She had wrapped a bolt of silk around her slim figure, and she looked stunning. It was held by one of Zenzie's *nivalas*, just under her throat. She looked so beautiful that tears came into my eyes.

Denaraz was in his dress uniform, as were the rest of us. As a Tyzaran, he was quite a bit taller than everyone except Seyal, so he was a duly imposing bridegroom.

When I got the nod from Mel, I walked forward to stand in front of them. The silver canopy of light far eclipsed me. It was the most stunning venue anyone could have ever chosen.

I went through the words slowly, my tongue tripping on some of the old-fashioned spelling. They sounded somber and binding.

Then it was over and Sibby turned in towards Denaraz. His crests were up. He bent down to touch her lips with his own, and she seemed to sway in towards him.

Then they turned to me. I read the final sentence. "As a solemnized representative of one of the Major Shells, I may and therefore *do* declare you to be husband and wife."

I looked around. Zenzara and Seyal had silly smiles on their faces.

Mel's shone with a sort of reflected happiness. My sister was radiant.

I peered at the paperwork. "It says here that there should be something called a honeymoon. What is that?"

Mel told me that it was a sort of holiday that newly-weds took to celebrate their changed status. I looked around in doubt. "So where can they go?"

But somebody had already thought of that. Sibby grinned across at me. "We are going out there," she said simply.

I gaped. She was indicating the outside of the ship.

"EVA? You have got to be joking!"

She shook her head. "Not. I am going, Mall, so don't even *think* about stopping me. Izan and I have the chance of having a 'honeymoon' nobody else in history has ever had, nor will ever have again, I think. We can celebrate our marriage in a truly timeless way."

"But ... but ..." I could hardly get the words out. "Wh-what if we come out of the time freeze just as you are outside the ship? You could get sublimated!"

"We won't. I have finished the calculations, and at the rate time is passing currently we still have fifteen hours before the Exceptional Point will release us."

My mouth was opening and closing like a fish. "You ... you have to be joking."

"Not only am I not joking, but you are all going to do the same thing. We will do it in shifts."

"Now I know you have gone mad!"

Denaraz grinned. "Come on, Rye, you know you would love to go out there. None of us will ever see anything like it again."

Seyal nodded. So did Zenzara.

Mel had tears running down her cheeks. "I would like to go outside. We are leaving Sammy here. I want to feel close to him for the last time."

Seyal edged closer to her. "I will go with you, Mel. We will say goodbye to him together."

I gave up. It was perfectly clear to me that the whole of my crew had been in some way affected by the Exceptional Point. If Sibby was right, and I had no doubt that she would be, then we had fifteen hours before time would unfreeze for us. That gave plenty of margin.

I blew out air. "Fine. But only for an hour each. I am not risking any more than that. Zenzara and I will go out last."

Sibby skipped around the console and Zenzie looked excited.

Mel clapped her hands for silence. "First we toast the bride and groom," she told us in a more solemn tone. She held up her glass. "To Izan and Sibby."

Seyal and I raised our own glasses.

"Izan and Sibby!"

"Sibby and Izan!"

Zenzie looked with some interest at the liquid in her glass. "What is this?" she asked Mel in a curious tone.

"It is called champagne," she told her. "I found a few bottles in the store. It is one of the typical drinks to toast a newly married couple."

"Is it alcoholic?" Zenzie's face lit up. Mine clouded over.

"Yes." Mel's eyes slid to me. "Just a little."

I was in the process of opening my mouth when Zenzara tipped the whole drink down her throat. She choked a little, coughed, and then swallowed.

I watched with some amusement. The Tyzaran girl's face looked surprised and then alarmed as the liquid burned somewhat as it went down. Then her whole face flushed red.

"It has bubbles," she managed to get out. Her voice was squeaky. "Very ... very nice." She looked around at us all and saw that we were laughing at her. "What? What did I do?"

"You didn't toast the couple," I told her.

"Oh yes. Sorry." She looked in my direction, perhaps to see if I would allow Mel to refill the empty glass. I shook my head.

She raised the empty glass, her face still pink. "To Sibby and Denaraz!"

One hour later, we shut the newly-weds into an airlock and opened the outer door. They drifted out with an expression of sheer wonder on their faces.

When they came in, the only thing they did was shake their heads. Words failed them.

Mel and Seyal had the same experience. They, too, seemed unable to translate the experience into language.

Zenzara and I were ready, but I can't say that I really felt a compulsion to submerge myself more in this strange phenomenon. However, I knew that Zenzie would never forgive me if I didn't, so I checked her EVA suit and then my own as we shuffled into the airlock and waited for the exterior hatch to open.

We had all decided to remain tied to the interior of the airlock, though Sibby had insisted on using some non-conductive bands, just in case there was a residual difference of potential. We were still mindful of what had happened to the suited *Chibuzo* attackers.

Zenzie and I loosely tethered ourselves together and then allowed ourselves to float freely, only attached to *Nivala* by the non-conductive bands. We lay on our backs, faces out towards the canopy. We drifted gently, our eyes riveted on the panorama in front of us.

The angular momentum that had existed in the hypersphere had been conserved, so the energy enveloping us curled around the invisible walls of the Exceptional Point. The strands of energy twisted in and around the canopy, the silver threads flashing and dimming again as they moved within the shimmering white background.

I don't think I have ever seen anything quite so mesmerizing in all my life. If I had been free, I might have allowed myself to float away from the ship and into the surrounding luminescence. It certainly drew me.

I don't think I could ever explain it in words. It was like submerging yourself in the most wonderful painting ever made, becoming one with it. It made part of me cry and part of me rejoice, all at the same time. It was vast. It was boundless. It collapsed the senses.

I have no idea why it should have felt almost mystical. I am not a particularly spiritual person, yet it seemed I could feel Sammy out there. Eshaan and Didjal, too. I could visualize the painting that Eshaan would have completed if it had been given time.

The experience was very moving. It was like a state change, but for people. I felt as if I would be able to reach out and touch the whole of my past and the whole of my future. It was all there, hanging frozen and burnished in the white light and the network of shimmering filaments. All I could do was stare. Wonder.

I felt completely relaxed. But I couldn't close my eyes. I couldn't look away from the surrounding dome of pure energy.

Then I felt a sort of prickling feeling in my mind. It was lightly intrusive, but it didn't seem threatening. I closed my eyes for a second to block the sights in front of me. This felt different to the strings of energy that were spinning past my eyes. This was something deep inside my mind. It was somehow even bigger and yet smaller at the same time.

Something touched me inside my brain.

I may have jumped.

Zenzara had pulled herself closer to me. She was examining my face. She looked surprised. Her head was tilted to one side, evaluating me.

I gave a shrug. *What?*

She pointed to her head, and then to mine.

It took me a moment, and then another strange flutter, deep in my own head, made me realize what she meant.

The Chakrans!

The Chakrans were trying to link to my human brain.

I closed my eyes again and let my consciousness fall back inside the blackness. I was aware of a shiver of awareness that seemed to be fizzing through my mind. It was quite extraordinary.

My eyes snapped open. I tried to telegraph a question to Zenzie. *What should I do?*

She shook her head and used her two hands to push down on the empty space in front of her. *Relax. Accept it.*

I tried. Really I did. I forced my eyes open again and tried to concentrate on the Exceptional Point again. There was a vague sense of tumbling disquiet and then it vanished. A shiver ran up and down my spine. The hairs on the nape of my neck stood on end.

It was gone. Whatever had or hadn't just happened, was over. I deflated. I felt as if I had been tested and found lacking. I shook my head at Zenzara. She returned a small grimace.

I turned briefly back to the surrounding lacework of energy. Our time was up. Incredibly, a full hour had passed.

Denaraz had been right. None of us would ever see anything like it again.

When Zenzie pulled her helmet off, once we were back on board *Nivala*, she was scathing.

"Ugh! Your brain is all wet!"

"You were inside it?"

She was repulsed by the idea. *"Euw! No!* But I felt the Chakrans explore it. It is horrible! Mushy!"

"I think it is a fairly standard human brain. It might not be the latest model, but it has served me reasonably well so far."

"Well, they don't like it. It is far too busy for them. They seem surprised you can get one coherent thought out of it."

"I am sorry to disappoint them."

"They were hopeful they could eventually create a Nexus in a human. With all external links halted it was a good moment for them to attempt contact."

"And they have changed their minds after visiting with my mind?"

"Yes! Of course they have. They could never exist inside that! They think it is chaotic. They need a sense of peace to share a mind."

"I'm surprised they found it in your brain."

That made her pause for thought. "Are you insulting me?" she demanded.

"A little."

She began to laugh. "I guess you are right. They don't like mine much either. They say I am all over the place most of the time."

"Please tell them that my ... damp ... mind is at their disposal should they be looking for a home for their Nexus."

She made a face. "Sorry. They say humans are too full of water. They can't find enough focus."

"Yes. I have the same problem sometimes."

She nodded. "No wonder. I am surprised you can think at all."

"Thank you."

The others had come up. "Well? What did you think?" Sibby asked, giving my hair, which had been flattened by the helmet, a tousle.

I couldn't deny the effect. "You were right. Unforgettable."

She seemed relieved. "It was, wasn't it? But you were right to limit us to an hour each. Time here is accelerating now. We probably only have another few hours before the Exceptional Point releases us."

"Will that be dangerous?"

She frowned. "I don't think so. The radiation will have dispersed during the time we have been frozen here. As soon as the canopy of energy evaporates, we can be on our way."

"Mel?"

Mel turned to face me. She appeared almost embarrassed. "I felt Sammy. When I was out there." She tilted her chin at a defiant angle. "I know you will think I have lost my mind, but I swear I felt his presence. He was at peace. I got to say goodbye to him."

I kept silent. The sensations I had experienced outside the ship were too personal to share. In any case, I wasn't sure of what I had witnessed. I reached down to press Mel's forearm, though. "I am glad, Mel. That will help."

She gave me a watery smile. "It has."

"Do you think you can work?"

She straightened her spine. "Of course, Captain."

I lowered my voice. "I am so sorry, Melly."

She laid her hand over mine for a brief moment. "I know. Thank you, Rye."

She walked away. Her life would never be the same again. Neither would mine. I was going to miss Sammy very much. Didjal and Eshaan would leave a tremendous gap, too. We had only known them for a short time, but they had become such important members of the team that I didn't know what we would do without them.

The Exceptional Point released within ten minutes of Sibby's revised estimate. One minute the silvery wisps were still whirling around the ship, the next they had gone and we could see the night sky again.

I leapt to the consoles to scan our surroundings.

There was nothing left. *Chibuzo*, the asset dump and the hypersphere were gone forever. All the instruments were picking up was a small background glow – a hum really. The residue of an explosion far beyond a nuclear blast. Just a small remnant vying with the background radiation. It didn't even register on the radian toxicity monitor. We had been held frozen inside the Exceptional Point for so long that almost all of the effects had disappeared.

A deep scan picked up nothing. A whole ship had been vaporized with nothing to show for it. It had been turned to dust and that dust had been flung out in an ever-expanding shell. I supposed that at least none of its occupants would have felt anything. Or had time had slowed for them at the end, too? Who knows? I was beginning to realize that there were very many things that we hadn't even begun to understand.

The disappearance of the Exceptional Point had brought normalcy back to the bridge. The light was sparse again; automatic reactivity had switched itself off and the viewport was showing only darkness outside the ship.

The routine of ship life felt a little too flat, a little too ordinary. So many things had happened in the last day that we had all been changed, chastened by the experience.

"Where to, Captain?" asked Seyal as soon as the necessary checks on the engines had been undertaken.

We needed to remove ourselves from the vicinity, and fast. The Omnistate would not be long in coming to see what had happened out here in the far reaches of their solar system. They would want to find their lost battleship. Their vanished asset dump. I wanted to be a long, long way away when that happened.

Also, our carbon bubble was offline. Sibby had told me that it would take her at least a day to reconfigure it to the old parameters. We needed to move, now.

I let my gaze wander around the bridge. It was over. It was all over. It was time to go home.

"Set a course for Ulon Prime," I told her. "The mission is over."

Books in Interstellar Enforcement Series:

Termination Shock (Book 1)
Interdicted Space (Book 2)
Exceptional Point (Book 3)

Next to come:

Inescapable Drift (Book 4)